THE BERLIN
CONSPIRACY

ANOTHER BUCK AND DOLLY ACTION NOVEL
by William Penn

The Berlin Conspiracy

CreateSpace
An Amazon.com Company
7290-B Investment Drive
North Charleston, SC 29418

ISBN: 144990985X
ISBN:-13: 9781449-909857

Printed in the United States of America

Also by William Penn

The Grand Conspiracy

The Panama Conspiracy

In memory of our beloved mothers: Lois Rafferty and Laura Edith Rennie Hamilton

List of photographs to be found at:
www.buckanddolly.com

1. The Rock of Gibraltar and Gibraltar Airport, with Africa in the distance
2. The Great Siege Tunnel gun ports
3. Gun crew demonstrates how the cannons were used
4. Aircraft carrier deck
5. The Hotel Eibsee with the Zugspitze above
6. The Zugspitze Ski Bowl
7. The Sonn-Alpin restaurant
8. The front of the Wannsee Mansion
9. View of the Wannsee Mansion from the lake
10. Germans boarding the LuftCondor charter in Berlin

ACKNOWLEDGEMENTS

Almost without exception, the authors write from first-hand knowledge of the countries visited by Buck and Dolly Madison, the only exception hitherto this novel being the caves of Tora Bora in Afghanistan. We continue that tradition in this novel; however, it has been necessary to borrow some expertise here and there. While we have been to London several times, we have yet to be invited to dinner at Buckingham Palace. For those details, we are indebted to our long-time Army friends Brigadier General and Mrs. Peter M. Dawkins. However, the conversation between the Royal Couple and the Madisons is our own fabrication.

Special tips of the beret go to Colorado Aviation Hall of Fame laureate, Babette André, who improved our fractured French and to retired Associated Press reporter, Joe McGowan, for his first-hand knowledge of Islam.

Dolly's expertise in the martial arts is borrowed from our son, J. Matthew Hamilton, who holds black belts in all five of the traditional martial arts and, in addition, earned a black belt in Kajukenbo, that most lethal form of street fighting.

For first-hand knowledge about the Boeing 727, we are grateful to our friend and retired FedEx pilot, Captain Tom Chaffin. We thank our long-time friend and former neighbor, and one of the Forty Living Legends of American Aviation, Emily Howell Warner, for providing us with an hour in a full-motion simulator for the Boeing 727.

For their hands-on experience on using the ventral exit door of the Boeing 727 as a parachuting platform, we are grateful to Leigh Fairbank, the former head of the Parachute and Aircraft Test Section of the U.S. Army Airborne Board. We thank L.H. "Bucky" Burruss, the author of five insightful novels about military life and the former deputy commander of Delta Force, for his helpful critique. For his expertise in journalism, we are grateful to our friend and former U.S. Air Force officer, N. Dale Talkington, who read the manuscript in its penultimate state and offered some very helpful advice.

We thank our Colorado neighbor, Gary A. Wright, for leading his reconnaissance platoon to the top of the Matterhorn and the Zugspitze. While we have been to Berlin a number of times, we are grateful for the assistance of Colonel William J. Lacey, Jr., who began his illustrious military career in Berlin and knows that city very well. We are proud to have served on active duty with all of these fine officers.

At one time, our aviation colleague, John Pfeifer, served on active duty as the Public Works Officer at Camp David. His insights into the layout and workings of Camp David were invaluable.

Once again, we are grateful for the computer expertise of our Grand Lake neighbor, Steve Batty, who, in 2001, conceived the idea of putting color photographs of the important geographic features of our novels on the Internet instead of having them within the printed pages. We continue that practice at: www.buck-anddolly.com in the hope readers will have their computers at hand when they come to those places in the novels where we invite their attention to the photographs. Steve Batty designed the front and back covers. We are grateful to Clark V. Kays for the cover photography.

For her assistance, we also thank Marilyn Chang, the volunteer Librarian/Archivist at the Wings over the Rockies Air and Space Museum – a "must-see" for aviation buffs visiting the Denver area.

We are truly grateful for the assistance of these friends and that of our son. If there are any errors of fact, they are ours and ours alone.

✡ ✡ ✡

PROLOGUE

Langley, Virginia. January, 1994

Mir Aimed Kasi observed the main gate of the Langley campus of the Central Intelligence Agency through field glasses. Speaking to Aliyah, his young and very beautiful, dark-haired assistant, Kasi said, "Over 20,000 people work inside those 258 acres or, if you prefer, 104 hectares. Within such a large universe we are going to find at least one of those 20,000 who, for one reason or another, will work for us. If it proves too difficult, we can shift our operation over to the State Department. One way or another, we will create a mole to do the bidding of Allah, be He glorious and exalted."

"But Mr. Kasi," said his assistant, "we don't look like them. We don't speak American English that good. We are only here on temporary work visas. How could we possibly develop what the British and the Americans call a 'mole' inside such formidable targets? What if we get caught? The Americans could put us in prison. I might not see my parents and my sisters and brothers ever again."

"My dear, with President Trimmer now in office, we have little to fear from his Department of Justice and the FBI. He and his wife are more likely to use them for domestic political purposes.

"Besides, little Aliyah, we will use the strategy of the indirect approach. If your English reading skills were better, I would commend to your reading the writings of the British strategist, Sir Basil Liddell-Hart. Sir Basil believed the most effective way to reach one's goals is by indirection.

"In this circumstance, we will create what the Americans would most like to see created: a grass-roots organization of Muslims dedicated to the more pacifistic teachings of the Prophet Muhammad, may his name be praised. This organization will be the basis for what we will tout as the Million Muslim March against what the Americans and British like to call 'the radical Islamists.'

"We have ample funding from certain friends in Saudi Arabia, Syria, and Iran. Triple M, as it shall come to be called, will attract those Muslims who are against jihad. In due course, we will deal with them appropriately. But, for now, they will be what Lenin called: 'useful idiots.' Moreover, we are sure to find an American Muslim or two whom we can inflame with the desire to commit random acts of violence against Americans – even commit violent acts inside the supposed security of American military installations.

"One of the programs operated by Triple M will be an Arabic language school offering instruction in our language to one and all. The Triple M language school will have what U.S. intelligence needs most – a way to train more of their case officers and agents in Arabic. I predict the CIA will soon say only those who are fluent in one or more languages will be admitted to its top leadership positions.

"It is through the school where we will make contact with large numbers of U.S. government employees. Eventually, we will identify a few worthy of attempts at recruitment. Some of them will be sympathetic to Arab culture. And, as they begin to learn more about our culture, they will become even more sympathetic to our cause and to the plight of the Palestinians. That's always the way with language learning. Initially, the student becomes enamored of the new culture, although the student may, in later years, find the new culture's glow wears off and the inherent flaws in any culture become evident and the folk ways of his or her new-found friends can even become irritating. We want to recruit our prospective moles while 'the bloom is still on the rose,' as the English like to say.

"Bear in mind the CIA and the U.S. Department of State have a long history of drawing their staff from the so-called 'ruling class,' the blue-blood families of America's Eastern Establishment – people who are often anti-Semitic. We will play on their bias against Israel and their inclination to overlook the violence of the Palestinian Liberation Organization and that of Hamas."

"But will we really try to turn out a million Muslims to march against jihad?" asked Aliyah.

"Don't be ridiculous, my dear. The Triple M staff will keep post-poning the date of the march on the grounds that such an under-taking requires much time and effort. Meanwhile, Triple M will operate as a major tool for our own counterintelligence efforts and as a major avenue for us to penetrate the U.S. government and develop a mole or moles. We will harness America's Political Correctness Movement to the benefit of Allah, be He glorious and exalted."

"Mr. Kasi, you have a brilliant mind."

"In all honesty, my dear, these ideas are not original with me. After the communists came to power in Russia, they set up something they called: 'The Trust.' They duped everyone into thinking The Trust was an anti-communist organization designed to restore the Czar or a Czar to power. The Trust, of course, was run by what would later become the KGB. Like honey attracting flies, the anti-communist aristocrats flocked to the Trust. The Trust appeared so real even British intelligence was duped, to include their famous spy-of-spies, Sidney Reilly."

"So what happened to the people who joined the Trust?"

"When Lenin had all their names, they were all rounded up and shot."

"So, what will be my role? Am I to remain here in America or am I to return to Gaza?"

"Aliyah, my dear, my chief, Mr. Ayman al-Zawahiri, says you are to stay here with your Palestinian relief organization. The U.S. Department of State will be happy to extend your visa again and again. You will have plenty of time to do your real work. Yours will be the work of years, not just months."

"And that is?"

"Money, friendship, favors, drugs and sex are the mother's milk of any effective intelligence-gathering organization. At some point, we will identify a CIA or a high-level State Department employee for you to seduce. Armed with ample photographic evidence, we will make the recruitment pitch. It's the oldest game in the business, and often works."

"But, Mr. Kasi, you know I come from a good family. I am a virgin. I know nothing of sex."

"Aliyah, as your name implies, you are of the highest social standing. But draw the curtains, my dear, and I will teach you all you need to know."

✡ ✡ ✡

CHAPTER ONE

Over the Atlantic Ocean. December, 2007.

Looking through the windshield of the chartered LuftCondor Boeing 727, Buck and Dolly Madison stared out into a midnight-blue sky decorated with planets and stars. Now and then, a distant meteor streaked across their view. On the western horizon, the Sun was about to set. Thirty-thousand-feet below, the lights of some of the cities along the Atlantic coastline of North America were just beginning to appear.

The darkness of the Atlantic Ocean was relieved here and there by the twinkling lights of trans-Atlantic ocean liners and by the lights belonging to merchant freighters making for safe harbor along the Atlantic seaboard or starting out on voyages to the Old World.

Buck Madison, who knew very little about the Boeing 727, was in the captain's seat. Dolly Madison, who knew even less about the 727, was on Buck's right, in the seat normally occupied by the first officer or co-pilot.

Standing behind Dolly was Fraulein Heidi Schnell, the Boeing 727's senior flight attendant. The airliner's captain was bound, gagged, drugged, and stowed on the floor of the flight deck. One of Heidi's sensible heels was firmly planted on the groin of the unconscious captain.

"Excuse me, *Herr Doktor Oberst* Madison," said Heidi. "Please do not take this false. I know you and *Frau Doktor* Madison are both pilots, but have either of you ever flown a Boeing 727 before?"

"Not really," said Buck. "But I do play a lot of video games."

"*Frau Doktor,* vat is he saying? Is your husband making some kind of American joke? A crack wise?"

"Heidi, you must forgive Buck. When he is nervous, he makes what he thinks are jokes. But, at 30,000 feet, flying an airplane he has never flown before, he's not all that funny."

"Seriously, Heidi," said Buck. "I did spend an hour in a Boeing 727 flight simulator at the United Airlines flight-training center in Denver. I was instructed by aviation legend Emily Howell Warner, the first woman to be hired as a pilot by a scheduled U.S. airline. As an airline captain, Emily led the first all-female flight crew. Heidi, you would like her."

"Ja, that is all well and good, but vas the simulator realistic enough for you and *Frau Doktor* Madison to get us safely to Dulles International Airport?"

"Heidi, the 727 simulator was so realistic when a female pilot accidently set it to Sex Mode; she had to go on birth control."

"Okay, Buck," said Dolly. "That's enough!"

For many years, Heidi Schell served the CIA as a covert asset. It was a way of picking up a little extra money for her eventual retirement. Heidi was well aware that Colonel Buck Madison and Dr. Dolly Madison, like so many retired intelligence couples (called Honeymooners, in the trade), had been pressed, post-9/11, to return to service.

In Berlin, after all the other passengers boarded the aircraft, Heidi beckoned the Madisons up the 727's aft boarding stairs. She seated them in front of the aft galley. Heidi made them feel welcome but, otherwise, treated the two Americans as if they were complete strangers. That, of course, was a lie. Heidi was well aware of the Madison's secret mission across Europe.

Now, Heidi listened carefully as the Madisons discussed a yellow, sticky note they found stuck to the 727's radio console. Scribbled next to the numeral "one" was a hand-written latitude and longitude. Next to the numeral "two" was a different latitude and longitude. Heidi watched as Colonel Madison reached into the captain's Jeppesen chart case. He selected a particular World Aeronautical Chart and handed it to Dolly.

"The first lat/long plots just north of Frederick, Maryland," said Dolly. "The second lat/long plots on top of the White House. So, the first officer wasn't lying when he confessed he and the captain planned to crash this aircraft into the White House."

"In all my years with LuftCondor," said Heidi, "I have never seen either of them. Do we know their names?"

"Actually, we do," said Buck. "After I put the first officer down for his little 'nap' in the aft lavatory, I checked his passport. He's Fritz Schmidt. The captain's passport shows him to be Hans Schmidt. Apparently, brothers-in-crime. Anymore questions?"

"Herr Oberst, you still haven't answered my first question. Soon, I must go back into the passenger cabin to assure our passengers and my flight attendants we can land safely. If I have no confidence, zay vill detect it in my voice."

"Heidi, I detect it already," said Buck. "You are losing a bit of your normally, perfectly-posh English accent. No matter. All your passengers are Germans. Speak to them in German. But try some deep breathing first."

"Okay, *Herr Oberst.* But are you sure you can land this airplane?"

"The landing may be a little bumpy," said Buck. "But I think it will be a good one."

"What Buck means by one of his 'good' landings," offered Dolly, "is that LuftCondor might be able to use this Boeing 727 again – someday."

"Now, Dolly's making jokes," said Buck. "Okay, off you go, Heidi. Use your best *Hoch Deutsch* to tell the passengers the truth. Then, tell them not to worry because two of the world's best pilots are going to fly them safely to Dulles. Tell them there is nothing to: worry about, worry about, worry about, worry about, worry about, worry about…"

Shaking her head, Heidi left the flight deck. Buck and Dolly looked at each other, knowing they were both scared spit-less. To keep his sweaty palms from showing, Buck donned the captain's Nomex flight gloves.

"Buck, do you think Heidi is as scared as we are?"

"I'd say Heidi is more scared than we are."

"Buck, do you really think we can pull this one off?"

"I once knew a naval aviator who claimed he could fly any airplane, to include the box it came in. But then, he was a naval aviator. Full of male bovine excreta."

"Buck, you didn't answer my question."

"I know."

"Maybe, the answer is in here," said Dolly, as she opened the Dash One, the operating manual for an aircraft neither of them had ever flown before.

✲ ✲ ✲

CHAPTER TWO

Tora Bora, Afghanistan. November, 2001.

He was a simple jihadist in the service of al-Qaeda. His full name was Adbullah Aziz Muhammad Wazwaz. His superiors called him Corporal Muhammad and his friends simply called him: Muham-mad. During the brief visit of Colonel James Buckley "Buck" Madi-son to Osama bin Laden's secret redoubt in the Tora Bora region of Afghanistan, Corporal Muhammad had been entrusted for a few hours to guard Colonel Madison, who was serving at the time as the personal envoy of the president of the United States.

But, one week after Colonel Madison departed Tora Bora carrying a videotape and a message from Osama bin Laden to the Ameri-can president, something went terribly wrong. The diesel fuel required to power the generators supplying the electricity needed to operate Osama bin Laden's kidney dialysis machine turned into a gelatin-like substance. Dr. Pandit Singh, the East Indian physi-cian who treated Osama bin Laden for diabetes and renal discase, gave Mr. Abu Amed, Osama bin Laden's chief-of-staff, the bad news: Within weeks, without a fresh supply of usable diesel fuel, their leader would die of what Dr. Singh thought was renal disease, although he wasn't sure. It could be something else entirely.

Abu Amed ordered every camel, donkey and horse in the region to be loaded with jerry cans of diesel fuel and be driven up to the secret redoubt. But Abu Amed's orders were hardly out of his mouth when aircraft belonging to the United States and the United King-dom began a saturation bombing campaign across the Tora Bora region of Afghanistan. None of the hardy beasts of burden reached the secret caves. They and their drivers were blown to bits. The burning diesel fuel they carried on their backs made pre-cooked feasts for the birds of prey by day and for the jackals by night.

Inside the cave complex, the silence of the generators was omi-nous to those who had lived underground for so long and gotten used to their incessant droning. Each day, Osama bin Laden's skin grew more and more yellow in color. He had no appetite. Dr. Singh used so many IV needles to deliver nutrition, hydration and morphine to the arms and legs of Osama bin Laden that his veins began to resemble those of a heroin addict. Dr. Singh was fighting a losing battle. With no kidney function left, the toxins in bin Laden's blood could no longer be removed. Septicemia began to set in. Finally, there was nothing more Dr. Singh could do. The mullahs pushed him aside.

Despite increasing amounts of morphine, the pain from the sepsis grew so severe Osama bin Laden became delirious. The mullahs leaned close to bin Laden's deathbed as they tried to decipher his ravings. As best they could tell, their leader was losing or had lost his faith. He seemed to have no confidence in getting to join with Allah and the Prophet Muhammad in Paradise. He kept mumbling something about never obtaining the promised seventy-two virgins as his reward. Instead of being serene as death approached, bin Laden grew increasingly disturbed and angry.

This caused the mullahs great distress. Surely, this man who killed or who had ordered the killing of so many thousands of infidels should know in his heart that Allah and the Prophet Muhammad were waiting to receive him in Paradise. Surely, if any Muslim should, Osama bin Laden should be confident of spending eternity in the arms of the seventy-two virgins.

Knowing his time was near, Osama bin Laden asked to be alone with Abu Amed. In a barely audible whisper, bin Laden instructed Mr. Amed to have his friend and adviser, Ayman al-Zawahiri, brought to Tora Bora – an order Abu Amed decided to ignore – at least, for the time being.

Next, bin Laden instructed Abu Amed on the disposition of his remains: His body was to undergo the ritual cleansing; however, under no circumstances were his robes to be removed. His body was to be carried dressed just the way it was and buried deeply in the ground. The grave site was not to be marked in any way.

Assured his most trusted aide would do as instructed, Osama bin Laden asked for the mullahs to be brought back into his room.

But, just before he died, Osama bin Laden began to chant: *Allah Akbar, Allah Akbar, Itback el Yahud.* (Allah is great. Allah is great. Death to the Jews.) The mullahs offered up prayers. But then, Osama bin Laden suddenly rallied. He opened his eyes, sat up in bed and cried out, "Insul-Swiss!" With that, he fell back and breathed his last breath. One of the bewildered mullahs reached down with his right hand and closed the terror-filled eyes of Osama bin Laden.

True to one part of his pledge, Mr. Abu Amed made sure his master's robes were not disturbed. He made sure the remains were taken directly to the grave just outside one of the entrances to the cave complex.

After the body of Osama bin Laden was lowered into the grave and the grave site and the surrounding area covered with large rocks no predator could remove. Abu Amed summoned Dr. Singh to his quarters.

"What does 'Insul-Swiss' mean?" asked Abu Amed without inviting Dr. Singh to sit down. "Why would Osama bin Laden shout out the words 'Insul-Swiss' before he died?"

"Sahib, I think my patient suffered from diabetes as well as renal disease. Maybe even from Addison's disease. I have long thought some of these conditions were brought on by the overuse of steroids when Mr. bin Laden was very young. As is often the case, the diabetes brought on the renal disease."

"Get to the point, Singh! I asked for the meaning of Insul-Swiss, not a course in medicine or pharmacology."

"Of course, Sahib. Insul-Swiss is the brand name of a type of insulin produced in Switzerland. It is the brand Mr. bin Laden used for almost his entire adult life."

"What is it about Insul-Swiss that would create such an impression on Mr. bin Laden, to the point 'Insul-Swiss,' instead of '*Allah Akbar*,' would be one of the last words he uttered on this earth?"

"If I tell you what I suspect, you must give me your word of honor to cause me no harm."

"All right, Dr. Singh. You have my word of honor. For the sake of Allah, be He glorious and exalted, get to the point!"

"As you know, Sahib, I am not a Muslim. I am Hindu. But both our faiths share a common aversion to certain animals. We Hindus will not kill cattle. Nor will we partake of their flesh. You Muslims have an aversion to swine. You are not supposed to ingest any of the parts of a pig."

"Dr. Singh, I need no instruction on the basic tenets of my religion. So what does insulin have to do with pigs?"

"About ten years ago, when I was first engaged to care for Mr. bin Laden, I did a thorough review of all of his many medications. During my review, I happened to come across an article in the *Journal of the American Medical Association.* The article revealed how Insul-Swiss, which was the world's leader in insulin medications, had just changed the way it formulated insulin. The new way was to use recombinant DNA. But the article also discussed the former way of making insulin."

"If you don't get to the point of all this, I *will* have you shot!"

Swallowing hard, Dr. Singh said, "Prior to using recombinant DNA to make insulin, Insul-Swiss made its insulin from the pancreas of cattle and pigs."

"Pigs! Did you say pigs?"

"I am afraid so, Sahib. Some batches of Insul-Swiss were made entirely from cattle pancreas. Other batches were made entirely from pig pancreas. Just before the change-over to recombinant DNA, a mixture of cattle and swine pancreas was used."

"Was Osama bin Laden aware of what you just told me? Did he know some fool before you came along was injecting him with products made from swine?"

"He knew his insulin was made by Insul-Swiss. But I am sure he knew nothing about its formulation, past or present. When I came upon the truth, I made an oath to myself. I vowed to go to my grave before I would tell him Insul-Swiss was once made from the pancreas of pigs. For my part, I made absolutely sure we only used batches of Insul-Swiss made entirely from recombinant DNA."

"Did Mr. bin Laden ever show any signs he was aware of how Insul-Swiss was originally formulated?"

"Not until just recently. In fact, it was the night when Colonel Madison departed. Mr. bin Laden called me to his bedside and asked to see all of the vials of Insul-Swiss in my medicine cabinet. He seemed terribly upset about something."

"So, you brought him the vials. Then, what happened?"

"He put on his reading glasses and he inspected each and every one of them. He read every label."

"Did he say anything?"

"Yes, Sahib. He asked me if I was sure the contents were made from recombinant DNA. I assured him we were using recombinant DNA. But I thought it rather odd for a person like Mr. bin Laden to be conversant with the term: recombinant DNA. I certainly never said anything to him along those lines. In the ten years I served as his physician, we never discussed insulin at all, other than a brief mention when it was time for his injections."

"At this moment, Dr. Singh, I would wager you and I are the only ones in this entire Tora Bora complex who know anything about the time when insulin was made from pigs."

"Yes, Sahib, I would say you are correct. Why is that important?"

"Because our cause, our Jihad against the American infidels and the Jews, would suffer a great blow if it became known Osama bin Laden cannot join Allah, be He glorious and exalted, and the Prophet Muhammad, may his name also be praised, in Paradise, you must promise never to reveal this information to anyone, ever!"

"Of course, Sahib. I have never spoken of this to anyone, except to you."

"Yes, Dr. Singh, you have been our master's faithful servant for many, many years. And, I thank you. That is all, Dr. Singh. You may go now."

"Thank you, Sahib. But what are you thinking about the way our master died? Are you thinking, as I am, that this had something to do with the visit of Colonel Madison?"

"Yes, Dr. Singh. I am thinking Colonel Madison caused the diesel fuel supply to go bad. If you recall, Colonel Madison did spend some moments alone with our master. I'm thinking Colonel Madison may have told Osama bin Laden about the various formulations of insulin made by Insul-Swiss."

"Is there anything we can do?" asked Dr. Singh.

"Yes, we will never speak of the insulin again. But there remains the question of what caused the diesel fuel to go bad? I can do something about that, beginning with the questioning of everyone here who had any contact with Colonel Madison."

After Dr. Singh departed, Abu Amed summoned three of Osama bin Laden's most-trusted bodyguards. He instructed the guards to find Dr. Singh, take him outside, shoot him, and cremate the remains. Dr. Singh was an infidel and the Koran authorizes Muslims to deceive infidels. Then, Abu Amed sent for Corporal Muhammad.

When Corporal Muhammad appeared in the office of the chief-of-chief, he was asked to describe in detail his contacts with Colonel Madison. With pride, the corporal recited how he was selected by Mr. Abu Amed himself to be a member of the escort detail on the night when the American officer was dropped off by helicopter. He recalled how he was assigned to guard Colonel Madison when Mr. Amed allowed the American to go to the exercise area to Mr. Amed's stationary bicycle. After Colonel Madison finished his work-out, he escorted the American back to his cell. Then, he stood guard over the American until his relief came. Muhammad recited how he led the party that took Colonel Madison back to the location where the American helicopter was to pick him up.

Muhammad's rendition of his contacts with Colonel Madison exactly matched the recollection of Abu Amed. But there remained some questions about the time when Colonel Madison was in the corporal's exclusive care.

"When you conducted Colonel Madison to the exercise machine area and back, was he in your sight at all times?" asked Abu Amed.

"I was with him at all times," said Muhammad, shading the truth.

"Was there a time when you might have fallen asleep?"

"Oh, no sir," said Muhammad. "That would be a breach of my duties as a guard."

"If such a breach occurred, what is the punishment for that?" asked Abu Amed.

"Death," said Muhammad, as perspiration began to break out on his upper lip.

"What if I told you it is important for me to know if Colonel Madison had an opportunity to leave the exercise area and visit the fuel-storage area? What if I told you I would forgive a breach or, shall we call it a lapse, such as falling asleep? Would that refresh your memory?"

"I swear by Allah, be He glorious and exalted, I was never asleep while in the presence of the American."

"While I would like to believe you, Muhammad, it will be necessary to make sure you are telling me the truth."

With a nod to a squad of jihadists standing just outside the entrance to Abu Amed's office, Muhammad was grabbed from behind and thrown on the ground. Terrified, he shrieked, "Please, please! I am innocent! I fought off the drug! I swear I did!"

"You fought off a drug?" asked Abu Amed. "What drug?"

"Before Colonel Madison got on the exercise machine, he made us some tea. I drank some of it. It made me sleepy. I think he put some kind of poison in it. But I swear I did not sleep."

"Not good enough Corporal. I shall have Sergeant Zaghal make sure your memory of those hours with Colonel Madison is accurate. Take him away!"

Kicking and screaming, Corporal Muhammad was carried off into the inner recesses of the cave complex. He was stripped naked. Rope was scarce, so his tormentors didn't bother to tie his hands. They just drove wooden stakes through his hands and feet and into the ground. When he passed out, they threw cold water on him and put smelling salts under his nose.

A field telephone – a Red Chinese copy of the old U.S. Army EE8/A field telephone – was set on the ground next to the writhing Muhammad. Wires were run from the two terminal posts on the telephone to the penis and testicles of Corporal Muhammad.

Sergeant Zaghal was about to turn the crank on the signal generator when Corporal Muhammad decided to confess to sleeping on duty.

Just how long he was unconscious Muhammad did not know. But when he awakened, the American was standing over him. He recalled having a terrible headache. The American gave him some aspirin. Then, the American asked to be escorted back to his cell. That was all he could remember.

Sergeant Zaghal left to report the results of the interrogation to Mr. Amed. Fifteen minutes later, Sergeant Zaghal returned to a sobbing Corporal Muhammad. The guards pulled the wooden stakes out of the hands and feet of Corporal Muhammad. The bleeding corporal was placed on a litter, and carried outside. Sergeant Zaghal used Muhammad's AK-47 to shoot him right between the eyes. Because of his disgrace, Muhammad was not buried. Instead, his body was carried out into the Afghan night to be eaten by the jackals and the birds of prey.

Now, Abu Amed knew what he needed to know. He knew who set in train the events that killed his master. The death of Osama bin Laden would be avenged. He began to form a plan to bring about the torture and death of Colonel Madison and all those dear to Colonel Madison. Money would be needed. He would return to his home in Saudi Arabia, obtain a fresh supply of money from his contacts within the Saudi royal family, and put his plan into operation. Meanwhile, he would move the al-Qaeda headquarters into the Federally Administered Tribal Area of Pakistan an area that was, for political reasons, beyond the reach of the governments of Pakistan and, more importantly, beyond the reach of the Americans. If his rival, Ayman al-Zawahiri, wanted to join them in Pakistan, so be it.

✳ ✳ ✳

CHAPTER THREE

Ouray Ranch Presidential Retreat. September, 2006.

As they stood in the icy-cold rapids of the Colorado River about a mile downstream from the Lake Granby High Dam, the trio cast their flies into the pools and eddies formed by the rapids. The rushing waters pressed against the backs of the rubberized waders that kept their feet warm and dry.

The president of the United States turned to Buck and Dolly Madison and asked, "Does it bother you that the violent events you two have experienced over the last few years have been written up by others? You could do your own publishing, you know. You might even make a little money at it. After all, almost the entire world stood still when satellite TV showed the two of you being forced to walk the plank off of your cruise ship near the Panama Canal."

"We might," said Dolly, flicking her fly into a promising pool. "Buck and I even joke about being 'unknown celebrities,' hoping we could tell our own story our own way, and yet, without losing our privacy, without losing the quiet way we are trying to live in retirement."

"Dolly, are you suggesting you two are already in the process of writing a book?"

"Yes, Mr. President," admitted Buck. "In fact, it is almost finished. As you can well imagine, it deals with terrorism directed against the United States."

"I suspected as much," said the president. "Are you doing it as non-fiction or fiction?"

"The book we hope to publish is non-fiction," said Dolly. "I know this must sound terribly immodest; however, I suppose we are famous for keeping Castro from disrupting a major portion of

Colorado's water distribution system and for stopping the Red Chinese from blowing up the Panama Canal. So, just to keep the record straight, we've written down what happened. If we can find a publisher, we'll donate the proceeds, if any; to a fund for military families who have lost loved ones in Iraq and Afghanistan."

"What's the title of your work-in-progress?"

"We call it: *Walking the Plank to Freedom*," said Dolly. "It's just a memoir about the strange happenings we've experienced since Buck retired from the Army and since I retired from the Agency. What about you, Mr. President? You are getting toward the end of your last term. Will you be writing a memoir?"

"Someday, I suppose. It would probably be a good idea to set the record straight. I suspect some who might follow me in the Oval Office will not be kind."

"Any idea about who that might be?" asked Buck.

"These things run in cycles, so I fear the other party will take over."

"So, if that is the case, will it be a female?" asked Dolly.

"Right now, I'd say President Trimmer's wife has the best shot. It's hers to lose. But there's a relative unknown waiting in the woodwork for her to slip. Actually, I'd be more comfortable with her, even with the baggage her husband brings. Anyone with zero executive experience gives me pause. So, I'm eager to get this al-Qaeda business concluded. I'm not at all sure the other party has the will to defeat those who would destroy us. I do, however, have an idea I'd like to discuss with you.

"Unfortunately, what I have in mind would be another terrible imposition on the quiet life you are trying to lead in retirement; however, I wouldn't ask it of you unless I thought it really important."

"Like what?" asked Dolly, starting to reel in a Red Quill the trout didn't seem to want.

"I need you to finish your book, your memoir, or whatever you decide to call it. Then, as soon as it becomes a best-seller, I want you to go on a book-signing tour across Europe."

"Mr. President," said Dolly, "we can finish our book all right; however, whether or not it becomes a best-seller is way, way beyond our control. That's up to the readers."

"Dolly, I beg to differ. I can name several political figures who manipulated their books onto *The New York Times* best-seller list. Former House Speaker Jim Wright comes to mind. He induced labor unions and other groups beholden to him, or trying to win his favor, to purchase thousands of copies of his book. There must be stacks of them still in warehouses, sitting around unread. I suspect the same about books written by a certain former president and a certain former first lady. Too bad the newspapers publishing those best-seller lists don't do more to prevent such trickery."

"Are you saying there's a way to do the Speaker Wright scam with our book?" asked Buck.

"Yes, there is. Intelligence and propaganda agencies the world around own what they call 'proprietary companies.' As you would know, Dolly, the CIA created Air America to deliver supplies and agents into Indo-China during the Vietnam War. In fact, some intelligence agencies own or control entire publishing houses.

"So, let's say you finish the book you are working on right away and it gets into the hands of one of the Agency's proprietary publishing houses. Eclectic House is one that comes to mind. Why, I'll bet it would hit the top of a number of best-seller lists in no time. First thing you know, there would be a clamor for the authors to go traveling all over the world signing books and doing interviews. I know certain authors who might be very attractive to al-Qaeda. Who might help us surface Abu Amed and his chief lieutenants."

"Why the focus on Abu Amed?" asked Dolly.

"Here I go again relying on tips given to us by allied intelligence agencies. That didn't work out very well for us in Iraq. But I'm hearing Abu Amed is planning to create a mutant form of al-Qaeda. The Cambridge-educated Amed is smart enough to realize the original al-Qaeda model isn't working anymore in Iraq. In fact, what's left of al-Qaeda is hiding along the fringes of Pakistan and Afghanistan.

"I'm told Abu Amed wants the Islamic jihad to become more Euro-centric, to use the loose immigration laws of socialist Europe to populate Europe with Muslims. Because we do not, at present, have an intelligence agency able to penetrate Abu Amed's inner circle, I think it is imperative to find out who they are and take steps to take them out, to include Mr. Amed."

"Mr. President," said Buck, with a frown, "if I'm reading you correctly, you are suggesting our book would be given the phony best-seller treatment and then we go overseas just begging for Abu Amed to take his revenge out on us."

"You got it, Buck," said the president, as he finished reeling in his line and the three started wading toward the river bank. "Actually, I'm more interested in the capture of Abu Amed and his closest lieutenants. Let's sit on those tree stumps over there. I can't think of a more secure environment. Let's rest a spell and I'll tell you what I have in mind."

The Secret Service agents hidden discretely along the banks shifted their positions accordingly. After the three fishers found places to sit, the president said, "As far as public diplomacy goes, I think your book tour should be sponsored by the State Department under the auspices of something over at State having to do with cultural-exchange programs and whatnot. As far as your covert mission goes, playing mouse to Abu Amed's cat, the CIA could play a major role."

"Pardon me, Mr. President," said Buck. "Lots of brave men and women work in the field for the CIA's Clandestine Services and for the Office of Technical Services; however, Dolly and I have lost confidence in some of the CIA's bureaucrats at Langley. Mostly the fault of President Trimmer, I might add. But if one of the dissidents over at Langley decides this book tour isn't a good idea, we'll all be reading about our actual mission in *The New York Times* before breakfast. The same goes for the State Department. If our so-called ship-of-state were actually a ship, the leaks to certain reporters would have sunk it long ago."

"Look, I'm well aware certain elements within the CIA and the State Department do not agree with my foreign policy. The Agency, I have learned to my chagrin, has several on-going culture wars within. Unfortunately, many of the operatives who understood the spirit of former Directors Allan Dulles, McCone and Helms are long gone."

"Mr. President," said Buck, "your predecessor's first pick for DCI would have worked out okay; however, when he balked at hiring one of Trimmer's girl friends, Trimmer refused to meet with him. So, he quit. But it was Trimmer's second pick for DCI who really harmed the Agency. For some reason, he detested the field hands, preferring to put analysts with no practical experience in charge."

"I have no bone to pick with intelligence analysts. For heaven's sake, Dolly was an analyst, an interpreter-translator. But she stuck to what she knew, which wasn't trying to recruit and run agents in a hostile environment."

"Because the so-called new culture is so clueless about developing human intelligence resources, if they do get a morsel of supposedly 'real' intelligence they seize on it like a vulture on road kill. When a foreign intelligence agency told them Saddam Hussein was on the brink of possessing his own nuclear arsenal, that little morsel kept passing around the intelligence horn until it came back to the Agency embellished as the 'slam dunk' intelligence that took the Allied Coalition into Iraq. Instead of being based on HUMINT, we ended up acting on RUMINT, if you will."

"Buck, we'll let the historians play the blame game," said the president. "Right now, we need to drain the swamp of jihadists. But since it's your lives I'm putting on the line, you tell me how you would organize your mission."

"I suppose," said Dolly, "we cannot escape how Buck's foray into Tora Bora against bin Laden may have put us both under a lifetime *fatwah*. Without meaning to be so, Buck and I are in a no-win situation. While Cuban intelligence might no longer be a threat, al-Qaeda is a threat for sure. I suspect the CIA, the State Department and the so-called mainstream media are not going to wish us well either."

"Dolly, I hear what you are saying, so I'm hoping Buck's military background might be brought to play here. What say you, Buck? Have you got any ideas?"

"Mr. President, when your former Secretary of Defense discovered the Agency and the State Department could not produce timely, actionable intelligence, a special intelligence-gathering unit was formed within the OSD."

"Yes, I authorized it," said the president.

"Right now, OSD-Intel is headed by a former subordinate of mine, Brigadier General Jack McClure. Long ago, Jack was one of my company commanders. Now, Jack and his staff operate out of the National Military Command Center, the NMCC, down in the bowels of the Pentagon."

"Been there many times," said the president.

"If we are going on this mission, Mr. President, I would like Jack McClure to be our controller. If so ordered by you and the SECDEF, Jack and his staff could monitor us 24/7 and respond to our needs. If we do smoke out any key Abu Amed operatives, some outfit is going to have to take him or her or them off our hands. You can't expect two middle-aged retirees to engage in armed combat with Abu Amed and the remnants of al-Qaeda. We will have to have a way to call for backup. For sure, Dolly and I will need secure, 24/7 satellite-communications gear."

"I agree. But do you see any roles for the Agency or State?" asked the president.

"Well, I suppose Agency snatch teams or its private contractors could render anyone we catch to some place for interrogation. As for State, the diplomatic pouch could be used to make sure we have what we need at each stop along the way.

"If the Islamic jihadists are supposed to attack us during our travels, then we will need some means of self-defense. Not the sorts of things the airlines will let us carry. If your plan is for State to provide some sort of cultural cover for our tour, it would be logical for us to visit the U.S. embassies or consulates along our way. We could pick up our self-defense items at embassies or consulates. We could turn our weapons back in before we have to submit to any TSA-like security screening."

"But what if we are attacked as soon as we deplane?" asked Dolly. "What if we are attacked before we can reach an embassy or a consulate?"

"That could be a role for the CIA," said Buck. "The Agency could have a case officer meet us at each airport. But it would have to be an officer with enough moxie to run a proper surveillance detection route. We could do a bag-swap shortly after we get off each airplane."

"You mean you would carry the same kind of handbag on each leg of your tour and someone from the Agency would come to each airport with an identical bag stuffed with your weapons," said the president. "I think I read about that one time in some espionage novel."

"Exactly," said Buck. "Dolly has a travel bag she carries on a shoulder strap. General McClure could procure several of them and make sure each CIA station has an identical bag on hand, each one containing our self-defense items."

"Tell you what," said the president, "I'll arrange for this General McClure of yours to control your mission and to be spring-loaded to respond 24/7 to your needs. I'm sure DOD can round up some small, satellite telephones to link you to the NMCC. But those kinds of details we'll leave to you and General McClure. As soon as I have the SECDEF with us on this and General McClure appointed as your controller, I'll have my National Security Adviser let you know. At that point, you two can proceed with General McClure. After you finish your book and we can do the 'marketing' to get your book on top or near the top of the best-seller lists, you will need to go to D.C. for a series of briefings. So, plan on all this taking the better part of a year to get set up.

"By the way, when you are jetting around Europe, you might start work on the book after this one. You could take a notebook computer or one of those MP3 player gadgets with you. After each encounter with Abu Amed or whatever happens, you could record your thoughts."

"Please, don't encourage him, Mr. President," said Dolly. "But I do have another concern: Benjamin Franklin observed: 'Three people can keep a secret as long as two of them are dead.' Just how many people or agencies would be 'witting,' as the spooks say, about what Buck and I will actually be doing?"

"There will be myself, my National Security Advisor plus the SEC-DEF, General McClure, and his staff in the NMCC. The DCI and someone on his staff will have to direct a case officer in each country you visit to deliver your bag of self-defense items. You may want to get some of those items from the CIA's Office of Technical Services. Of course, the cultural affairs people over at Foggy Bottom will have to arrange your public appearances; however, they don't need to know your actual mission – just your itinerary."

"Mr. President," said Dolly, "that's tantamount to saying the details of our mission will appear on the front page of *The New York Times* before we leave Grand County, Colorado."

"Yes, Dolly, but think of it this way: The typical leaks we suffer from the usual suspects at State or at the Agency will help us attract the attention of the people I want captured."

"Yes, so what happens when we are attacked?" asked Dolly. "Will there be some kind of ready reaction force to come to our rescue? Again, if we are unable to deal with the attackers ourselves, there has to be some sort of backup."

"That's why I like your idea of having OSD-Intel back your book-signing tour. General McClure should be able to provide a number of assets such as Army Special Forces, Navy SEALs, Delta Force, you name it. And, since certain elements within the Agency and State are going to leak some of the details anyway, we might as well call on the field elements of the Clandestine Service to provide some muscle in certain countries."

"Mr. President, military back-up might work in NATO countries. But what if we go to places where U.S. forces are not stationed?"

"Again, that's where the Agency's Clandestine Service could come in handy. You know, you are forcing me to refine my thinking about your mission. So here's the deal. You will only go where we can make backup available. In other words, your book-signing tour will only go to countries where we have diplomatic missions or where the countries visited are members of NATO. Okay?"

"Well, I suppose we might as well be hung for a sheep as a goat," said Dolly. "I'll come up with a laundry list of self-defense items to fit in my shoulder bag."

"You name it. You got it. You send that list to General McClure," said the president. "Look, Julius and Emily have invited all of us for lunch. Let's hike up to the Warner's house and have some trout."

✲ ✲ ✲

CHAPTER FOUR

Southern Waziristan, Pakistan. September, 2007.

Abu Amed, Osama bin Laden's former chief of staff, was having a bad day. Even though southern Waziristan offered slightly more creature comforts than the old headquarters in the Tora Bora region of Afghanistan, Wana, the capital, still caused Abu Amed to feel like he was in a prison. Packed in with thousands of Pakistanis and hundreds of Taliban refugees from Afghanistan, his Cambridge-refined nose hated the sweaty smells of unwashed bodies and the bluish haze created by the open smoking of hashish.

While both southern and northern Waziristan were places hostile to the police forces of former Pakistani President Pervez Musharraf, it still wasn't a good idea to risk his life by strolling through the crowded lanes running like spider webs here and there. With a million-dollar price tag on his head, Abu Amed had many reasons to be cautious. U.S. Special Forces or Navy SEALS, or a missile from a Predator or a Global Hawk might kill him. Still, he felt safer in Wana than farther north near Peshawar where his rival, Ayman al-Zawahiri, was in hiding.

Southern Waziristan would have to do for now. Seated before him in a half-circle on the luxurious Persian Rug presented to him by Osama bin Laden himself, were some of the men who might well hold the key to al-Qaeda's future. Two of them were not impoverished Islamic zealots. But then, neither was Abu Amed whose wealthy family preferred living the "good life" in Monaco and Cannes to the family home in Wahhabi-restrictive Saudi Arabia.

Both Tarik Hussein and Mohammad Gobanifar had what Abu Amed was looking for: money and motive. Tarik Hussein, the former head of Iraqi intelligence, had access to some of the Swiss bank accounts established by Saddam Hussein to harbor the millions of dollars stolen by Saddam Hussein from the U.N.'s Oil-For-Food Program. For religious reasons, Gobanifar hated the

Great Satan. Gobanifar, the current head of Iranian intelligence, enjoyed almost unlimited access to the millions of dollars being generated from the Iranian oil fields of Isfahan.

But both of their governments lost millions by financing Fidel Castro's abortive attempt to assassinate Presidents Trimmer and Popov. More importantly, both men suffered considerable personal embarrassment when Castro's plot was foiled by a middle-aged couple who, without meaning to do so, got in the way. Abu Amed's promise of the capture of Colonel James Buckley "Buck" Madison and his wife, Dr. Melissa Rennie "Dolly" Madison was what brought Tarik Hussein and Mohammad Gobanifar to Wana.

The other men who were seated on the almost priceless rug were Abu Amed's lieutenants for personnel, intelligence, operations and logistics. Clearly, al-Qaeda, or what was left of it, was organized along military lines. In fact, when Abu Amed was a student at Cambridge, Professor Buck Madison was invited to lecture there on leadership. Almost in passing, Dr. Madison made reference to the way the American military organized for both peace and war: personnel, intelligence, operations and logistics. Years later, when tasked by Osama bin Laden to put the al-Qaeda organization together, Abu Amed recalled what he learned from Colonel Madison that day in Cambridge. When the time came, he structured al-Qaeda the same way.

Gobanifar and Hussein understood English quite well. Some of Abu Amed's lieutenants spoke Arabic, some spoke Farsi. For this mixed audience, they would just have to understand Abu Amed's upper-class English.

"My brothers, this is probably the last time we will be able to meet here in the comfort of the Kasbah of Wana. The infidels are closing in on us here. And we never know if the feckless Pakistanis will try to stop them. The faithful in Afghanistan tell me the American Special Forces have infested our former headquarters across the border at Tora Bora. But that is of no consequence. I have an entirely new vision of our mission and what we must do to carry out that mission."

Anxiously, the men seated in the circle bent forward to learn what Allah, or at least Abu Amed, held in store for them.

"Allah willing, be He glorious and exalted," announced Abu Amed, "some of us are going to Berlin where we will establish a new base of operations."

"Berlin?" the word erupted from the mouths of his lieutenants at the same time along with a babble of questions: "Why Berlin? Who will carry on the fight to restore the Taliban to power in Afghanistan? Who will lead the efforts to assassinate the infidel leaders we must kill. Why must we travel so far from the resting place of our beloved Osama bin Laden?"

"Be calm," ordered Amed. "We must be realistic. Afghanistan has a new constitution giving strong powers to the Afghan president. The United States has bought and paid for so many of the tribal chiefs that I fear betrayal. Afghanistan will take care of itself. But just as the British and the Russians found Afghanistan to be ungovernable, so it will be for the United States and its NATO allies. Chaos is the natural order of Afghanistan. Besides, if the American Left comes to power, it will run up white flags all around the world. So, we need not risk our remaining resources in Afghanistan and Pakistan. Now, we must go where we can be of better service to our cause.

"As I am sure you are aware, al-Qaeda, as the core of our movement to restore the Caliphate, has weakened under the leadership of Ayman al-Zawahiri. The Great Satan and its allies have al-Zawahiri reduced to sending out periodic video tapes in an effort to regain control of our Islamic-jihadist movement. In desperation, Ayman al-Zawahiri may be planning another operation on the scale of the September 11th attack on the American mainland. Unfortunately, such an attack might reunify the infidels the way they were unified on September 12th. That would not be good.

"We need the infidels to continue to fight among themselves. In America, political partisanship is trumping patriotism. Moreover, liberal judges and greedy lawyers are making it more difficult for the infidels to penetrate our networks. So, for the moment, America is not our problem.

"We must also face the problem of al-Qaeda elements not under any kind of central control conducting operations against the infidels. So far, the operations of these elements are not well planned and have been poorly executed. One of their botched sabotage attempts in Great Britain was embarrassing. The solution, my friends, is for us to relocate our operations to the heartland of Europe. We must become the heart and soul of al-Qaeda, leaving Ayman al-Zawahiri in his dingy cave and to his own devices.

"At Cambridge, I became familiar with the writings of Sir Halford John Mackinder, the genius who invented geo-politics. Sir Halford said whoever controls the heartland of Europe controls the central mass leading to the control of the world. That is why I have chosen Berlin as the site for our operational headquarters. Al-Zawahiri can theorize all he wants; however, actual operations require high-speed control and direction from a headquarters located in the midst of the infidels. If al-Zawahiri is content to operate at the speed of couriers on the backs of donkeys, so be it.

"Al-Zawahiri is convinced Pakistan, the only Muslim nation with nuclear weapons, is the main prize. Al-Zawahiri may have a point; however, Pakistan is too far east and too far removed from the heart of the Middle East, the Arabian Gulf, the Mediterranean, the Balkans and the heartland of Europe. If al-Zawahiri succeeds in gaining control over Pakistan and its nuclear weapons, will he have gained anything useful? No. He will only bring a rain of cruise missiles and bombs down upon his head and, in the wake of that, he gives the infidel Hindus their opportunity to control Kashmir forever.

"Now, listen carefully. I have some new missions in mind. First, we must plan and carry out attacks on Europe and the United States.

Done properly, the retribution for those attacks will not rain down on us in Berlin, but rather, on al-Zawahiri in the Northwest Frontier Province.

"Meanwhile, our other mission will be to direct, as best we can, the repopulation of Europe with people who accept Allah, be He glorious and exalted, as supreme and who will live by the dictates of the Prophet, may his name be praised."

"But didn't the Palestine Liberation Organization try to repopulate Israel with Muslims and fail?" asked Gobanifar.

"Yes, the PLO failed for now. The PLO failed because of the collapse of the Soviet Union. Suddenly, thousands of Jews were free to leave the USSR and resettle in Israel. For that temporary change in the demographics of Israel, we can blame the infidel Ronald Reagan.

"As I say, the change was only temporary. We are, once again, gaining on the demographics front. Let me assure you the population of Europe with Muslims is going along quite well. For example, in Great Britain, where we have two million of our faithful, the second-most popular name recorded with the British Birth Registrar is: Muhammad, or variations thereof. Moreover, some British courts are allowing Muslims to live under the Law of Sharia.

"Meanwhile, I have not forgotten Colonel Buck Madison and his wife, Dr. Dolly Madison. Granted, they don't amount to a biting fly on the behind of a camel, but we cannot allow ordinary people like the Madisons to go unpunished. The Madisons, according to my sources, will embark on a tour of Europe. The world must learn that affronts to Allah, be He glorious and exalted, and to our cause do not go unpunished. From Berlin, it will be easy to track their movements and swat them as we would a fly on the butt of an ass, if you will excuse my mixed metaphor.

"As the number of the faithful increase, we will gain seats in the parliaments of Europe. You saw the cowardice of many European editors and publishers when we protested the Danish cartoons that depicted the Prophet, praise be His name, in an unflattering manner. You saw how we murdered the sodomite van Gogh for his blasphemy against Allah, be He glorious and exalted. The Europeans are like a flock of castrated sheep. So, even without being in the majority, our elected brethren can assist in the fragmentation of the European Union."

"But Abu," protested Tarik Hussein, "the European Union is adding more nations to its numbers. How can you say it is 'fragmenting'?"

"At Cambridge, I learned nations act – first, last and always – in their own national interest. As Lord Palmerston said, 'Nations have no permanent friends or allies, they only have permanent interests.' Palmerston's truism means the differing permanent interests of the European nations spell eventual doom for the European Union.

"The so-called integration of the European nations reached its high water mark in November, 2002, when the United Nations Security Council voted unanimously to take stern measures against Saddam Hussein if he did not comply with the U.N.'s previous 16 resolutions. That was the last moment of accord in the halls of the United Nations. When the Great Satan insisted force could be used to enforce compliance, France, Germany and Russia broke away. France and Germany broke away because some of their leading politicians were receiving oil vouchers from Saddam Hussein. Russia broke away simply because its actions are almost always directed against the Great Satan.

"While most of the European countries sided with the United States – especially those recently released from the yoke of the atheist Soviet Union – each time the European Union adds another member, it adds another nation which will, ultimately, act in its own self-interest. Mark my words, while it will not happen right away, the European Union, like the League of Nations before it, will fail. It will be a case where the individual parts will prove to be greater than the whole.

"So, my friends, we are going to live for a time in a villa one of our operatives has rented for us on the shore of the Wannsee, a lake lying inside the Steglitz-Zehlendorf district of Berlin.

"Tarik Hussein, you will find Berlin most interesting. When Hitler was in power, the uncle who was raising and educating Saddam Hussein was Khairallah Tulfah, a disciple of Haj Amin al-Husseini, the Grand Mufti of Jerusalem. The Grand Mufti worked hand-in-hand with Heinrich Himmler's Gestapo and the SS to exterminate thousands of Jews. The Grand Mufti recruited 20,000 Muslim volunteers for the SS. Working side-by-side, Muslims and the SS eliminated many of the infidel Jews in Hungary and Croatia. It was from the teachings of his uncle and the Grand Mufti that Saddam Hussein learned to hate the Jews and to distrust the British.

"On the opposite shore from our rented villa will be the Wannsee Mansion, the place where the Nazi leadership plotted the destruction of Europe's Jews. At some point, I plan for us to visit the Wannsee Mansion. We will pose as members of the German Council on American-Islamic Relations which, as you may know, is a covert arm of our brothers in Hamas. We will say we are simply peace-seeking Muslims trying to understand how supposedly rational men could plot the destruction of an entire race. I trust the irony will not be lost upon you.

"Moreover, and this is all I have to say to you on the matter, al-Qaeda long ago placed certain operatives in Washington, D.C. Their mission is to spot, recruit and train some spies within the U.S. government. At one time, they had some success; however, they are now under the control of Ayman al-Zawahiri. Go now. Pack your things. We are moving to Berlin."

✡ ✡ ✡

CHAPTER FIVE

Washington, D.C. November, 2007.

When *Walking the Plank to Freedom* was headed toward first place on *The New York Times'* best-seller list, Buck and Dolly were summoned by the president to Washington for a round of briefings. First stop was the Pentagon.

Right on time, the Madisons were ushered into the office of the Secretary of Defense. The Secretary, as was his custom, was working at his stand-up desk. Turning his attention to the doorway, the Secretary came over to shake their hands.

"It is a pleasure to meet you, Dr. Madison, and this husband of yours," said the Secretary shaking both their hands. "Buck, your service record is over there on my other desk. You had quite a career during your 20 years with us."

"Thank you, Sir," said Buck. "Your predecessors kept farming me out to other branches and services, so I got the idea the Army was just a place to be between being seconded to other agencies."

"Actually, Colonel, the people in career 'mangelment,' don't tell them I said that, were probably just trying to make you into a 'purple-suiter,' someone who could see beyond the parochial interests of just one service."

"Actually, Mr. Secretary, Dolly's the international purple-suiter. During her time with the Agency, she went back and forth between Langley and Hong Kong quite a bit. She got to work with State, with MI-5, the FBI, and even the Secret Service."

"Given the assignment you two have 'volunteered' to take on, I suspect both of you will need all the skills and experience you have. Look, I just wanted to say 'hello' before you go down in the bowels of this place and see your old friend, Brigadier General Jack McClure. Buck, I understand you and Jack McClure go way back."

"Yes sir. When I commanded an airborne battalion in Germany, Jack was our best company commander. If it can be done, Jack will figure out a way to do it. Dolly and I are pleased you have assigned Jack to monitor our somewhat phony book-signing tour."

"As you know so well, this project is the president's baby; however, I am perfectly okay with it. Thank you for stopping by. I won't detain you any longer. General McClure is waiting."

Brigadier General Jack McClure was watching the entrance to the National Military Command Center as Buck and Dolly were escorted inside by one of the SECDEF's military aides. McClure had not seen the Madisons in a decade. He noted that Dolly was still the tall, trim, blue-eyed blond that made her look like she belonged on the Swedish ski team. Buck's hair was grey, almost white. But, otherwise, Buck looked pretty much the same: Still about 190 pounds, six-foot tall, tanned and fit-looking, despite being well-past the age of military retirement.

After the ritual handshake with Buck and a hug for Dolly, McClure said, "Buck, it's been awhile since I was a captain and you were my battalion commander. I feel like I have aged more than either of you."

"You may feel that way, but you don't look it either," said Dolly, as McClure escorted them toward his office just off to the side of the command center.

The visit to the NMCC was a first for the Madisons. As they followed General McClure, they noted the huge plasma screens showing the locations of the Pentagon's military assets around the world. For every time zone, there was a large clock. A dozen or so staffers wearing headsets were seated in front of computer screens or quietly moving about to confer with other staffers. It looked like Houston Mission Control during a space launch. But, instead of NASA staffers, the NMCC was packed with personnel from all of the Armed Forces. The personnel ranged in rank from very senior NCOs to Army and Air Force colonels and Navy captains.

Buck and Dolly were fascinated as they watched a TV screen showing a female U.S. Air Force captain in a dark room somewhere, probably near Las Vegas, remotely piloting a Predator drone. Her aircraft looked down on a Toyota pick-up kicking up dust as it sped across some desert on another continent.

Before the Madisons could enter General McClure's office, one of the staffers interrupted long enough to ask permission for the Predator to fire on the speeding truck.

"What's the intel say?" asked McClure.

"We have a high probability the pick-up is carrying some al-Qaeda types to a meeting with Taliban leaders."

"Take 'em out," ordered McClure. Within moments, the NMCC staffers were high-fiving each other.

"It didn't take you long to decide that," offered Buck.

"Well, if I wait too long, the lawyers get involved and we have a mess on our hands like the time back in late 2001 when the lawyers would not let us fire on a convoy known to be transporting Mullah Muhammad Omar. The military commander took the blame. Actually, it was the lawyers that FUBARed that one. Mullah Omar has been on the loose ever since. Mullah Omar, may his name be damned, has cost us and the Afghans a lot of lives.

"The upside of the Predator is its ability to take out the bad guys without risk to our troops on the ground and it does it with either zero or little collateral damage. The downside is the possible psychological impact on the operator who, after dispatching a truck full of terrorists to Islamic Paradise, simply goes home at the end of his or her shift, picks up the spouse and they take their kids to the soccer match. Then they come home and cook dinner.

"Buck, you and I have been in actual close combat. So, we understand kill-or-be-killed situations, making it easier for us to pull the trigger on a firearm or easier to throw a hand grenade or easier to order an artillery strike or an airstrike. The young men and women operating the Predators or other armed, remotely-piloted aircraft are in no physical danger. They operate in air-conditioned comfort.

"So, it is difficult to equate the effective work they are doing to the valor of our troops in the field who are at enormous risk and enduring terrible hardships while doing essentially the same job: killing the enemy.

"Hopefully, they read a lot of St. Thomas Aquinas and St. Augustine on the theory of the Just War. If not, we may have a bunch of head cases on our hands.

"The effectiveness of the program, however, is so great that you know the radical Islamists are going to enlist the aid of the ACLU and all the lefty lawyers they can find to claim Predator strikes are unauthorized assassinations. They will claim the Predators violate the Geneva Conventions or they violate the Executive Order against assassinations.

"No matter that the enemy slaughters thousands of innocent men, women and children. When the enemy causes collateral damage, it is no big deal to those who do not want us to win the war on terror. But if we cause any collateral damage it is the end of Western Civilization as we know it.

"Moreover, we have some administrative issues. Our operators are flying a sort of aircraft. Should they get flight pay? They are engaging in a form of combat. Should they get combat pay? They do some distinguished 'flying.' Should they get the Distinguished Flying Cross?"

"Talk about a mixed blessing," said Dolly.

"But where are my manners?" said McClure, as Buck and Dolly were ushered into McClure's tiny office and sat down in front of his desk.

"Would you like some coffee or tea?"

"Thanks, but no, Jack," said Buck. "We have more briefings today. I suppose the SECDEF has filled you in on what the president wants you to do."

"Yes, I was even summoned along with the Secretary to the White House to hear it directly from the president himself. You two must be nuts to accept a mission like this. But, I'll guarantee you one thing: Every facility, every person you see here in the NMCC will be at your beck and call 24/7. You call, we haul. I will be sleeping with a personal communicator that will allow you to talk to me, satellites working, at any time, night or day.

"In fact, here are your own communicators," said McClure, extracting what looked like ordinary cell phones from a box on his desk. "As you can see, these look like Blackberries, iPhones or whatever. They have all the functions you would expect from those sorts of gadgets, only what you now have in your hands can be switched to a satellite mode that will send whatever you have to say, either voice or text, via satellite, here to the NMCC and to me wherever I am 24/7.

"Unless you are indoors, the GPS function will allow the NMCC to know the position of your phone within about two meters. What's more, we can tell which signal is which. Dolly, the phone in the blue case is yours. The black phone is for Buck. The pound sign is the panic button. Whether the phone is turned on or off, if you press the pound sign, we will know you are in a world of hurt and need us to send someone to your rescue. Try not to need it."

"But if we do need your help, who or what have you got lined up?" asked Buck.

"It depends on where you are along your tour. Wherever possible, I'll be calling on the Delta Force or DEVGRU, which used to be Navy SEAL Team Six, or the Special Forces to bail you out. If one of them is not close enough by, we've made a deal with the Agency to call on their case officers. They have some armed assets scattered about, some legal, some illegal. We'll try not to use the latter."

"I hate to sound like a lawyer," said Buck. "But did the president sign one of those 'finding' things required by Congress?"

"No need for that Buck," said McClure. "You are not being sent to assassinate anyone. You are going abroad to promote and sign your book. If you are attacked, you have an inherent right to self-defense. If some 'tangos,' our short-hand for terrorists, get killed, it's between the tangos and Allah."

"Okay. But, if we get taken captive," said Buck, "I hope the Delta Force will come get us."

"If we have to use Delta, here's the thing to remember: When they break into the room or jail cell, or tent or wherever you are held captive, you drop to the floor and stay still. The Deltas are excellent shooters. They are required to fire several hundred rounds each day. They can pick the fly specks out of the pepper, if you will pardon the expression.

"Dolly; speaking of shooting, I understand you are the better shooter in your family. You were on your university rifle team. Won some trophies I hear."

"I'm okay with a rifle or a shotgun. Buck's better with handguns."

"But you're the one who bagged the Cuban we thought was Ilich Ramirez Sanchez, AKA Carlos the Jackal."

"He wasn't Carlos, the Jackal?"

"Hell, no. He was just one of Fidel's many illegitimate children. The terrorist you shot was just a Carlos wannabe. He was such a bullshitter. He just wanted everyone to think he was the Jackal. Actually, the real Jackal was locked up in a French prison."

"'Whoever he was," said Dolly, "he had to be nailed before he blew Buck to smithereens." Dolly did not mention what she did to the two terrorists who killed her precious, canine-American, Scooby-doo.

"Dolly is better at the martial arts than I am," said Buck. "She's a Kajukenbo Black Belt."

"What's that?" asked McClure.

"Basically, it is the art of dirty street fighting. It means she holds black belts in Karate, Judo/Jujitsu, Kendo, Karate, and Kung Fu. A Kajukenbo Master also knows all the lethal or 'killer strikes,' as they call them."

"Good grief," said McClure. "Dolly, how did you acquire all those skills?"

"Growing up in the New Territories outside of Hong Kong, we missionary kids, in addition to absorbing Cantonese and Mandarin, needed something to do. At the time, the name Kajukenbo was not known to us. We were simply learning the martial arts. Later, someone in Hawaii came up with that catch-all name. The Ka is for Karate, the Ju is for Judo/Jujitsu, the Ken is for Kendo and the Bo is for boxing, which the Chinese call: Kung Fu."

"Do you ever spar around with Buck?"

"No. Buck didn't grow up with it. He's more of a gun or knife person. But he did rig up a big body bag for me to kick. Now and then, I'll go out in the garage and give the bag a few blows."

"Let's hope neither of you have to do anything physical," said McClure. "Now, let's get to your list of requirements. Dolly, I understand all your self-defense stuff needs to fit in bags that look exactly like the shoulder bag you walked in here with today.

"Stacked over there on my bookcase are two dozen shoulder bags just like yours. Based on the list you provided, we've filled one of those bags as a sample for you to examine. If you go over and lift it, you'll find it is fairly heavy; however, not so heavy as to arouse suspicion. Loaded just the way it is, it weighs precisely 11 pounds or five kilos. If you decide to add anything, be sure to weigh it, and add it to the total weight. Let me know what you add and I'll do the same for a model shoulder bag we'll keep right here. After you receive your bag, Buck gets about half of what's in there.

"Inside, you will find a .380 Walther PPK/S. The PPK/S has a longer grip than the original PPK so it can be fitted with the Crimson Trace laser sight, which it has. That's for Buck. There's a left-handed shoulder holster for Buck, along with an inside-the-belt holster, and even an ankle holster. Buck, depending on what you are wearing, you can choose between holsters. For your book signings, you'll be wearing a coat and tie. For travel, wear whatever is comfortable.

"Inside, you will find a Taurus Judge Revolver outfitted with the Crimson Trace laser grip sighting system. As you know, you can load the Judge with .410, 2.5-inch shotgun shells and/or with .45 Colt pistol rounds. Dolly, the Judge is for you.

"When you are walking along with the bag hung from the shoulder strap, you can have your gun hand inside the bag and resting on the weapon. You can fire it from inside your shoulder bag; however, it would be better if you have a .45 Colt round in the first chamber. That would make a smaller hole than the .410. But don't worry about it. As you can see, we have more bags. We only have one of you.

"Also, for Buck, is an Emerson CQC-7BW folding-knife. Buck, at $228 bucks a pop, I have to say you have good taste in knives."

"You got off easy," said Buck. "I could have asked for a Smitherman done in Damascus steel."

"In any event, the president said you might capture people. In aid of that, you will also find two, seven-inch, hard-leather saps. We've included three sets of plasti-cuffs. You can use those to hold your captive or captives until we can get someone to you who can render them elsewhere.

"Here at DOD and over at the Agency's Office of Technical Services, we've come up with some gimmicks that probably weren't around when you guys were active. For example, we've included a pair of suspenders or, as the Brits say, 'braces' for you, Buck. What makes them different from ordinary suspenders is the Det-cord hidden inside the elastic straps. Inside the elastic, you'll find two 36-inch lengths of Det-cord. There are slits where you can reach in to grab the Det-cord and pull it out."

"But I always just wear a belt," protested Buck. "My Master Parachutist Wings are on the buckle."

"Fine, you can wear your normal belt and buckle as well," said McClure. "People will just think you are paranoid about your pants falling down. So, get over it, Buck.

"As you know, Det-cord is harmless without a detonator. So, we've hidden a detonator inside on of those super-fat Montblanc pens. Unscrew the cap, take out the detonator, and attach the detonator to one end of a piece of Det-cord. Pull the pin on the detonator. You have five seconds to hide behind something."

"Why do we need the Det-cord?" asked Buck.

"It crosses my mind you guys might be the ones who are captured. There is nothing like a few wraps of Det-cord for cutting some bars or chains or whatever."

Dolly, picked up the bag, put the strap over her right shoulder, stuck her hand inside the bag and felt around.

"Is this piece loaded?"

"No. But when you receive it in the field, the cylinder will be holding five rounds. Three of them will be .45 Colt; two of them will be .410 birdshots."

"I can also feel the Walther in the bottom of the bag," said Dolly, pulling out the shoulder holster for Buck.

"Here, Buck, try this on," said Dolly.

"Bond's the name. James Bond," said Buck, slipping into the shoulder rig.

"He's impossible," said Dolly, as she laid the rest of the bag's contents on McClure's desk.

"You'll also find some Inferno Pepper Spray, and two of those Sure-Fire combat flash lights that will temporarily blind an assailant. Inferno contains two interesting ingredients: Oleoresin Capsicum, which gets in the eyes and burns like fire. It also contains black pepper. The black pepper causes the target to sneeze which forces the target to inhale deeply of the Oleoresin Capsicum, and when the Oleoresin Capsicum gets into the lungs it causes the target to collapse. Long term, it is harmless. But, short-term, it renders the target helpless.

"Speaking of helpless, we have also included some vials of Ketamine. As you may know, Ketamine is a powerful sedative. An injection of Ketamine disassociates the brain from the rest of the body. The victim, as it were, loses control of his or her ability to make their arms and legs function as normal. Do not ever, ever let some veterinarian use Ketamine on your beloved canine-American. In fact, Ketamine is banned for use on humans with the exception of certain highly-trained physicians. But we don't mind using it on tangos because it renders them harmless for long periods of time.

"This will come as a shock to you; however, you are both now diabetic. You each have diabetic dog tags and the necessary paperwork to show why you are carrying some hypodermic needles and some vials appearing to be full of insulin. Not so. They are filled with Ketamine.

"Plus, we took the liberty of including some personal items we figured you would probably carry in a shoulder bag like this one. You know, tooth paste, tooth brush, hair brush, compact, lip gloss, the items you would want to use in any event."

"Jack, you must think I'm a lot younger than I actually am," said Dolly, as she pulled two tampons out of the bag.

"Well, you look so young I think we could be forgiven; however, that's not why we included the two tampons."

"Then, why on earth for?" asked Dolly.

"Well, you know how inventive GIs are. Ever since we've included so many women in the armed services, tampons have been part of the supply system. In both Iraq and Afghanistan the troops discovered that a fresh tampon is just the thing to insert into a bleeding wound until a medic can crawl or walk over to apply a proper dressing.

"Actually, you could carry the tampons in any of your bags; however, I just wanted to bring their usefulness to your attention."

"What if we need a black bag job or some place bugged or a lock picked?" asked Dolly. "What do we do?"

"Dolly, your Agency jargon is showing. The Agency is going to station some teams from the Office of Technical Services along your route. As you know, they have the skill sets to do all kinds of technical penetrations. It's hard to imagine a scenario where you'll need that kind of help; however, someone from OTS won't be far away."

Dolly extracted a jewelry case from the bag. She asked, "What's this necklace? This looks like costume jewelry. Oh, Jack, you are too kind."

"Actually, not kind at all," said McClure. "The necklace is the latest model of the old SRR-100 radio receiver. It is a counter-surveillance device. You wear it around your neck and it can detect the presence of hostile surveillance teams. Basically, it is just an induction coil. If a surveillance team is talking on radios or painting you with any kind of electronic beams, you will feel the necklace get a bit warm. Not hot. Just warm enough that you will feel it."

"Thank you, Jack. I shall wear it always and, when I do, I shall be thinking of you. Does this require a thank-you note?"

"If you come home safely, that will be thanks enough."

"Do you know why Junior Leaguers do not attend sex orgies?" asked Buck.

"No, but I'm afraid you are about to tell us," said McClure.

"It's because they can't stand the thought of mailing out all those thank-you notes."

"Okay, Buck, for you, the computer geeks made up a special laptop for you to carry. It looks and works like a regular Dell or whatever; however, in addition to working in the usual Wi-Fi environment, it also has a satellite-texting capability. We recognize you won't be able to have this computer with you at all times. So, we expect the other side to gain access to your hotel room and to your computer to see what's inside. We get around this by installing a separate word-processing program, one that is unlikely to be discovered.

"Use the regular WORD program to write your next book or whatever. But use the hidden word-processing program to compose and send text messages to me. Just open the hidden program, write whatever you want to tell us. It will be encrypted automatically. Switch the laptop into satellite mode. Then, take the laptop outdoors and you can uplink your file to one of our satellites that downlinks here at the NMCC. As you will see, we've made improvements to the old Short Range Agent Communication system. It is now long-range. When you hit ENTER, the laptop sends up a burst communication lasting only a fraction of a second. Only we here at the NMCC can decrypt it."

"That's great," said Buck. "The president did suggest I start working on a new book. If I am seen typing away, it would just add to our cover, our legend. In fact, I already have something to write about. They say, when writing a play, if you have one of the characters place a pistol on the mantle in the first act, you better make sure that pistol gets fired before the final act is over. Jack, you've given us plenty to write about."

"Buck, let's hope you don't have to fire any weapons. Remember, you are supposed to be spreading good will and understanding to the cultural elites of Europe."

"Right," said Dolly, rolling her eyes, "Do I get a bag swap when we get off the plane in London?"

"There is no bag swap until Paris. In London, MI-5 will have some of their 'hard men' on hand at London Heathrow. You might not see them. But they will have your back. You are going to be hosted by Buck's old friend, Kirk Forsyth, the Deputy Chief of Mission, and his lovely wife, Judith. Kirk will have you picked up at Heathrow.

"Look for a black, Jaguar XJ. Yes, we know the XJ has an aluminum body. That's why it's been armored. Also, it's the long-wheel-base model. You'll feel like you're in a limo. And, I might add, that your ride was built when Jaguar was owned by the Ford Motor Company. So, don't think the embassy didn't buy American.

"The DCM's driver is retired MI-5, a former 'hard man.' Not someone you would want to cross. Your driver will take you directly to our embassy on Grosvenor Square. Livingston Biddle, our Ambassador to the Court of St. James, expects you to make a brief courtesy call. He will want a photo taken. The ambassador will make some excuse as to why he won't be going with you and the Forsyths to the Buckingham Palace later than evening. Truth be known, he wants to come back here for some sunshine. After you make nice-nice with Ambassador Biddle, your driver will take you to the DCM's residence in time for lunch. I've seen the DCM's digs in Mayfair. They are rather nice."

"Hold the phone," said Dolly. "Did you say we are going to Buckingham Palace?"

"Yes. The Queen is having one of her 'intimate' dinners. Not many guests. You have been invited. I'll get to that in a minute.

"You will stay overnight with Kirk and Judith. Buck, your Army Blue Mess Uniform and an appropriate gown for Dolly are already in a closet in one of the guest rooms in the DCM's residence. After lunch, you should even have time for a nap. We want you to look sharp for the Queen. Also, the next morning you must be at Harrods for a book-signing and for every day after that you are going to be on the go.

"That evening, the armored limo will take the four of you to Buckingham Palace. Both the Queen and Prince Phillip are well aware of your previous dust ups, as the Brits like to say, with Castro's intelligence service, the Red Chinese, and maybe even with al-Qaeda. We are told the Royals were watching in living color as you two were being forced to walk the plank off the Scandia *Seawind.*

"The Palace has been provided two copies of *Walking the Plank to Freedom.* So, you can expect the Royals have read it, or have been briefed on the story line. They may even ask you to sign a copy for them. Just sign something like 'With respect' and your names. Don't get fancy.

"Either Kirk or Judith will brief you some more on how to address the Queen and Prince Phillip in conversation. When you first meet the Queen, Buck, you are expected to make a slight bow. If you were the American president, you would not bow. American presidents do not bow to royalty or to the heads of any other states.

Dolly, it is not required of non-Brits; however, you should curtsy. Judith Forsyth will go over all that with you.

"These so-called intimate dinners are something new for the Queen. She likes to play the role of the peace-maker. Do not be surprised when you see she has invited people who, for the sake of public appearances, cannot stand each other. But, under the Royal roof, she finds world figures of all stripes and spots can find a few moments of respite from how their followers think their leaders should behave. She thinks some Royal glitter and some fine things to eat and drink might heal old wounds and even build new friendships. Anyway, the dinner is not just for you. It just worked out that you get to attend. More luster for your book tour, and something you can add to your next book. Buckingham Palace is so heavily guarded we don't think al-Qaeda will try anything there.

"The next morning, the armored limo will take you to Harrods for your book signing. But at Harrods you might encounter trouble.

"Your driver will park outside under the cooperative eyes of the local police. Besides, the limo has diplomatic plates and is immune from parking tickets, something that drives us nuts here in D.C. and in New York. Your bags will already be packed and loaded into the limo for your flight to Paris. You will not be returning to the DCM's residence. After the book signing, the limo will take you directly to the airport for your flight to Paris.

"When you get to Charles de Gaulle International Airport, you will need to take a taxi to your hotel. But, before you can hail a cab, you must proceed out of customs. Straight ahead you will see some payphones on little pedestals. They are not actual booths like you find in England or back in the States. Anyway, that's how France Telecom does it at de Gaulle. Look for two payphones that are close together. While you are calling to tell me you are in Paris, place your shoulder bag on the floor just to the right of your right foot. Just remember: 'right,' okay?"

"We are charter members of the vast, right-wing conspiracy," said Dolly.

"Buck, while Dolly is talking to me, you do counter surveillance. If Dolly's necklace gets warm, something is up. Dolly, a case officer will come to the payphone to the right of yours. He will set a bag identical to yours on the floor. Your bag will be taken by 'mistake.' From that point on, you two will be armed. But I hope not dangerous. Clear?"

"By George, I think she's got it," responded Buck.

✧ ✧ ✧

CHAPTER SIX

Blair House, Washington, D.C. November, 2007.

Eager to attract attention to the success of *Walking the Plank to Freedom*, the president let it be known the Madisons would be staying across the street from the White House at Blair House, the mansion President Truman fixed up for visiting dignitaries. The mainstream media took note, giving even more ink to the Madison's book. Alternatively, the president could have put the Madisons up in the Lincoln Bedroom of the White House; however, a previous president so shamelessly "rented" the Lincoln Bedroom to political contributors the current president only allowed his relatives, either by blood or marriage, to stay there.

Instead, briefers from the National Security Agency (NSA) and the CIA were brought through a back door to a small apartment inside Blair House. Because the Madison's mission would be taking place outside the continental United States, no one bothered to invite the FBI.

The NSA briefer, who introduced himself as Mr. Duncan de Mille was one of those grey-faced technocrats; however, he brightened up as he told Buck and Dolly he would be taking his wife to the Kennedy Center later that evening for a performance of Swan Lake. Obviously, the expense-paid drive down from Ft. Meade, Maryland, was a boon for the de Mille family.

The CIA briefer, Mr. Catesby Fawkes, was another matter. His chalk-striped suit, striped shirt, paisley handkerchief in his suit jacket and foulard tie gave Fawkes the air of being Bond-Street foppish. Fawkes' almost-white hair suggested he was over-age-in-grade. He must have either screwed up some operation or somehow ticked off his superiors to end up doing a flunky job like running over to Blair House to brief a couple of middle-aged retirees.

Mr. Fawkes' nostrils flared as if encountering a bad smell when he learned the Agency was subordinated to the DOD for the so-called "book tour." Clearly, being the "baggage handler" for Brigadier General Jack McClure was not to his liking. Nevertheless, he assured the Madisons he would see to it the case officers stationed in Europe would manage the bag swaps called for in their itinerary.

Right before they departed, both briefers, however, expressed skepticism about the Madison's mission. The NSA briefer said they could read some, but not all, of Abu Amed's message traffic. He said Abu Amed and his lieutenants were using multiple, throw-away cell phones. The Patriot Act was of enormous help; however, the courts were applying more and more constraints by ruling the monitoring of cell phone conservations constituted a "warrant less" search. He said Ayman al-Zawahiri was using very few electronic communications. Even so, the NSA felt al-Zawahiri was planning some sort of operation inside the USA, the nature of which was yet unknown.

Having done what they were ordered to do, the two briefers bade the Madisons farewell and slipped out the back door.

Seeing no need to go out, Buck called the Blair House kitchen. Buck ordered two salads, some grilled chicken for Dolly and a medium-rare steak for himself. Within the hour, their meal was delivered. After dinner, Buck worked awhile on their next book. Dolly fussed with their packing. The next morning they would be over at Foggy Bottom for the meeting with the Under Secretary of Public Diplomacy and Public Affairs and with some of the lesser officials from the Bureau of International Information Programs.

✻ ✻ ✻

CHAPTER SEVEN

Foggy Bottom. November, 2007.

The black Lincoln Navigator provided by General McClure deposited Buck and Dolly at the front entrance to the Department of State. The driver said he would be waiting for them when they came out.

A personal meeting with Buck's former Infantry School classmate, the Secretary of State, would have raised a lot of eyebrows because it was not the custom for the Secretary to spend his valuable time with authors simply going abroad as part of one of the Department's cultural programs. Besides, the Secretary had not been told the details of the Madison's actual mission. One never knew whose side the Secretary would take. And that went double for his talkative deputy and his left-leaning chief-of-staff.

The Madisons presented their credentials at the reception desk. Buck told the cheery receptionist they were expected by Ambassador Clayton Frederickson. The receptionist made a phone call.

Ambassador Frederickson was the scion of an old-line East Coast Establishment family. The Frederickson family made its fortune in banking and in oil. The family had a history of belonging to country and luncheon clubs with "restricted" memberships. But, under pressure from the Anti-Defamation League, Frederickson resigned from a Virginia country club which had yet to initiate a member of the Jewish faith.

Frederickson was a leader of the entrenched State Department bureaucracy known to favor Arabs and Iranians over Israel. However, at one time, a number of Jews were prominent in the U.S. Diplomatic Corps. They were seen as a useful bridge between Christians and Jews in the Middle East. In fact, the post of Ambassador to Turkey was, at one time, reserved for Jewish diplomats. But, after 1920, all that began to change as the latent anti-Semitism of the East Coast Establishment became more manifest. In fact, by 1948, if the courageous Harry Truman had not been the U.S. President, the U.S. Department of State would have thrown the fledgling State of Israel to its Arab neighbors.

As a result of spending his boyhood summers at his family's seaside villa in Tunis, Frederickson was fluent in both French and Arabic. Following graduation from Groton and Harvard, he served with distinction in a number of posts across northern Africa and in the Middle East.

In fact, Frederickson was a favorite of the previous president and served, at one time, on the staff of President Trimmer's National Security Council. His rise to ambassadorial rank in the State Department was not hurt by the Frederickson's generous contributions to President Trimmer's political campaigns, his contributions to the coffers of President Trimmer's wife, or by the promise of further contributions to President Trimmer's Presidential Library.

After about five minutes, Ambassador Clayton Frederickson debouched from a nearby elevator. The ambassador wore a tweed jacket with leather elbow patches, chino slacks, and a button-down Oxford-cloth shirt with a foulard tie, and a golfer's tan. Dolly noted his tassel loafers and his British regimental-style moustache.

After brief greetings, Ambassador Frederickson bowed the Madisons into the waiting elevator. Arriving on the fifth floor, Frederickson led them to an ornate conference room.

"We have you at a disadvantage," said Ambassador Frederickson. "We know who you are; however, we are probably new faces to you. Dr. Dolly Madison and Colonel Buck Madison, allow me to present my colleagues who will clearly and distinctly pronounce their names."

With all names distinctly spoken and all hands politely shaken, Ambassador Frederickson indicated the two empty chairs at one end of the long conference table as belonging to Buck and Dolly. As expected, none of the FSOs possessed Joe or Bob or Jim or Chuck or Bill as first names. Instead, their first names were: Thornton, Wythe, Winthrop, Erskine, Crocker and Cabot. Dolly had never seen so many vested-suits and paisley bow-ties. The room felt like a posh London men's club. Or, like the Georgetown Club, over in Georgetown. The room held the faintest whiff of expensive, lavender-based after shave. For sure, it wasn't Stetson.

"Well then," said Frederickson, "Let us begin. Ladies and gentlemen, the Madisons, both of whom, I might add, have more degrees than a thermometer, are going off on a tour of Europe under the auspices of our very own Bureau of International Information Programs. Their book tour is for the purpose of helping our friends in other lands understand the nature of the terrorist threats we have been facing both here in this country and even on the high seas. So, ladies-first, as it were. Dr. Madison, have I correctly stated the nature of your task?"

"Yes, you have, Mr. Ambassador," said Dolly. "As some of you may have read, Buck and I were living in peaceful retirement high in the mountains of Grand County, Colorado, when a group of terrorists, under the direction of the Cuban Intelligence Service, tried to blow up some key dams and tunnels related to the storage of water in Colorado. My husband and I just happened to be in a position to, shall we say, interfere.

"Our resulting and unwanted notoriety led to what we expected to be a rather relaxing engagement as lecturers on a cruise ship which, unfortunately, caused us to experience an attempt by the Red Chinese and other Cuban intelligence operatives to sabotage the Panama Canal in concert with what would have been an attempt by the Red Chinese to invade Taiwan. We just happened to be position to disrupt the plan to sabotage the Canal. That, in turn, caused the Red Chinese to abandon, for now anyway, their plan to invade Taiwan. Our book, *Walking the Plank to Freedom* provides an account of what I just described to you."

"Thank you for that brief summary, Dr. Madison. But, for the purpose of today's discussion, I must say that we, here at the Department of State, do not use the term: Red Chinese."

"Fair enough," said Dolly. "Why don't we just call the Red Chinese 'commies' and the folks on Taiwan, 'our allies'?"

"Do you have any expertise in the area?" asked Frederickson, archly.

"Probably not as much as some; however, I was born in a Presbyterian mission near Shanghai. My father was a missionary. But after Chairman Mao's thugs beheaded my father in front of his congregation, my mother carried me as a babe-in-arms to Canton where we stayed for awhile before fleeing to find more permanent refuge inside Rennie's Mill Mission in the New Territories just outside of Hong Kong.

"Our escape was made possible by a former member of the O.S.S. After university, I suppose I had a natural leaning toward the Agency.

"My amah was Cantonese. So that was my cradle language. Mandarin is my second language. English I learned a bit later. I spent most of my career with the Agency in Hong Kong, serving as an analyst/interpreter."

"Well, I dare say you do know something about that part of the world," said Frederickson, looking very uncomfortable. He shifted the subject. "Now, Colonel, tell us a bit about your military career."

"I jumped out of perfectly good airplanes. Spent some time working for the Director of Central Intelligence, as the saying went back then, did a couple of years detailed to the Air Force, spent a year at the Naval War College where I met Dolly. Mostly, I was a grunt who spent two years in Vietnam, to include almost two months in Cambodia. As Dolly said earlier, we were perfectly happy to be retired in Grand County, Colorado, when some of Castro's terrorists tried to blow the place up."

"Colonel Madison," said Frederickson, "I have often wondered why you folks would jump from perfectly good airplanes. It seems a bit too dangerous for my taste."

"Yes, Mr. Ambassador," said Buck. "Parachuting does seem dangerous to a great many. I've even known Air Force pilots who said their airplane doesn't have to be perfectly good. They are still not jumping.

"That aside, since 9/11, a lot of us are doing the unexpected. These days, when I pick up a book to read, non-fiction or fiction, the first thing I do is check to see if it was written prior to 9/11 or after 9/11. Books written prior to 9/11 seem, well, so innocent.

"As some here in Washington know, but apparently not all, we are engaged in a war like no other before it. If we believe what the Islamic jihadists say and write, they do not intend to stop killing until all of us are dead. So, the purpose of our book tour is to provide our erstwhile European allies a better understanding of the threat we should be facing together – instead of the U.S. going it pretty much alone."

To a person, the briefers were aware of how the Madisons were, to put it diplomatically, not well-liked in Havana and Beijing and within what was left of the al-Qaeda organization. All of them expressed a concern for their welfare and placed special emphasis on topics related to their personal safety while abroad. Some of the briefers even told them how to guard against SARS and the Norwalk Virus. Neither Buck nor Dolly could detect any of the briefers were aware the book tour was anything more than what it was purported to be.

Due to the recent unpleasantness with France and Germany, the political situations in those two countries were given special attention. When the desk officers and the cultural affairs officers were finished, Ambassador Frederickson summed up the session by wishing them a safe journey and expressing the desire of the Department of State to help them in every way possible. They were invited to stop by the U.S. Embassy or consulate in each country on their tour for an update briefing on the local situation. Apparently, Frederickson and his colleagues had not been told how Agency case officers, operating under diplomatic cover from U.S. Embassies and Consulates, were going to be doing bag swaps with Dolly.

Buck and Dolly thanked the panel for devoting their time to the briefing. Ambassador Frederickson escorted them to the main entrance where the SUV was waiting to take them back to Blair House. After they were dropped off at the back entrance to Blair House, Dolly asked, "So, what do you think?"

"Typical State Department pukes," said Buck. "They spend their days reading cables from diplomats out in the field and their evenings attending cocktail parties along Embassy Row. I think they operate on the principle even a blind squirrel finds an acorn now and then."

"I detect you are not enamored of our Foreign Service Officers," said Dolly.

"When I worked in the Pentagon, relations were so strained with State we used to say we needed to exchange ambassadors with the State Department and vice versa. Once they have their language training and get posted to a particular country, they tend to be captured by their hosts and do more representing of the view points of their hosts back to the United States rather than representing the view points of the United States to their hosts.

"I felt some of that when I went through the total immersion course for German at the old Army Language School. As you know so well, Dolly, there is much to like about almost every culture. Learning the language makes you want to buy into what appears to be something new and different. When you start to spend your days and much of your evenings working and socializing with your in-country counterparts, it's easy to see the world more through their eyes and to give less credence to the way world events would be perceived from the point of view of your own culture.

"For example, on the eve of World War I, Turkey could have joined forces with England and France or joined forces with Germany and Austria. Turkey chose the losing side. Had she joined with England and France, she would have come out of World War I the Great Power her geography suggests Turkey ought to be.

"But Turkey's leader, Enver Pasha, served as a military attaché in Berlin. He spoke German quite well. So, he got caught up in the Germanic *Kultur*, which he admired. He kept pushing for Turkey to side with Germany and Austria. The second factor was when the Royal Navy screwed up and allowed two German warships to slip through the Mediterranean to Istanbul. That unfortunate demonstration of British ineptitude helped tip the scales toward Germany.

"Still, language learning is good in a sense because it can give us a better understanding of what our allies and our possible adversaries really think and what they might do in the future. In other words, it helps us do a better job of measuring their intentions. Just don't fall in love with any of them.

"As you know, in the world of military intelligence, we always look at two factors: capabilities and intentions. Given our satellite and other technical intelligence-gathering abilities, we have a pretty good handle on the missiles, tanks, ships and troops we might face someday. In other words, we do know a great deal about the capabilities of those who would harm us.

"But discovering and measuring the intentions of a potential adversary is much more difficult to do. So, I suppose there is something to be said for training your diplomatic corps to be so lovey-dovey with their foreign counterparts. Yet, I swear some of them go overboard and become more sympathetic to their host nations than they are to the U.S. of A. I think some of them are charter members of the 'blame-America-first crowd.' Dr. Jean Kirkpatrick nailed it when she spoke of the 'blame-America-first-crowd' and caught the attention of President Reagan. That's how she got to be our U.N. ambassador and to be in Reagan's cabinet."

"You may be right," responded Dolly. "My problem is so many of them don't seem like real Americans. You know, the Americans of Middle America. Fly-over Country, if you will. They don't seem to have much in common with our farmers, ranchers, and factory workers. The typical American. How are they supposed to represent the people of the United States, when they are so 'foreign' in their dress, their manner of speaking and in their Chablis and Brie tastes? They probably wouldn't be caught dead in a Walmart or a Sam's Club.

"But then, few of the foreign diplomats whom I've met are representative of the work-a-day folks of their own nations either. So, I suppose when elites meet to eat, it all works out."

"Dolly, if you want real Americans, check out the Foreign Agricultural Service, the FAS. There you will find men and women with degrees from our agricultural and mechanical colleges. Many of them come from farm and ranch families. I've seen FAS officers at work in the field. They actually have calluses on their hands. They will roll up their sleeves and will help install an irrigation pump or whatever is needed to 'drain the swamp,' if you will. But I suspect the FSOs make them check their boots for manure before they let them back into the embassy for the cocktail hour.

"If you've had enough of D.C., let's ask to be checked out of Blair House and sent on our way back to Colorado. We need to get our home front secured before we can head for Europe."

"Let's do it," said Dolly.

✵ ✵ ✵

CHAPTER EIGHT

Denver International Airport. December, 2007.

Arriving back home to pack their bags for Europe, Buck and Dolly were greeted by the Secret Service couple, Benny and Beth Cornwell, who were posted to Lake Granby to watch their home and Prince, the Madison's Old English Sheepdog, while they were on their book-signing tour. Seeing his human companions again, Prince would have wagged his tail off, if he had one.

The Cornwells were pleased with their temporary duty. Beth Cornwell was recovering from a gunshot wound she suffered while conducting a reconnaissance for a presidential visit to a Third World country. Benny Cornwell was on administrative leave, without pay, so he could finish his doctoral dissertation for The George Washington University. If all went as planned, the Madisons would be back in time for the Cornwells to have Christmas with her parents out in Wray, Colorado.

If Madison's book tour were to take advantage of pre-Christmas sales, Buck and Dolly had little time to spend back home. Hurriedly, Dolly went over some check lists having to do with when to operate the heat tapes inside the roof gutters and when to have them off. She explained when to expect Waste Management to collect the trash, and how to operate the snow plow for the driveway, and how to operate the snow thrower for the upper deck. Given the average seasonal snow fall of 30-feet, these were important tasks. Maintaining a home at an elevation of over 8,000 feet above sea level, especially in winter, requires care and attention. Yet, for the Madisons, the extra effort was more than repaid by the extraordinary scenery and the relative isolation from what they felt was an outside world gone mad.

Buck and Dolly checked and rechecked their packing lists. They would need business attire for the book signings. Business casual for travel and leisure wear, and exercise wear if they were to have any hope of keeping in shape. Bags stacked on the entry deck, they were at last as ready as they were going to be.

All too soon, it was time for Buck and Dolly to bid a reluctant farewell to their canine-American and to the young couple. Mr. Robert Price, of the Federal Protective Service, arrived in an unmarked government SUV to escort Buck and Dolly on the two-hour drive from their secluded home near the Lake Granby High Dam to the Denver International Airport.

Ever since the Madisons foiled the Red Chinese-Cuban plot to block the Panama Canal, the president felt they needed to be protected from possible terrorist retaliation. So, Mr. Price plus three more FPS agents were their almost constant companions and, of course, friends. But, with Buck and Dolly leaving for an extended period, the FPS detail was being relieved for awhile by the Cornwells.

After passing through Granby, Tabernash, Fraser and Winter Park, the drive over the 11,315-foot Berthoud Pass was, as always, spectacular. Fortunately, the road over the pass was now three-lanes, making the drive much safer in winter and summer. Once on the Denver side of the pass, Buck fell asleep. Dolly chatted with Bob Price. Two hours later, as Special Agent Price parked momentarily at the curbside check-in for SkyAir Airlines. Buck and Dolly alighted from the government SUV and started their heavier luggage on its way to London Heathrow Airport via Dulles International Airport.

"So long," said Agent Price, extending his hand to Buck, "you are pretty much on your own now. I hope whoever thought this caper up knows what he's doing."

"Think of it this way, Bob," said Buck. "We get an all-expense trip to promote our book about terrorism. We could never have afforded to travel in such grand style on our own. Unfortunately, getting shot at may be part of the deal."

"Just keep your head down, Colonel. Dr. Dolly, don't take any more risks than you have to. If your plane doesn't go today, you have my cell number. I can come back and get you."

"Thank you, Bob, for the care you've given us these many months. Were it not for you and your fellow agents, the tangos might have gotten us already. But if this caper, as you call it, works, we and all Americans may be able to sleep a lot easier in the years to come. And, thanks for the ride down the mountain. You be careful going back to your family. Give Rose our best. Just before our plane takes off, we'll call you on your cell phone to let you know we are on our way."

Because of heightened security requirements, passengers were told to arrive at the terminal two hours prior to their scheduled departure times. Experienced travelers, they had their little 3-1-1 bags at the ready and their Velcro-strapped travel shoes that were easily gotten off and back on.

Buck and Dolly whizzed through the TSA's primary screening in the Jeppesen Terminal and boarded the underground train for Concourse B. When they got to their boarding gate, the electronic arrival and departure board indicated their flight to Dulles was going to depart 30 minutes late. That meant they would have over two hours to kill in the boarding area.

Initially, they were the only persons next to their boarding gate. But shortly after they took their seats, they noticed the arrival of an olive-skinned man wearing a well-tailored business suit. The man took a seat, pulled a newspaper from his briefcase and started reading. Now and then, he would look over the top of his newspaper to steal a look at Buck and Dolly.

"Dolly, don't turn around," said Buck. "But when you can do so without being obvious, check out the chap in the Saville Row suit reading *The Times* of London. I suspect he's just the first of several al-Qaeda minders we may encounter along our way."

Dolly stood up to adjust her cargo pants, the kind with so many pockets you can never remember where you put things. As she walked over to check the electronic departure board again, Dolly's eyes swept across and then beyond the man.

Resuming her seat next to her husband, Dolly said, "The English-cut suit and *The Times* are a bit much for Denver."

"Apparently, he's thinks he's going to fly with us to Dulles and maybe even to London. I'd love to get a look at his ticket."

"Buck, when you say 'thinks,' are you suggesting our minder isn't going to make our flight?"

"Well, at the least, we can make his life pretty miserable. For him to be here in the boarding area, he has to have a valid airline ticket and a photo ID. He's gotten his boarding pass, and he's been through the primary security screening. Because of TSA's fear of 'profiling,' you can bet our Arab-looking friend will not get any secondary screening which, as we know, is reserved for blue-eyed blonds with over three ounces of nail polish, and blue-haired, grandmothers with knitting needles.

"Unfortunately, what I have in mind for our 'friend' over there depends on his going through another x-ray screening. So, we'll have to be sure he gets screened again. We don't have anything better to do for the next hour so. Let's work on it."

"What do you have in mind?"

"Did you see that Chinese fast-food shop we passed on our way to this gate?"

"I also saw that French restaurant, *Pour La France.* They might even serve escargot."

"Actually, I prefer fast food."

"Buck, stop with the jokes. Of course I noticed the Chinese fast-food place. I even saw a Chinese woman at the cash register. What about it?"

"That's good. So, please go back there and order something that comes wrapped in metal foil. Using your Chinese, I want you to charm the cashier into loaning you something I can cut with. You may have to trade her something or pay her."

"But Buck, suppose she is not allowed to have anything sharp."

"Actually, the food service vendors inside this area can't operate without the knives or other sharp objects they need to slice and dice their food. It's one of the many weaknesses in the TSA system. With the help of a food-vendor accomplice, already-screened sky-jackers could be slipped all kinds of weapons."

After an animated conversation with the young Chinese woman tending the cash register, Dolly returned carrying a Chinese take-out carton. Inside the carton was an assortment of Chinese dishes capped with metal foil. In exchange for a knife, Dolly had to give up her Power Ball ticket.

"When I said try to get a knife, you got a really sharp one," said Buck, slipping the knife into his leather flying jacket. As they picked around in their food, Buck secreted the metal foil in one of the pockets of his jacket. He did the same with the lid to the cardboard carton. Then, Buck headed off to the men's room.

Once inside one of the stalls, Buck took out the cardboard lid and drew a fairly accurate outline of a small semi-automatic pistol. In his mind, Buck tried to picture the outline of a .380 caliber Walther PPK, James Bond's weapon of choice.

Carefully, Buck cut along the outline until it became a reasonable replica of a Walther PPK. He wrapped the replica in the metal foil and slipped it into his jacket.

Rejoining Dolly in the boarding area, Buck explained the need to distract the al-Qaeda minder long enough to insert the phony pistol shape into one of the outer zipper compartments of the minder's briefcase. Dolly went off to return the knife to the Chinese cashier.

Meanwhile, Buck decided he needed something more than just planting the phony pistol. The minder was sure to be stopped when the x-ray machine detected what the TSA screeners were sure to think was a hidden pistol. But the scam would quickly be uncovered and, if their minder was quick-witted enough, he could claim he was merely the victim of someone's practical joke.

As General George S. Patton, who was fluent in French, liked to say: *L'audace, l'audace, toujours l'audace.* Getting up from his seat, Buck walked over to where their minder was seated and asked, "Pardon me, Sir. Do you know how much time we will have on the ground in Chicago?"

The minder was taken off guard. "Chicago? I do not think we stop in Chicago," the man replied in French-accented English. "This is supposed to be a non-stop flight to Dulles International Airport. My ticket does not show a stop in Chicago."

"Could we check?" asked Buck. "My wife has our tickets. Could I look at yours?"

"But, of course," said the man, as he took out his ticket.

Buck knew the plane from Denver to London was only stopping at Dulles to refuel. The ticket showed a Mr. Abdul Sharif was planning to be with them all the way to London Heathrow.

"Ah so, you are correct," said Buck. "This *is* a direct flight to Dulles. I was mistaken. Pardon me. Now, I must telephone my friend in Chicago. I will tell him we will not be able to see him today. Thank you for your help."

"It is nothing," said Abdul Sharif, returning to his newspaper.

When Dolly came back from the Chinese place, Buck pretended to use his cell phone. Putting the phone away, he slipped Dolly a piece of paper with the name of their suspected minder. Buck walked over to the agent at the boarding-gate lectern and asked, "Do you know what kind of meal service we'll have on the flight to Dulles and on to London? While our plane is being refueled at Dulles, I might want to deplane briefly to buy something more to eat."

"Sir, in first class, the cabin attendants will be serving a nice lunch about mid-way along your flight to Dulles," said the gate agent, with a smile. "You shouldn't be hungry."

"Thank you. That's good to know. By the way, would you have a diagram of the cabin interior? You know, one of those safety cards you find in the seat pockets. I always like to know where the emergency exits are located."

"Here you are, sir," said the agent, handing Buck the cabin diagram.

Buck took the diagram back to where Dolly was guarding their carry-on luggage. With a felt-tip pen, Buck placed an "X" on the plane's aft lavatory and added the words: *Placez-vous la bombe ici. Itbak el Yahud!*

"Dolly, keep an eye on our friend over there. I need to walk away and call Bob Price. I'm hoping Bob, as a card-carrying member of the Federal Protection Service, can convince the TSA to have Mr. Sharif subjected to secondary screening."

When Bob Price heard what Buck and Dolly were planning to do, he laughed so hard he almost ran off the road.

"How do you plan to insert the phony gun and the diagram in his briefcase?" asked Dolly.

"Let's try the old caffeine trick," said Buck. "In the early days of the Cold War, the 513ᵗʰ Intelligence Corps Group kept surveillance on the Soviet Military Liaison Mission based across the River Main in Frankfurt-Sachsenhausen. When we caught the Russians taking photographs inside an off-limits area in West Germany, we would block their sedan so it couldn't move and then demand they give us their film canisters. Initially, they would always refuse.

"At a minimum, the Russkies knew we were going to detain them at least long enough for them to miss the vodka-hour back in Sachsenhausen. Just to be 'friendly,' we gave them lots of cups of hot coffee. Eventually, the Russians would have to choose between giving up their film canisters and wetting their pants.

"I've been watching Mr. Sharif. He was carrying a cup of coffee when he took his seat over there. His bladder must be getting pretty full. We still have at least an hour before our plane departs. Let's get some tea for you, some coffee for me and a great big coffee for our new-found pal, Abdul Sharif."

Coffees and tea in hand, Buck and Dolly wheeled their carry-on bags over to where Mr. Sharif was seated.

"Sir," began Buck, "would you mind watching our luggage while we use the restrooms? As a token of friendship, please accept this cup of coffee. Okay?"

"Yes, of course. I would be pleased to watch your luggage. And, I thank you for the coffee; however, that was not necessary."

"Our pleasure," said Buck, as he and Dolly went off to their respective restrooms. Abdul Sharif sipped his fresh coffee as he watched his new-found 'friends' withdraw. Buck and Dolly took a great deal of time in their restrooms. When they returned to Mr. Sharif and their luggage, Mr. Sharif's coffee cup was almost empty.

"Please allow us to return the favor," said Buck. "If you wish to use the facilities, we will be happy to guard your luggage."

At first, Mr. Sharif declined the offer; however, as time went on, he became more and more restless. Finally, his bladder could not take it anymore. He was experiencing what the TV advertisements call: "embarrassing urgency."

"Yes," said Sharif. "Please do watch my luggage. I shall return shortly."

When Sharif was out of sight, Buck and Dolly made a careful search of their own carry-on bags to make sure Mr. Sharif had not done them any "favors." They found none.

Quickly, Buck slipped the phony handgun into one of the zippered pockets on the outside of Sharif's briefcase and slipped the cabin diagram into another. While Sharif was in the men's room, two TSA agents, who had been tipped off by Mr. Price to interrupt the flight of Mr. Sarif but, otherwise, let the flight proceed, arrived at the boarding gate for the flight to Dulles. The agents set up a portable, magnetometer screening arch and a folding table alongside it.

Just before the boarding process started, the gate agent said all passengers would be required to walk through the screening arch. The agent explained that secondary screening was merely a randomly-applied security procedure.

But Abdul Sharif seemed wary. He let others go ahead of him. Buck and Dolly hung back as well so they were just in front of the reluctant Mr. Sharif. The Madisons cleared the screening arch with no problems and were rolling their carry-on bags down the jet-way when they heard a buzzer go off behind them. Looking back, they saw Mr. Sharif putting his brief case and carry-on bag on the portable inspection table.

As one TSA inspector was applying his high school French to the cabin-safety diagram, his partner was pulling out a set of hand-cuffs. Mr. Sharif shot Buck and Dolly a dark look. Buck and Dolly responded simultaneously with rude hand gestures and darted down the jet-way.

Their flight was delayed while the lavatories were inspected. No bomb was found. The flight was allowed to proceed, almost on schedule.

Within hours, word of Mr. Abdul Sharif's capture and interrogation reached Mr. Abu Amed in his rented Berlin villa on the banks of the Wannsee. But the report came too late to get another agent on the flight from Dulles to London. Obviously, Sharif was out-witted. Such bungling could not be tolerated. If and when released from police custody, Mr. Abdul Sharif would be debriefed by al-Qaeda operatives. Then, arrangements would have to be made for someone to care for Sharif's wife and children.

✫ ✫ ✫

CHAPTER NINE

London -Heathrow International Airport. December, 2007.

After landing at Heathrow, Buck and Dolly rolled their carry-on luggage to the baggage carousel they hoped would deliver the rest of their baggage from the long flight from Denver. When all their bags were accounted for, they entered the queue for British customs. They had nothing to declare. Their passports were in order. Without further delay, they were admitted to the Commonwealth of Her Britannic Majesty, Queen Elizabeth II.

If any MI-5 "hard men" were watching over their arrival, neither Buck nor Dolly could detect them. Just outside the taxi rank, a shiny-black, extra-long, Jaguar XJ was waiting.

The driver introduced himself as Mr. Cartwright. He would be in charge of their transportation.

He invited Buck and Dolly into the spacious rear seats. Copies of *The Times* of London were in the seat pockets. Mr. Cartwright mentioned the center armrest was also a bar. They could help themselves. Buck and Dolly declined the offer.

Mr. Cartwright put their baggage in the boot, as the British call it, and off they went to the American Embassy in Grosvenor Square.

The first order of business for Buck and Dolly was to pay a courtesy call on the American Ambassador. But as they were being escorted up the embassy steps, they couldn't help but notice two elderly men. One was dressed up to look like Adolph Hitler. His companion was wearing a vested, black suit with a winged collar. He was made up to look like Neville Chamberlain.

Even though it wasn't raining for a change, the Chamberlain character held a black umbrella over his head. The Chamberlain figure and Hitler bowed to each other and then shook hands. They hugged each other and smiled for the cameras as tourists took their photograph. Then, when Chamberlain turned his back, the Hitler character would stab Chamberlain between the shoulder blades with what must have been a rubber knife. Chamberlain would fall to the ground.

After a moment, Chamberlain would get back up. Then, he and Hitler would start their little charade all over again.

Buck and Dolly hurried on up the embassy steps. After they were cleared by the U.S. Marine guard at the entrance, they were escorted by a young Foreign Service Officer to the Ambassador's office. Following introductions and some small talk, they were asked to recount the circumstances of their "execution" and to detail their surreptitious return to the Scandia *Seawind*.

The session was about to end with a photograph of the smiling American Ambassador standing in between Buck and Dolly, when the Ambassador said, "I'm afraid my schedule won't permit me to accompany you this evening to Buckingham Palace. I've just been informed of some family business requiring my presence back home.

"Not to worry. Kirk Forsyth, my deputy chief-of-mission, and his lovely wife, Judith, will be standing in for me and taking you to the Palace. You already know Kirk and Judith who have asked to be your overnight hosts. The Palace has been informed of my circumstances." With that, Buck and Dolly were excused.

As Buck and Dolly were going down the Embassy steps, the Hitler and Chamberlain characters maneuvered to intercept them. Rather than risk a collision, Buck and Dolly came to a halt.

"Colonel Madison, Dr. Madison, we have been reading in *The Times* about your book tour. Please allow me to introduce myself and my colleague. I am Sir George Hambleton and this is my friend, Sir Simon Cohen. He, of course, is not the late and unlamented Herr

Hitler. Nor am I the late and unlamented Neville Chamberlain. Please accept this little envelope. It contains my card.

"We, and our colleagues have maintained this peaceful vigil outside your Embassy since shortly after the end of the war that killed so many of our fathers, brothers, mothers, sisters and cousins We act out our attempts at impersonation at noon each day, rain or shine, every day of the week except Sundays."

"What exactly are you protesting?" asked Buck.

"Oh, we are not protesting. We are memorializing. The umbrella I carry is symbolic of the former British Prime Minister, Neville Chamberlain, the man whose appeasement of Herr Hitler made inevitable the deaths of our loved ones and the other horrors of World War II.

"As you may recall, Prime Minister Chamberlain always carried his black umbrella wherever he went. He gripped his umbrella in one hand while he held in his other hand the piece of worthless paper he carried back from his capitulation to Hitler. Chamberlain declared the piece of paper represented, 'Peace for our time.'"

"But why do you maintain your vigil in front of the American Embassy?" asked Dolly. "After all, America came to your rescue."

"You are entirely correct, Dr. Madison."

Sir George was about to launch into a further explanation when one of the ubiquitous Bobbies of the London Metro Police was prompted by one of the Marines to get the Madisons into the stretched Jaguar purring quietly at the curb.

"Unfortunately," said Sir George. "I see your security people are pressing you to depart before we can state our case in full. So, please just keep my card and please do contact us when the promotional tour for your new book is over. As you can see, Sir Simon and I are getting up in years. Please, do not tarry."

"I'll give it some thought," said Buck, slipping the envelope into the pocket of his raincoat.

"Naturally, you will want to make some inquiries about us. I trust my business card will lead you back to us, someday. Good day to both of you and Godspeed."

Sir Simon, came to attention, clicked his heels, and rendered the Nazi salute.

Following their encounter with Chamberlain and Hitler, the Madisons were whisked away from Grosvenor Square.

CHAPTER TEN

Berlin-Wannsee. December, 2007.

Although Abu Amed was feeling the pinch of the financial noose being tightened around the neck of his diminished organization, he rationalized the rental cost of an elegant villa right on the shore of the Wannsee was justified. Of course, he wasn't about to hang out a sign saying: "Al-Qaeda Headquarters-Europe." Still, he felt the need to make a not-so-subtle signal to his operatives throughout the world and to his European agents, in particular, that al-Qaeda was still a movement of some substance.

Across the mammoth desk in the villa's oak-paneled study, Abu Amed kept an array of throw-a-way cell phones. If he kept the calls to his operatives to less than a minute-per-phone before the phone went in the trash, he was pretty sure he could frustrate attempts by the National Security Agency to listen in. Still, the most secure communications were achieved by the use of messengers and one-time code pads. But the messengers were slow and some of his operatives were dumber than camels. It took some of them all day to encrypt or decrypt the simplest message.

Although he possessed a guest-worker permit issued to a Christobal Garcia-Diego of Spain, Abu Amed had no intention of being very much out and about in Berlin. His operatives would have to come to him. Re-building and expanding al-Qaeda-Europe would take time. Patience was not one of his virtues, but he was resigned to the reality his organizational work would take years. Yet, to rally the millions of his co-religionists already residing in Europe to his cause would require something spectacular on his part. He would have to think of something to show the weakness of Ayman al-Zawahiri. Meanwhile, the pursuit of the Madisons would give his agents something to do.

In that regard, his agents would have to do much better. Both the Fox News Channel and CNN carried the story of the arrest of Abdul Sharif in Denver. Now, in London, the fate of the Madisons would be in the hands of the youth, Najib el-Shaabi.

✼ ✼ ✼

CHAPTER ELEVEN

DCM Residence, London. December, 2007.

The residence of the Deputy Chief of Mission, usually referred to as the DCM, is on a quiet side street in Mayfair not far from the Embassy itself. Typical of the posh neighborhood, the residence suggests an understated elegance. But Buck and Dolly noted the decorative ironwork covering the windows was extra thick, designed more to protect the occupants than for Edwardian beauty.

A morning-coated butler wearing white gloves attended the door. The butler looked at them as if they might be the people who came to empty the dust bins. The butler's imperious stare made Buck and Dolly feel like looking down at their shoes to make sure they were clean enough to enter.

Shortly, Buck and Dolly were greeted by Kirk and Judith Forsyth. Then, following an elegant lunch served by the butler, Buck and Dolly were shown to an upstairs bedroom where their evening clothes were already laid out. A seamstress was on hand to make any needed alternations. Buck's uniform was perfect. But because it was winter, General McClure arranged for Buck to have the Army Blue Mess Uniform instead of the Army White Mess Uniform Buck had worn on board the Scandia *Seawind* that fateful summer.

The hem on Dolly's gown needed to be shortened somewhat. Other than that, General McClure's arrangements for them were perfect. After the seamstress took the gown away for the slight alternation, the butler told them a nap was the next item on their schedule. But Buck and Dolly were so intrigued by the encounter with Sir George and Sir Simon they asked to have another word with Kirk and Judith.

"Who are those people standing out in front of the Embassy?" asked Buck.

"We get all kinds of demonstrations in Grosvenor Square," said the DCM. "Actually, we take the demonstrations as a left-handed compliment to our sole super-power status. One of our colleagues over in the British Foreign Office tells the story about the year 1948 when protestors attempted to set fire to the American Embassy in Athens. One British Foreign Service Officer turned to a colleague and said, 'Oh for the days when they used to burn our embassies.'"

"The two gentlemen who confronted us were: Sir George Hambleton and Sir Simon Cohen," said Buck.

"Ah, the ring leaders," said Forsyth. "Those two, and about a dozen or so others, are the survivors of some of the people killed during World War II. Sir George's father flew Spitfires in the Battle of Britain. He fought off the Luftwaffe fighters too long, ran out of fuel, and crashed into the English Channel. Sir Simon, who was an investment banker, lost his father, mother and his sisters to the ovens of Dachau. Sir Simon was knighted because of his generous efforts to help the families of the victims of the Holocaust. After the war, Sir George made a fortune with a brokerage firm in the City. When he gave away most of his fortune to various charities, he was knighted by the Queen."

"But why are they holding their vigil in front of our Embassy?" asked Dolly. "They should be in front of the German Embassy. How about the French Embassy over the Vichy Government's collaboration with the Nazis?"

"The basis of their anger with the United States is because of our pre-World War II Ambassador's involvement with the infamous Cliveden Set."

"I've heard of them," said Dolly. "They were a group of anti-Semitic English aristocrats who spent their country weekends at Cliveden Manor, praising Hitler's so-called reforms."

"Right Dolly," said Buck. "And, the doyenne of Cliveden Manor was the American-born, social climber, Lady Nancy Astor – the woman whose anti-Semitic, pro-Hitler views were so detested by Sir Winston Churchill. But I don't see why the treacherous Cliveden Set causes Sir George and Sir Simon to be holding vigils in front of the American Embassy. Why is that?"

"They are out in front of our embassy every day except Sunday because back in the 1930s, the American Ambassador to the Court of St. James, Joseph P. Kennedy, was a member of the Cliveden Set. In fact, Ambassador Kennedy was so pro-Hitler and so anti-Semitic it became necessary for President Roosevelt to recall Kennedy to the United States."

"So, you are saying Sir George and Sir Simon or their colleagues stand out here almost every day at noon to remind the United States that appeasement of dictators leads to wider wars and to the deaths of millions of innocent people?"

"You got it, Buck," said the DCM. "It may also be their subtle way of warning the British government about the dictatorial nature of jihadist Islam."

"Well," said Buck, "I admire their tenacity. I suppose some kind of organization is needed to make sure their vigil gets conducted every day. Does it have a name?"

"Probably, but we don't know what it is," said the DCM. "Despite the efforts of MI-5, we know very little. Our guess is they think they are born-again, Knights of the Round Table."

"Oh, I like it," said Dolly. "Buck, put them in this book or the next one."

"Look," said Kirk, "we all face a long evening at the Palace and you two will have an even longer day tomorrow at Harrods and then you have to fly to Paris. Let me suggest we all have some rest before we dress for the evening."

✻ ✻ ✻

CHAPTER TWELVE

Soho, London. December, 2007.

Nineteen-year-old Najib el-Shaabi listened quietly as Abdullah el-Jabar instructed him on his mission. The thought of blowing himself to bits inside Harrods Department Store terrified him. But what choice did he have? His older sister back in Yemen was forced to have sex by one of her father's brothers. Fearful of exposure, the uncle told the local mullah the girl had seduced him. According to letters Najib received from his mother, she suspected the mullah and the uncle entered into a conspiracy. They were demanding money to keep quiet. If she could not produce any money, the mullah would go to the mosque and denounce his sister. Following that, she would be dragged into the public square and stoned to death to restore the honor of the family. Najib's mother told her son an Arab charity was offering $25,000 U.S. dollars to families producing martyrs to die for the glory of Islam.

Najib's mother did not know the $25,000 came originally from Saddam Hussein's robbing of the United Nations Oil for Food Program. But then, she would not have cared either.

Abdullah el-Jabar was offering a way for Najib to be, not just a martyr, but also a hero to his sister, to his mother, to his entire family, and also a way out of the drudgery of his back-breaking job unloading fish in the Covent Garden fish market. Besides, his temporary UK work visa was about to expire. Even so, Najib was so scared he could barely comprehend Abdullah el Jabar's instructions on how to set the timer to blow up the 18.18 kilos (40 pounds) of Semtex inside his schoolboy's backpack at the same moment when Big Ben struck noon the next day.

✲ ✲ ✲

CHAPTER THIRTEEN

Buckingham Palace. December, 2007.

Too excited to sleep, Buck and Dolly just lay on their backs, held hands and stared at the ornate, pressed-tin ceiling. After awhile, Buck and Dolly got up, showered and donned their evening dress. Dolly was gorgeous in the replica of the black evening gown she wore when she flipped the now dead Federico Rivera the finger and walked the plank. The London-made version of Buck's mess jacket was much finer and better tailored than the old uniform Buck had tailor-made on-the-cheap so many years ago in Hong Kong. His four rows of miniature medals were correct in every detail. Obviously, General McClure had access to Buck's DD Form 214, the official record of military service.

"Should I wear the counter-surveillance necklace?" asked Dolly.

"Not fancy enough," said Buck. "Besides, everyone there is going to be under all kinds of surveillance, your neck would be warm all evening long. I'd leave it behind. Wear your pearls."

At the agreed-upon time, Buck and Dolly joined the Forsyths in the drawing room for a fortifying cocktail prior to their departure for Buckingham Palace. The Butler served French 75s in chilled champagne flutes. Kirk was in evening diplomatic attire adorned with some of the medals he earned as a Marine during Gulf War I. Judith and Dolly both looked ravishing in their floor-length gowns.

"Just so we are clear," said Kirk, sipping his drink, "Judith will go over the reception-line drill and the way the Royals are addressed in conversation."

"Dolly, not being a British subject," said Judith, "you are not required to curtsy. But I suspect you will. Buck, you lead, Dolly follows," said Judith.

"Do I curtsy?" asked Buck.

"Buck, cut it out. Pay attention," said Dolly.

"First in line will be Major General Sir Robert McKelvey. He will be serving as the host. Tell Sir Robert: 'Colonel Madison and Dr. Madison.' Sir Robert will repeat what you say with enough volume so both the Queen and Prince Phillip can hear it.

"When you first address the Queen, call her: Your Majesty. Buck, as you bow and the Queen shakes your hand, you introduce Dolly to the Queen. Say: 'Your Majesty, my wife, Dr. Madison.' Dolly, looking at the Queen, extend your hand and curtsy if you wish. After that, the Queen is addressed simply as: Ma'am.

"When you come to Prince Philip, the Duke of Edinburgh, address him as 'Your Royal Highness.' It's the same drill, but, Dolly, no curtsy. You both just shake hands. Then, simply address him as: 'Sir.' Any questions?" asked Judith.

"Judith, are you sure my gown is okay?" asked Dolly.

"Yes. Palace protocol calls for long sleeves, a long skirt and nothing cut low in front. So, your gown is perfect."

"What happens if we screw up?" asked Buck.

"You must serve two years before-the-mast in the Royal Navy," answered Kirk.

After their drinks were finished, the butler entered the drawing room to announce their limousine was waiting outside. The butler put Dolly, Judith and Buck in the rear seat. The driver assisted Kirk to the front passenger seat. The drive to Buckingham Palace took all of five minutes. After the guards made a brief sweep for hidden explosives, the armored Jaguar glided into the Palace grounds.

Buckingham Palace is actually built around a hollow square large enough to provide parking for up to 300 cars. The driver knew the Buckingham Palace parking drill quite well. So, after discharging the foursome right at the front steps to the main entrance to the Palace, he turned the limo about and went to wait with his mates in the Palace parking lot.

Only 20 couples were invited to dine on this particular evening. The "small" dinner party was a relatively recent departure for the Royal Family because their earlier practice was to entertain up to 400 guests at a time. But now the Queen and Prince Philip were seeking a different format, one in which they could bring people of opposing views together, and one in which the Royal Couple could have more informal contact with the distinguished company they invited to sup with them.

The Forsyths and the Madisons were among the first to arrive. Immediately, they were taken in hand by Prince Philip's military aides-de-camp and by the Queen's ladies-in-waiting. Amidst welcoming words and polite banter they were escorted into the White Drawing Room. Hanging over the mantel and dominating the White Drawing Room was a large portrait of Queen Victoria. Servants, dressed in uniforms reminiscent of the Edwardian Era, circulated bearing trays of what had to be actual Champagne.

Given the age of Buckingham Palace, Buck and Dolly expected the interior of the Palace to be somewhat worn and faded, even shabby. The opposite was the case. The splendor of the Palace was startling. The walls were adorned with damask brocade rendered in two shades of white. Soft, warm candlelight glowed everywhere, giving the feeling everyone was being lighted to take part in a Technicolor motion picture set at the height of Great Britain's power.

From the gilt-edged portrait frames to the ornate furniture to the thick carpets, every artifact was clean, polished, and even, pristine. While the Monarchy might be considered faded by some, the condition of the Palace suggested otherwise.

Prince Philip's chief-of-staff, retired Royal Army Major General, Sir Robert McKelvey, playing the role of "host," was clearly in charge. Sir Robert and his more junior aides-de-camp made sure all of the guests were introduced to each other and had an opportunity for some social chatter. Sir Robert made everyone feel as much at home as one could feel amid the intimidating splendor of Buckingham Palace. This was not the Forsyth's first dinner at the Palace. This occasion, however, was far more intimate and, even for experienced diplomats such as Kirk and Judith, it was a bit daunting. Needless to say, for Buck and Dolly, it was more than daunting, it was overwhelming. They felt like two country mice come to town.

Kirk and Judith maneuvered Buck and Dolly about the room so they could meet some of the other guests. The Forsyths already knew some of the other members of the diplomatic corps as well as some of the military officers detailed to the household staff.

The guests were an eclectic assemblage. A rabbi was talking with a mullah. A Greek Cypriot was talking with the Turkish ambassador. The German and the French ambassadors and their wives were enjoying the Queen's libations. A Roman Catholic Bishop was talking with an Episcopal Bishop. The Georgian ambassador was talking with the Russian ambassador.

To overcome their disquiet, Buck and Dolly fell back on the tried and true method of the skilled conversationalist: don't talk, ask questions of others. One of the Queen's ladies-in-waiting seemed to take a shine to Buck, so he took the opportunity to ask her how one became a lady-in-waiting.

But, before the lady-in-waiting story fully unfolded, one of the military aides asked if he could have a word with the Madisons. After a few whispered words from the aide, Buck and Dolly, with questioning glances back toward Kirk and Judith, dutifully followed the aide who led them to a small, but even more ornate, room just off the White Drawing Room. Suddenly, Buck and Dolly found themselves face-to-face with Queen Elizabeth II and Prince Philip, the Duke of Edinburgh.

The Queen was wearing a gorgeous, full-length gown of pale blue under a box jacket trimmed with real diamonds and pearls. Clutched in her hand was a small purse matching her pale-blue gown. On top of her head was a small silver crown studded with diamonds. Prince Philip's naval uniform was bedecked with an impressive array of decorations he earned during World War II combat operations.

Buck and Dolly said their lines perfectly, Dolly did her curtsy. Hands were shaken all around. Nearby, another military aide was holding a copy of *Walking the Plank to Freedom*.

The Queen said, "Colonel Madison, Dr. Madison, would you be so kind as to inscribe a copy of your book for us? We would be honored to add your book to our library."

Quickly, Buck and Dolly did as they were asked. The two aides withdrew, taking the inscribed book with them. Now, Buck and Dolly were alone with the Queen and Prince Phillip.

The Queen began again, "Your president has reminded our prime minister that 170 of our subjects were on the ship the two of you prevented from destruction. Moreover, our grandson, Prince Harry, is a veteran of the fighting in Afghanistan.

"Colonel Madison, we know something of your earlier mission in Afghanistan. Of course, we have no official way of knowing; however, we are willing to wager you were successful with your task.

"For the reasons we have just stated, we think it appropriate for you to be included in the next Honours List. The list, however, will not appear for another six months. Since the mission you have now undertaken is extremely hazardous, we want to take this occasion to express our appreciation in a tangible way.

"Neither of you are citizens subject to the Crown. So, what we are about to do is only honorary; however, this limitation does not diminish our heartfelt appreciation for what your have done. But this recognition carries with it a two-edged sword, if you will pardon the double meaning. Until the next Honours List appears, what we are about to do must remain a secret between you, Prince Philip, the prime minister, the cabinet secretary, and we. Are we all agreed?"

"Yes, Ma'am," responded Buck. Dolly simply nodded her "yes."

The Prince went over to the table, picked up a ceremonial sword and handed it to the Queen.

"If both of you would be so kind to kneel, we are about to dub you Knight Commanders of the Order of the British Empire."

Buck and Dolly did as they were told. With Prince Philip looking on, the Queen touched Dolly on each shoulder saying, "We dub thee, Lady Melissa Rennie 'Dolly' Madison."

Touching Buck with the sword in similar fashion, the Queen said, "We dub thee Sir James Buckley "Buck" Madison."

Handing the sword back to Prince Phillip, the Queen said, "Arise, Sir James, and arise, Lady Dolly."

With Buck and Dolly standing again, Prince Philip handed each of them a small, leather-covered box. The Royal Coat-of-Arms was encrusted in gold gilt on each box.

"Inside," said the Queen, "you will find the medallions representing your new status as Knight Commanders of the Order of the British Empire.

"After the next Honours List is published, you are entitled to wear them when and where you see fit; however, we suspect your innate modesty will place these medallions in a place where they will never see the light of day. But, I must confess, what we have just done here this evening is extraordinary. But then, what the two of you did aboard the Scandia *Seawind* was more than extraordinary.

"It is our custom to chat with our new Knights and Ladies for about 15 minutes. Unfortunately, because we must all make our appearances shortly. We will postpone our chat to later this evening when it is expected for us to take a few moments with each of our guests."

"Ma'am, we are both astonished and grateful," said Buck as he slipped his leather pouch in his pocket while Dolly did the same into her purse. "We will strive to merit your Majesty's continued respect and that of the British people."

"We are sure you will, Sir James. Or, maybe I should address you as Sir Buck? No matter. For the rest of this evening, you are Colonel Madison and Dr. Madison. You may withdraw."

Miraculously, an aide appeared. He escorted them back into the White Drawing Room.

"What was that all about?" asked Kirk Forsyth.

"Her Majesty wanted us to sign a copy of *Walking the Plank to Freedom,*" said Buck. "Apparently, she wanted to get it out of the way before they make their appearance."

After a half-hour of conversation, the assemblage was directed out of the White Drawing Room and into the Blue Drawing Room to be received by the Queen and the Prince. The walls were done in blue brocade with ornately-framed portraits hung high on the walls. The frames alone must have cost a fortune.

Just as Judith predicted, the first person they encountered in the reception line was Major General Sir Robert McKelvey. When it was their turn, Buck said to Sir Robert, "Colonel and Dr. Madison."

Turning to the Queen, Sir Robert announced, "Your Majesty, Colonel and Dr. Madison."

"So good of you to come," said the Queen, showing no sign of their earlier encounter. Dolly performed the ritual, but not obligatory for non-British subjects, curtsy. The Queen looked into their eyes, gave their hands a gentle squeeze and then turned her head to listen to hear Sir Robert's next introduction.

As Prince Phillip shook their hands, he said, "After dinner, please save some time for me to learn more about your most interesting exploits."

When the reception line was depleted, the guests were invited into the Red Dining Hall. As Buck and Dolly approached the doorway, a footman for each of them stepped forward and escorted them to their places. The footmen stood directly behind each diner. Surrounded by the footmen Buck felt like paraphrasing Custer at the Battle of the Little Big Horn: "Where the hell did all these footmen come from?"

The Red Dining Hall was done in a deep Chinese red. More portraits adorned the walls. The dining table must have been nine-feet-wide and over 40-feet-long. Candles cast a warm glow all along the dining table. All the glassware sparkled like diamonds. The silver gleamed. The napkins were folded just so. Dolly felt like she was inside a Technicolor, high-definition, movie scene and the director was about to shout: "Action!"

The Queen and the Prince entered the Red Dining Hall and took their places half way down the length of the table and on opposite sides of the table from each other. In the British tradition, husband and wives were not seated side-by-side. Whoever planned the event seemed to know who had what languages. While everyone present spoke English to some degree, it was helpful for those with limited English to be able to turn either to their left or to their right for a bit of help.

For the moment, no one was saying anything. A Bishop of the Church of England cleared his throat and then asked for a blessing on the Queen and on all assembled. The prayer was so ecumenical all religions seemed to be included and none excluded.

When the prayer was finished, the Queen sat. All sat. To Dolly's delight, she found herself sitting between the art collector and Sir Robert.

"Sir Robert," said Dolly. "I'm sure you have heard this before. You remind me of the American actor, Richard Gere."

"Yes, Dr. Madison, I hear that now and then. I try not to let it go to my head. And might I say that you look a lot like the American actress, Loren Hutton, only with perfect teeth."

"Well then," said Dolly. "It looks like Hollywood has come to Buckingham Palace. And let's not forget Judith Forsyth who looks a lot like Sandra Bullock."

"Yes, I have had the pleasure of meeting Mrs. Forsyth here at the Palace on a number of occasions. I dare say she adds beauty, grace, and charm to any evening."

The dinner proceeded delicious course by delicious course. When it was time to withdraw the plates for a course, enough servants were there to withdraw everyone's plate at the same time. When the next course arrived, enough servants were there to serve all the guests at once.

The footman assigned to each guest stood back next to the walls, never moving, but ever watchful. Over in one corner of the room, a string ensemble performed Bach. Buck was seated between two ladies. One was German. Her English was sufficient to the level Buck resisted the temptation to show off his excellent German. The German lady sported enough diamonds to start her own jewelry store. Buck's other companion was the lady-in-waiting with whom Buck had spoken earlier. Buck asked her to continue her story.

"Actually, we are all of royal blood, albeit relatively minor. Most of us are war widows with either grown children or no children. Being a lady-in-waiting gives us something useful to do."

"So, what are your actual duties?"

"What do we do? Whatever the Queen wants us to do. When she bids us to do so, we keep her company. Some of us travel with her. She knows our lips are sealed, so she can speak her mind without worry. And yes, the tabloids are always trying to get us to say something about the Royals and about life inside these walls. That, however, would be the end of our time here and would bring disgrace upon our families." Buck wanted to ask if ladies-in-waiting got paid, but thought better of it.

When the Queen finished her meal, she gave her head a tiny nod and her footman pulled back her chair. The Queen stood. When the Queen stands, all stand. No matter if they finished their meal or not. The footmen pulled back all the chairs. Then, the aides ushered everyone back into the Blue Drawing Room where after-dinner drinks were offered. For those needing the "facilities," discrete signage pointed the way.

Meanwhile, the Queen and Prince Phillip began to circulate freely, but separately, among their guests. Apparently, the Queen had dismissed her ladies-in-waiting and the Prince had dismissed his aides, leaving the two Royals to wander about on their own. Eventually, Buck and Dolly found themselves in a threesome with Prince Phillip.

The Prince was eager to learn more about the Madison's relatively recent ordeal. After all, that was the reason they were invited. The Prince wanted to know the details of how Buck and Dolly were brought on board the rescue submarine and how they were able to leap from the submarine to get back on board the Scandia *Seawind*.

The Prince then shared a vignette from his own days as a World War II naval officer which he smoothly turned into a series of questions about the nature of the current terrorist threat and how the Madisons thought the war against terrorism would play out.

Buck allowed that was anyone's guess; however, it was clear Great Britain and the United States were not going to quit until the terrorists are defeated, even if some of the "old" European powers failed to come along. Buck couldn't resist a quote from World War II General George S. Patton who said, "I'd rather have a German Division in front of me than a French Division behind me."

The Prince slapped his knee and laughed so hard nearby guests stopped their conversations to look at the Prince and the Madisons. The laughter attracted the Queen's attention. She glided over to join the Prince.

"Well," said the Queen. "You certainly struck my husband's funny bone. May we be let in on the story?"

"Of course, Ma'am," said Buck. "We were just discussing, somewhat indirectly, the desire of the French to play a role in world affairs which is no longer merited by their economic or military status."

"There are those who think the French are an international laughing stock," said the Queen. "Of course, we can't endorse such a view in public. As for the antics of the French within the United Nations, we will quote one of my predecessors who said, 'We are not amused.' Now, Colonel Madison, let us exchange French jokes. We will go first. Later, I'll get my husband to tell me the joke you told him."

"We rather like," said the Queen, "what your writer, Mark Twain, said about France. He said, 'France is a country with neither summer nor winter nor morals. Other than that, it's a fine country.'

"Now, it's your turn, Sir…ah, Colonel Madison."

"Your Majesty, do you know why the French celebrated their World Cup victory so wildly?"

"No, Colonel, we do not."

"Because it was the first time the French ever won anything without the help of the British or the Americans." That earned Buck two Royal smiles.

"While the story is amusing, the underlying truth of it makes us sad. We lost two generations of our youth in two world wars to restore freedom to France, and your country lost well over a million of your finest, as well," said the Queen, as she turned to Dolly and changed the subject.

"Dr. Madison, it is not our habit to spend much time watching television; however, we must confess being spellbound by the sight of you and your husband out on the bow of the Scandia *Seawind*. Of course, we were not privy to your gun duel with that dreadful woman. But we are told you showed both compassion and courage in dealing with the Cuban agent, Regina Rivera. In fact, you put us in mind of your Alexander Hamilton who, in effect, allowed Aaron Burr to fire the first shot in that ill-fated duel. Only, in your case, your *noblesse* yielded a much more satisfactory outcome."

"Your Majesty, I could not let Regina Rivera run into that booby-trapped electrical vault with her baby strapped to her back. I felt if I could get her to put the baby out of harm's way, then I could win a western-style shoot-out. Fortunately, Regina Rivera panicked and I didn't have to fire my weapon."

"For a girl raised by Christian missionaries in our former Crown Colony, Dr. Madison, you seem to have developed a number of lethal skills," said the Queen.

"Ma'am, my husband says the female of the species is the more deadly. I try not to disappoint him."

"Nor have you disappointed us," said the Queen. "We wish you well on your book tour and we pray the good Lord will keep you safe during your journey. And may the good Lord continue to bless the special relationship our two peoples have enjoyed for so long. Your president understands our special relationship full well. We pray that those who follow him into the Oval Office will understand it as well.

"The late Sir Winston Churchill used to say: 'We are one people, separated by a common language.' We find it amusing," said the Queen with a wink.

Then, the Queen and the Prince withdrew, signaling the end of a splendid evening. The guests were escorted back to the main entrance where their sedans and limousines were awaiting them.

Across the square from Buckingham Palace, one of Abu Amed's agents aimed a captured Soviet night-vision monocle through the wrought-iron fence as the Queen's guests came down the Palace steps to mount their sedans and limousines. The entire area was abuzz with security agents and vehicles belonging to Scotland Yard and, presumably, MI-5. The agent was pleased with his orders to merely observe the Madisons, rather than make an attempt to kill them. From a discrete distance, he followed their limo back to the residence of the DCM. Once the Madisons were inside the DCM's "fortress," the agent retired to his SoHo flat to use multiple cell phones to render his surveillance report to Abu Amed in Berlin.

✫ ✫ ✫

CHAPTER FOURTEEN

Harrods Department Store. December, 2007.

At 0900 hours the next morning, when Buck and Dolly reached the front entrance to Harrods, the manager of Waterstone's, Harrods vaunted book department, was present to greet them.

"How do you do," he said. "My name is Edward Higgins." Hands were shaken all around.

"If you don't mind too terribly," said Higgins, "it would be a good idea for us to take the freight lift to the third floor. The pallets containing your books have just arrived. The first of them were put on board the lift in the basement. The car is here now and we can take the books on up with us. My staff will have some of them on a display island in time for our opening at 10:00 a.m."

The lift, made by Otis, the French manufacturer, looked like a relic from a 19th Century French hotel. Basically, an open metal cage with an accordion gate attached to the framework on one side. Mr. Higgins pulled the gate aside and bade them enter. If the lift could be described in one word, it would be: rickety. When it jerked to a stop at the third floor, Mr. Higgins pulled the accordion gate to one side. Mr. Higgins bowed them out of the car and onto the third floor.

Two workmen in blue smocks were waiting for the car. After the Madisons and Mr. Higgins vacated the elevator, the workmen entered the car to wrestle the pallet of books out onto the floor.

While Mr. Higgins showed Buck and Dolly the desk set up for them to greet customers and sign their books, the workmen placed a sales island just outside the elevator. They decorated the island with a green baize cloth and then piled the island high with copies of *Walking the Plank to Freedom*.

When the workmen were finished, they boarded the elevator car, closed the accordion gate, and descended to the basement to load more books.

Not long after the store opening, Mr. Higgins felt the gathering crowd of at least 50 was sufficient to merit his opening remarks. Mr. Higgins explained the books were to be found on the display island adjacent to the freight elevator. Patrons were to pick out a book or books, take them to a nearby cashier for payment and then present themselves and their book or books to the desk where Dr. Madison and Colonel Madison would inscribe them however they wished.

Mr. Higgins gave the crowd a few words of introduction designed to incite the purchase of *Walking the Plank to Freedom* after which he turned the floor over to the Madisons. Dolly responded to the kind introduction and made some remarks about their recent close calls in dealing with the terrorist plots hatched by Fidel Castro and the Red Chinese.

Their remarks concluded, Buck and Dolly sat down at their desk and started signing books. They made good eye contact with each reader and took a fair amount of time to listen to what each person wanted to stay. Some of those in line had watched, in real-time, as Buck and Dolly were forced to walk the plank off the bow of the Scandia *Seawind*. Others saw the interminable re-plays on BBC Television. After an hour of listening, talking and book signing, the Harrods staff brought Buck and Dolly some tea and scones. The manager reappeared to draw everyone's attention to free tea and scones over at a sideboard.

The Madisons were aware Harrods started out as a grocery store and prided itself on its 22 in-store restaurants. The scones with whipped cream and strawberries were the best they had ever tasted. Apparently, the Arab owner of Harrods was maintaining some of the store's best English traditions.

At the rate they were signing books, Buck and Dolly estimated several pallets of books would be needed before the day was over.

After the brief break, the Madisons continued to take their time with each patron. Buck and Dolly held dozens of interesting conversations with their growing army of fans. They heard from a number of eccentrics who were there, not so much to buy their book, but to expound on their favorite conspiracy theories. Buck and Dolly wondered if some of the eccentrics were just taking a break from the Speakers' Corner over at Hyde Park in order to speak to a more or less captive audience at a book signing. But most of the people in the queue seemed sincerely interested in what they could learn from the ordeals Buck and Dolly experienced. Several of them asked if the things the mainstream media wrote about their foiling of the plot to assassinate the American and Russian presidents were actually true.

Buck said he and Dolly only did what any patriotic person would have done under the circumstances. Buck modestly dismissed much of the media accolades as the products of imaginations on steroids. Their disclaimers convinced no one.

The line of book buyers waiting for their books to be autographed seemed endless. In anticipation of hearing Big Ben strike noon, Buck decided he needed to get up to stretch his legs. Wandering over to a counter full of bar accessories, Buck spotted something he always wanted, a pneumatic wine cork popper. A friend told him the "Cork-It" wine opener was carried by Harrods. The "Cork-It" was on Buck's shopping list.

The device eliminated all that twisting and pulling associated with conventional wine openers. All one had to do was stick a long hollow needle down through the cork and then start pumping air through the needle down into the wine. After about a dozen injections of air, the cork would come popping out without the usual damage to the cork. The clerk helped Buck sort out the needed amount of British money and Buck was the proud owner of a "Cork-It."

As Buck was making his way back to Dolly, he noticed a young man standing at the back of the line. His overall appearance and his backpack suggested a young Arab sent to England to get an education or maybe just in England on a work permit. Either way, the boy was perspiring heavily and looking nervously in all directions. The young Arab kept checking his wrist watch as if he must be somewhere at a certain time. He was clutching a copy of *Walking the Plank to Freedom.* A sales slip was sticking out from inside the book. To Buck, the boy looked as nervous as a liberal at a NASCAR race.

Buck said, "Hello. I'm Buck Madison. What is your name?"

The young Arab was speechless. Suddenly, he was confronted by one of the people he was supposed to kill.

"I am... ah, ah, Najib," he responded, forgetting to use his false name.

"Let me have your book," said Buck, as he tried to take the book from the young man's hands. "You obviously have an appointment somewhere. I can save you some time by signing it right here. What time is it, anyway?"

But the young man, who was perspiring and giving off the odor of week-old fish, would not give up his grip on the book. In fact, the young Arab was almost rigid, as if his feet were set in concrete. His only movement was to turn one wrist so he could see the face of his watch.

"My goodness," said Buck. "You've perspired all over the dust jacket and made quite a mess of it. Ink has run onto your hands and also spoiled your shirt. That won't do."

Now, the book was the prize in a tug-of-war. But Buck kept pulling until he got the young Arab in between the sales island and the elevator shaft. Meanwhile, the boy kept casting glances at his wrist watch. The boy kept moving his lips but no sound was coming out of his mouth. Now, truly alarmed, Buck examined the book more closely. The book was connected to the boy's backpack by some sort of electrical wire or lanyard.

The blue-smocked workmen had gone off somewhere, leaving the open gate on the elevator car unguarded.

Buck said, "Tell you what, Najib, let's move over to the display island. For free, I'll give you a fresh copy of this book."

Najib realized there was no plausible way to resist. Buck's firm grip on the book steered him to the display island. When they reached the display, Buck gently placed a second copy of *Walking the Plank to Freedom* on top of the copy Najib was holding so firmly. Then, Buck pushed the young Arab into the elevator.

Buck pulled the accordion gate closed. Reaching quickly through one of the openings in the gate, Buck pushed the button to order the car to descend into the basement. The elevator began its rickety descent. As he disappeared down the elevator shaft, the young man screamed: "Allah Akbar! Allah Akbar!"

As Big Ben struck the hour of noon, a massive explosion shook the building. A tongue of orange flame shot up the elevator shaft. Then, the orange flame gave way to a column of white smoke boiling up from below.

At the sound of the explosion, Dolly vaulted over the signing desk, bowling over a couple of blue-haired ladies. Following on her heels was a rush of customers headed toward the elevator shaft.

"Buck, what happened?" asked a breathless Dolly.

"Someone started a fire," said Buck, as he used his cell phone to speed dial a special number for Scotland Yard.

After a few moments of mass confusion on the third floor, the manager of the bookstore reappeared to assure everyone the authorities had everything under control. He announced The Bagel Factory would be sending up complimentary bagels, cream cheese and smoked salmon for those who cared to stay and partake. That was agreeable to all.

As Buck was spreading cream cheese on a freshly-baked Harrods bagel, an Inspector from Scotland Yard came up the stairwell to ask: "Colonel Madison, may I have a word?"

He produced credentials showing he was Chief Inspector Thomas Griffin. The Chief Inspector said he had been instructed by Special Branch to extend every possible courtesy to the Madisons. It only took a few moments for Buck to relate how his discovery of the bomb in the would-be assassin's backpack caused the man to flee. Chief Inspector Griffin was keen to have a detailed description of the man.

"You see, Colonel Madison, until we have time for a DNA analysis, there is not enough left of that person down there for us to identify," said Griffin.

After describing the young Arab, Buck said, "Hopefully, no one else was hurt."

"Not likely," said Griffin. "It was lunch time. The shipping department lot were off for some fish and chips and a pint or two."

"That's good news," said Buck. "However, I would have to say our jihadist friend was not particularly good at contingency planning. You should always leave yourself a way out. Chief Inspector, if you need more information, we can be reached in Paris for the next few days at the Georges V or, as the French say, the *Cinq*."

With a slight bow, Chief Inspector Griffin said, "I'm sorry if I've inconvenienced you and your lovely wife in any way." Chief Inspector Griffin put his notebook back in his suit coat and went back down the stairs.

✫ ✫ ✫

CHAPTER FIFTEEN

Charles de Gaulle International Airport, Paris

Originally the Madisons were booked on "Air Chance" (Buck's nickname for Air France). But after the cozy business relationship between former French President Jacques Chirac and Iraqi President Saddam Hussein was exposed, U.S. agencies weren't buying anything French whenever they could help it.

Due to a strong tailwind, the British Airways flight from London to Charles de Gaulle International Airport arrived 20 minutes ahead of schedule. After claiming their checked baggage, they cleared customs and passport control in Terminal 2. Rolling their bags along with them, Buck and Dolly made their way toward the rank of telephone stands. They were pleasantly surprised to see a young man in a chauffeur's uniform holding a hand-lettered sign that said: "Madison." Glad not to have to rustle up a taxi, the Madisons walked over to the chauffeur to inquire if they were the people being provided with limousine service.

"*Mais, oui*," said the young chauffeur. "The Embassy of the United States of America has given me, Omar Rahman, the honor of taking you to your hotel. I am at your service. Please call me Omar."

Pointing through the terminal's glass façade, Omar Rahman indicated a black, Citroen limousine parked at curbside. Steamy exhaust fumes in the cold winter air revealed the engine was running. The trunk stood open in anticipation of their baggage. Two gendarmes were keeping watch over the limousine. The letters "CD" on the license plate explained why the limousine was allowed to loiter at curbside and why the gendarmes were being so compliant.

"Please, allow me to place your baggage in the truck of the limousine," said Omar.

"Perhaps later," said Buck. "For the moment, leave them here. Please go out and stand by the car. We will join you in a few minutes."

According to the plan, the delivery of the weapons package was to be done at the first set of payphones just outside the passport control point. Buck stayed with their baggage and did counter-surveillance while Dolly went directly to the payphones. Her necklace remained cool. Dolly set her shoulder bag down next to her right foot.

Almost immediately, a young man in a business suit placed an identical bag beside hers. He picked up Dolly's bag and quickly walked away with it.

"Hi, Jack," said Dolly into the non-secure phone. "We're at CDG. Everything's on schedule. We'll call you from the hotel." General McClure expressed his satisfaction and hung up. Dolly picked up the shoulder bag and walked back toward Buck.

Buck said, "I suppose the best thing to do is rearm ourselves as soon as we can."

"Yes, we can take turns carrying the bag into the restrooms," said Dolly. "But this bag seems awfully heavy. Jack McClure said my bag would weigh 11 pounds. That would be five kilos."

Buck nodded his head toward the airline ticket counters that ran the length of the concourse. Selecting one of the attractive Air France ticket agents, Buck went over and said, *"Pardon. Je pense mon sac est trop lourd. Pouvez-vous me dire combien il pèse?*

"Naturellement," said the agent, batting some mascara-laden lashes at Buck. After placing the bag on her scale, she said, *"Votre sac pèse dix kilo."*

"Merci," said Buck, taking the bag back over to Dolly.

"Dolly, she says your bag weighs ten kilos. That's 22 pounds, twice what it is supposed to weigh."

"Buck, I think we've been had. At the Farm, they taught us there are no such things as coincidences. Like the limousine and this bag. What say we get rid of this bag while we wait to see if another bag shows up?"

Taking the bag and some French francs in his hand, Buck walked over to the station for the baggage handlers. Addressing one of them Buck said, "*Pardon, Monsieur. Voici, un pourboire.*"

Pointing outside to the limousine idling at the curb, Buck said, "*Veuillez avoir ce sac effectu au limousine et placez lui dans le tronc. Merci.*"

Taking advantage of a large, and conveniently placed potted plant, Buck and Dolly watched as the suspect bag was taken out to the limousine. The baggage handler placed the bag inside. Omar left the trunk open and resumed his wait for the Madisons to summon him to collect the rest of their luggage.

Buck and Dolly walked back over to the payphone she had used to call General McClure. No sooner had Dolly gotten there when a fresh-faced and nicely-dressed male in his late 20s came along and set his shoulder bag on the floor. He seemed perplexed there was no bag to pick up. He looked at his wrist watch. He looked around in all directions.

"Hello," said Buck, showing his own passport. "Can you show me some ID?"

The young man reached into an inside-pocket of his suit coat and showed Buck his impressive U.S. Diplomatic Corps credentials.

Satisfied, Buck said, "Well, Mr. Clancy, it looks like the bad guys got here before you did."

"Sorry, we were held up in traffic," said the young case officer.

"No matter," said Buck. "Somebody took off with Dolly's clean bag. Do you know if the Embassy sent a limousine for us? Because, if not, the limo you see idling out there at the curb is a trap."

"My instructions are to leave a bag and to pick up a bag. That's all I know except you are supposed to hail a taxi. Then, my partner and I are supposed to do counter-surveillance on your ride to the *Georges Cinq.* Nobody said anything about sending a limousine."

As the three of them stood looking out at the limousine, the chauffeur was joined at the curb by an Arab in a western business suit who looked furtively around before he started slapping Omar across the face with both hands. Poor Omar looked as if he were going to pee in his pants.

"Just as a precaution," said Buck, "I think we need to take cover behind that concrete pillar."

Looking around from behind the pillar, Buck watched as Omar and his hostile companion were peering into the trunk. Buck had just pulled his head back behind the pillar to report on the scene outside the terminal when the limo exploded in a fiery ball that obliterated the two men, set the limousine on fire, destroyed the nearby revolving door and took out about fifty feet of glass wall. Shards of glass blew through the concourse wounding dozens of innocent bystanders. Fortunately, the two policemen had wandered off to check other cars and were only blown off their feet. Now, they were back up, running around in frantic circles and blowing their whistles like Keystone Kops. Safe behind the concrete pillar, the Madisons and the young agent were untouched.

"Time to go," said Buck, as the three threaded their way through a sea of on-rushing emergency responders and walked away from the blast area. The young case officer led them outside to a Mercedes sedan and said something to his partner. The CIA officers threw the baggage in the trunk. The four of them sped out of Terminal 2, headed for downtown Paris.

"Scratch two more al-Qaeda," said Buck. "But it seems we are going about our mission retail, rather than wholesale. Anyway, French Quarter here we come."

"Buck, that's in New Orleans," said Dolly.

"I know. I mean the quarter of Paris that hasn't been taken over by Muslims. That's about all there is left."

"So, I hear. But at this rate," observed Dolly, "our little operation is going to take forever and our luck can only hold out so long."

Clearly upset by the unexpected turn of events, the two CIA officers decided the best thing to do was to say nothing. They would simply drop their unexpected passengers off at the *Georges Cinq* then go back to the embassy and tell their boss what happened. Obviously, something was compromised somewhere.

When the Madison's attempts at small talk were met with monosyllabic responses, Buck and Dolly gave up and the four rode the rest of the way in silence.

En route, Dolly dug into the shoulder bag and produced the three weapons. She gave Buck his PPK/S, his shoulder holster and two clips of ammunition. Pulling the slide back slightly, Buck made sure there was a round already in the chamber and the safety engaged. Dolly checked her revolver. All five chambers were full with three .45 Colt rounds and two .410, 2.5-inch shotgun shells. The laser grip functioned properly. Buck donned his shoulder holster and slipped the Walther in place. Dolly kept one of the mini-saps and gave the other one to Buck. The suspenders with the Det-cord could stay in the bag.

Dolly made sure her revolver was secure in its firing position inside the shoulder bag. As long as they didn't attempt to go through any security screening employing a magnetometer, they could remain armed until it was time to board the plane for their next destination.

☆ ☆ ☆

CHAPTER SIXTEEN

Paris

The *Georges Cinq* turned out to be just as elegant as it was touted to be. But Buck and Dolly were so tired from the events of the preceding 48 hours they simply flossed and brushed their teeth and crawled between the sandalwood-scented sheets.

The next day, the book signing at the Paris International Book Store drew a nice crowd of mostly American ex-patriots. The event also provoked a number of people who were out in the street tearing their hair, gnashing their teeth, and beating their breasts – and that was just the French.

Over a hundred Islamists were holding up signs in Arabic and French denouncing the Madisons as capitalist, running-dog infidels. Eventually, the gendarmes grew weary of guarding the door to the book store and suggested it was time for the Madisons to bid their fans *au revoir*. Departing out the back door, Buck and Dolly caught a taxi to the *Georges Cinq*.

Refreshed enough to notice their surroundings, Buck and Dolly found the *Cinq* was infinitely more comfortable than when Buck and Dolly, some years earlier, pitched a tent in a camp ground on the banks of the Seine. Shortly after they showered, the front desk called to say a messenger with flowers was waiting in the lobby. The messenger gave his name as M. Bouquet.

Very funny, thought Buck, as he asked to have the flowers brought to their room. When the messenger came to their door, he handed Buck a bouquet of roses, took his tip, and departed. Buck checked each rose for any "bugs" planted inside. Finding none, he handed the bouquet to Dolly. She carried the bouquet into the bathroom.

After turning the cold water on full force, Dolly plucked an envelope out of the flowers. "Buck, the flowers are from the U.S.

Embassy," whispered Dolly. "The note says we've been declared *persona non grata.* We are no longer welcome in France."

"Darn," said Buck. "Not even the five-minute Louvre tour for us. Let's give Jack McClure a call and see what's up. Turn off the water."

For the best satellite connection, Buck went out into the hotel's Marble Courtyard. "I see our friends in striped-pants want us out of here," said Buck.

"Not only that," said General McClure, "we must change your itinerary somewhat. NSA says you've got Abu Amed's shorts all in a wad. He's not happy with the way things went in Denver, at Harrods and at Charles de Gaulle Airport. He's scrambling to reallocate his personnel. Buck, we need to give him time to do that.

"Tomorrow, we want you to fly to Barcelona and catch a cruise ship to Gibraltar. The ship is the *Capriana.* The cruise line only has four ships; however, they are all new and, I'm told, rather nice. It will take you a few days to cruise down the east coast of Spain and around to Gibraltar. For now, the rest of your stops are on track; however, everything will be set back about a week later than we planned. No big deal. Try not to walk off any more gang planks. The cruise line has you booked for one night into a tourist hotel in Barcelona before you board their ship the next evening. When you get to Gibraltar, I've made reservations for you at the famous Rock Hotel. Winston Churchill used to stay there. Tell Dolly, M. Giroux, the day-shift concierge at your hotel, has her clean bag. Before you leave for the airport give him the weapons bag. Don't worry. He works for us. Gotta run. Out."

Just as Buck finished replaying his brief conversation with Jack McClure, the front desk rang again. Another message was at the front desk. Buck asked for the bellman to bring it up. After tipping the bellman, Buck and Dolly went in the bathroom and turned the water back on.

The envelope contained airline and cruise ship tickets plus their hotel confirmations for Barcelona and Gibraltar.

"I see we stay one night in Barcelona and board the cruise ship the next day," said Dolly. "I've always wanted to visit the tapas bars along *Las Ramblas*. We'll have time to do that and maybe even visit a museum or something."

Booting up the laptop, Buck said, "Also, this will give me time to work on our book. I can't wait to write about what happened to the basement of Harrods and to the front of Charles de Gaulle Airport. But I was hoping our break would come later on at a time when we could return to the Zugspitze for a day of skiing."

"Well, you did propose to me up on top of the *Zugspitze*. It would be rather nice to go back up there."

"We could take the cable car from Lake Eibsee to the *Schneeferner-haus* at the top. It would be like one of those James Bond movies."

"Hopefully, you won't be on top of the cable car doing Kung Fu with Blofeld's goons."

"Dolly, that's what I have you for."

"The Zugspitze should have good skiing this time of year," said Dolly. "But who knows what will be waiting for us in Barcelona or along the way to Gibraltar?"

"George Bernard Shaw once observed that: 'Marriage is like a bad meal, with the dessert served at the beginning.' For me, this change in itinerary, giving us more time in Gibraltar, is like a dessert. Gibraltar conjures up thoughts of Lord Nelson and the Battle of Trafalgar, of being under siege by the French and the Spanish, of the caves with their gun emplacements, of the imposter who helped disguise the actual date of the D-Day invasion by posing as General Montgomery. I could go on and on."

"I'm sure you will," said Dolly. "Speaking of dessert, this is the City of Love, you know."

"I thought it was the City of Light."

"Whatever. *Je t'aime.* How's that for foreplay? Turn out the light."

CHAPTER SEVENTEEN

Barcelona

As they deplaned at Barcelona's surprisingly modern international airport, Buck and Dolly were looking forward to the next day when they would board the cruise ship. According to the itinerary, the ship would take them to Menorca, to Mallorca and then down the east coast of Spain, through the Strait of Gibraltar, and around to the famous Rock itself.

During the long walk to the baggage claim, Dolly felt her necklace heat up. Buck stopped to tighten a shoelace while Dolly looked to see if anyone behind them made a quick stop. As they resumed their walk toward the baggage pick-up, Dolly said, "He's the one in the black beret. Let's see if we can get him in a photograph. If he follows us all the way to the baggage area, try to get next to him alongside some other tourists. I'll take his picture."

Later, while they were standing in line to go through passport control, Buck used Dolly's satellite/cell phone to send the photo and to talk with Jack McClure. Jack said his staff would try to ID the guy in the black beret. If the guy turns out to be a tango, Buck and Dolly were to find some way to ditch him before the cruise ship sailed.

On the other side of passport control, an English-speaking miss was holding up the sign of their cruise line. She was a welcome sight. After she gathered her flock of passengers, she led them to a waiting area where she gave them an orientation briefing. She assured the passengers the cruise line would see to it that their heavier luggage would go directly from the airport to their cabins, only she called them: staterooms. All they would need to have for the night would be carry-on bags, any medications, briefcases, laptops, purses and other small, carry-on items.

With those details out of the way, she ushered them toward a waiting tour bus for the ride to their overnight hotel. But before Buck and Dolly could get on board, a woman struggling to manage way too many pieces of luggage bumped into Buck spilling her bags on the ground. Buck and Dolly helped her back to her feet. The stranger walked off with Dolly's "clean" shoulder bag. The weapons bag was on Dolly's shoulder. The second "bag swap" was complete. Dolly sensed the weight of the bag was as it should be.

The hotel used by the cruise line was neither Barcelona's best nor its worst. It was typical of the kind of hotel chosen by German businessmen when they travel on business. *Burgherlich*, as the Germans would say.

Because their ship did not depart until late the next day, the cruise staff explained the numerous attractions one could experience in Barcelona. Dolly picked up a brochure about the Picasso Museum. Buck wasn't enthusiastic about Picasso, but finally agreed to sign the roster of those who were slated to leave the hotel for the Picasso Museum at 1100 hours the next day.

Once inside their hotel room with the door locked behind them, they unpacked, holstered their weapons, hung up their clothes and got some exercise by walking down to *Las Ramblas* for some tapas and wine. The vaunted *Las Ramblas* turned out to be a touristy street of tapas bars, some of them pretty seedy. But then, they sort of expected that. They tried a couple of the nicer-looking establishments. The food was okay, albeit greasy. The local wine was excellent. Eager for a good night's sleep, they took a taxi back to their hotel. Dolly's counter-surveillance necklace did not heat up. But if they were under surveillance they didn't care. There were so many rough-looking characters skulking around *Las Ramblas*, it could have been anyone of them.

After they got ready for bed, Buck got out his notebook computer to update the log he was keeping. "In this counter-terrorism genre, aren't we supposed to be working for really stupid people in D.C. who don't understand what it is like to be working in the field?"

"Buck, you know I don't read much fiction. But yes, all those police-procedure shows on TV always have the good cops working for stupid or corrupt bosses. The same with the intelligence agency shoot 'em ups."

"For sure, Jack McClure isn't stupid or corrupt. But we've got a leak somewhere. It's like Abu Amed knows everything we are doing, knows where we are going to be next."

"With Eclectic House and the State Department publicizing our appearances, your Mr. Abu Amed doesn't need a leak. What worries me is how he knows about my shoulder bag. Thank goodness, the bag that was blown up at Charles de Gaulle Airport was a clean one.

"McClure's working on it. Maybe, he'll tell us the answer tomorrow."

The next morning Buck and Dolly found the hotel's breakfast room to be pleasant and sunny. The outside wall was almost entirely of glass interrupted only by a set of French doors. The windows looked out onto a colorful, flower-laden patio. But, due to the slight December chill and an early morning rain shower, none of the diners were taking their breakfast on the patio. Dolly was in the process of applying what the British call "the throttle" to her tea bag when she noticed Buck punching numbers into his cell phone.

She started to ask what on earth he was doing when Buck nodded toward a table next to the French door. An East Indian Dolly had not noticed before was trying frantically, and without success, to open the door and, via the patio, flee the breakfast area.

"This is Colonel Madison," she heard Buck whisper into his cell phone. "A thief is trying to leave the premises via your patio."

"Who was that?" asked Dolly, as Buck hung up.

"Mr. Garza, the house detective," said Buck, putting his cell phone away. "I made his acquaintance early this morning when I went down to get a newspaper. He warned me to watch out for purse-snatchers. Apparently, Barcelona is overrun with petty thieves. He gave me his cell phone number."

As the Madisons watched the East Indian struggle with the door, Dolly reached into her shoulder bag. When the East Indian finally got the moisture-swollen door to open, he burst out onto the patio. But when he saw he was about to run right into the arms of two members of Spain's *Guardia Civil*, the thief turned around and ran back into the breakfast room. As he came abreast of where the Madisons were sitting, Dolly shot him right in the face with a dose of Inferno Pepper Spray.

As predicted by General McClure, the pepper caused the "victim" to inhale sharply, drawing the burning chemicals deep down into his lungs. Staggering around blindly and howling with pain, the thief thrashed around in circles, causing the breakfasting guests to flee up the stairs. Finally, he bounced off a solid wall, sending him crashing to the ceramic-tile floor. Just at that moment, Mr. Garza rushed down the stairs to retrieve the stolen purse. The *Guardia Civil* handcuffed the sobbing thief and carried him like a sack of potatoes out the patio door.

"*Gracias*, Colonel Madison," said the detective. "Our humble establishment is in your debt. We have been trying to catch that particular thief for some time. Our hotel is in your debt."

"It was nothing," said Buck.

"Dolly, this is Detective Garza."

"How do you do?" said Dolly, extending her hand.

"It is a pleasure to meet you, Senora Madison," said Detective Garza.

"Please join us," said Buck

"*Gracias,* Colonel Madison. *Por favor,* just allow me to go up to the lobby and return the victim's purse. She will be so relieved. Otherwise, her vacation would have been spoiled."

"We await your return," said Buck.

On his return and while Buck and Dolly finished their breakfast, Detective Garza spent almost an hour explaining the modus operandi of the local thieves. He said the main objective of the ring of thieves was not so much cash but rather credit cards which their couriers took to cities all over the world. A credit card stolen in Barcelona could be in Casablanca the next day, in Tangiers the next, then on to London and even Miami. Meanwhile, the thieves could run up credit card charges to the top limit of a particular credit card.

Fortunately, if the cardholder reported the theft right away, the cardholder was only charged a few U.S. dollars. Unfortunately, the losses suffered by the credit card company had to be distributed across their entire customer base in the form of annual fees or by higher interest rates.

Because they would be going to the Picasso Museum, Buck concentrated his questioning of Detective Garza on thievery in that part of the city. The Madisons learned the city's many art museums are favorite hangouts of the city's pickpocket fraternity. Buck expressed his misgivings about the museum trip, in general, and Picasso, in particular. Detective Garza was not surprised. After Detective Garza took his leave, Buck suggested they slip out the back of the hotel and grab a taxi.

"But we will get to the museum well before 1100 hours," protested Dolly.

"I know," said Buck. "But I figure the guy in the black beret has seen the sign-up sheet in the lobby by now. So, he'll probably try to pick us up again at the entrance to the Picasso Museum. We can use the extra time to figure out how to deal with him. McClure said to lose him."

After a taxi driver dropped them off at the entrance to the narrow alley leading to the Picasso Museum, Dolly said, "Now, tell me
again why you don't like Picasso as a person?"

"Because he lived in Paris during the Nazi occupation and was a
Nazi collaborator. His international fame gave him considerable
influence with the German High Command in Paris. But when
his agent, the Jew who helped make him famous, was arrested by
the Gestapo, Picasso wouldn't lift a finger to save him. On top of
that, Picasso was a notorious womanizer and abuser of women.
Anything else you'd like to know about Picasso?"

"Yes, how can someone who is so obviously politically incorrect be
the object of such acclaim and veneration?"

"Because the lefties love him."

"How can that be when he collaborated with the Nazis?

"During the Spanish Civil War, Picasso was a card-carrying member of the Communist Party."

"Now, I don't want to visit his stinking museum."

"Well, we're here now. Let's see who is dumb enough to go in."

As they stood across the narrow alley, they watched tourists from
many nations queue up at the cashier's window. But as they
watched, Buck noticed something strange. On a large sign posted
behind her, the admission ticket prices were posted; however, the
prices varied based on day-of-the-week or adult or child. Buck
noticed the cashier gave the lowest price to Spanish-speaking customers. But when approached by apparently well-heeled Americans or Brits, there was always a lengthy discussion as to which
price was appropriate. The cashier always seemed to insist on the
highest posted price and, sometimes, on a higher price not even
posted. As a consequence, several of British and American tourists
put their wallets back in their pockets and walked away.

"Bingo," said Buck. "The cashier lady isn't really interested in selling those folks any tickets. She is more interested in causing them to get out their wallets and then put them away again. That's so someone out here in the crowd can see where they keep their wallets. This fits what Detective Garza was telling us at breakfast."

"Look, Buck," whispered Dolly. "See the man over there. He just fell in behind that American couple who refused to pay the high ticket price. He's following them along the alley."

"Let's go," said Buck, as they hurried past the man and caught up with the American couple.

"Excuse me," said Buck, as they drew near.

Startled, the male asked, "Do we know you?"

"No, not at all," said Buck. "But you are being followed by a pickpocket. We just thought we'd let you know."

"Well, thanks," said the man, looking around. "Where is he?"

"Oh, he's the one staring intently into the store window back there," said Dolly, "Isn't it strange for a man to take such an interest in pots and pans?"

"How can we thank you?" asked the man.

"By putting your wallet in an inside coat pocket," said Buck.

"I'll do it," said the man. "May we buy you a drink?"

"No, we have a ship to catch," said Buck. "But thanks, anyway."

"Now what?" asked Dolly, after the American couple moved on down the passage way.

"We try to hire us a pick-pocket."

With Dolly trailing behind, Buck walked over to where the pick-pocket was reading the prices on pots and pans for about the 20th time. As Buck approached, the pickpocket started to bolt. But, when Buck held out a $20 dollar bill, the man remained in place.

"Don't worry," said Buck. "I'm not going to call the police. But I think I would like to engage your services."

"Me?" asked the man, obviously another East Indian. "You want to hire me?"

"Yes, I do. You see, we are being followed by someone who might try to do us harm. I would like to look inside his wallet. I don't want his money. You can have his money and his credit cards. But I want his passport. I want to know who he is. And I want to keep his passport. For a fee, would you be willing to help us?"

"I charge $100 U.S dollars, in advance. Plus I get the money and credit cards in his wallet."

"Done," said Buck, slipping the man a couple of $20 dollar bills.

"You said you would pay $100 dollars."

"Correct. When I get his passport, you get the other $60 dollars."

"Fair enough," said the pickpocket. "Let's go into that tapas bar over there. They know me."

After they were seated and after a cup of tea was served to the East Indian and the Madisons received glasses of sangria, the man extended his hand to Buck and said, "My name is Sukumarin; how-ever, everyone here calls me Suku. You may call me Suku."

"For the brief time we are partners," said Buck, "you may call me Sahib, and the lady here, Memsahib."

"As you wish, Sahib."

Buck turned on the digital camera function of his cell phone. He caused the phone to display the color image of the man they photographed at the airport. Suku studied the image.

"He appears to be a light-skinned Arab," said the pickpocket. "Could be Syrian."

"Whatever," said Buck. "You just need to bring us his passport and let us have the wallet long enough to photograph whatever other ID is in his wallet."

"ID, Sahib?"

"I'm sorry," said Buck. "We Americans are given to abbreviations. By ID, I mean identification."

"Yes, I see. Does he always wear the long trench coat shown in the photograph?"

"It's certainly not out of place in Barcelona in December," said Buck.

"The length of the trench coat poses a problem; however, there is always a way. I will need to make some preparations. There's a back room here where we can be alone. Please follow me."

As Suku and the Madisons passed the barmaid, she gave Suku a knowing wink as she followed along to close the door to the back room behind them.

"This will only take a minute," said Suku, as he rummaged around in a wooden chest from which he produced a plastic squirt bottle like the ones used to hold mustard. Next, he found a bottle of what looked like Hershey's chocolate sauce, some wooden matches, some strange-looking powders and a ceramic bowl. He mixed the powders with the chocolate sauce. Then, Suku took out a pocketknife and carefully scraped the heads of the several matches into the mixture. He produced what looked like Dunhill cigarette lighter and set fire to the mixture. Immediately, a foul odor arose from the ceramic bowl.

"That smells like you-know-what," complained Buck.

"Yes, Sahib, it does. That is exactly what it is supposed to smell like."

Satisfied with the odor, Suku added some water and stirred the mess with a plastic spoon until it reached a consistency suitable for pouring into a plastic squirt bottle.

"Suku, I'm not sure why you are playing with your chemistry set, but we are due at the Picasso Museum at 1100 hours," said Buck. "We need to get moving."

"Yes, we do. Now, please, I want you to walk back to the Picasso Museum. Hopefully, the man in the trench coat will be waiting there for you. But don't go into the museum. Instead, I want you to walk along the alley that leads from the Picasso Museum to the front entrance of the Church of the Navigator which is just across the street from this tapas bar. My associate, whom you have not met, will be in hiding. As your man goes by the church, my partner will spray his leather trench coat with what your follower will think is human excrement. He will be appalled. I will come to his aid.

"First, I pull out my handkerchief and offer to clean his coat. Then, I will show him his trench coat is so heavily soiled that we need to rush into the toilette of this tapas bar where there is water. Inside the toilette, I will get some paper towels and start wiping the front of his coat so I can take his passport. Telling him to finish wiping the front of his coat, I will lift the tail of his trench coast and remove his wallet. I will hand the wallet and the passport out the door of the toilette to the barmaid who knows to be standing by. She will bring them to you. After I've helped clean his trench coat as best can be, I will usher the man back out onto the street. Sometimes, I get a tip for my kindness.

"Now, I will tell you how to find the rear entrance to this tapas bar and how to re-enter this room: When you hear me shouting to your follower that he has *merde* all over his coat, you go into the main entrance to the Church of the Navigator. Drop some coins in the poor box, if you wish. But turn left and go right on out the side door. You will see the alley that leads to the back of this bar.

"Stay in this room until the bar maid comes back here with the man's wallet. Please take what you want, Sahib. But leave me the money, any credit cards and my $60 dollars. Do you understand?"

"Yes, we do," said Buck.

Quickly, the Madisons left the tapas bar and headed for the Picasso Museum. When they reached the cashier's window, Buck asked the price of admission for two adults for a half-day ticket. Speaking English, the cashier quoted an outrageous price that was not posted. Buck declined to pay. Shaking his head, Buck turned away, putting his wallet in his left hip pocket. He and Dolly began their stroll along the alley toward the Church of the Navigator, playing the role of unwitting tourists. The man in the black beret was following along. Suku was following him.

When they came to the Church of the Navigator, the Madisons heard some shouting behind them. They ducked inside, dropped a coin in the poor box and quickly exited out a side door and scooted through the passage way that led to the rear entrance of the tapas bar.

After a few minutes, the barmaid hurried into the back room to hand the "victim's" wallet and his passport to Buck. Dolly's cell phone camera was at the ready. Buck briefly examined the man's passport and gave it to Dolly to be photographed. Buck didn't bother to count the Spanish pesetas. He removed every ID-type item from the wallet and arranged all of them on the table. Dolly took a close-up photo of each one.

Just as Dolly finished putting the ID items back into the wallet, Suku came in from the alley. Dolly handed Suku the man's wallet and the $60 dollars. Suku pressed his palms together, bowed his head, and was gone.

Once outside, Suku took the victim's credit cards and the pesetas out of the wallet, wiped the wallet clean of any fingerprints, and tossed the wallet into the gutter.

As the Madisons left via the back door, they could hear their minder screaming at the barmaid in broken English about the robbery. He ordered her to call the police. In equally halting English, the barmaid said her telephone wasn't working; however, there was a police station just a block away. She advised him to go there and report the theft.

Meanwhile, Buck and Dolly walked back to the museum. On the way, Dolly paused just long enough to send her photographs to General McClure. They hired a taxi for the return trip to their hotel. Before entering the hotel, Buck gave General McClure a call.

"How the hell did you steal that guy's passport?" asked McClure.

"Jack, I'm disappointed you would think we would steal anything. Actually, we hired a professional to do it. So, who is he?"

"The passport doesn't belong to the face on the photo," said McClure. "He's the same tango you photographed yesterday at the airport; however, we could not make a match with a name until just now when you sent the passport photo. He's Abu bin Kahlil, one of Abu Amed's lieutenants. So, do not let that clown get on board your ship.

"Buck, you need to know the president has gotten some angry calls from Number 10 Downing Street and from the Elysee Palace. The blow-out of Harrods basement and the destruction of the glass front of Charles de Gaulle Airport are giving the president second thoughts about your mission. I'm hoping the time you'll be spending on that cruise ship will allow matters to cool off a bit."

Buck briefed Dolly on the conversation with Jack McClure. "So, now what?" asked Dolly, as they reentered their hotel room and threw themselves on the bed.

"Accordingly to our cruise instructions, we are supposed to be in the hotel lobby at 1600 hours to catch the bus to the cruise ship for an 1800 hour sailing. That gives us plenty of time to have lunch here in the hotel, take a nap and go downstairs to watch the fun.

"Without his passport, it is highly unlikely Mr. Abu bin Kahlil, is going to be able to sail with us on our wonderful voyage through the western Mediterranean. I think we will be treated to the pleasure of watching him try to get his money back."

Knowing they would be feasting on the cruise ship later that evening, they went to the hotel dining room for some crisp salads and a bottle of excellent Spanish wine. Then they took a 90-minute nap.

Refreshed, Buck and Dolly dressed for the bus ride to the ship and for all the bon voyage festivities. Carry-on baggage in hand, they joined the other passengers in the lobby of the hotel. Buck and Dolly made sure they were among the first to board the bus. Looking down the aisle they saw the lady who bumped into them at the airline terminal. In her lap was a shoulder bag matching Dolly's. Dolly took a seat beside her. With Buck standing in the aisle as cover, they exchanged shoulder bags.

When they got to the dock Mr. Kahlil was already there, engaging in earnest conversation with the representative of the cruise line who kept shaking his head and saying something to the effect of: No passport, no cruise. As the time for the departure of the cruise ship drew closer and closer, Mr. Kahlil became more and more frantic. Eventually, he stopped harassing the cruise line representative and went to a dockside phone booth. Apparently, he was calling for a back-up or a replacement. In any event, Mr. Kahlil was very unhappy to be without his credit cards and without his passport in a foreign land. Buck and Dolly did a high-five.

As the ship cast off and the bow-thrusters spun it around to go into the ship channel, Buck waved at Mr. Kahlil. When Buck was sure he had Kahlil's undivided attention, Buck made a rude hand gesture and went inside.

✫ ✫ ✫

CHAPTER EIGHTEEN

The Western Mediterranean

By the following dawn, the cruise ship was alongside the dock in Mahon, on the island of Menorca, the sister island to the much larger and better known Mallorca. The only other vessels in port were some corvettes of the Spanish Navy tied up over at the naval station on the other side of the harbor. The Madisons decided to go ashore for two reasons: they wanted to get some exercise and Buck wanted to purchase a bottle of mayonnaise in the port where mayonnaise was invented.

In 1756, the French, to the surprise of everyone, defeated the British fleet in a naval battle just outside the Port of Mahon, which is pronounced as: mayon. To celebrate, the French admiral ordered a feast prepared. His chef wanted to make a sauce made of cream, egg yolks and, lemon juice; however, he could not find any cream. He had to substitute olive oil. By accident, he invented mayonnaise.

For her part, Dolly was not as keen on mayonnaise as Buck because of what it did to her figure and her cholesterol. But Buck always dismissed her concerns by saying, "That's why we have the Mayo Clinic."

The steep steps leading up from the dock to the old Fortress overlooking the harbor provided the exercise they were looking for. They had fun poking around in the many shops in the Fortress which had been converted into a shopping mall on the inside. There was even a grocery store in what was originally a dungeon but now served as a basement. Buck kept looking for mayonnaise made in Mahon; however, he soon learned mayonnaise was no longer made in Mahon. He settled for mayonnaise packaged back on the Spanish mainland. On the way back to the ship, they did a counter-surveillance routine. Dolly's necklace gave no sign of surveillance. They spent the rest of the day exploring the ship, using the ship's self-service laundry, taking naps and doing what couples do when they feel secure and rested.

At only 40,000 tons, the *Capriana* was small by 140,000-ton mega-ship standards. But it was clean and comfortable. The staff members, mostly recruited from the Baltic States of Latvia, Estonia and Lithuania, were efficient. But like their homelands, they were rather cold.

The ship's library was paneled in a rich walnut and lined with books. It exuded the aura of an English or Scottish manor house. Dolly enjoyed curling up in one of the leather chairs with a book while Buck sat at a library table with his laptop. Each day, Buck would compose a report for General McClure, go out on deck and send the report in a quick burst. With no sign of al-Qaeda, the daily reports must have been pretty boring. But the initial chapters of the Madison's book-in-progress covering the events in London, Paris and Barcelona made lively reading.

By the morning of the second day, they were docked in the Port of Mallorca. More for exercise than anything else, Buck and Dolly walked the long pier into town. The most interesting part of the walk was the array of mega-yachts riding in their slips or farther out at anchor.

"Where do you suppose all this money comes from?" asked Dolly.

"Who knows? I don't think it's from using grocery coupons."

A counter-surveillance routine produced negative results. Dolly's necklace remained cool. Apparently, Abu Amed wasn't going take any risks on small islands. The next few days were spent stopping each morning at the larger ports along the Spanish coast. Disgusted with the thieves of Barcelona and the post-Madrid Spanish cave-in, the Madisons did not feel like spending any money ashore. The ship was their resort. They had feared the book-signing tour would be a long and dangerous ordeal. Instead, it was turning into a real vacation.

"If we ever go to Dijon, I wonder if we can find mustard?" mused Buck.

The leisurely pace gave Buck even more time to work on their next book. Dolly used much of her time to work out each day in the well-equipped gym. The gym attendant, a young man from Thailand, bragged how he knew something about kick boxing. Dolly talked him into being her sparring partner. After getting his butt seriously kicked several days in a row, the young Thai allowed as how a crew member should not be kick boxing with the passengers.

During their last night on board, the ship transited the narrow Strait of Gibraltar. Just as dawn bathed the east side of the Rock of Gibraltar in sunshine, the *Capriana* was maneuvering in the long shadow cast by the west side of the Rock onto the peaceful harbor that looked out toward the Atlantic Ocean. The docking at the long pier went smoothly.

✫ ✫ ✫

CHAPTER NINETEEN

Gibraltar

Of all the places on the book-tour itinerary none possessed greater appeal for Buck than the British Crown Colony of Gibraltar. The idea of venturing to the place where Europe and Africa almost touch each other, separated by less than eight miles across the Strait of Gibraltar was like a magnet to Buck. Then to, was the prospect of standing at Nelson's Anchorage where the survivors and the dead of the Battle of Trafalgar were brought ashore. For the allied invasion of North Africa, the Rock provided the headquarters for General Eisenhower and his staff. They might even see the dining room where the British used an actor bearing a remarkable resemblance to British Field Marshal Bernard Montgomery to dupe the Nazis into believing the real Montgomery was dining on Gibraltar on the evening of the 5th of June, 1944. The Rock was as full of history as the Rock's supposedly rock-solid geology was full of holes.

Buck and Dolly proceeded on foot to Main Street. Because their itinerary called for them to leave the cruise ship in Gibraltar, they arranged to have their baggage delivered to the Rock Hotel. Dolly, of course, kept her clean shoulder bag. Buck took only his brief case with the laptop inside as they strolled along the dock and into the town. The book signing wasn't until 1:00 p.m. local time, so they had plenty of time to check into the hotel and walk over to the book store. [See photo of the Rock, the Bay of Gibraltar, and the airport at: www.buckandolly.com/BerlinConspiracy.]

Their first order of business was to meet their contact. He was supposed to be waiting at the Royal Yacht Club. As they walked along, they had to laugh at an advertisement posted on a wall by a local underground newspaper called the *Ape Sheet*. The tabloid was trying to compete with *The Times* of London. The advertisement read: "Last year, 500 Gibraltarians left *The Times* and went *Ape Sheet.*"

When they arrived at the Royal Yacht Club, they had just reached the cloak room when a silver-haired gentleman stepped forward to introduce himself.

"Good morning," he said, with a slight bow toward Dolly. "Allow me to introduce myself. I am Colonel Jack Dawes, formerly of the Royal Army, but now retired here on the Rock. If you are the Madisons, then I have something of yours."

"We are the Madisons," said Buck, extending his hand. "This is my wife, Dolly."

"How do you do?" said Dawes, as he extended a shoulder bag exactly like Dolly's. Looking around to see if they were being observed Dawes said rather loudly, "There seems to have been a mix-up. Somehow, you got my bag, and I got yours. Terribly sorry. I trust you will find everything in order."

"I'm sure I will," said Dolly. "Actually, we didn't need any of your condoms. I hope you weren't caught unprepared," said Dolly, testing to see if Dawes' urbane British demeanor could be ruffled.

Without missing a beat, Dawes said, "Please call me Jack. Perhaps, you will join me here for a drink come about sundown?"

"Colonel, I mean Jack," said Buck, "we would be honored to join you; however, we must first check into our hotel and take care of some other details. Let's exchange cards so we have each other's cell phone numbers. I assume we have cell service here?"

"Oh, indeed. It's rather good except, of course, deep inside the Rock. Thank you for your card. I look forward to hearing from you.

"Dolly, I'm so sorry about the bag mix-up. Your Botox and Buck's Viagra were of no use to me," said Dawes, putting paid to Dolly's earlier jab.

With that, the Madisons took their leave and Colonel Dawes retreated into the dark, mahogany-paneled recesses of the Royal Yacht Club.

As Buck and Dolly hiked up to the Rock Hotel, Dolly said, "So, that's what the resident MI-6 agent looks like. The very image of the retired colonel living the good life in a sub-tropical climate while enjoying decent public utilities, clean water and without the crushing tax burdens of living in England. I wonder if the other side knows who Dawes really is?"

"I'm not sure we do. He reminds me of Sir Nigel Lawson, one of Prime Minister Thatcher's cabinet officers. He's the one with the beautiful daughter who has her own cooking show on BBC-TV and the Food Network. She's a knock-out. I watch her all the time. Never miss her show."

"What does she cook?"

"I don't know."

"Buck, you are impossible."

Just before they checked into the Rock Hotel, they found one of those Red English Telephone Boxes. While appearing to use the telephone box, Buck used his satellite cell phone to call General McClure.

"How was the cruise?" asked General McClure.

"Restful," said Buck. "In fact, I got quite a bit done on our next book. Dolly worked off all the extra food in the gym. What have you got for us?"

"The NSA is picking up telephone traffic indicating some Spanish jihadists are planning to enter Gibraltar with another car bomb."

"I seem to recall some group tried to blow up a car bomb here a few years back," said Buck.

"Yes, the IRA was plotting to blow up the British Army Band on Gibraltar. But the SAS got wind of it early-on and took out the IRA chaps before they could kill anyone. The faint-of-heart thought the SAS was too hasty. Tried to have the SAS shooters brought up on charges. But the inquest showed the SAS intervention was timely and proper. The SAS killed three IRA gunmen. Left alone, the IRA would have murdered scores.

"Today's concern is the jihadists will try to bomb you, Dolly and your fans at the Green Parrot Book Store. You can cancel the book-signing, you know."

"I don't think so. Our mission is to draw them out. Hiding won't accomplish anything. We'll stay on schedule. I suppose from here we fly to Lisbon, then to Munich and, finally, to Berlin?

"Yes, but stay loose. Anytime I suggest a change in your itinerary to State, they get upset. The Agency doesn't seem to care one way or the other. As long as they don't run out of shoulder bags full of weapons, they are fine. I assume you have made contact with Colonel Dawes and gotten your bag. Prior to your flight to Lisbon, give your weapons bag back to him."

"That's affirmative," said Buck. "As instructed, we met Colonel Dawes at the Royal Yacht Club and made the swap. He seems like a stand-up fellow."

"Yes, he's one of their best. Look, I have other fires to put out. Keep your heads down. Oh, almost forgot. The president insists you must not harm the Rock's pet Barbary Apes. Out."

When they reached the Rock Hotel, Buck asked the concierge to recommend the best way to see all one could see on Gibraltar in one day. The concierge recommended a tour bus that just happened to be operated by his cousin. He said the tour bus called at the Rock Hotel each morning at 10:00 a.m. The tour would be over by tea time. Buck filled out the form and made the reservation for the next day.

The décor of their room was in the grand British Colonial style. The balcony was guarded by an iron railing. The balusters supporting the railing were linked together to create the feeling that the railing was made out of entwined grape vines. About 12 feet below were some lush and well-manicured topiary. The balcony afforded a magnificent view across the Bay of Gibraltar and across the way to the Bay of Algeciras and the southern coast of Spain. Down below, they could see the *Capriana* resting at the pier, being prepared to depart that evening for Casablanca.

Leaving Dolly to unpack, Buck's went to the concierge for directions to a store catering to hikers. Not far from the hotel, he was able to buy two backpacks each large enough to carry his notebook computer and the other "necessities" from Dolly's shoulder bag. Each backpack contained a hydration unit for either water or wine. Having eaten way too much on the cruise ship, they opted to skip lunch and proceed directly to the book store. But, as was their habit, they put a strand of Dolly's hair across the top of the door before they closed it shut.

The afternoon book signing at The Green Parrot was well-attended, mostly by British ex-pats who preferred the climate of Gibraltar to the so often rainy England. In the wake of the London subway bombings and the foiled plot to blow up about a dozen airliners en route to America, the Brits were very keen to learn more about how Buck and Dolly were able to foil two plots engineered by the communist governments of Cuba and Red China.

During the question and answer session Buck happened to mention his interest in the Battle of Trafalgar. That was a mistake because virtually everyone in the room considered him or herself to be an expert on the subject.

Colonel Dawes was in the audience, standing way in the back. He lingered behind after the others were gone. He even volunteered to help the bookstore staff box up the handful of unsold books. He seemed to be known by many of the people there. At just over six-feet-tall wearing a blue blazer with a regimental tie and tan slacks, he cut a rather dashing figure. His pencil-thin mustache made him, as Gilbert and Sullivan might say: "The very image of a modern major general."

Turning to Buck and Dolly, he pretended they just met. "I realize we haven't been introduced; however, I am Colonel Jack Dawes, wounded a bit in the Falklands and the SAS put me out to pasture. If you have some time, I'd like to treat you to a drink at the Royal Yacht Club."

During World War II, "Jackdaws" was the code name for a British intelligence operation that sent female agents to infiltrate Nazi-occupied Europe's largest telephone exchange. Was Jack Dawes a cryptonym appropriated by their new acquaintance or was he just yanking their chain? Whatever his real name, it did not matter. But then, if he really was Sir Nigel Lawson, maybe they would get to meet his famous daughter.

"Jack Dawes," said Buck. "Are you *corvus monedula?*"

"Unfortunately, bird watchers pull that old chestnut on me quite often. Are you a bird watcher?"

"I'd like to be; but Dolly here would kill me."

"Colonel Dawes, you must forgive my husband. What he thinks passes for a sense of humor, does not."

"You must call me Jack. That way, I won't have to call your husband colonel or you doctor."

"Jack, Dolly and Buck it is then," said Buck. "And we rarely turn down an offer of drinks or a chance to gaze upon some sailboats."

"Indeed, we can do both. In fact, I would be pleased to show you my sailboat, even though it is for sale."

"And why is that?" asked Dolly. "Surely, you aren't giving up the joys of sailing for one of those horrible stink pots."

"No, indeed, I just want to go back home and buy something a bit smaller to sail during Cowes Week. Also, I have a Cessna Skylane, a gussied-up Cessna 182, tied down here at the airport. I use the Cessna to fly back and forth to England. But with Dame Thatcher gone, our economy is shot to hell. So, keeping both a sailboat and an airplane here is getting a bit pricey. For now, one of them has got to go."

"Both of us have some hours in the Skylane. In fact, we've owned two of them. They are wonderful airplanes. What's your sailboat?" asked Buck.

"It's an American boat, a MacGregor 26X. Do you know it?"

"What a coincidence," said Buck. "That's the same boat we sail on our lake back home. We'd love to see your boat."

"When we get to the Royal Yacht Club, I'll show you the 'for sale' card I've posted on the bulletin board. All the pertinent details are listed, to include my asking price."

"If the price is right and if we can quickly work out the details of the ship's papers, Dolly and I might be interested in buying your boat." Dolly shot Buck a glance that looked like the first chapter of a new book entitled: *Are you out of your cotton-pickin' mind?*

The Royal Yacht Club was only about two hundred yards down-hill from the bookstore. The interior was paneled in dark wood, the walls were festooned with coats-of-arms. The trophy cases were lined with the loving cups awarded at previous regattas. It was old-world British Empire. Several Royal Navy officers were at the long mahogany bar. One of them detached himself from his fellows long enough to greet Colonel Dawes and give him a pat on the back.

The veranda looked out over the yacht basin. Even though the place was packed with thirsty members, both inside and out, Colonel Dawes was escorted immediately to what must have been "his" table out on the veranda. Right next to the railing, it afforded a close-up view of the sailboats bobbing in their slips or tugging at their moorings.

Dolly was excited about the chance to visit the Royal Yacht Club. Buck was even more excited by the prospect of looking at the Mac-Gregor 26X belonging to Colonel Dawes. In their excitement, and taking too much comfort in the commanding aura of Colonel Dawes, they gave little thought to counter-surveillance. If they were paying attention, they might have detected the two men who followed them from the Green Parrot to the Royal Yacht Club.

Abu Amed's men didn't look Anglo enough or even Spanish enough to be admitted to the club without being questioned by the Yeoman Warder posted at the entry, so they slipped around to the side and found several young people sitting on the sidewalk just below the Club's veranda. Some of them were warming their backs against the veranda's stone foundation while watching the sun beginning to sink into the Bay of Algeciras. The minders put their backs to the wall in the hope of overhearing what the Madisons were saying to Colonel Dawes.

"Who was the distinguished naval officer who spoke to you?" asked Dolly.

"Captain Ralph Goulds, a mate from the Falklands War. He's the skipper of the Royal Navy corvette you see out there."

Colonel Dawes ordered a Guinness. Buck and Dolly did the same. After their drinks came and the waiter left, Jack Dawes said, "Well, now you've seen the bulletin board with the particulars of my Mac-Gregor 26X, what do you think?"

"Wow, I like the fact you have a 90-horsepower motor," said Dolly. "The most we've ever seen before is 50-horse. You even have a remote-controlled spotlight. Your boat is loaded with accessories: a GPS, a chart plotter, a roller-furler jib, and a bimini top."

"Actually, that's not a jib on the furler. It's a 135-percent genoa. The genoa gives me some extra speed. But if you want some real speed, pull up the twin rudders, dump out the water ballast, full throttle that 90-horse motor, and Bob's your uncle. You can do about 26 miles-per-hour.

"I'm sure you know the MacGregor 26 was designed to motor the 26 miles from Los Angeles or Long Beach to Catalina Island and then rig for a weekend of sailing around the Channel Islands."

"Yes, we even know a song about the 26 miles to Catalina Island," said Dolly. "But does the length of the boat at 26-feet have anything to do with song?"

"I don't think so," said Dawes. "The MacGregor 26 is also designed to be carried on a trailer. So, 26-feet is about as long as it can be without having the width end up being too wide for trailering without a special permit. My guess is the song and the length of the boat just happens to be a coincidence.

"But tell me, Buck, why would you want to buy a sailboat here in Gibraltar. Don't you have other stops to make on your book tour?"

"Actually, we do. Three days from now, we are supposed to fly to Lisbon. So, I figure we have enough free time to sail ourselves to Lisbon. The people who have been trying to blow us up might put a bomb on the plane. We always like to have a back-up, as a former Army boss of mine liked to say."

"That's why I keep the sailboat at the ready," said Dawes. "Like you, I never know what the next day will bring.

"I have enough charts on board to get you all the way back to England. Relatively speaking, Portugal's not that far. She's already fitted with long-range gas tanks, so if the winds are fickle, you can, as Dolly might say: stink-pot along."

After they finished their drinks, Colonel Dawes said, "Well, let's go have a look."

Colonel Dawes' boat was named: *Falklands Folly*. Seeing Buck and Dolly puzzling over the name, Colonel Dawes offered, "Her name suggests the folly of thinking that Prime Minister Thatcher would abandon British subjects and leave them to the tender mercies of the Argentine junta."

After a walk around the exterior and a tour of the cabin, Buck said, "Well, Jack, she's in Bristol condition. I wish our MacGregor 26 looked this nice."

"Well, I do try. As a widower, I don't have much else to do."

"Maybe, you should take this boat back to England to find someone to share her with," said Dolly, ever the match-maker.

"I dare say the pickings are rather slim around here," said Dawes. "So, I'm hoping you are correct."

"Could you give us a moment?" asked Buck. "I think Dolly and I would like to have a word."

"Of course," said Dawes.

After they moved out of earshot, Dolly asked, "Why do we need this sailboat when we have a wonderful sailboat almost like this one back in Colorado?"

"We don't. But it's good to have some other way out of here. We've made no secret of our plan to fly out of here on an airliner. I worry the aircraft could be sabotaged. A lot of innocent passengers could be killed. We have more than enough 'discretionary funds' to buy Jack's boat. And that's without bargaining, something the English aren't keen on anyway. So, if he can bring us the ship's papers and will agree to provision the boat for a sail to Lisbon, I say let's buy that beauty. We can call Jack McClure and tell him the sailboat is our back up plan."

"Okay. I do like the idea of having options," said Dolly.

As they returned to the *Falklands Folly*, Colonel Dawes was making a show of polishing a ship's bell made of brass.

"Okay, Jack," said Buck. "We want to purchase your boat; however, we have some conditions. We'll meet your asking price, no questions asked; provided, you can produce a clean bill of sale, all the necessary ship's papers to operate in the waters we discussed, full fuel tanks, enough potable water and provisions for a week of sailing and all the charts we will need to go from here to Portugal. If you can do that, we'll meet you at the Barclays Bank tomorrow and present you with your asking price. Our publisher, Eclectic House, has set up a draw account for us against the advance on our next books. So, we can do this at the bank either in dollars, pounds sterling or Euros, you name it."

"Actually, the place is called Barclays Wealth Private Clients International. I have an account there. Yes, dollars would be nice. I can do all you ask by early tomorrow morning. We could meet as soon as the bank opens. That way, you could get on with your sightseeing. I'm very keen for you to take a tour of Nelson's Anchorage, see the lighthouse, and go up to the Upper Galleries. The views from up there are spectacular."

The three of them shook hands on their deal. But, before they parted, Dolly asked, "Jack, who has to know about the sale of your boat to us?"

"For now, only the bank. She is registered here in Gibraltar. She gets to fly the Red Ensign marking her as a British boat. As such, she is entitled to the protection of the Royal Navy. Perhaps, best of all, I do not have to pay the European Union VAT or a sales tax. For the moment, I don't plan to tell anyone my boat has been sold. Not even the Royal Harbor Master.

"But on this tiny Rock, secrets don't keep long around here; especially, from the Spanish across the way. But I try. Many of our workers commute each day from Spain. Some of them work for Spanish

Intelligence. They know who I am, and I know many of them. But we keep it civil. *Noblesse oblige,* that sort of rot.

"I know you must be tired, but would you like to come back here this evening so I can treat you to dinner?"

"How kind of you," said Dolly. "But we need to stay close to our hotel. If you don't mind, we will just have a bite there. You are more than welcome to join us. Our treat."

"I think not. I'd best go to my flat and check up on the boat's paperwork. The Barclays Wealth opens at 9:00 a.m. Let's just meet there in the morning. I will have the necessary paperwork in hand."

"Done," said Buck. "Thanks for selling us the *Falklands Folly.* If we need to use it, we promise to take good care of her."

Abu Amed's minders watched outside the yacht club as their quarry and the Briton shook hands and took leave of each other. Still watching their weight, Buck and Dolly quietly shared a Caesar Salad in the hotel dining room. After leaving a wake-up call at the front desk, Buck and Dolly took the stairs up to their room. But as they approached the door, they noticed the telltale they left over the top of the door had fallen to the carpet.

Listening carefully, they heard the sounds of someone or something moving around inside their room. Dolly pulled her revolver out of her shoulder bag. Fearful one of the famous Barbary Apes was pillaging their room, and not wanting the president to hear from the prime minister how she killed one of Gibraltar's prized attractions, she rotated the cylinder to position one of the .410 shotgun shells as the first round to fire. Buck put his Surefire combat light in one hand.

Just before Buck pushed his key into the door lock, they looked at each other and then took a deep breath. When Dolly nodded, Buck inserted the key and pushed the door wide open. The combat light brilliantly illuminated the fleeting backside of a man scrambling over the iron balcony railing. Startled by the light, the man lost his balance and fell. But not before Dolly fired a shotgun shell through the decorative balusters. That was followed by a loud yelp and the sound of bushes being crushed down below

"Did I hit him?" asked Dolly, running out onto the balcony.

"Hard to tell," said Buck, searching the garden with his combat light. "The faux grape leaves stopped a lot of the blast. Still, some of the birdshot must have gotten through. I'll bet our visitor will be running around holding his behind and looking for someone with a pair of tweezers and the skill to extract a bunch of lead BBs."

"Surely, you don't think I would shoot someone with something so environmentally incorrect as lead?"

"He's just lucky you didn't give him a free colonoscopy with one of those .45 rounds."

The hotel's thick stone walls muted much of the sound of the shotgun blast. No one came running to see what happened. But the phone did ring. It was the front desk asking if they heard a sharp noise. Buck said he dropped his suitcase off the bed. Satisfied, the person at the front desk rang off.

Dolly called Colonel Dawes on his cell phone to tell him what happened. Colonel Dawes said he would tip off the local medics to be on the lookout for someone wanting to have birdshot removed from his nether regions. Assured Buck and Dolly were no worse for wear, Dawes found the episode very funny. He would see them at the bank.

Two of the tangos were outside the Rock Hotel waiting for their comrade to finish the search of the Madisons room when he came limping over to them holding the back of his pants. After a quick and embarrassing examination, it was determined the wounds were not life-threatening. He would, however, need first aid and some painful plucking of birdshot from his behind. They decided not to report the botched search to Abu Amed.

Using a series of cell phones, they told Abu Amed the Madisons and a Colonel Dawes spent some time talking about a sailboat. The trio went down to the dock to inspect a boat called: the *Falklands Folly*. Amed told them to post a watch on the sailboat. If it departed the harbor, he would arrange to have it sunk.

The minders also reported the Madisons made reservations for a guided tour of the Rock. Unaware of the botched search, Abu Amed told them they did a good job. They were to return to Spain. Other agents would deal with the Madisons inside the Upper Galleries.

☆ ☆ ☆

Right on time the next morning, Buck and Dolly met Colonel Dawes at Barclays Wealth. The funds were transferred to Colonel Dawes' account and the necessary papers were handed over to Buck and Dolly. If the *Falklands Folly* was to be used to get them to Lisbon, Colonel Dawes would be kept informed. If they decided to fly on the airline after all, Colonel Dawes was to keep the boat and sail it back to England. Buck said they might have more business in England someday. If so, they might reclaim the *Falklands Folly* and even sail it to Newport, Rhode Island.

Buck and Dolly returned to the Rock Hotel in time to board the tour bus which began with a ride over to Nelson's Anchorage, the place where, in 1805, the wounded and dying from the Battle of Trafalgar were brought. The remains of some who died are buried there. Buck was particularly fascinated by the 100-ton Victorian Super Gun, the mammoth artillery piece guarding the Atlantic side of the Rock. While Buck was looking at the huge, 1870-built cannon and learning it could fire one 2,000 pound round every four minutes out to a range of eight miles, Dolly noticed two bearded men who were not with a tour guide. They were standing off to the side, appearing to be interested in the 100-ton cannon.

The tour guide put them back on the little bus for the ride out to Europe Point at the very tip of Gibraltar where Europe almost touches North Africa. They stood in the shadow of the Trinity Lighthouse so important to the shipping making passage through the narrow 7.7 nautical mile strait. In the distance, they could just make out some low-lying hills where Muslim herders and farmers were, no doubt, going about their daily rituals.

Turning to Buck, Dolly said, "I had no idea Europe and North Africa are so close in terms of distance."

"Unfortunately, unless something changes, the cultural and religious divide is more like the distance between Earth and Mars," said Buck.

From the lighthouse, the bus chugged up higher on the Rock to the entrance to the 32 miles of caves that are inside the limestone formation the world knows simply as the Rock of Gibraltar. As Buck and Dolly were soon to see, the inside of the Rock is like Swiss cheese, the reason why that old slogan: "Solid as the Rock of Gibraltar" now rings a bit hollow.

After the bus negotiated a series of switchbacks, they came to the entrance of the Upper Galleries of the Great Siege Tunnels. In addition to a ticket booth and the archway for a magnetometer, the entrance was guarded by manikins dressed as the gunners would have appeared during the Great Siege of 1783 when a combined force of over 100,000 French and Spanish troops tried to overrun Gibraltar and wrest it away from the British. [See photo of the Great Siege Tunnel gun ports at: www.buckanddolly.com.]

"We can't get through the magnetometer carrying our weapons on our bodies," whispered Dolly.

"Let's put them in our backpacks," whispered Buck. "Maybe we can get them in that way."

Once the tour group was assembled in front of the magnetometer, their tour guides explained the Upper Galleries were full of artifacts under the protection of the Royal Society in charge of preservation. Moreover, the Barbary Apes were infamous for rip-ping apart backpacks and purses in a quest to find even more food than the generous amounts of food already provided to them by the Gibraltar Tourism Board. Therefore, all backpacks, purses and briefcases must be stored in lockers at the entrance. Buck shot a worried glance at Dolly. Her face reflected her own misgivings as they deposited their backpacks in one of the lockers.

After everyone from the tour bus was inside the tunnel entrance, their guide explained how the Great Siege came about and how the British forces on the island responded to it. Mainly, by creating tunnels inside the Rock that led to gun ports or embrasures from which the British could fire cannons down onto the ranks of the advancing French and Spanish forces and also rake the invader's support ships with cannon fire.

Back at the tunnel entrance, a man claiming he needed to use his cricket bat as a cane and his companion, who stuffed several Brit-ish pounds into the shirt pocket of the gate guard, were admitted without question.

After winding around in the tunnels for some time and stopping now and then to peer through the gun ports down onto the town of Gibraltar and out toward the arching coastline of Spain, the members of the tour group came to the gun port of most inter-est to Buck and Dolly. From its opening, they could peer down onto the short land bridge linking Gibraltar to Spain and onto the unique airport that links Gibraltar by air to the outside world.

To make the tour more interesting, a complete cannon crew was there in the regalia of 1783. Their function was to demonstrate the steps necessary to prepare the cannon for firing. At first, Buck and Dolly didn't see the cannon because it was pushed away from the gun port and back up a fairly steep slope into a darkened recess that almost hid the cannon from view. The guide explained when the cannon was not actually firing out the gun port it was withdrawn and held back up in the darkened recess by chains. So doing, kept the cannon safe from counter-battery fire and also served to keep the narrow passageway clear for the ammunition bearers serving the gun ports farther along the path.

When the guide signaled him to do so, the gunnery sergeant ordered some of his crew to slip along one side of the cannon and up into the recess where they could be heard unlocking and un-wrapping the chains holding the cannon in place. The guide cau-tioned everyone to stand to the side because if the cannon were to get away from the gun crew it would come racing down slope and, given its weight, could cause serious injury to anyone in its way.

Two soldiers placed wheel chocks in front of the cannon's two wheels. That done, the gunnery sergeant ordered the men holding the chains attached to the trails of the cannon to begin the process of letting the cannon move slowly down the compacted track lead-ing from the recess to the gun port. On command, the crewmen in charge of the wheel chocks would advance them downhill a foot or so as the chains were loosened a bit.

When the cannon was resting on the flat of the tunnel floor, the crew went through a mock drill of loading the cannon with gun power and a cannon ball. Then, the gunners pushed the cannon outward unit it was sticking out the gun port and aimed downward as if to shred the lines of advancing infantry or to sink any French or Spanish ships in the Bay of Gibraltar. [See a photograph of the gun crew at: www.buckanddolly.com.]

Once the brief mock demonstration was over, it took the entire gun crew to push the cannon back up into its recess. They chained the cannon back in place and removed the wheel chocks. Everyone thanked the gunnery sergeant and his crew. Tips were handed out. The gunnery sergeant barked an order. The gun crew stomped about in the British manner and quick-marched back to the tun-nel entrance.

After the tour group saw all the exhibits inside the Upper Galler-ies, the tour guide said they would be free for the next half-hour to poke around in the tunnels as they pleased; however, they must be back at the entrance to the Upper Galleries within the time allotted.

Buck and Dolly found the free time quite agreeable because Buck wanted to revisit the gun port that looked out over the airport on the land bridge between Gibraltar and Spain. As they poked along, Dolly noticed they were being followed by the bearded men seen earlier at Nelson's Anchorage.

"Buck," whispered Dolly, "Don't look back. I just saw the two men from Nelson's Anchorage. They stop at each gun port and look out. But they don't seem like tourists to me."

"One way to tell," said Buck, "let's slip back up behind this cannon and see what happens. If they walk on by, they might be tourists. But if they double back like they are searching for us, we may be in trouble."

A few minutes later, the two men came to a halt at the gun port overlooking the airport. In Arabic-accented English, one of them called up into the darkness behind the cannon, "Colonel Madison, it will do you and your wife no good to hide up there behind the cannon. My brother and I have you trapped. You come down here so we can talk. Or, we will climb up there and kill you. It is your choice."

"Stall 'em," whispered Buck, as he pulled a foot of Det-cord from his suspenders and started wrapping it around the chain securing the cannon in place.

"Yes, you have us trapped." called Dolly. "But I have some information of interest to Mr. Abu Amed. He will be unhappy with you if you kill us. I will come down and tell you something of what I know. Besides, if you kill us up here, our blood will be down there at your feet. The Royal Police will use it to track you down for our murders."

"Dr. Madison, stop talking and come down here immediately or we are coming up there!"

Unscrewing the cap of his faux Montblanc fountain pen, Buck whispered, "Dolly, keep buying time. I've got to get the detonator rigged to the Det-cord."

"I'm coming down," called Dolly, as she inched slowly down the incline. When she was on a level with the two terrorists, she saw the one to her left was trying, without success, to unfold some kind of knife. Apparently, he didn't understand the blade would not unfold until he slid he unlock button into the correct position. The terrorist to her right was holding what looked like a cricket bat.

Instead of waiting for them to attack, Dolly decided to put her Kajukenbo skills to the test. Knowing the bat would be relatively easy to disarm compared to the knife, she moved toward the tango with the cricket bat, putting as much distance between herself and the tango with the knife as possible. If she could gain control over the bat, she might have a chance to defeat the knife.

She knew pain would be her ally. If she could get in close enough and start inflicting debilitating pain on her opponent fast enough and often enough, she would have a chance. As she moved toward the man with the cricket bat, she hesitated just long enough for him to begin his back swing, and then, with perfect timing, she charged right at him. As the man swung the bat downward with his right hand, Dolly stepped in close using her left hand to Monkey Grip the inside of his wrist and to deflect the bat away to her left. At the same moment, she used her right hand to Eagle Claw at his eyes.

Still pushing the bat away, and stepping under his right arm, she pulled her right hand down, raking her fingernails across his face. Blinded, the tango could not see Dolly recoil her right arm and deliver a Crane Strike to his right floating ribs, expelling the air from his lung. Gasping for air from the Crane Strike, the man bent toward her making it easy for Dolly to slip her arm around the tango's neck. Her hips acting as a fulcrum, Dolly quickly changed her foot work thrusting her right hip into the man's pelvis, altering the tango's center of balance. While controlling the man's weapon arm with her left hand, Dolly executed a classic box-step hip throw and sent him, heels over head, to the ground. Barely a second passed between the sound of his thigh bone breaking against the hard-packed ground and his loud scream of pain.

Putting her right hand behind the man's still-extended right arm, she joined her two hands together over the cricket bat handle and rotated his wrist, her hands and the bat clockwise. The man had no choice but to release his grip on the bat lest the twisting maneuver rip out all the muscles in his right arm, shoulder and upper back.

Gripping the bat, Dolly hit the downed tango squarely in the testicles. Then, quicker than a windshield wiper on high, she slapped the front and back of both his knees with the bat. When he tried to rise up, she hit him on top of the head with the butt of the bat handle, aiming for the soft spot on top of the cranium. He was out cold. Dolly spun to deal with the man who had finally figured out how to unfold his knife.

Then, Dolly realized, *oh my God, the man has a Karambit, the knife with the curved blade designed to gut animals and humans.*

The Karambit has a finger loop at one end, a palm sized handle, and a five-inch talon-shaped blade. The design of a Karambit makes it almost impossible to disarm in hand-to- hand combat without getting sliced to ribbons.

The blade was in the tango's right hand. As he swung the gleaming Karambit in a horizontal slashing motion at her midsection, she got out of her assailant's line-of-attack by stepping quickly to her right. Using the edge of cricket bat, she struck the inside of the tango's right wrist with a blow that should have caused him to drop the knife. But the tango had his right index finger inside the index-finger hole of the Karambit.

With a backhand stroke, she slashed the cricket bat against the tango's right clavicle. She heard the bone crack. His right arm went limp. Then, with an upward stroke of the bat, she hit him in the groin. His left hand went to protect his testicles from more blows, leaving his knees unprotected. Dropping into the Lion stance, she slapped both his knees with the edge of the bat.

Disabled from head-to-toe, her attacker started to fall forward, but Dolly used the tip of the bat to straighten him up so she could smash her right foot deep into his solar plexus, sending him reeling backward.

Trying to fall forward instead of on his back, the tango twisted around. He succeeded in falling on his face; however, his index finger was still caught in the Karambit. As he fell, the tip of the Karambit slid off the side of his sternum and sliced into his heart.

Unaware her attacker was dying; Dolly grabbed his ankles and pulled him on top of his unconscious comrade. But, when she saw the trail of blood left across the pathway, she almost fainted. Breathing heavily, Dolly ran back up the slope to Buck.

"Buck, he must have fallen on his knife. I swear I didn't stab him."

"I know you didn't," said Buck. "But it may not look that way to the Royal authorities. So, lest the Royal Police hold you for murder, let's get rid of the evidence. Get your hands over your ears and look away from the cannon. After the explosion, help me get the cannon started downhill."

With a loud pop, the Det-cord severed the chain tethering the cannon from rolling downward. With almost no effort, Buck and Dolly got the cannon in motion and headed down the gun-carriage track toward the two terrorists.

Just then, the man who wielded the cricket bat at Dolly woke up. Buck's only regret was they didn't use the camera in his satellite phone to record the look of absolute shock and horror on the man's face as he realized the on-coming cannon was going to carry him and his bloody colleague out the gun port and into space.

Slipping and sliding down the cannon track, Buck and Dolly reached the gun port and looked straight down. A cloud of dust marked where the cannon hit a narrow gravel road far below and then bounced into a minivan, knocking it off the road. As Buck and Dolly watched, the minivan tumbled end over end until it was lost from sight in the green foliage. When the dust on the road settled, the mangled bodies of the two tangos and the half-buried cannon became evident.

As they would learn much later, the cannon did not kill any innocent civilians, although almost certainly the tumbling minivan must have bewildered some of the Barbary Apes. Unfortunately, the vehicle hit the concrete roof of one of the many cisterns used to collect the Rock's precious rainfall. The minivan broke through the concrete roof and disappeared.

After Dolly brushed the dirt from the knees of her cargo pants and ran a comb through her hair, they made their way back toward the entrance and caught up with the rest of their tour group. When one and all were once again assembled, their guide asked, "Did everyone have a good time? Did you see anything of interest?"

Buck and Dolly just looked at each other and then shook their heads. They reclaimed their backpacks, found everything in order, and got back on the tour bus.

☆ ☆ ☆

CHAPTER TWENTY

Gibraltar

When they returned to their hotel room, the telltales placed on top of the entry door, on top of the door to the wardrobe, and in the drawers of the vanity were missing. Buck nodded toward the still open door and they retreated back out into the hallway.

"This isn't working," whispered Dolly. "Now, they must be searching our room in broad daylight. It looks like the tangos know everything about us and about accommodations. Frankly, I'm afraid to be boarding the airliner for Lisbon tomorrow. I think we need to go to Plan B."

"You mean get on the *Falklands Folly* and sail for Lisbon?"

"Precisely. Let's give Colonel Dawes a call and tell him to meet us at his former boat just after dark."

The commotion caused when the cannon came bursting out of the Upper Galleries came immediately to the attention of Abu Amed's minders stationed outside the Rock Hotel. When they called Amed, he knew right away something was seriously wrong. He ordered the minders to tell those staking out the sailboat to be alert. The airline terminal was to be kept under surveillance as well. Under no circumstances were the Madisons to leave Gibraltar alive.

After requesting and receiving permission from the front desk for a late check-out, Buck and Dolly went shopping for as much bottled water and tinned food as they could fit into their backpacks and their luggage. Then they made arrangements with the concierge to have their other luggage delivered to the Royal Yacht Club. Finally, they called General McClure to give him a situation report.

"Yes, Buck, I am already well aware of what happened up on the Rock. In addition to hearing from the British prime minister about the destruction of Harrods basement, the president has now heard from the prime minister on the subject of the destruction of a prized and irreplaceable antique cannon and the dropping of a minivan down inside one of Gibraltar's water reservoirs. Fortunately, they now get their water from a desalinization plant. But you have damaged part of their strategic water reserve. Could you please limit your activities to the destruction of just the tangos and reduce the amount of collateral damage?"

"Jack, the cannon is indestructible. The reservoir can be fixed. I'm sure the Royal Engineers can fish the minivan out of there and make it hold water again. We are truly sorry; however, the tangos didn't leave us any choice up there. As far as we know, none of the locals were hurt. Not even one of those blasted Barbary Apes."

"In that you are correct. No locals, no apes. Just two more tangos. Still, the prime minister wants you two off the Rock."

"Okay. We want permission to go to Lisbon by boat."

"We monitored your large cash withdrawal at the Barclay Bank this morning. Does it have anything to go with going to Lisbon?"

"We bought Colonel Dawes' sailboat."

"You think you can sail from Gibraltar to Lisbon in time to make your next book signing?"

"Properly rigged for motoring, a MacGregor 26 can do about 26-miles-per-hour. We could make Lisbon on time."

"And why don't you want to take the nice airliner between Gibraltar and Lisbon?"

"Because we suspect there will be a bomb on board. If we are on the passenger manifest, we might be responsible for the deaths of a bunch of innocent airline passengers."

"Okay. Sail the boat. Or, motor. Whatever, it takes. Give me position reports in case I have to adjust your schedule in Lisbon. I won't cancel your airline reservations. That way, your minders will have to stake out the airport to see if you actually board. Out."

As darkness fell, Buck and Dolly checked out of the Rock Hotel and took a taxi to the Royal Yacht Club. Colonel Dawes, drink in hand, detached himself from Captain Goulds.

"I'll stand you to a bon voyage drink," offered Colonel Dawes.

"Sorry, no time for that," said Buck. "If and when we get to London, I'll stand you to a round at the White Swan. They have rare, roast-beef sandwiches to die for."

You're on," said Colonel Dawes. "I've told the Royal Harbor Master the *Falklands Folly* will be putting out this evening. He just assumed I would be at the helm. No cruise ships will be making port until dawn. But you still have to watch out for small freighters and the mega-yachts. The approaches to Gibraltar are teeming with mega-yachts. If you get too close to them, they will light themselves up like the Las Vegas strip. I think their owners like to show off their toys. It's one of those my yacht is bigger than your yacht things.

"You'll be in Spanish territorial waters for most of the night. Sometimes, the Spanish put out some small patrol boats. Since the Madrid bombings, the Spanish have gone Pablo-wobbly on us, kow-towing to the Islamic jihadists."

"Pablo-wobbly?" questioned Dolly.

"Yes, cowardly. Like Hemingway's character, Pablo, in *For Whom the Bell Tolls*. You may recall it was his wife, Pilar, who possessed the... ah, *cojones.*"

"I do recall," said Dolly. "I often think of Buck as Robert Jordan."

"Let's hope Buck doesn't have to provide covering machinegun fire for you to escape tonight," said Dawes.

"Fortunately, on this moonless, December night, with your radar reflector stowed below, I rather doubt they could see you anyway. Once you leave the harbor, let me suggest you douse your navigation lights. You will, I trust, keep a sharp eye out for other vessels.

"Well then, she's ready to go. With the exception of the personal floatation devices, the PFDs, I removed all my personal items: photos of my sainted wife, and of my lovely daughter – those sorts of things."

The good Colonel saw them on board the *Falklands Folly*. When the motor was running smoothly, he cast off their dock lines. Colonel Dawes wished them Godspeed and wondered if he would ever see the Madisons and his beloved *Falklands Folly* ever again.

After donning the PFDs left for them by Colonel Dawes, Buck and Dolly motored slowly inside the long, curving breakwater behind which dozens of small craft were pulling gently against their moorings. To make sure he did not hit any of them, Buck used the remote-controlled spotlight to advantage. Once clear of the harbor, Buck killed the motor and pushed the button to cause the motor to tilt upward, bringing the propeller out of the water. With practiced hands, Dolly dropped the centerboard fully down, hoist the mainsail and unfurled the genoa. She trimmed the sails so the main and the genoa were working together to attain the maximum Venturi Effect.

The western reaches of the Costa del la Luz lay to starboard. Across the bay, the lights of Algeciras were twinkling. The lights of the big oil refinery were not a pleasant sight. In 1982, during the Falklands War, the Argentine military tried to use Algeciras as the base for Operation Algeciras – which was a failed attempt to damage the British military facilities on Gibraltar.

During the day, the shoreline, chock-a-block with the concrete condos favored by the hoards of northern European vacationers and ex-pats, had baked in the hot sun, creating an off-shore breeze. But with darkness, the cool waters of the sea took over, reversing the wind to an on-shore breeze. Moreover the stretch between Gibraltar and Cadiz was tidal making the journey either faster or slowing depending on your direction and the time of day or night.

Buck looked at the chart and took up a southwesterly heading that would allow them to round the port of Tanrifa and then turn to the northwest toward Portugal. With Tanrifa known as the windsurfing Mecca of Europe, high winds could be a problem. For now, however, a 10-knot wind was coming over their portside. Dolly trimmed the sails a bit more. The weary couple settled back on a long beam reach they hoped would carry them beyond Tanrifa.

Despite their precarious circumstances, Buck was pleased they would sail by Cadiz from which Columbus set sail in 1492 in search of the East Indies. That was the same year the Catholics finally wrested back control of the Iberian Peninsula from the Muslims. But of even greater interest to Buck was the realization they would be sailing through the waters where Lord Nelson fought and won the Battle of Trafalgar. Other than getting killed by a sniper, it was Admiral Nelson's finest hour.

As they sailed westward, Buck was surprised at the number and size of the pleasure craft making their way along the Costa del la Luz. Navigation lights were everywhere. Buck knew the red and green navigation lights on the bow of the *Falklands Folly* should be on, but escaping the jihadists took precedence over the rules of the road. He turned them off, making the *Falklands Folly* completely dark.

The sea state was so calm boredom and fatigue began to take their toll. Dolly was about to nod off when the cockpit was hit with a blinding spotlight. From behind the spotlight came the loudhailer-powered voice of someone speaking Spanish-accented English, ordering them to heave-to.

In Spanish waters, why English? Whoever was ordering them to heave-to must already know who they are. Once more, the fix is in, thought Buck.

Buck's response was to aim the *Falklands Folly's* own Xenon 1,000,000 candle-power spotlight at what he assumed was a Spanish patrol boat. Buck hoped the Xenon light would blind whoever it was to what he and Dolly would be scrambling to do.

Buck told the adrenaline-jolted Dolly to roller-furl the genoa, douse the mainsail, and raise the center-board. To anyone watching, it would appear they were heaving-to. Buck pressed a button on the gear handle, starting the propeller on its short journey back down into the water. Quickly, he pulled up the twin rudders and tied them off. Then, Buck reached down behind the transom, grabbed the handle for the bilge-drain port and pulled it fully open. With the port open, 1,500 pounds of water ballast would escape the bilge within minutes. After a shot of primer and a twist of the ignition key, the 90-horse motor sprang to life. Buck gave the motor full throttle.

The *Falklands Folly* shot forward out of the Spaniard's spotlight and into the blackness. The Spaniards swung their spotlight, trying to keep their quarry illuminated. The Spaniards didn't bother with any warning. A volley of green tracers erupted from behind the Spaniard's spotlight, but fell behind their mark. From the weapon's uneven bark and the green tracers, Buck could tell it was an AK-47, the favorite weapon of the Islamic jihadists.

In minutes, the 1,500 pounds of water ballast were drained into the Bay of Algeciras. The *Falklands Folly* got up on her step, planing faster and faster into the darkness. After Dolly got the hastily-flaked mainsail streamlined to the boom and lashed in place, the Falklands Folly maxed out at almost 26 miles-per-hour. Now and then, searching bursts of green tracers would try to find them, but without success. Alarmed by all the gunfire, the large pleasure craft bobbing in the Bay of Algeciras lighted up like Las Vegas and started sounding their horns. The tracer fire stopped. Apparently, the patrol boat did not want to incur the wrath of the millionaires in the Bay of Algeciras.

Using her cell phone, Dolly called Colonel Dawes to report their predicament. Dawes said he would alert the Royal Harbor Master to their impending return. He would ask Captain Goulds to rush his corvette to their defense. After an hour of pounding along in the *Falkands Folly* at flank speed, they passed port-to-port with the British corvette as it raced seaward to protect the British-flagged *Falklands Folly*. Captain Goulds ordered his signalman to use the blinker light to signal: "Tally-ho!" In response, Buck turned on his navigation lights and blinked his spotlight to signal a "Thank-you" to Captain Goulds.

As Buck and Dolly neared the breakwater, the *Falklands Folly* reduced speed and started threading its way through the boats moored between the breakwater and the docks. Nearing the dock, Dolly threw a line to an anxious Colonel Dawes. Quickly, the *Falklands Folly* was made secure in its usual berth.

"We were ambushed," explained Buck. "Someone tipped them off. I think we have to go to Plan C."

"Which is?" asked Colonel Dawes, climbing on board.

Inside the privacy of the cabin, Dolly whispered, "Plan C means we scrap the trip to Lisbon. We need a time-out. We need a different itinerary. We need to go to Italy."

"You mean change your airline reservation from Lisbon to someplace in Italy?" asked Dawes.

"No, I mean for you to fly us to Italy in your Cessna Skylane."

"My dear, I would love to do that; however, my Skylane would run out of fuel somewhere out over the Med. Unlike flying in the U.S., we can't just be flying around at night. Socialist officialdom insists on knowing what everyone is doing at all times. So, landing in either Spain or France will not do."

"I figure we are about 1,000 miles from Italy," said Buck. "What if we could arrange to land on an American aircraft carrier, say, half-way between Gibraltar and Italy?"

"Could you really do that?" asked an incredulous Dawes.

"I don't know. But let's check," said Buck, as he punched in the numbers on his satellite phone.

When General McClure answered, Buck said, "Jack, in addition to the two tangos we blew out the Upper Galleries of the Rock, al-Qaeda has Spanish tangos all over this place, even at sea. We just got ambushed at sea by what we think was a Spanish patrol boat. Someone tried to hose us down with an AK 47."

"Do you have a Plan C?"

"Colonel Dawes is willing to fly us off the Rock in his Cessna Sky-lane. With Spain and France so uncooperative to American inter-ests right now, we figure Italy is the place we need to go. But, to do that, we need to land on an aircraft carrier somewhere between here and Italy. Can you arrange it?"

"Let me check with one of the naval aviators assigned to the Com-mand Center. Where would you want to land in Italy?"

"I know the airport in Pisa. My former airborne battalion staged a couple of operations out of there."

"Buck, promise me you and Dolly won't go anywhere near that tower."

"Okay. We promise not to go near the tower. Actually, at Camp Darby, just south of Pisa, there's an Armed Forces Recreation

Center. I thought Dolly and I could hole up there while we get our new itinerary sorted out. I think we need to scratch Lisbon off the list. If Abu Amed is in Berlin, the sooner we get there the better. Maybe we should just concentrate on Munich and Berlin."

"I'll think about all that. In fact, the State Department wants your entire tour cancelled. The president, as usual, is hanging tough. Hold on, while I check with my Navy desk."

After a few minutes, McClure came back on the line. "A Carrier Strike Group of about 12 ships, headed by the *USS Enterprise*, it's getting ready to make a port call on Mallorca. But right now, the CSG is about 100 miles north of the neighboring island of Menorca which looks to be about half-way between Gibraltar and the Italian mainland. Would that work?"

"Yes, we are familiar with both islands. The cruise ship stopped for a few hours at each of them. Jack, did you know mayonnaise was invented at the Port of Mahon?"

"On some other occasion, I would be fascinated to learn more about the invention of mayonnaise. Instead, let's talk about the *Enterprise.*"

"I thought the *Enterprise* was in Norfolk for a 16-month overhaul."

"She came out last month and took her strike group to the Med. How come you know so much about the *Enterprise?*"

"In World War II, my second cousin was the original's air boss, and later, her skipper. I take a special interest in her. That's why. So, how do we radio the *Enterprise* for landing instructions? And, does she have any 100 octane, low-lead avgas? If not, she's useless to us."

"I have a naval aviator at my elbow right now. A Navy Captain no less. He says when you get within VHF radio range, call the *Enterprise* on 121.5. I wonder if his picking the international emergency frequency suggests your landing on an aircraft carrier will be an emergency."

"Anyway, my helpful Navy staffer here, who claims to be the world's best naval aviator, is telling me aircraft carriers keep some 100-octane avgas on board for some of the older and smaller aircraft used to deliver the mail from the various Fleet Post Offices in the Med. He also says the *Enterprise* can broadcast a VOR signal on 113.8. You can use your Skylane's VOR receiver to find the carrier. Call me when you get there.

"Oh, by the way, Colonel Dawes should be brushing up on his short-field landing technique."

"The good Colonel doesn't know it yet, but Dolly will be flying. She's a whiz at short-field landings. With the carrier turned into the wind and Dolly using full flaps, she should get us on board in one piece. Do you have more advice?"

"Yes, tell Dolly not to land short on an aircraft carrier. It can be done, but only once. Out."

✲ ✲ ✲

The *USS Enterprise*

On board the *Enterprise*, the ship's captain and the admiral commanding the carrier strike group were somewhat amused by the unusual request coming from the National Command Center.

"The flight deck crew should find this unexpected exercise quite interesting," said Admiral David "Davy" Jones.

"Lieutenant Commander Farris, one of my LSOs, is a private pilot," said Navy Captain Ken Horn, the ship's skipper. Farris even owns a Cessna Skylane. We'll have Commander Farris on deck as the LSO.

"Civilian planes don't have tail hooks, so the arresting cables won't do us any good. In fact, I'll tell the air boss to have all four cables pulled aside. Otherwise, even retracted, the cables could rip the gear off that Cessna. Admiral, I'm confident we can take them on board. Whether the aircraft will be in condition to leave again will depend on the skill of the pilot."

☆ ☆ ☆

CHAPTER TWENTY-ONE

Gibraltar Airport

With the Royal Yacht Club closed for the night, Buck and Dolly huddled outside against the sea wall, savoring the warmth that lingered from the setting sun. Colonel Dawes went off to his nearby flat, to fetch what he called his "kit."

"Okay," said Dolly. "We land on the *Enterprise*. We refuel. Then what? Where do we land in Italy?"

"I'm leaning toward Pisa."

"Buck, please. Not now. Besides the tower, what's at Pisa?"

"Just south of Pisa is Livorno. The U.S. Army has a big logistics and ammo storage facility at Camp Darby. Better yet, Camp Darby is also an Armed Forces Recreation Center. We can find a place to stay there while General McClure and the president decide our next move.

"My airborne battalion staged out of Camp Darby a couple of times. But the airport we want is Galileo, almost in downtown Pisa. The *Aeronautica Militare*, the Italian Air Force, shares the airport with the commercial airlines."

"What about Colonel Dawes?"

"With his MI-6 connections, I'm sure Colonel Dawes can work through the international paperwork to fly his plane from Italy through Austria and Germany and back to England. Or, maybe, he will want to go back to Gibraltar to be with his, I mean, our boat. Actually, I suppose all that is up to folks who control Colonel Dawes. For sure, your illegal take off from Gibraltar Airport using his airplane will have to be sorted out."

"What do you mean 'my' illegal take-off? Surely, you will be in an Italian prison with me."

"I promise to visit you every single day, even bring pizza."

"Okay, but no anchovies."

At that moment, Colonel Dawes returned carrying an overnight bag. "I am ready to go; however, I must confess to being somewhat apprehensive about landing on the deck of an aircraft carrier at night. In fact, I'd be apprehensive to do so in broad daylight. I'm a bit rusty, you know."

"If you don't mind, Jack, Dolly is very good at short-field landings. She could be in the left seat. You fly co-pilot. I'll take a snooze in the back."

"Well, young lady, I'm game if you are," said a visibly relieved Dawes.

The trio, the Madisons with just their backpacks and Colonel Dawes with his overnight bag, walked from the Royal Yacht Club basin, around the soccer pitch, and onto the airport. They did not report in to the aerodrome officer. Instead, they walked very quietly to where Colonel Dawes' Cessna Skylane was tied down at the back of the ramp. Dolly got into the left seat while Colonel Dawes and Buck did the ritual pre-flight checks on the aircraft. Colonel Dawes pulled out the tiny step stool used to check the fuel caps on the top of the wings. Both of the extended-range fuel tanks were full, just as Colonel Dawes said they would be. They did not test the navigation lights or the rotating beacon on top of the tail or the landing light in the nose.

When the step stool was stowed, the tie-down ropes were dropped, the wheel chocks were cast aside, and everyone was strapped into their seats, Dolly started the engine. The oil pressure indicator needle moved immediately into the green, Then, Dolly asked

Colonel Dawes to flip the airplane's avionics master switch to the "on" position.

Although they were not going to land there, Colonel Dawes programmed the on-board GPS for *Aerop de Menorca* (MAH). He made sure their transponder was turned off. To avoid flying over Spain, Dolly told Jack and Buck they would not head directly for Menorca. Instead, they would fly for awhile on a heading of 90-degrees into the western Mediterranean to get clear of the Iberian Peninsula. Then, they would turn north and take up the GPS course heading for Menorca. Once they crossed over Menorca, they should be able to receive the VOR signal from the *Enterprise*.

"At this unseemly hour, let's not bother the chap up in the tower," said Colonel Dawes. "We have 6,000 feet of runway in front of us and we are at sea level. The wind is calm, so we are not plagued with that infamous Levanter wind. No need for flaps. Please don't run the manifold pressure needle up into the red. Keep it at the top of the green."

"Roger that," said Dolly, as she taxied the aircraft into position at the west end of the runway. "Buck, you ready back there?"

"Let's roll," said Buck, tightening his seat belt even tighter across his waist.

Suddenly, the tower radio frequency came alive with: "Unknown aircraft, what the bloody hell do you think you are doing?"

Dolly ignored the call, made sure the autopilot was off, brought the engine up to take-off power, and released the brakes. They only used 800-feet of runway and were off. Hoping to stay below any of Spain's shore-based radars, Dolly stayed 100-feet above the water for the next 30 minutes. When they were well clear of Gibraltar, Dolly climbed to 8,500-feet above-sea-level, re-trimmed the controls for hands-off cruise flight, set the heading bug for 90-degrees, and engaged the autopilot.

Buck sat up enough to see over Dolly's right shoulder. He noted the heading of 90 degrees. Colonel Dawes nodded back toward Buck his satisfaction that Dolly was doing just fine. Buck took off his headset, slumped down in his seat, and went to sleep. Buck was still sleeping when Dolly decided they were far enough to the East. She disconnected the autopilot from the heading-bug indicator and slaved the autopilot to the GPS. The GPS, already set for *Aerop de Menorca* by Colonel Dawes, gave a ncw heading to the autopilot. The autopilot smoothly turned the aircraft onto a northerly heading.

After flying for almost three hours, Dolly and Colonel Dawes noticed the fuel indicator needles were leaning more toward empty than full. Theoretically, a factory-new Skylane could fly about 1,000 miles without refueling, so the approximately 500 miles to reach the *Enterprise* should be no problem; however, as experienced pilots, both of them knew the fuel indicators were only truly accurate twice: Once, when the tanks are completely full and, again, when the tanks are completely empty.

When they neared the southern coast of Menorca, the needle on the VOR started to twitch. It was coming to life. Colonel Dawes switched the set so they could hear the Morse code identifier for the VOR in their headsets. As they did that, Dolly rotated the omni-bearing selector knob on the side of the VOR receiver until the needle centered on the dial. At the top of the dial, she could read the radial she needed to track inbound to the *Enterprise*. She switched the autopilot off of the GPS and put it to tracking the VOR signal inbound to the *Enterprise*.

"Okay," said Dolly, as the auto-pilot gently turned the aircraft to the new heading. "Jack, please put the number one radio on 121.5. Get Buck to wake up and put on his headset."

When they reached the north coast of Menorca, Dolly pressed the push-to-talk switch on her control yoke and said, "*Enterprise,* this is a Cessna Skylane inbound for landing, *Enterprise*."

"Roger, Cessna Skylane," said a disembodied voice. "We'll call you: Skylane One. You call me LSO. That stands for Landing Signals Officer. How's that?"

"Skylane One it is. Do you have Skylane One on radar?"

"Only for the last two hours. Of course, we had a little help from an Airborne Warning and Control System, a friendly AWACs provided by 6th Fleet. But we do need you to turn on your transponder and set it to 1200. The radio was quiet for a minute, then:

"Okay, Skylane One, radar sees you squawking 1200. We have ceased air operations for the night. So, you are our one and only customer. Well, not quite. We just launched a search and rescue helicopter. It will stand off to the side and be able to assist in the unlikely event that you end up in the drink."

"That's reassuring. Now, how about some landing instructions?" asked Dolly.

"Roger that. The wind is out of the North at 15 knots. We are coming to a heading of 360 degrees. We will be steaming forward at 20 knots. So, you will be landing into a 35 knot headwind. We would offer you an ILS approach, but our ILS uses UHF frequencies. Unless you have a very unusual Skylane, all your radios are VHF. Correct?"

"Affirmative," said Dolly. "We don't have UHF. *Enterprise*, we are about 30 minutes south of your position."

"Roger, Skylane One. We are standing due north of Aerop de Menorca. Our radar shows you headed right toward us. Now, listen up. Instead of the Navy's usual race-track approach, we are planning to take you on board with a visual, straight-in approach. Set your power and your flaps to attain a 500 foot-per- minute rate of descent for now. That's not exactly how we do it with our jets, but in your case, it should work. [See photograph of the carrier deck in the daylight at: www.buckanddolly.com.]

"When you are about five miles out, you'll see a horizontal row of green lights on the port or left side of the landing area, about midway down. You'll also see a bright amber-colored ball right in the middle of that row of green lights. The amber ball is what we call the 'meatball.' It is designed to give you a three-degree glide slope. If the meatball is above the horizontal row of green lights, you are too high. If the meatball is below the row of green lights, you are too low. Keep adjusting your pitch and your power until you can keep the meatball steady on line with the row of green lights. If you get way too low, the meatball turns red and I'll tell you to go around and try again. Do you have an angle of attack indicator?"

"Negative."

"Okay, you will just have to rely on your airspeed indicator. What's your stall speed with full flaps?"

Dolly looked over at Colonel Dawes. Via the intercom, Dawes said, "With full flaps, the manual says 49 knots or 56 miles-per-hour."

"Forty-nine knots," radioed Dolly. "But the manuals always fudge a bit. I would be more comfortable at 60 knots. Would that work?"

"Okay," said the LSO. "With the 15 knot natural headwind and with the ship making 20 knots, you have, in effect, a 35 knot headwind. Theoretically, at 60, you will be coming aboard at 25 knots. That's plenty slow, so you shouldn't run out of deck. But you still need to get your wheels down on the deck as near to the stern as possible. Fortunately, the sea state is relatively calm so the deck is pretty stable right now.

"But be aware there is a burble of air right at the stern. It might try to suck you down too low. Maintain a tad bit of power all the way down. And be prepared to add a touch more power to get through the burble. I know it's counterintuitive, but I don't want you chopping your power completely, thinking you've got the landing made.

"Also, on approach, make sure you have your prop control all the way forward. With the blades almost flat, they will help you slow your speed. If I tell you to go around, give me full power and have your co-pilot raise your flaps to 20 degrees. Full flaps would hinder your go around."

"Roger," said Dolly, her palms starting to sweat.

Colonel Dawes raised his left thumb to indicate he understood about the flap setting for a go-around.

"Okay, Skylane One. You can turn on your landing light now. I'm going to light up our landing deck."

Suddenly, what had been an indistinct shape down somewhere in the blackness of a moonless night became ablaze with the center-line and the runway-edge lights of what now looked like a mini-ature airfield. Dolly radioed, "LSO, I have the airfield…ah carrier, in sight. I also have the meatball."

"Roger, Skylane One. You are looking good. Fly the meatball and your airspeed, stay aligned with the deck. You are probably used to that 500 foot-per-minute rate-of-descent I gave you earlier. But now, I need you to cut that in half. Give me full flaps now and 250 feet-per-minute. Can you do that?"

"Wilco," responded Dolly, as she adjusted her throttle. Colonel Dawes pushed the flap level down to the full position. Colonel Dawes confirmed she was at 60 knots. Dolly's palms were sweating even more as she heard the LSO say: "Cleared for the approach."

The deck in front of her was rising up and down like a hobby horse. Moreover, it seemed to waddle some from side-to-side. Try-ing to focus on all the motion in front of her and keeping her airspeed at 60 was giving Dolly an industrial-sized headache. *How do naval aviators land those big fighters on this moving monster? No wonder they have egos as big as their airplanes.*

"You're steady on 60 knots," said Colonel Dawes, leaning to his left to see the airspeed indicator better.

With Skylane One hanging in the air just above a stall, the meatball started to sink. Dolly pushed the throttle forward like giving a horse a gentle touch of spur. The aircraft rose just enough to get the meatball aligned again with the horizontal row of green lights.

The LSO said, "Cleared to land."

But as the Skylane approached the stern, the air burble tried to force the craft too low to reach the runway. Dolly gave the engine another burst of power and the meatball went up too high. She had to fight the temptation to chop the power completely and pull back the yoke, causing the aircraft to float too long along the runway and then not have enough runway left to do a go-around.

Instead, she pulled the throttle back to just enough power to help her maintain the runway alignment, and she applied just enough back pressure to keep the nose gear from hitting the deck before her main gear. They felt the thump as her main gear planted firmly on the deck, but not hard enough to bounce her back up in the air. As she chopped the power, Dolly let the nose gear ease down onto the deck.

Skylane One was solidly on board the *Enterprise,* but the rolling of the ship made it difficult to maintain the runway alignment. Dolly did a tap dance on the rudder pedals to compensate, and the nose of the aircraft steadied on course down the runway centerline. She slipped her feet to the top of the rudder pedals to access the brakes. Dolly bit her lip as she worried about burning out the brakes on the airplane.

But the ship's forward speed, the natural wind coming over the deck and Dolly's firm brake pressure combined to halt the aircraft just 50 feet from a disastrous dive down into the wake of a massive ship making 20 knots.

Dolly gave the engine a touch of power as she turned the airplane 180 degrees, and then braked to a full stop. She killed the engine and set the hand brake. Colonel Dawes gave her the victory sign. Buck patted her on the back.

Immediately, Skylane One was surrounded by a hoard of sailors wearing a variety of multi-colored vests. Their leader signaled for Dolly to release her hand brake. Crewmen took hold of both wing struts and walked Skylane One off to the side and placed her on top of an elevator platform. Then, the airplane seemed to sag a bit as both wings and the tail were tied securely to the deck of the elevator. Two sailors laid short lengths of red carpet on the deck beside each cabin door. Their leader gave Dolly a hand salute and the deck gang moved off to assist the SAR helicopter that had just landed at the other end of the flight deck.

Buck cast a wary eye around what he knew to be some of the world's most dangerous real estate. He lost one of his best friends when a magnesium flare was mishandled on the deck of the *USS Oriskany*. Forty-four officers and men were killed in the resulting fire. On the *Enterprise*, 27 were killed and over 300 were injured on when a tow tractor parked too near a Zuni rocket hanging from under a F-4 and the tractor's exhaust ignited the Zuni.

When Buck and Dolly and Colonel Dawes finished climbing down from the airplane, Admiral Jones and Captain Horn were standing by.

"Welcome aboard the *USS Enterprise*," said the skipper. "I am Captain Ken Horn. Allow me to present Admiral Jones."

"Thank you for taking us on board," said Buck. "I'm Buck Madison. This is my wife, Dolly, and this is Colonel Jack Dawes. You got us out of a terrible situation on Gibraltar."

"Our pleasure," said Admiral Jones, as they shook hands all around. "That was a very nice landing. Which one of you did that?"

While Dolly held up a still-sweaty palm, she noticed Skylane One descending out of sight via the elevator.

"Well, Dr. Madison, you've given Captain Horn's crew something different to do in the wee hours of the morning," continued Admiral Jones. "While the crew tops off your tanks with 100 low-lead, come inside and we'll have a cup of something warm. You look like you could use a drink. As a rule, we don't serve alcoholic beverages on a Navy vessel. The ship's surgeon can, however, make an exception for flight crews who have had a difficult experience. I think you qualify. Captain Horn and I will watch with envy while the surgeon finds you something stronger than the bilge that passes for coffee up on the bridge."

An elevator took them up to the ship's bridge. At 20 stories above the water, the view from the bridge was, in a word, towering.

"If I may ask," said Colonel Dawes. "Just how long is this ship?"

"About the length of the Empire State Building," replied Captain Horn, as he directed them to enter his sea cabin just aft of the bridge. While a mess steward stepped away to fetch their drinks, Admiral Jones suggested a message be sent to General McClure telling of their safe arrival aboard the *Enterprise*. The Madisons and Colonel Dawes were readily agreeable; however, Dolly suggested the message include the fact that Skylane One was not damaged in anyway. That drew a smile and wink from Buck.

As they sipped their drinks, Captain Horn explained how the *Enterprise* is home to over 6,000 men and women of the U.S. Navy and carries over 80 combat aircraft. Admiral Jones told how the ship is powered by two nuclear reactors that can go 20 years without refueling.

Buck could not refrain from sharing memories of his second cousin who commanded the original *Enterprise* during World War II and that another naval aviator, the fabled Oklahoma University football coach, Bud Wilkinson, served on the *Enterprise* during World War II.

After awhile, the discussion turned to launching Skylane One on to Italy. The ship's meteorologist was summoned to provide an outlook briefing. He opined that the flight to Italy could be conducted under Visual Flight Rules all the way to Pisa; however, about half-way en route they would probably see some clouds over Corsica. It was decided Colonel Dawes, as owner of the aircraft, would be the pilot and Dolly would act as co-pilot. Once again, Buck would be in the backseat. Only this time he planned to resume work on their book. If asked by the Italian authorities, Colonel Dawes would say he had taken off from Menorca.

Communications between the Spanish possession and Italy not being the best, they were unlikely to be challenged.

Graciously, Admiral Jones gave his relatively spacious stateroom over to Buck and Dolly. Captain Horn gave his cabin to Colonel Dawes. With dawn approaching, Captain Horn would remain on the bridge. Before they all said goodnight, it was agreed Skylane One would take off for Pisa at 0900 hours. After launching Skylane One, the *Enterprise* and its carrier strike group would steam back toward the promised port call on Mallorca.

The next morning, the SAR helicopter was launched. Then, with the *Enterprise* steaming at 20 knots into a 15-knot head wind and with Colonel Dawes using full power and 20 degrees of flaps, the take-off of Skylane One was uneventful. After climb-out, Colonel Dawes adjusted the throttle and the prop control for best fuel economy and then connected the autopilot to the GPS for a direct course to Pisa.

On board the *Enterprise*, the arresting cables were put back in place. Normal flight operations resumed. The off-duty sailors shined their shoes for the pending port call. Later that day, the *Enterprise* received a Beta Zulu (great job!) signal from the President of the United States.

☆ ☆ ☆

CHAPTER TWENTY-TWO

Galileo International Airport, Pisa, Italy

The landing at Pisa was mercifully uneventful. Colonel Dawes asked for taxi instructions to the fuel facility. After Buck and Dolly went inside the General Aviation terminal to use the restrooms. Colonel Dawes watched carefully as a line boy topped off the fuel tanks. During the refueling, a customs inspector wandered over, talking on his cell phone to someone. With a jolt, Dawes remembered the weapons inside the backpacks belonging to the Madisons.

When asked by the customs inspector if he had anything to declare, Dawes handed the inspector a large bundle of Lira. The inspector nodded and then walked off still talking to some honey who was apparently giving him a ration of crap about something he did or failed to do.

When Buck came back outside, he conferred with Dawes about the refueling and customs. Buck gave Dawes money to cover the refueling and for the bribe for the customs inspector. Then, Buck called Jack McClure on the satellite phone.

"So you cheated death once again," said General McClure.

"Dolly who got us on board the *Enterprise* in fine shape. Just now, Colonel Dawes landed us here in Pisa. Do you have any instructions for us?"

"Affirmative. Colonel Dawes is to get in touch with his betters at MI-6. They will be telling him to come home to London. The fix is already in with the Italian, Austrian and German air traffic authorities. He is cleared to fly his bird back to England.

"As for 'your' sail boat back in Gibraltar, it has been confiscated by the Royal Governor of Gibraltar to be sold and the proceeds used to repair the damage you did to that gun port in the Upper Galleries and to rehabilitate the heavy cannon you allowed to leap out onto the Royal subjects down below. With regard to the dead tangos, the Queen instructed the PM to tell the Royal Governor that you must have been acting in self-defense. So that's the end of that; however, you did scare the crap out of a tribe of Barbary Apes.

"If you had killed one of those blasted apes, we would never hear the end of it. Legend has it if the Barbary Apes leave Gibraltar then the Spaniards will take Gibraltar away from the British. So, during World War II, Churchill had dozens more Barbary Apes captured over in Morocco and imprisoned on Gibraltar. Although I think the term these days is 'rendered.'"

"I suppose you think your Barbary Ape story is more interesting than how mayonnaise was invented," said Buck. "But I told you that cannon was indestructible. All it needs is for some skilled carpenters to re-create the wooden gun carriage and give the tube a polishing. All shiny, it will be as good as new."

"Buck, you miss the point. The bloody Royal authorities want it to look like it did back at the time of the Siege in 1783. We are lucky they don't make you go back there to help the Royal carpenters."

"What about the minivan?"

"Oh, the Royal Engineers fished it back out of the water reservoir. They patched the concrete roof. Uncle Sam is getting a bill for that as well."

"Anything else we need to know?"

"Yes, the two tangos you blew out the side of the Rock were working for the Spanish branch of al-Qaeda. But the Brits put out a story that the tangos were Basque separatist. They blew themselves up to make a political statement.

"There's no problem with the State Department about Lisbon. In fact, the fewer stops you make, the happier State seems to be. Munich and Berlin are still on; however, we are setting those dates back by one week. The NSA says Abu Amed is planning some kind of meeting with his lieutenants in Berlin. But he is having trouble getting all his tangos assembled. Apparently, they are coming from Pakistan, Afghanistan, Iraq, and Yemen and from all the Muslim countries cooperating with Al-Qaeda-Europe.

"When the meeting takes place, we want you and Dolly to be in Berlin. Also, the NSA says Ayman al-Zawahiri is planning some kind of operation. They can't tell if Abu Amed and al-Zawahiri are acting in concert or not. They may have some of the same left-hand, right-hand coordination problems we have.

"In any event, you now have a week off to mill around somewhere until it is time for you to be at our consulate in Munich. Do you know where it is?"

"Actually, I was stationed over in nearby Augsburg for almost two years. No sweat."

"You still have your weapons?"

"We have them in two backpacks. We ditched Dolly's empty shoulder bag on Gibraltar. Also, we are short one each 2.5-inch shotgun shell."

"That reminds me. At the Royal Infirmary, the Royal authorities arrested a tango whose non-royal butt looked like a piece of Swiss cheese. He claimed he was cleaning his shotgun and it went off. How a tango could hold a shotgun so he could see to clean it and then shoot himself in the butt escapes me. Anyway, the Royal Police didn't buy his story. Since he can't sit down, the Royal Confinement Officer has him in orange jump suit walking around with a broom and a dustpan picking up ape poop.

"Tell Dolly that was one well-placed shot. Before you board the flight from Munich to Berlin, the Agency will have to relieve you of those backpacks and give Dolly a clean shoulder bag.

"How do you plan to get to Munich?"

"We could go by train or plane; however, we don't want to put other passengers at risk unless there is no other way for us to travel. We plan to rent a car for drop-off in Munich. Now we have some time to kill, we might head for Garmisch and ski on the *Zugspitze*. Up there is where I proposed to Dolly. I think the altitude must have affected her judgment. Obviously, she said: 'yes'."

"Yes, too much altitude is the cause of many errors in judgment. Alcohol makes it worse. Look, Buck if you encounter any tangos, just tell us where to find them and I'll send someone to render them somewhere for safe keeping. But if there is violence before we can get there, it would be nice if you could limit the collateral damage. Don't destroy any national treasures. For example, the *Hofbrauhaus.*"

"That would be a national disaster. Meanwhile, we'll take our leave of Colonel Dawes and start heading for Garmisch-Partenkirchen."

"No problem. Gotta go. Out."

✯ ✯ ✯

CHAPTER TWENTY-THREE

Berlin, Abu Amed's Wannsee Villa

"They are gone," said one of the minders who survived the Madison's brief visit to Gibraltar. He was calling from Algeciras, Spain.

"How can they be gone?" asked Abu Amed.

"We can't find them. The Madisons checked out of the Rock Hotel late yesterday afternoon. But the sailboat boat they bought is still here. In fact, the Royal authorities have it chained and padlocked to the dock. The airplane belonging to that retired British colonel took off during darkness for somewhere. My contact says the airplane had no authorization to do so. He says the Royal authorities are going to charge the aircraft owner with some kind of aviation violation for taking off without permission."

"That's the answer, then. The colonel took the Madisons with him. But where? Spain, Portugal, France? It has to be somewhere within the range of a small aircraft. Italy would be too far. But the Madisons could be anywhere. My brother, I am going to put the arm out for the Madisons in every country between Gibraltar and Berlin."

"Put the arm out?" asked the minder. "I do not understand."

Proud of his command of American idiomatic speech, Abu Amed explained American police forces use the term "put the arm out" when they wish for someone, even fellow policemen, to be found and brought to the police station.

"We have cells everywhere," said Abu Amed. "We have taxi drivers, waiters and waitresses in hotels and restaurants, desk clerks at car rental agencies, airline ticket counters, hotel reception desks, maids, and janitors. The only area where we are short is bartenders. When you are unfamiliar with alcohol, it is hard to be convincing as a bartender. So, unless the Madisons spend all their time in bars, we stand a good chance of finding them.

"I must ring off. I have important business here in Berlin," concluded Amed.

✵ ✵ ✵

CHAPTER TWENTY-FOUR

Garmisch-Partenkirchen

At the car rental desk, Buck and Dolly presented their international drivers licenses to the young man who looked like he could be from South Asia, either Pakistan or India or even Afghanistan. His impeccable English was redolent of Oxbridge and yet was a bit sing-song.

Buck asked for and got a Mercedes CLK 350, although Buck really wanted to try a Fiat-Abarth because a friend owned an Abarth sports car back in the mid-60s that looked like fun. The charge for dropping off a German Mercedes in Munich was a lot less than dropping off an Italian car.

The 350 would be plenty fast for the Autostrada, and even the Autobahn. Buck was eager to get in the left lane and start flashing the high beams, known in Germany as "the death ray." German drivers loved to flash the "death ray" at any driver who dared to go too slow in the left lane.

Fortunately, their satellite phones had GPS capability. When the GPS acquired all the satellites it was going to get, Dolly told the GPS she wanted to go to the Brenner Pass. The GPS responded with a map showing the turns they needed to take to leave the airport. After changing the scale of the map display, Dolly saw the network of highways they would use to take them to the Brenner Pass or *Passo del Brennero*.

Once the shiny red Mercedes was on its way, the desk clerk told his co-worker he needed to visit the toilette. While he was there, he made a phone call giving the model, make and license number of the car just rented to two Americans. Abu Amed's arm extended deep into Italy.

The GPS told Buck and Dolly the distance to Munich was over 300 miles. Not far by Texas standards, but a long way by

European standards. They took turns driving north to Milano, to Trento and on up to the Brenner Pass. With the advent of the European Union, border formalities were almost non-existent. The passage from Italy into Austria was a non-event; however, someone was posted at the Brenner Pass to look for a Mercedes 350 bearing a certain license number. As Buck and Dolly crossed over the Brenner Pass into Austria, a phone call was made to Berlin.

Approaching Innsbruck, they recalled their honeymoon when the Club Med owned a hotel above Innsbruck at Lizum.

"Do you remember your dispute with our Austrian ski instructor?" asked Dolly.

"If you mean the gal who was teaching the hopping up and down method that went out with waxed barrel staves, the answer is: *Ja*. But the food at Club Med was terrific."

"Memories are made of that. Maybe we can make some new ones up on the *Zugspitze*."

"We've stayed down below at the Hotel Eibsee before. Let's stay there tonight. We can take the cable car or what the Germans call a *Seilbahn* to the peak tomorrow."

"What about skis, boots, poles, that sort of stuff?"

"There's a rental shop up there. It's called the Sonn-Alpin."

When Buck was a troop commander in Germany, he sent his troopers on Adventure Training, squad-by-squad or even platoon-by-platoon to climb the *Zugspitze*. By Colorado standards, the *Zugspitze* was not all that tall. It is a little bit less than 10,000 feet above sea level. But the *Zugspitze* rises up sharply from its surrounding terrain, over 5,000 feet, so it makes the impression of extreme height. The hiking approach favored by Buck was via the *Partnachklamm*, a narrow canyon leading up to the ridge line separating Germany from Austria. With one foot on one side of the ridge, the climber is in Austria, while the other foot is in Germany.

Even for his fit paratroopers, it was an all-day climb. They delighted in scrambling all the way to the very summit and taking photographs of each other hanging onto the peak's signature golden cross. Other than making the ascent without falling off into Austria, their only requirement was to bring Buck a photograph of their unit clustered around the golden Cross mounted on the peak. For a more difficult Adventure Training exercise Buck sent his reconnaissance platoon to Switzerland to climb the Matterhorn. Photographs of these Adventure Training exploits adorn the walls of Buck's den.

"Have you ever stayed overnight at the top, at the *Schneefernerhaus?*" asked Dolly.

"Yes, back when it was an Armed Forces Recreation Hotel. But we gave it back to the Germans. Now, I think it's just a place to eat and drink. But it is still where the Seilbahn and the cog train arrive. To get down into the ski bowl of the glacier, we have to take another bahn. It's called the *Gletscherbahn.* Because the ski area is on a moving glacier, it is difficult to have regular chair lifts. So, they have a bunch of drag lifts. But I hear there is one six-seat chairlift down lower. I can't imagine how they engineered it on a moving glacier. Also, there's another bahn coming up from the Austrian side of the *Zugspitze.* It's called the *Tiroler Zugspitzbahn.*"

"I've always liked the Hotel Eibsee. It has, what's that German word?"

"*Gemutlichkeit.* It means cozy and comfortable."

When they registered at the Hotel Eibsee, Dolly looked around to see if any of Abu Amed's minders were lurking around. Other than a janitor with what looked like a bad spray tan, the few people in the reception area looked pretty Germanic or even French. After Buck and Dolly received their room key and headed up the stairs, the janitor decided the registration desk could do with some more cleaning. After giving the guest register a brief look, the janitor put aside his feather duster. He went outside to use his cell phone.

Their room in the Hotel Eibsee met their expectations. While it wasn't large, it had a big bed piled high with the thick feather bedding so beloved by the Germans. The windows looked out toward the Zugspitze. In summer, the flower boxes outside the windows would have been overflowing with red geraniums. But, in winter, they were empty. The en suite bathroom had a large bath with one of those shower devices non-European tourists used to mistake for telephones and the kind of bidet some tourists thought were foot-baths.

After they had their showers and were lying on the bed in the thick, terrycloth bathrobes provided by the hotel, Buck got out his notebook computer to bring the notes for their next book up-to-date.

"Dolly, isn't this the point in the espionage novels when the lovers make love?"

"Let's see. During the previous day, the female engages in some serious live-saving hand-to-hand combat, that evening they were almost blown out of a sailboat by some kind of Spanish naval vessel, they had to make an illegal takeoff from a British airfield, they had to land on an aircraft carrier out in the middle of the Mediterranean Sea, so the next day they could fly to Italy and then drive clear across Italy into Austria and Germany after which they take a shower and make love? Buck, that's only in the movies; however, with a good night's sleep, in this *Gemutlichkeit* environment, it might be possible in the morning. Meanwhile, Goodnight."

The next morning, Buck and Dolly went down to breakfast. They were up early and had the breakfast room almost to themselves. They feasted on freshly baked, hard rolls, strawberry jam, real butter and soft-boiled eggs. Buck pronounced his coffee superb. Dolly had her usual pot of Earl Grey.

Then, dressed in layers against the cold, they made their way to the *Seilbahn*. Because the top of mountain was still shrouded in thick clouds, the cable car was empty. But the first part of the steep climb, before they entered the bottom of the cloud deck, was breathtaking. Just as in the James Bond movies. [See photograph of the Eibsee with the Zugspitze above at: www.buckanddolly.com.]

The deep blue of the Eibsee, and the town of Grainau and Garmisch-Partenkirchen were spread out below. If the fog bank ever went away, they knew from the very top they would be able see into Austria, Italy and Switzerland. Just then, the *Seilbahn* penetrated the bottom of the cloud deck. All the gorgeous scenery disappeared.

After several minutes of seeing nothing but each other, the cable car began to sway a bit as they all do when they are slipping into the steel jaws of the arrival station. When the *Seilbahn* came to a full stop, the side doors opened and they were able to step out onto the perforated-steel arrival deck.

Buck led the way across the metal platform to where they would catch the *Gletscherbahn* down into the ski bowl and the Sonn-Alpin rental shop. But the view on the way down was no better. The *Zugspitze* was still shrouded in the clouds.

Undaunted, they rode the *Gletscherbahn* downward. The last time they were on the *Zugspitze* to ski, there was no Sonn-Alpin. In fact, an avalanche knocked down some of the original cable-car supports for the *Gletscherbahn*. Halfway down, the cables for the *Gletscherbahn* were buried in the snow.

From what they could see of the Sonn-Alpin, it was a large base lodge built in the traditional style of the Bavarian-chalet. Through the fog, the lights from inside the building were giving off a warm and inviting glow. When they got close enough to peer through the windows of the ski shop, Buck and Dolly saw two men who looked very out-of-place and very uncomfortable.

To combat the biting cold, the men wore *keffiyeh* wrapped around their necks like scarves. They were Yasser Arafat look-a-likes. A lot of hand gesturing was going on at the rental desk, a sure sign of language difficulties. Buck and Dolly loitered outside the ski shop, picking up tourist brochures to cover their faces. Finally, the two men seemed satisfied with their skis, boots, poles, helmets, and goggles. An attendant helped them get into their ski boots. Walking like new-born colts, they struggled toward the outside door lugging their unfamiliar gear.

The men clomped along in their ski boots not knowing how to hold their skis and poles and dropping various items as they stumbled along. When one of the men bent over to retrieve a dropped ski glove, the back of his parka rode up, revealing the pistol he was carrying in an inside-the-belt holster.

"So much for concealed-carry," said Dolly.

After Buck and Dolly picked out their skis, boots, helmets and goggles and got everything fitted, they looked around outside for the two men, but the fog was still so thick they could barely find their way to the drag lift that would take them to the very top of the ski bowl. Buck knew, if the fog ever lifted, they would be able to look over the ridge and see down toward the Austrian village of Ehrwald. He asked the clerk about the *Tiroler Zugspitzbahn*. Due to the fog, it was not operating as yet. Indeed, the fog was still thicker than week-old pea soup. Although neither of them had been on a drag lift in some time, they were able to manage. But, once they got on the drag lift, if they hadn't been connected by the rope they would have almost lost each other.

After sliding off the drag lift at the top, they held hands as they shuffled off the side. Buck checked his watch. "It's still early. Let's just stand here on our skis and wait for awhile. The wind is starting to pick up. Hopefully, that will clear the fog away."

Voices carry very well in fog. Buck and Dolly could hear more people coming up the rope tow. Someone down below was having trouble staying connected to the drag lift. Male voices in some kind of foreign language were making sounds like swearing born out of frustration and fear.

"If they actually make it up here, see if you can get them to speak French," suggested Dolly.

Buck called down into the fog in French, offering words of encouragement. One of the men responded in Arabic-accented French. Buck suggested they use an overhand grip on the t-bar. Another voice thanked Buck for his suggestion. Unknown to the Madisons, the first man lost his grip on the drag rope and was being pushed upward only by virtue of the strength of the arms and legs of the second man.

Buck and Dolly were not worried about being recognized. They were covered from head-to-toe in ski gear, to include helmets and goggles. They looked like typical German or Austria or Italian or Swiss skiers hoping for a sunny day on the *Zugspitze*. When the two huffing, puffing and swearing men fell off the drag lift, Buck and Dolly rushed to assist them. The *keffiyeh* marked them as the men seen in the ski shop. Buck helped up the man known to be packing a pistol in the small of his back.

Continuing in French, Buck asked them if they skied before. Embarrassed, the two men answered in the negative. One of them explained their presence in such unfamiliar circumstances because they had been hired by the American consulate in Munich to deliver an emergency message to an American couple thought to be skiing on the *Zugspitze*. Something terrible was happening back in America. The couple must be found and notified. It was a matter of life and death.

Buck said he thought the couple they sought passed by only moments before. But they disappeared into the fog. In any event, the Americans could only be a few steps away. Buck said if they didn't mind a helping hand, he and his companion would be glad to get them pointed in the right direction. [See photograph of the Zugspitze Ski Bowl at: www. buckanddolly.com.]

The men readily agreed. So, Dolly took one of the men by his left elbow. Buck took the other man by his right elbow. Coaching them in French, Buck explained how to do a herringbone with their skis. When the men got their ski tips spread out wider than the tails of their skis, the four of them began to make some progress up the slope.

Because of the times Buck took his troops up on the ridge line separating Germany from Austria, he knew, despite the fog, almost exactly where they were. After about twenty herringbone steps up the slope, the snow under their skis leveled off. Buck sensed they were now balanced on the ridge line separating Austria from Germany. One step too far and all four of them would be making an unplanned 5,000-foot drop onto the Austrian village of Erhwald.

Buck reached across and hit Dolly on her right shoulder. That was the signal to stop and get ready. Then, Buck shouted, "*Au revoir, sheet heads!*" In unison, Buck and Dolly pushed the two men ahead of them as hard as they could.

When the bottom dropped out from under their skis, the two men let out blood-curdling screams. The screams had something to do with Allah. Then, the screams grew fainter and fainter and fainter. Finally, there was silence.

"They say the first step is always the hardest," said Buck. "I'm told that first step is over 5,000 feet."

"Chairman Mao said the longest journey begins with a single step," said Dolly.

Not long after the two tangos took their surprise visit to Austria, the clouds holding the top of the Zugspitze so tightly in their moisten-laden grip began to blow away. Beyond Austria, the peaks of the Swiss Alps began to appear. It felt like Germany, Austria and Switzerland lay at their feet.

"Look, there's the six-seat chairlift down below," said Dolly. "Let's ski down and give it a try."

The rest of the morning was spent using almost all the drag lifts and also the six-seat chairlift. The sun was so brilliant they stopped to rub sun protection on their faces. By noon, they were ravenous. The large deck of the Sonn Alpin was the perfect place for lunch. They chose bratwurst with sauerkraut and mustard washed down with large steins of the local beer. [See photograph of the Sonn-Alpin at: www.buckanddolly.com.]

As they were basking in the sun, Dolly said, "I can tell you have something on your mind. When you get up in places like this and have a few beers, I know you are trying to put the world into context. So, what's on your mind?"

"You know me too well, Dolly. Yes, I was thinking about all the cold nights our troops spent on maneuvers in the German woods and at the major training areas where we fired our weapons. Granted, it was in our national interest to confront the Soviets over here instead of our homeland. But I was just wondering what we bought for the people of western Europe during the 55 years between the end of World War II and the end of the Cold War? As you look around, Dolly, what do you see?"

"I see a lot of people doing a lot of hum-drum jobs in a half-vast manner while they think about their next month-long vacation. I don't see the kind of drive or ambition we see in the States."

"Yes, what I see are western Europeans who just want a dull state job, a small car, a little apartment, a big pension, a short work week, four-to-six weeks of vacation on the beach, and a leftist government that tells them what to do and when to do it. I'm not sure the hard work we put into defending this place bought us much that is worthwhile. It's like we made George Orwell's book *Nineteen Eighty-Four* come to life. While we saved them from Stalinist communism, it looks like they have settled for what they think is some kind of Utopian Socialism. I wonder who they think is going to pay for all this?"

"Uncle Sugar paid for most of their defense concerns so they have more money to spend on consumer goods. In fact, we are still paying."

"What about the *Bundeswehr*? Didn't the German Army get out in the cold and soldier along with you?"

"Yes, some of their troops were very good. The Germans had some good equipment. They learned a lot when they got their butts kicked by the cold, the snow and the mud in Russia in World War II, so their tanks and trucks are designed to do a better job next time."

"Next time? Do you think the Russians and the Germans will go at it again?"

"Neither country has defensible borders. That makes them paranoid. So they raise large standing armies. Large standing armies tend to be used. Poland lies between them. Neither Russia nor Germany knows what to do with Poland except to have it as a buffer. Fight over it.

"Turkey is the country to watch. With one foot in Europe, one foot in Asia and sitting astride Russia's access to the Mediterranean, Turkey is in the catbird seat. If Turkey can stay a secular nation and not be taken over by the radical Islamists, Turkey can become the world power it would have been had Turkey not chosen the losing side in World War I.

"But I wonder how long the industrious Germans and Austrians will be willing to support the laid-back lifestyles of the Spaniards, Italians and Greeks? These cradle-to-the-grave entitlement programs must be paid for by somebody.

"The Greeks want 14 month's pay for 12 month's work. How long will that last before the bills come due and the Greek government is bankrupt? Just the mention of any kind of belt-tightening brings the labor-union workers out into the streets.

"In the long run, I suppose, the forward deployment of our troops and their dependents into Western Europe was the thing to do; however, in the end, we may have saved them from atheist communism and they, in turn, have turned the opportunity we bought for them into atheist, left-wing, socialist states whose people have no vision beyond getting their pensions and heading for the beach. I get the feeling they are like soap scum circling the drain while the Muslims keep making babies."

After awhile, the food, the drink, and the sun made them sleepy, so they checked their ski equipment back in and boarded the *Gletscherbahn* back up to the peak. With the fog long gone, the ride back down on the *Zugspitzebahn* to the Hotel Eibsee was spectacular from top to bottom. With regret, they knew they would probably never see the *Zugspitze* again.

Before entering the Hotel Eibsee, Buck used his satellite phone to call General McClure. It was morning in D.C.

"Scratch two more tangos," said Buck. "But Jack, we were just minding our business up on the *Zugspitze* when we encountered two tangos spouting some male bovine excreta about being messengers for our consulate in Munich. They were each wearing *keffiyeh* around their necks and one of them was packing a pistol inside his belt. Also, they spoke Arabic and French."

"So, you killed them because they wore *keffiyeh*?"

"No, because they spoke French."

"Buck, be serious. Will there be any repercussions?"

"Not in Germany. But there might be in Austria."

"But you're in Germany. Right?"

"True. However, the two tangos fell off the south side of the *Zugs-pitze* and landed in Austria."

"Will there be any blowback to you?"

"Negative. But we think it is time for us to drive the 100 miles or so to Munich."

"Tomorrow afternoon, you are set for a book-signing at the *Amerika Haus* in Munich. The following day, you fly to Berlin. Someone from the Agency will take your rucksacks and provide a clean bag for Dolly for the flight to Berlin."

"How's the president holding up? Is he still game?"

"He's still hanging in there. It looks like Berlin may be our only chance to redeem this mission as worth all the time, effort and, of course, the danger to you and Dolly. As much as I dislike the term, we need a much bigger body count from you two."

"You sound like LBJ. Do we get any brownie points if we can bag the very top leadership of al-Qaeda?"

"Affirmative. But let's get it done so you guys can come home for Christmas. I'm getting tired of sleeping with this phone in my ear."

"We hear you, Jack."

"Good luck in Munich. Out."

✷ ✷ ✷

CHAPTER TWENTY-FIVE

Munich.

Because of its central location, they checked into the Hotel *Vier Jahreszeiten* (the Four Seasons). Within walking distance of the *Hofbrauhaus* and the English Garden, the *Vier Jahreszeiten* was a good choice. Because the morning after the book signing would be free, they decided to keep their rental car and make a side trip to nearby Dachau.

After showering in the luxury hotel, they dressed like back-packing tourists on holiday and headed to the *Hofbrauhaus* for a platter of wiener schnitzel with German-fried potatoes and sauerkraut. Their meal finished, they linked arms with some new-found German friends and swayed from side-to-side, singing some of the traditional German beer-hall songs. With the exception of some non-German tourists, everyone in the massive hall seemed to know the German lyrics. Even the tourists understood the melodies and the rhythm. In the singing, the swaying and the beer-drinking, the entire hall was unified.

Buck and Dolly could not help but think about how the beer halls of the 1930s had been the places where Germans drank and sang and thought about the greater glory of the Germanic peoples. They even imagined their fitness to rule the world. As some Germans liked to say: *Immer besser bei uns.*

Given the propaganda saying the Treaty of Versailles was unduly harsh upon the defeated Germany of World War I, no wonder the Germans were relatively easy recruits to the Nazi Movement. Buck and Dolly could visualize Hitler's brown-shirted thugs stilling the crowd inside the *Hofbrauhaus* so the relatively unknown former German Army corporal of Austrian birth could bewitch the assembled drinkers with his soaring rhetoric and dramatic gestures.

Stuffed with their evening meal, they wove their way back to the *Vier Zahreszeiten* for a good night's sleep. When morning came, and after more *Gemutlichkeit,* Buck suggested they walk up to the *Hofgarten* and then on to the English Garden. En route to the *Hofgarten,* Dolly noticed something she did not expect to see.

"Buck, why, in the middle of downtown Munich, would a shop be selling and renting surfboards?"

"Because you can actually do some pretty good surfing not far from here on a tributary of the Isar River called the *Eisbach.*"

"*Eisbach?* Doesn't that mean ice-river or stream?"

"Yes, it does. But even the bitter cold of winter does not keep some fanatical surfers from surfing a portion of the *Eisbach.* After we visit the memorial I want to show you at the northeast corner of the *Hofgarten,* we'll walk over to see the famous surfing wave known as the *Eisbach Welle.* "

Buck led Dolly to a place where they found a block of black granite sticking up out of the ground. It wasn't huge. But you could not miss it. It was the memorial to the White Rose Group.

"I just wanted you to see not all Germans fell for the rot being spewed by Hitler," said Buck. "This is a memorial to a group of Germans who spoke out against Hitler – a university professor and some of his students. They were executed as an example of what would happen even to Aryan intellectuals who opposed the Nazi regime."

They stood there for a few moments thinking about how terrified those "good" Germans must have been as they drew their last breaths on earth. After a while, Dolly asked, "How were they executed?"

"Hitler had them decapitated."

"Oh, my God! I take it Hitler wanted to make the point that even 'thinking' against him was a crime."

"No doubt. The professor and his students were certainly non-violent. All they did was print some anti-Nazi pamphlets and scrawl some anti-Nazi graffiti on some walls. It cost them their heads."

After a brief stroll, they came to the English Garden, the largest park in central Munich. Near the Isar River, they found the bridge overlooking the tunnel outlet where the waters of the *Eisbach* are constricted into a channel so narrow the water shoots out with such a force that it forms a perfect wave for surfers. They leaned against the bridge railing and looked down into the raging Eisbach channel.

The *Eisbach Welle* is not a wave to compete with those off the coast of Hawaii, but it forms a perfect standing wave of remarkable consistency and height. Even so, the *Eisbach Welle* is not for beginners. Dangerous rocks are downstream from the wave. Those unfamiliar with the *Eisbach* can get killed. The channel of the *Eisbach Welle* is so narrow only one surfer at a time can be on the wave. Buck and Dolly were fascinated as they watched a line of wet-suit clad surfers courteously wait their turn to ride the wave.

"Buck, it is so unlike Germans to queue up like Brits and Americans do," said Dolly. "Germans usually run over anyone in their path to get in ski-lift lines or to get on a bus or train. What's going on here?"

"Yes, seeing Germans waiting in line is a phenomenon almost as unusual as the *Eisbach Welle* itself. But, as you can see, there is only room for one surfer at a time on the wave. I suppose necessity has become the mother of courtesy."

After the surfer on the wave rode it back and forth several times and got so tired he or she could not stand on the board any longer, the surfer would fall off the board, taking care to swim in the center of the channel to avoid the rocks lurking downstream. Almost immediately, the next surfer would throw his or her board down onto the roaring water and jump on top of it. Sometimes, they missed their board and it got away from them. Surfer and board would be washed downstream and out of sight. Undeterred, the next surfer would give it a try. Most of them were successful. But then, it was not a place for beginners, and most of them displayed great skill. Buck and Dolly were so fascinated by the *Eisbach Welle* they were late in hearing the gravel-crunching sound of someone sprinting right at them. "Drop!" shouted Dolly.

Just as they turned loose of the bridge railing and fell to the tarmac, a body slammed against the railing. From her prone position, Dolly launched an upward Karate kick that sent whoever it was up and over the railing. Scrambling back up to look, they saw the head of someone in civilian clothes bobbing along in the frigid and foaming waters of the *Eisbach*. A man was flailing his arms against the current. But when his unprotected head hit a rock, his arms went still. He was swept out of sight.

"Thank God for your sharp hearing," said Buck. "I never heard that tango coming."

"Unlike you, I didn't lose my hearing in Vietnam or Cambodia. Let's get out of here. The surfers might have seen us up on the bridge. Speaking of hearing, I suppose Jack McClure needs to hear about this encounter."

As they backtracked toward their hotel, Buck said, "At this hour, Jack should be asleep. We are six hours ahead of Pentagon time. Let's wait awhile. We are to be at *Amerika Haus* at 1500 hours for the book-signing. *Amerika Haus* is somewhat farther from the hotel than the English Garden, but we can walk it and still be there on time. At this point, I don't feel much like eating; however, I suppose we need to have a bite at the hotel."

During a rather subdued lunch, they worried about a visit from the local *Politzei*. Apparently, the surfers were focused on the water and had not seen the two Americans watching from the bridge. No one came to question them.

The crowd at *Amerika Haus* was not large. In all, they inscribed fewer than 50 books. Everyone present spoke English very well, so there was no need for Buck to speak German. During a short break, Buck stepped outside. He called General McClure to report the incident at the *Eisbach Welle*. McClure already knew a Saudi tourist had fallen into the *Eisbach* and drowned. He figured the Madisons had something to do with it. The body count was rising; however, not fast enough.

As Buck and Dolly left *Amerika Haus*, several protesters were walking up and down the sidewalk wearing sandwich boards. One sign said something about *Atomgegner*, meaning they were against atomic weapons. One of the sandwich boards said: "Free the Ukraine!" None of the protesters paid any attention to Buck and Dolly as they left *Amerika Haus*.

Rather than risk being spotted by any of the *Eisbach Welle* surfers, they had room service bring them their evening meal.

✫ ✫ ✫

CHAPTER TWENTY-SIX

Dachau

Only ten miles north of Munich, the drive to Dachau in the rented Mercedes 350 Sport Sedan did not take long. Even so, Buck had time to tell Dolly about his previous association with Dachau.

"In 1945, after the few who remained alive at Dachau were moved elsewhere for medical treatment and the place was fumigated, some of the original masonry buildings were still useable. Later on, a portion of the camp was used as a U.S. Army Post. At one time, the Department of Defense operated an elementary school for the children of the military stationed at Dachau and in the surrounding area."

"Just imagine putting 'Graduate of Dachau Elementary School' on your resume," said Dolly.

"Yes, from a PR standpoint, it doesn't seem all that smart. But with all the devastation, I suppose they had to use whatever buildings were still standing. In fact, a portion of one of the old buildings was used as a military confinement facility. Soldiers who had been convicted at the Special Courts-Martial or General Courts-Martial level were confined at Dachau."

"You must be kidding," said Dolly. "The U.S. Army was holding convicted GIs in Dachau? Are you sure?"

Buck paused to answer because another Mercedes doing at least 90-miles-per-hour was flashing the death ray, even though Buck was already in the right lane. After the maniac shot past, Buck said, "Back in the mid-60s, when I was commanding a mechanized infantry company in nearby Augsburg, we used to pay the troops in cash.

"On paydays, my jeep driver and I would strap on our M1911 semi-automatics and go to the post finance center where I would draw a month's pay for the enlisted men in my company. Some company commanders would delegate such duty to one of their junior officers. But I saw it as a chance to talk with each soldier as he came through the pay line.

"After I finished paying my own troops, one of the additional duties I had to carry out was to be driven over to Dachau and pay any troops confined in Dachau the one-third of their pay they had not forfeited by virtue of their convictions. Of course, the confinement officer then deposited the cash into a fund where it remained until the soldiers had served their time. Then, they got their money. Ironically, some of the soldiers left jail with more money than they had ever saved in their entire lives. None of my own troops were confined there. So, I was paying someone else's soldiers. Fortunately, there were only one or two.

"Most of my troops were in their late teens or early 20s. The Dachau camp had been liberated about the year they were born. Regrettably, I found many of our troops had little knowledge of what the Germans call: *die Hitler Zeit*, the Hitler time. Many were clueless about the horrors of the concentration camps like Dachau or Auschwitz.

"My jeep had two seats in the back. So, each payday I would pick two soldiers to ride with me and my driver over to Dachau. While I was in the confinement facility paying whoever was in there, my driver would escort our two passengers to see what remains of the barracks, the gas chambers and the ovens. We made the trip to Dachau many times. So, almost 30 troopers learned something they never knew before. Of course, they told their buddies.

"Today, there are people who try to deny the Holocaust ever took place. Well, my driver and I and those other 30 troops saw some of the remnants of the Holocaust first-hand."

When the directional sign pointed to Dachau, Buck made the turn retracing the path his jeep driver had driven so many times before. After parking the rental car in the visitor's lot, they joined one of the tour groups for a guided tour. The Dachau Museum provides a chilling history of the period 1933 to 1945 when man's inhumanity to humankind knew no bounds.

As Dolly looked into one of the cremation ovens, she asked, "How could a people known for great music, poetry and science commit these unspeakable crimes against other human beings, against humanity?"

"Dachau was the first of Hitler's concentration camps. Initially, it was for political prisoners. People who spoke out against the dictatorial powers Hitler had assumed. When the same political party controls the executive, legislative, and judicial branches of government and the media that can happen. God save us if it happens in America.

"But it wasn't long before Dachau became a killing factory for Jews, gypsies, homosexuals, for anyone Hitler and Himmler wanted out of their way. The exact number of how many were murdered here is unknown; however, the famous Pastor Niemoeller said the number was well over 200,000. Nazi records showed an even higher number as actually registered. But, toward the end of World War II, the volume of prisoners being transported here overwhelmed even the Germans' normally meticulous accounting system, so the actual number of murders might be closer to 250,000.

"Stalin, who murdered many, many more people than Hitler, is supposed to have said: 'The death of one person is a tragedy. The death of millions is a statistic.'

"One of Hitler's disciples was the Grand Mufti of Jerusalem, Amin al-Husseini. His primary aide was Kharaillah Tulfah. Tulfah was Saddam Hussein's uncle and mentor. Al-Husseini and Himmler were buddies. Al Husseini even insisted that Himmler allow him to witness the murders of dozens of Jews. So, Himmler put al-Husseini in charge of the Jewish concentration camps in the Balkans. Eventually, al-Husseini was made prime minister of the Pan-Arab world. His mission was to rid Western Europe and the Balkans of the Jews.

"But the tie-in was larger than just the nephew of Kharaillah Tul-fah; you can trace the tendrils of hatred for the Jews from Sayyid Qutb in Cairo to al-Qaeda in Afghanistan and Pakistan. So, what you see here today at Dachau was not just a one-time aberration. It is a pandemic of hatred for the Jews and for what Qutb and his disciples saw as the decadent Judeo-Christian West.

"Oddly enough, Sayyid Qutb had a Colorado connection. Many years ago, he got some kind of fellowship to study in the United States. Part of the time, he was a graduate student at Colorado State Teachers College in Greeley. Now, it is called: the University of Northern Colorado.

"Anyway, Qutb decided he hated the entire United States because of what he thought was the immoral behavior of the co-eds on the Greeley campus. Just think if he had gone to Boulder."

"Buck, it sounds like Qutb needed some serious sex counseling. Where was Freud when we needed him? We might have been spared this entire pandemic of hatred."

"Let's just say Qutb was of indeterminate gender. When he got back home, Qutb wanted to bring down the Egyptian government. Eventually, Qutb was thrown into a Cairo jail. There he met and influenced the thinking of Ayman al-Zawahiri who, in turn, influenced Osama bin Laden. Also, it didn't help when the Qutb visited the British Museum in London and saw many of Egypt's most valuable artifacts on permanent display.

"What ever happened to Qutb?"

"The Egyptian authorities got tired of his urging the Muslim Brotherhood to overthrow the existing regime. He was executed. That made Qutb a martyr."

After Dolly had seen more than enough of the barracks where prisoners were housed like cheeses on racks, the gas chambers and the ovens, the couple returned to the parking lot. They checked inside the hood and underneath the Mercedes for explosives. Finding none, they started back to Munich.

"Any thoughts?" asked Buck, as he maneuvered around a group of bicyclists.

"As we've been fending off the agents Abu Amed has sent to kill us, my thoughts have just been about survival, but now I'm thinking in terms of revenge. I know that's wrong. Damn it, Buck, these crazies don't deserve to live. I'm ready to move this operation up from the retail to the wholesale level."

"In Berlin, we may have the opportunity."

"But why do they hate us?"

"Because they've missed the boat called: Modernity. The teachings of their mullahs arrested their development into the ways of thinking and doing things appropriate to about the 13th Century. Today, when they look at the Judeo-Christian West, they see our much healthier living conditions and hate us for it. Apparently, they can't see their way to hating the mullahs who trapped them back in the 13th Century. They have to blame someone. So, they blame us.

"I think that explanation covers Joe camel-driver; however, events such as 9/11, that take a lot money, training and coordination, are the work of relatively upper-class jihadists who may detest western lifestyles yet harbor a strange form of envy – an envy born of the idea that some, maybe most, upper-class Europeans will always look down upon them. Envy turned to hatred."

"Well, I don't hate them for any of that," said Dolly. "I'm starting to hate them because of the unspeakable things they have done to the Jews and to others in the name of their religion. If I get Abu Amed or any of his agents in my sights, they are going to meet those 72 virgins a lot sooner than they planned."

✳ ✳ ✳

CHAPTER TWENTY-SEVEN

Munich to Berlin

The drive from Dachau to the Munich International Airport was almost devoid of conversation. Even the usually ebullient Buck was subdued. En route, they stopped by the American Consulate in Munich. The Marine guard made a phone call. A young "diplomat" came to the entrance. He said he would be pleased to take their rucksacks for safe keeping. He gave Dolly a "clean" shoulder bag.

After turning in the rental car, Buck and Dolly went to the LuftCondor counter and got their boarding passes for the flight to Berlin. Their luggage was "clean," so they had no problems with security. In the waiting area, they did not detect any of Abu Amed's watchers. Dolly's necklace remained cool. The flight from Munich to Berlin-Tegel would be relatively short, only two hours. But enough time for Buck to brief Dolly on his hoped-for reunion with their old friend, Walter Zantner.

The take-off was routine. As soon as the airliner reached its assigned flight level and the captain reduced engine thrust to permit conversation, Buck said, "As I'm sure you will recall, when I commanded an armored cavalry squadron up along the Fulda Gap, our regiment had a civilian interpreter-translator named Walter Zantner. Plus, many years prior to that, when I was a full-time spook, Walter and I worked together on some operations in West Berlin."

"Of course, I remember Walter, and Anna, as well. I was saddened when he left the regiment and went to work for the Lord Mayor of Fulda."

"Actually, Walter had a number of careers. During World War II, he was a Luftwaffe bomber pilot over London, then as an intel operative, then as interpreter-translator for the U.S. in Fulda, then for the Lord Mayor and, most recently, as a tour-boat operator in Berlin."

"Weren't Walter and his brother POWs in England?"

"Yes. Walter and his brother, Gerhardt, were born and raised in the Sudetenland of Czechoslovakia. They were in their late teens when Hitler marched into the Sudetenland and annexed it to Germany.

"Both boys were crazy about airplanes. The *Hitler Jugend* promised them an opportunity to learn to fly. They jumped at the chance and were sent to a glider school perched on a small mountain to the east of Fulda. You remember the *Wasserkuppe* because we used to ski up there. When Hitler renounced the restrictions placed on powered aircraft by the Treaty of Versailles, Walter and Gerhardt were sent to the Luftwaffe to learn to fly bombers.

"Although assigned to separate Luftwaffe squadrons, they both flew a number of bombing missions over England. Walter was shot down and ended up in a British POW camp. One day, Walter was singing in the shower when he heard a familiar voice coming from another shower stall. The voice was supplying the harmony to Walter's melody. Walter started checking the other shower stalls and there was Gerhardt. He had been shot down and captured as well.

"The two boys were model prisoners. Both loved to garden and worked raising vegetables for the camp. They were good at it and word got around to the local laird. So, they were sent to work on the estate of the titled family whose estate abutted the POW camp. Eventually, they got to know the lord and the lady of the manor. In fact, they charmed the estate owners so thoroughly the owners of the estate sought and got permission for Walter and Gerhardt to leave the POW camp and live in their gardener's cottage. Ironically, the gardener was off serving in the Royal Marines.

"Now, here's the really crazy part. The lord and lady liked the lads so much that Walter and Gerhardt were sometimes invited to take the evening meal with the owners of the estate. During this time, Walter and Gerhardt, both gifted language learners, perfected their posh British accents. After the war, both the Zantners had families. They were invited to bring their families to England for visits. It got to be a tradition. One year, the lord and lady would come to visit the Zantner families in Fulda. The next year, all the Zantners would go to England."

"Buck, truth *is* stranger than fiction."

"Before Walter married Anna, he worked on the secret tunnel the CIA dug into East Berlin to tap into East German and Russian telephone traffic.

"When Walter left the Agency, he came to work for the U.S. Army in Fulda, and later, the Lord Mayor. Then, after the fall of the Wall, he and Anna bought the tour boat they operate on Lake Wannsee. Walter writes to me now and then. He says he has a dock and a kiosk on the shore near the Wannsee Mansion. The kiosk serves as Walter's booking and ticket office."

"Wannsee Mansion," said Dolly. "I've heard of the big mansion where the Nazis held a formal conference to settle the Jewish question, the 'final solution,' as they called it."

"Exactly. People with an interest in the Holocaust go there today because the Wannsee Mansion is now a museum and conference center. Either before or after a tour of the museum or even as a break from a conference, people can engage Walter's boat for a tour around the Wannsee. Not surprisingly, many of his passengers are Jews who go there to try to gain some understanding of how supposedly rational people could conceive a plan to murder every one of them.

"Just before we left the States, I received a letter from Walter. Just chit chat among old friends; however, I am troubled by Walter's reference to his financial troubles. He said public interest in the Holocaust has waned over the years. Even more troubling is Walter's belief that, since 9/11, some folks are fearful radical Muslims might try to blow up the museum or sink his boat when it is loaded with Jews. His insurance premiums have skyrocketed. Anyway, I promised I would come see him, just for old time's sake and for a few beers."

"I'll go with you," said Dolly, "if I can have some Mosel or Merlot, instead of beer."

"No problem. Now, let's see if we can grab a short nap."

"Buck, you know I can't sleep on airplanes. I don't know how you do it."

"I find the noise and vibration to be soothing. It's like putting a ticking clock in the box with a small puppy."

"If you say so," said Dolly, searching the seat pocket for something in English to read. From Buck's lap she took the book he was reading. It was by Buck's favorite historian, Barbara Tuchman.

She flipped it open and started to read where it said: *"…to read the minutes of the Wannsee Conference of 1942 at which the grandiose plan for the Final Solution – extermination of Europe's Jews – was adopted, is hardly to believe the printed page. Not one of the thirteen departments of the German government represented at the meeting questioned the goal, only the methods. The immensity of the task suggests the numbers of Germans involved in it: lawyers to draw up the decrees, civil servants to administer them, virtually the whole of the SS to carry out the program, police and certain sections of the Army to assist them, trainmen and truck-drivers to transport the victims, clerks to keep the statistics, bank tellers to tabulate the gold teeth and wedding rings salvaged from the millions of corpses, not to mention the fortunate citizens who received Jewish property, businesses, and belongings…"*

Dolly closed the book and put it back in Buck's lap. How could anyone sleep after reading anything so chilling?

✻ ✻ ✻

CHAPTER TWENTY-EIGHT

Berlin

When they emerged from the arrivals gate, Buck and Dolly were met by Matthew "Mac" Macallan, an intelligence officer posted to the U.S. Embassy and operating under official cover as a diplomat. With so many photographs of the Madisons appearing in the European media as a result of their book tour and, of course, as a result of "incidents" that seemed to occur at almost every book signing, Macallan had no trouble identifying his quarry.

In his late 40s, the dark-haired, brown eyed, square-jawed, Macallan still looked like the former college linebacker he once was. He looked like a good man to have on your side.

"Welcome to Berlin," said Macallan, stepping forward to greet them. "I have your transportation waiting outside."

"Well, thank you," said Buck, "but could we see some ID, please?"

"How stupid of me," said Macallan. "I should have offered some ID right away. After what you two have been through recently, I can understand your caution."

"Do you go by Matt or Mac?" asked Dolly, after looking at the passport showing Matthew Macallan to be a member of the Diplomatic Corps of the United States of America.

"Everyone calls me: 'Mac'."

"Thanks for coming to meet us, Mac," said Buck, as they shook hands all around. "We are simply Buck and Dolly. I hope you'll be taking us to the Embassy. We seem to be running short on some of items we like to carry with us."

"Ah, well, I've been instructed to take you to the Hotel Adlon Kempinski where we have arranged a comfortable suite. Also, we can do the bag swap in my car. I've brought along Dolly's weapons bag and I'll take her clean bag.

"As I'm sure you'll recall, the Adlon is only about 1,000 feet or so from the Brandenburg Gate. You'll have a great view. That's the good news. But the bad news is your book signing for tomorrow has been cancelled."

"Cancelled? But why?" asked Dolly.

"Ahem, well, the sponsors got word of what happened to London's most famous department store, Charles de Gaulle Airport and other places scattered around Europe. Their insurance carrier nixed the book signing. That's the bad news. The good news is: While I arrange for your transportation back to the States, you will have ample time to see what Berlin is like since the Wall came down and since Berlin became, once again, the German capital. In fact, I gather I'm to keep you busy seeing the sights and staying out of trouble."

With a glance, Buck let Dolly know he liked the good news. No doubt meaning a chance to visit with Walter Zantner was virtually guaranteed.

After they climbed into Macallan's Ford Expedition and they were moving along for the 20-minute journey from Berlin-Tegel to downtown Berlin, Macallan handed the Madisons a scrap of paper and said, "Please memorize the address and the telephone number on the paper and then destroy it. It's on edible rice paper. That's the address of one of the safe houses we use. If you happen to get into trouble or trouble finds you while I'm working on how to get you from Berlin to Washington, go to that address and I'll come to your aid. The housekeeper will have your names. She will let you in. But let's hope you'll have no need to go there.

"By the way, Madame Ambassador sends her regrets about not being able to meet with you."

"Right," said Buck, sensing he and Dolly were now *persona non grata* with the entire U.S. Diplomatic Corps. "I'll bet she's crushed."

Their suite, on the top level of the Adlon, was nicely appointed. The view of the Brandenburg Gate was as promised. Buck and Dolly recalled a time in the early 1970s when they had stood near the Wall watching Soviet troops goose-stepping around the famous gate. Now, they watched with immerse satisfaction as traffic flowed freely around the horse-topped monument. Arguably, the Brandenburg Gate was one of Germany's most revered landmarks.

Surveying their suite, Buck said, "The president wasn't kidding when he said the Agency would see to it we are well-treated. In the old days, Walter Zantner and I had to stay in the Berlin Brigade's BOQ at the Harnack House in the Dahlem district."

"Hopefully, that kept you and Walter from dragging any Frauleins into your BOQ rooms."

"My dear, the plural of *Fraulein* is *Fraulein*, not Frauleins."

"Forgive me, great speaker of German. We, who only speak three dialects of Chinese, tremble before your skills."

While Dolly began the unpacking, Buck looked up Walter's tour boat operation in the phone book and placed a call. Walter picked up on the second ring.

"Walter, heir spricht Buck Madison. *Wie geht's?"*

Replying in his Oxbridge English, Walter Zantner said, "Buck, what a pleasant surprise! How are you, old chap? It's been donkey's years since Fulda. Are you in Berlin?"

"Yes, Walter. I'm here with Dolly. If you have time over the next day or so, we'd like to take a cruise around the Wannsee."

"Like most males, I have a crush on Dolly. So, do come by all means. Also, if you've never seen the Wannsee Mansion, I can arrange a private tour for you as well. I would invite you over to our flat for dinner; however, Anna is back in Fulda visiting with Gerhardt and his wife and I'm not a good housekeeper or cook. The flat is a bit of a mess."

"That's fine, Walter. We understand. Just sorry we won't see Anna. No, we haven't seen the Mansion. We've only read about the dreadful conference. Your invitation is accepted. What would be a good time for you, Walter?"

"Today, I have no bookings. But that is not unusual. How about noon? At the moment, I'm just mucking around with a pump to make sure the bilge is completely dry. Nasty business. But I'm almost done.

"For sure, I'll be finished in time for the booking I do have for late tomorrow afternoon. Do bring your appetite. I'll run get some things from my favorite delicatessen. I recall Dolly likes Mosel. I'll put a bottle on ice. We can tour the lake while we eat."

"Sounds wonderful," said Buck. "But can we come at 1300 hours instead? We are still unpacking."

"Take your time. Now that you are here in person, I do have something to discuss requiring extreme discretion. It's related to what I wrote in my latest letter to you."

"Walter, our lips are sealed."

"Well then, it's all settled. By the way, where are you staying?"

"The Adlon. We're under our own names. Just call the desk. They'll put you through."

"My word, Buck, you've really come up in the world from our old days in the Berlin Brigade's BOQ or when we guarded the Fulda Gap. Do you know how to find the Wannsee Mansion? Do you need transportation?"

"We have a map. Don't worry. We'll just take a taxi. Thanks for asking. We'll see you at 1300.

"*Tschues*" said Buck, signing off in Berliner slang.

✫ ✫ ✫

CHAPTER TWENTY-NINE

Berlin-Wannsee, Walter's boat

The day was cloudless. The shining December sun and the bracing temperature produced what Berliners proudly call: *Berliner Luft*. With the temperature in the 40s, Berliners, wearing their coats, hats, and gloves, were walking about with their faces turned upward to the December sun. As Buck and Dolly left the Adlon, the Brandenburg Gate was gleaming. The doorman escorted them into a waiting taxi.

Promptly at 1300 hours, the taxi deposited Buck and Dolly in the circle drive that fronts the Wannsee Mansion. But instead of walking directly into the Mansion, Buck and Dolly skirted around on one side and found the broad trail down through the thin band of woods between the Mansion and the shoreline.

The *Valhalla* was rocking quietly at the dock. Wearing a double-breasted, navy-blue sport coat over a white turtle-neck sweater topped off with a yachting cap, Walter Zantner watched as Buck and Dolly descended the grassy slope.

"*Willkommen*, Buck and Dolly!" said Walter, pumping Buck's hand in the typical up and down European fashion. Then, Walter took Dolly's outstretched hand. He gave the back of it a kiss to make any Frenchman envious.

"Oh my, Dolly" exclaimed Walter. "You are even more beautiful than I remembered. I have wonderful memories of the times we waltzed around in the Orangerie in Fulda. Dolly, my humble vessel and I are honored. Allow me to escort you on board."

"You are too kind, Walter," said Dolly. "Hopefully, the *Valhalla* only goes around the Wannsee and not to her namesake."

"Maybe, tomorrow, but not today," said Walter.

"They say tomorrow never comes," said Dolly.

"Well, tomorrow may be an exception."

Without further ceremony, Walter led them on board. He seated Dolly inside the cozy wheel house. After starting the old gasoline engine in neutral, Walter said, "I can no longer afford a deck hand, so I must do everything myself. Buck, would you mind giving me a bit of help?"

After casting off the dock lines, Buck returned to the wheel house. Walter engaged the clutch. The 40-foot *Valhalla*, leaving a trail of smoke, motored slowly out across the Wannsee, one of a chain of lakes along the River Havel. Once they were in the middle of the lake. Walter cut the engine and let the *Valhalla* drift along in the river's slow current.

With the exception of the wheel house and the brightly-painted and bolted-down passenger benches, the top deck of the Valhalla was open and flat. Aft of the wheel house was a small table surrounded by four deck chairs. The table was supporting a colorful umbrella advertising "Warsteiner" around its fringe.

Along with a spread of lunch meats and cheeses, Walter served a well-chilled bottle of wine. While it wasn't *Johannesburger Hoelle 1959*, it was more than adequate to the occasion. Drifting across the beautiful lake and looking at the huge mansions lining the shore was idyllic. While they made little sandwiches and sipped their drinks, Buck and Walter talked of old times in Fulda and the two different U.S. armored cavalry regiments headquartered in Fulda over the years since World War II. Then, the meal over, Walter cleared away their plates. That done, Walter sat back down and pulled a serious face.

"Due to the colder temperatures," Walter began, "we stop operating the *Valhalla* at the end of December. But still, I should have had more bookings this year. As you can see, I have no bookings today even though I could carry up to 40 passengers. With insurance, license fees, plus what I have to pay to have the dock next to the Wannsee Mansion, it is getting to the point where the finance company may repossess my pride and joy and put me and Anna out of business. If she burned diesel, it would a little better. But, as you know, compared to America, gasoline is prohibitively expensive. The environmentalists are after me to convert to a new diesel engine with a 'green' exhaust system. If I could afford to do so, I would. But I cannot. If we are to retire in Fulda, Anna and I need to realize some cash out of this boat.

"Again, Buck and Dolly, I must have your pledge to be discrete."

"Our lips are sealed," said Dolly.

"Okay, if my boat were to meet with an accident. Like an explosion, you know. I would be able to collect on the insurance and, finally, Anna and I could retire back to Fulda."

"Walter, just wanting to go back to your beautiful Baroque city is reason enough to blow up your boat," said Buck. "So, when and how do you plan the semi-tragic event?"

"I do have a rare booking tomorrow afternoon. *Herr Doktor* Manfred Langsam, the curator, told me an outfit calling themselves the Muslims for Peace will be renting his conference room for the afternoon. I wonder how they define 'peace'? Anyway, my friend, Dr. Langsam, suggested the Muslims conclude their conference with a boat ride around the lake. I'll buy Dr. Langsam a nice bottle of wine.

"While it gets dark early this time of year, the lights along the shoreline make for a pretty sight. Turns out, the tour group is staying in some villa almost directly across the lake from the Mansion. After I take them for a ride around the lake, all I have to do is drop them off at their bloody dock and Bob's your uncle.

"They even paid in advance. And I gave them a receipt. I was more than happy to take their money. But I think that's the last money the *Valhalla* will ever earn."

"May we see the receipt?" asked Dolly.

"Sure, I have it right here. Paid in full by the German branch of CAIR, whatever that is. Why? Do you know anything about them?"

"Only that the American branch of CAIR is considered to be an extension of al-Qaeda or Hamas," said Buck. "Just looking at the receipt, it seems a bit odd. You made it out to a Christobal Garcia-Diego. I would have expected a more Arabic name. For example, Abu Amed."

"What can I say? That's the name he gave me. But he looked more Arab than Spanish."

"That's okay," Dolly. "But we might want to be involved with this Christobal Garica-Diego person some way. For now, please tell us your plans for the *Valhalla.*"

"Okay, here's the deal," responded Walter. "It will be dark when the cruise is finished. So, I thought after I drop the bloody WOGs off at their dock. Then, a really bad accident happens to the *Valhalla*. Like, maybe, one of the passengers left a burning cigarette on board. A fiery spark must have fallen down into a gasoline-filled bilge. That sort of thing."

"Walter, old friend, we like your plan," said Buck, clapping Walter on one shoulder. "But we have a suggestion. The group planning to board the *Valhalla* late tomorrow afternoon is a collection of Islamic jihadists. They are terrorists. They are cold-blooded killers. The world would be better off if the *Valhalla* were to explode with them on board. Who knows how many more people they are plotting to kill? Do you think you could manage to destroy your boat with them on board but without harm to yourself?"

"Oh, yes. But, either way, I would ask you and Dolly to be here tomorrow. To be hanging around my little kiosk. The water is frigid this time of year. So, the lake patrol or someone will have to come quickly."

"It would be our pleasure to help you arrange your finances so you can get back to Fulda," said Dolly.

"Walter," said Buck. "While the terrorists are having their meeting inside the conference room, maybe you could get your friend, Dr. Langsam, to give us a private tour of the exhibit rooms. That way we'll have an excuse to be hanging around. We'll just have to make sure we don't run into Senor Cristobal Garcia-Diego, AKA Mr. Abu Amed.

"I'm sure Dr. Langsam would be pleased to accommodate two friends of mine."

"Tell me, Walter," said Dolly, "what's your plan for the demise of the *Valhalla.*"

"The bilge pump is designed to pump overboard any water collecting underneath the cabin sole. But what if a fuel line ruptured or vibrated loose? A fault in the fuel line would allow the bilge to fill with gasoline.

"One night I was doing maintenance on the engine. It was very dark down in the bilge. I noticed the bilge pump makes a spark when it switches on. If the bilge were to fill up with gasoline instead of water, the spark made by the bilge pump could ignite the gas vapors. Given full gas tanks, the explosion would be enormous.

"So, if I had to swim for shore tomorrow evening would you break open the emergency call box on the side of my kiosk and call for the fireboat and for the *Politzei?*"

"Walter, we are at your service," said Buck, with a smile.

✫ ✫ ✫

CHAPTER THIRTY

Berlin. Hotel Adlon Kempinski

Walter's Opel Cadet had seen much better days; however, it ran well enough to get Buck and Dolly back to the Hotel Adlon Kempinski. Although invited in for a drink, Walter begged off, saying he had some more work to do on his boat.

When Buck and Dolly checked for messages at the hotel desk, the clerk handed Buck a note.

As they walked toward the elevators, Buck opened the envelope and read the note to Dolly. The words purported to be from an old acquaintance who invited them for a drink in the bar.

"What do you think?" asked Buck. "Shall we see who wants to see us?"

"I wouldn't mind a nice glass of wine in a cozy place where I could rest my feet. Let's go for it."

After they entered the bar area, the maitre d'hotel for the bar came forward to greet them with a bow, "Ah, Colonel and Madame, your guest is waiting. He said he would like to have some privacy, so he is in our private club. Please follow me.

"This early in the day you and your guest have the club to yourselves. He is seated at that table over in the far corner. Have a pleasant afternoon," said the maitre d' as he withdrew.

"I don't recall inviting anyone to meet us here," said Dolly.

"Don't look at me. Let's go see what this is all about."

"Oh my, Buck," Dolly whispered. "If that's our guest, he's wearing one of those gosh-awful, chalk-stripe suits with a shirt and tie entirely all wrong. Even in this darkened room I can see that. All those stripes running in different direction would make a TV tube pulsate. Some American TV news readers do that. They look like Bozo the clown."

"There's no accounting for poor taste; however, I happen to know that chap buys all his western clothes on Saville Row. That suit probably set him back about 2,000 English Pounds."

"You know that fellow?"

"Yes, indeed. He claims to have attended my lecture at Cambridge some years ago. But, more importantly, that chap is someone I knew as Osama bin Laden's right-hand man. He's none other than Mr. Abu Amed.

"Oh, my word, that's the Saudi who held you captive for awhile inside Tora Bora? That's the one who has been trying to have us killed?"

"The very one. Let's go over and say *Shalom.*"

Standing up and making a bow toward Dolly, Mr. Abu Amed said, "Welcome to Berlin, my American friends. Colonel Madison, I have not had the pleasure of meeting the lovely Dr. Dolly Madison."

"Ah yes," said Buck. "Dolly, allow me to present Mr. Abu Amed, a distinguished graduate of Cambridge University, which accounts for his upper-class English accent. Mr. Amed is also the chief-of-staff to Osama bin Laden and, maybe even, Mr. Ayman al-Zawahiri."

"Forgive me," said Abu Amed, "my sense of protocol is lacking. I should have addressed you as Sir James and Lady Dolly. I suppose I should kiss your hand?"

"Actually, I had another place in mind," said Dolly, not hiding her irritation that Abu Amed knew about the Queen's supposedly secret ceremony.

"My husband has told me so much about you," said Dolly. "Now, we meet face-to-face; however, I assume you would prefer that I cover my face. But, somehow, I forgot to pack my *abaya* and my *ghotwa* for this trip."

"That will not be necessary, Lady Dolly. I lived in England long enough to understand different cultures have different customs. If you are not embarrassed by seeing me without my Arab *ogal*, *shumagg* and *thobe*, I am not embarrassed to gaze upon your face which, I dare say, is quite beautiful. And, I might add, your knowledge of Arab dress is most pleasing."

"Thank you, Mr. Amed; however, with typical American lack of patience for dancing around with deceitful platitudes, I must ask you: What is the hell is the point of this meeting?"

"Pardon me, Lady Dolly. Where are my manners? Please sit down."

Snapping his fingers, in the accepted German fashion at the waiter hovering just out of earshot, Abu Amed called, *"Herr Ober,* please bring your wine list. I'm sure Dr. Madison would like to select a Merlot."

A wary Dolly said, "I can't imagine that Buck and I are on your Ramadan card list. Again, what's the purpose of this meeting? Also, who's the host here?"

"Actually, because we are under your hotel roof, I'd like to think I am under your protection," said Abu Amed. "But that doesn't mean I won't stand you to a few drinks."

As she sat down, and without even glancing at the wine list, Dolly said, "Then, I'd like a glass of *Clos de L'oratoire Grand Cru St. Emilion*." Abu Amed did not even flinch.

"Would the year 2000 vintage be acceptable?" asked the waiter.

"Indeed," said Abu Amed. "Bring a bottle, please. Dr. Madison and I will share the wine."

Turning to Buck, the waiter waited for him to order.

"Sometimes, I drink beer; however, the beer I like is difficult to find."

"Sir, here at the Adlon, we stock virtually any beer you could possibly name," said the waiter, with pride.

"The beer I like is from Israel. It called: Nagila."

"Sir, I must admit I have never heard of Nagila," confessed the Waiter.

"Pity," said Buck. "It even has a nifty slogan."

"And what would that be?" asked Abu Amed, growing a bit wary.

"'When you are having only one: Then, Hava Nagila.'"

"Dr. Madison, is he always this way?" asked Abu Amed.

"No, Mr. Amed," said Dolly. "He is often worse."

"Seriously, I'll have some Laphroaig with a drop of spring water," said Buck.

When the waiter left to fetch the wine and the whisky, Dolly said, "I thought Muslims did not drink alcohol."

"One does what one must do to blend into one's surroundings," said Amed, with a shrug that would have made a Frenchman proud.

"I rather like your custom that guests are afforded protection from harm," said Buck. "How nice if we could erect a great big tent over the entire planet and declare we are all each other's guests."

"Once again, you please me that you find some merit in one of our basic concepts; however, such a tent would have to include Las Vegas and Hollywood and, as the English are wont to say, 'That simply won't do.'"

"I wasn't aware of this private club inside the hotel," said Buck. "But then, I haven't been in Berlin since the early 1970s. The décor is quite well done. It reminds me of a posh men's club in Washington, D.C. or London."

"You would probably know about those things, Sir James, I expect you belong to many fashionable clubs in America."

Irritated by Amed's smug use of the Queen's supposedly secret knighthood information, Buck said, "Yes, back home, we belong to Sam's Club."

"Since I have never heard of it, it must be quite exclusive," said Amed.

To keep from laughing, Dolly had to concentrate on folding her linen napkin into a small swan.

After the waiter served their drinks, Buck said, "Thank you for the drinks. Apparently, your intelligence sources are accurate as to our tastes as well as to our itinerary. Mr. Amed, you have made your point that your intelligence sources are better than ours. So, would you please knock off the Sir James and the Lady Dolly crap?"

"I'll try. But what does the lovely Dr. Madison call you at home?"

"Just before we were married, she asked if I preferred to be called Colonel, Doctor or Professor."

"And what was your response?" asked Amed, playing along with the old Henry Kissinger joke."

"That I really prefer: Your Grace."

"Colonel, as an avid reader of the life and times of Henry Kissinger, I must charge you with plagiarism. Besides, you told me that tired joke back in Tora Bora.

"Guilty, as charged," admitted Buck.

"You see, openness is one of the downsides of your society, my dear Colonel. Open source intelligence is all we need; however, it is nice to operate some moles here and there. But forgive me once more. I have failed to answer the question posed earlier by your lovely wife. The answer is I just wanted the three of us to sit together in the hope we could engage in what your pop psychologists call: values clarification. Then, there is, ah, one other item."

"Excuse me, Mr. Amed," interrupted Buck. "The differences in our respective values cannot be more clear. We celebrate a culture of life. You celebrate a culture of death.

"You send young suicide bombers, even children, to kill and maim innocent people in marketplaces, mosques or wherever you can find a large crowd. Our values tell us to defend ourselves. How do you reconcile the murdering of innocent people with the many Sura in the Koran that lecture against suicide and against the killing of innocents?"

"We don't always use violence to impact your society," countered Abu Amed. "Sometimes, we just take pleasure in harassing you."

"Harassing? How so," asked Dolly, sipping her wine.

"My agents tell me on Sunday afternoons in America some Muslim families take their children out to some of your larger commercial-service airports so their children can enjoy the sight of Americans having to remove their shoes to get through the pitifully inadequate shakedowns conducted by your Transportation Security Administration, your TSA. They enjoy watching Americans struggle to show the TSA their so-called 3-1-1 bags of fluids, none of which can be more than three fluid ounces.

"Of course, in flight, several of our comrades could easily combine the fluids in their 3-1-1 bags to produce an explosive large enough to bring down an airliner and all on board. The measures employed by your TSA are both amusing and woefully inadequate. Anytime it serves our purpose to down one of your airliners, we can penetrate your pitiful TSA defenses, and do so.

"What do you mean by woefully inadequate?" asked Buck.

"For starters, all of those laptop or notebook computers and cellular telephone your TSA allows on board contain lithium-ion batteries. If we could slip a half-dozen of our brothers or sisters on an airliner, they could find a way to remove those batteries from those devices and combine them to make a small bomb capable for rupturing the pressure vessel of an airliner."

"Okay," said Buck. "So, the TSA bans computers, cell phones and other devices containing lithium-ion batteries. Once more, you're screwed."

"Come, Colonel, be realistic. As long as males have one internal cavity and females have two internal cavities, even your most sophisticated scanners cannot detect certain explosive compounds inserted into those cavities."

"You mean a woman could carry enough explosives internally to bring down an airliner?"

"Yes, of course. As you know, binary explosives must be carried separately. Using condoms, she would carry one part in one cavity, the other part in the other cavity. Then it is a simple matter of going to use the restroom and removing the condoms. While there, the two explosives would be mixed together. Add a detonating agent from her 3-1-1 bag and you would have an explosion large enough to blow a large hole in the aircraft's pressure vessel. At high altitude, the sudden depressurization of the aircraft would cause the entire fuselage to rupture, bringing the entire aircraft to earth."

"But your 'shoe bomber' failed to make his explosives explode effectively," said Buck. "All your 'shoe bomber' did was burn his foot and end up in prison."

"We were just testing a concept. Now, we have decided the female jihadist offers a much larger 'bang-for-the-buck' as you American like to say."

"Why are you telling us this?" asked Dolly. "Don't you know we will report what you just said to our authorities?"

"Of course you will. But they are not so stupid that they have not figured this out already. The point is your government is never going to subject anyone to the kind of truly invasive search able to detect explosives in those internal cavities."

"Are you saying the TSA is wasting millions of dollars and pissing off millions of travelers to no effect?" asked Buck.

"No, my dear Colonel, the TSA's efforts are not entirely wasted. There are amateurish 'garden variety' madmen out there who have nothing to do with Islamic Jihad. I'm sure your TSA catches a few of them before they can do harm to an airliner.

"Actually, you should follow the practices of *El Al*, the Jewish airline, may they be cursed forever. *El Al* looks carefully at the individuals who want to fly on *El Al*. The Jews, may they be cursed, do the kind of profiling your liberal Left will not permit your government to do. Consequently, we are unable, thus far, to attack *El Al* aircraft.

"But, you see, our movement really doesn't need to bring down anymore of your airliners. Our goal is make the American public so weary of your so-called 'War on Terror' that you will turn inward, leaving us to achieve our goals in the Middle East, South Asia, and in Europe. In that, we are succeeding.

"But I must confess we face a long struggle and much of it is rather grim. So we are pleased to find some joy and to take comfort from watching Americans jumping through the hoops the TSA imposes on them. Meanwhile, if we do decide to take down more airliners, we have devoted women who are willing to do so."

"But how can you be so cavalier about taking the lives of innocent men, women and children and the lives of your devoted jihadist women?" asked Dolly. "I've read your Koran where it claims Islam is a religion of peace. Why are you doing this?"

"Admittedly, Lady Dolly, the Koran and the Hadith are sometimes difficult for people not raised in our culture to understand. But for every Sura you wish to quote against suicide or the harming of what you call 'innocents,' I can counter with a Sura or a passage in the Hadith to the opposite effect. You see, while we treasure all of the Koran, the later passages are the operative passages. The later passages are the ones that have force and effect today. Why are we doing what we do? Because the Koran commands to us wage jihad until Islam rules the world and Sharia is the law of every land.

"But you employ sophisticated missiles and other technologies against us. Just now, we cannot match you in that regard; however, we have something better than the computers guiding your sophisticated missiles. We have human brains trained and motivated to insinuate themselves through the cracks and crevices of your defensive systems and detonate massive explosions in your subways, tunnels, airports and any of your monuments to western technology. That is our way of leveling the playing field, as you Americans like to say."

"Look, Mr. Amed," said Buck, "we could sit here forever and never come to an agreement that one side is right and the other side is wrong. Besides, you and I already had this same conversation more than once when I visited you and Mr. bin Laden in the caves of Tora Bora. But if you want to convince Dolly, be my guest." With a hand signal to the waiter, Buck added, "Please, instead of Scotch, I'd like a Perrier on the rocks."

"It might be helpful to our discussion, Dr. Madison, if you had some understanding of how your culture has wronged my culture. You need to understand how our culture has been under attack by your culture."

"I don't mean to hurt your feelings, Mr. Amed," said Dolly, "but for most of my lifetime anyway, we Americans could not care less about your culture, Arab or Muslim or Islamic or whatever. That doesn't make us bad people. In fact, if the American geologist, Karl Twitchell, hadn't discovered oil in your country, only readers of *The National Geographic* would know Saudi Arabia even exists.

"Let me remind you, Mr. Amed, if the American Henry Ford hadn't figured out how to make automobiles affordable for ordinary people, the world would not need your oil and your people would be watching the camel races from the tops of sand dunes instead of from inside your air-conditioned Mercedes."

"Please do not patronize me with how your society will invent a way to turn water into gasoline and my people will be searching for food in the desert. Your society is much more at technological risk than ours."

"Oh, really? How is that?" asked Dolly.

"If we can detonate a magnetic pulse bomb above your country, you will be without your vaunted electron-based economy. After an electromagnetic pulse or EMP attack, everything you have containing a micro-chip will no longer work. The components that run your banks, your gas pumps, your factories, your airplanes, your agricultural machinery, your kidney dialysis machines, your life-support systems, your pharmaceutical companies, your hospitals, your water systems, will all be fried.

"A few provident people among your society will have kept cash on hand, will have stored away non-hybrid seeds for basic food stuffs, will have stored petrol, will have emergency generators, water wells, their own septic systems, and, most importantly, will have plenty of firearms and ammunition to stave off the attacks from their improvident neighbors who will attempt to take away what they have stored rather than watch their own children starve to death."

"That would be worse than a hundred 9/11 attacks!" exclaimed Dolly.

"More like a million times worse, my dear," said Abu Amed. "Your people have grown soft. They no longer have the skills to survive in an agrarian economy. Your masses of improvident people will kill your few provident people over packets of vegetable-garden seeds, over ammunition needed to kill game, over your last stores of life-sustaining medicines. You will be thrown back into the 18th Century.

"So, you see, in the end, my agrarian people, the people you dismiss as camel jockeys, will survive as they always have and we, the privileged few, will still have our Mercedes. Your people will be the people scratching the ground, trying to get something edible to grow in order to feed your starving children."

"Are you saying nothing in our society would work anymore?" asked Dolly.

"Maybe a few automobiles manufactured prior to 1970, before the advent of the microchip. If you have an old Volkswagen, you would be wise to keep it running. As they say, 'In the land of the blind, the one-eyed man is king.' Should we subject you to EMP attack, the person with the old VW would ride. The person with the most-recent Cadillac or even Hummer would walk."

"But the magnetic pulse attack would be our last resort. I think we can carry out lesser forms of attack designed to get your society to leave our society alone. It is my hope that those lesser forms of attack will lead to a negotiated settlement of our differences."

"Mr. Amed, you keep coming back to the theme that our society is attacking your society. Frankly, I don't see that as the case," said Buck.

"Yes, Colonel, you both fail to see al-Qaeda as a counterattacking force designed to stop you from attacking our culture."

"Okay," said Dolly, finishing her wine. "Let's back up. Explain how we have attacked your culture."

"First, let me say we do not fault your pursuit of technology: radio, television, satellite communications, medical research, aviation – all of those advances and more – we applaud. Unfortunately, you allow the worst among you to use some of these technologies for the worst of purposes."

"You mean the sewage that flows out of Hollywood depicting all that's bad in America and passing it off as the norm." said Buck.

"Yes, indeed, Colonel, it is sewage that appeals not just to the lowest dregs of your society but to millions in Asia and in all the developing countries. Even as Americans, you may not be aware of this; however, Hollywood makes some films you do not see in your regular theaters. They are marketed abroad at certain film festivals to film distributors who then show them to Orientals and others who want to see horrific torture and violence mixed with soft- or even hard-pornography.

"You see, the people who are envious of your society are quite willing to believe the worst about it. But the problem for us is the invasiveness of your electronic media. Try as good Muslim parents might to prevent it, our children are seeing nudity and seeing your God and our Allah, be He glorious and exalted, mocked. Our youth are being exposed to bizarre sexual behaviors, seeing homosexuality condoned, even seeing outright pornography."

"I take your point on that, Mr. Amed," said Dolly. "We have good Christian, Jewish, Hindu, Buddhist, or even Atheist parents who can't keep their children from being negatively impacted by all that sewage, as you and Buck call it."

"Right on," said Buck, nursing the drink quietly delivered by the waiter who quickly withdrew to the bar. "Look, Mr. Amed, all

Muslim-led countries are dictatorships. Surely, you can use your police to prevent your children from seeing and hearing what you don't want them to hear or see. Did you ever see an electronic device without an 'off' button?"

"Granted, we could and should do more in that regard, Colonel Madison. But you attack our culture in other ways. You have dozens of organizations, both governmental and non-governmental, that spend billions of dollars and untold hours trying to change our culture to make it more like yours. You want us to want what you want. We do not want what you want."

"Give us some examples," asked Dolly. "I know I don't wake up each morning asking myself what I can do today to undermine Islam or Muslims or Turks or Arabs or even those blasted Iranians."

Pulling a piece of paper from his suit pocket, Abu Amed said, "As you can see, I've prepared myself in the hope we could have this talk. May I read this list of organizations? These are the organizations that are undermining what we are trying to teach our children is the way of Allah, be He glorious and exalted, and the way of the Prophet Muhammad, may his name be praised, as well."

"Of course," said Buck and Dolly, their curiosity peaked.

After clearing his throat, Abu Amed began to read: "The American Civil Liberties Union, People for the American Way, Center for Democratic Development, Center for Constitutional Rights, Feminist Majority Foundation, Human Rights Watch, National Abortion Rights Action League, National Organization of Women, Global Fund for Women, Women Living Under Muslim Laws, International Gay and Lesbian Human Rights Commission, Al Fatiha Foundation (for gay, bisexual, and transgender Muslims), Women's Global Network for Reproductive Rights, Planned Parenthood, National Endowment for the Arts, Americans United for Separation of Church and State, Move on.org., NetRootsNation.org, the dailykos.org, Amnesty International, certain programs funded by the U.S. Department of State and the United Nations, and the Democratic National Committee."

"That's quite a list you have there," said Dolly. "Other than the U.N. and our State Department, I had no idea those groups were projecting themselves overseas into Islamic countries."

"It's not just Islamic countries, Dr. Madison. Many of the groups I just read to you try to change Muslims wherever they find them. In America, in Great Britain, wherever. Following World War II, these assaults against the way the Koran and the Hadith teach us to live have been like a red tide."

"Speaking of the Red Tide," said Buck. "I suppose while Dolly and I were focused on our small roles fighting against the Communists in the Cold War, we didn't realize the culture war we saw inside America between liberals and conservatives was being played out in other countries as well."

"Well, now you know. Hopefully, I've set the stage for what I want to propose to your president. *Herr Ober*, please, we would like another bottle of this most excellent wine and another, ah, Perrier."

✳ ✳ ✳

CHAPTER THIRTY-ONE

Valhalla

After dropping the Madisons off in front of the Adlon, Walter Zantner drove back to where the *Valhalla* was berthed on the Wannsee. Rummaging around in the ship's tiny wheelhouse, he found the grease-spotted and dog-earned diagram for the fuel system. The schematic showed a drain plug very low down at the forward end of the main fuel tank. Taking his tool kit, Walter went down below into the engine compartment.

The main fuel tank was located on the boat's centerline and just aft of the foot of the ladder leading down into the engine compartment. The cabin sole was made out of strips of mahogany and holly. A hatch in the cabin sole gave access down below to the bilge pump. After opening the hatch, Walter pulled the fuel drain hose out from its recess and placed it at the base of the bilge pump.

Then, his experienced hand selected the proper wrench from the tool kit. Gingerly, he applied the wrench to the hexagonal drain plug. But it wouldn't rotate. Taking some WD-40 from his toolbox, he sprayed the drain plug with the fluid and resigned himself to a wait of several minutes before trying again. When he tried again, he was rewarded with the turning of the drain plug. Raw gasoline started seeping down into the bilge.

Quickly, he retightened the drain plug and set the wrench to the side in readiness for what he planned to do the following day. Walter wiped up the fuel spill with a paper towel. Turning to the bilge pump, he reached down to the base of the bilge pump and found the float that causes the pump to activate. He pushed up on the float and was pleased to see the electric spark that was created when the float came up high enough to trigger the pump to start pumping water out of the bilge and over the side. As long as the bilge contained only water, the spark created no danger. But a bilge filled with the fumes of raw gasoline was an entirely different matter. Walter closed the hatch, but did not dog it down.

Returning to the upper deck, he located his personal floatation device, his PFD. When submerged in water, the PFD was designed to inflate automatically. Too expensive to be provided for all on board, the PFD was there for Walter's own use. It was light and compact, allowing Walter to move about his boat quite easily.

At the very stern, he opened a locker built into the transom. Walter stowed his PFD in the locker. Donning the PFD would be his last act before leaping from the stern of the *Vahalla* and into the cold, cold waters of the Wannsee.

✣ ✣ ✣

CHAPTER THIRTY-TWO

Baden-Baden, Germany

After the fall of the Berlin Wall, the spirit of reunification moved LuftCondor to recruit some former MiG fighter pilots from the defunct East German Air Force. Although some former fighter pilots have a tendency to yank and bank their aircraft in ways that would scare the daylights out of commercial airline passengers, a few of the out-of-work MiG pilots proved docile enough to fly passengers for LuftCondor. Two of LuftCondor's East German recruits were the brothers: Fritz and Hans Schmidt.

The brothers Schmidt grew up in East Prussia. As with so many Prussians, they considered themselves a cut above the masses, even though they did not have the coveted "von" in front of their family name. Their lack of nobility did not, however, stop them from inserting the "von" when they were in foreign lands where there was little chance of being exposed. They even had some phony business cards showing them as Fritz von Schmidt and Hans von Schmidt. Had they been born earlier, their temperaments would have made them easy recruits for the *Schutzstaffel (SS)* or the *Gestapo*. Both pilots detested Jews, Slavs, Gypsies, and anyone they considered non-Aryan.

The brothers "von" Schmidt had never bothered to marry because they found any number of female flight attendants who were happy to take care of their physical needs. Not a few flight attendants had been initiated into the "mile-high" club by the Schmidt brothers who, more often than not, would bid to fly together as captain and first officer on the long transatlantic flight from Frankfurt to the East Coast of the United States and back. Being of the exact same size, they would trade uniform jackets with one brother wearing the four stripes of captain while the other wore the three stripes of the first officer. As a practical matter, the brother who was the least hung-over got to wear the four stripes and sit in the pilot's left seat.

Sometimes, while one of the brothers flew the aircraft the other brother and a willing flight attendant would lock themselves in a lavatory to conduct a "mile-high club" initiation. In fact, some of their female flight attendants had been initiated more than once.

But living the high life was expensive, made even more so by their penchant for risking their LuftCondor pay in the posh casinos of Baden-Baden and Monte Carlo. They were more adept at flying than gambling.

Overtime, they were befriended by the Arab whose oil money allowed him to buy their favorite casino in Baden-Baden. The multi-millionaire Arab even flew them on his jet and hosted them on his 250-foot, mega-yacht anchored in the Bay of Monte Carlo. In the midst of astonishing luxury, they were wined and dined and supplied with as much female companionship as they could handle. And, when the brothers lost heavily at his casinos, the Arab was more than happy to advance them some serious amounts of money so they could attempt to recoup some of their losses.

But then the bills came due. One evening in Baden-Baden, drunk and broke, they were directed to a suite of offices where they were confronted by a German wearing something the Schmidt boys had never seen before: a scarlet tuxedo jacket with a plaid cummerbund worn over black tux trousers. Instead of the usual high-roller treatment, the casino manager did not ask them to sit down or offer them anything to drink.

"*Meine Herren*, as you know, you are deeply in debt to the owner of this casino. That means you have three choices. You can pay up right now. Or, you will be killed. Or, you can agree to my proposal."

"What if we don't like your proposal?" asked Hans.

"I am offering you both a carrot and a stick. If you carry out your duties satisfactorily, your casino debts are cancelled and you each receive $50,000. That's the carrot. The stick has to do with your aging parents. We know they live in a retirement home in Weimar.

If you refuse my offer, then my men will subject your parents to a very slow and painful death."

"I think we would like to hear your proposal," said Fritz Schmidt.

"On a certain date, there will be a LuftCondor charter flight from Berlin to Washington Dulles International Airport. The aircraft will be a Boeing 727. We want you to put in a bid to be the relief crew for that charter. But the flight will not terminate at Dulles Airport. It will crash into the White House.

"Bist du verrueckt!" blurted Hans.

"No, Herr Schmidt, I am not crazy. Nor is my employer, Mr. Ayman al-Zawahiri. What you are going to do will put the stamp of Mr. al-Zawahiri on the world-wide jihadist movement once and for all. Once I explain your mission, you will understand.

"Meanwhile, I appreciate your concern for your own lives. Even though you spend your time whoring around, your miserable lives will be spared. Prior to the crash, you will parachute to safety."

"But, sir," protested Hans, "ever since the escapade of the infamous D.B. Cooper in America, the rear stairs of most of the Boeing 727s have been disabled."

"You are almost correct, Herr Schmidt. On some of the 727s, something called the 'D.B. Cooper Vane' was installed on the outside of the rear stairs. It looks like a small ping-pong paddle. But that will not be the case with the 727 you will be flying. That particular Boeing - is currently in service in Africa where jet ways and even rolling stairs are not common. The ventral air stair on your particular LuftCondor charter will work quite well."

"But what if LuftCondor switches equipment at the last moment?" asked Fritz. "What if we get a 727 with the vane installed?"

"During your pre-flight inspection, you should be able to find the vane. Put a small hack saw in your flight bag. Detach the vane from the aircraft and hide it in your flight bag. You do conduct a pre-flight inspection, do you not?"

"Of course, we do," said Fritz. "We may act…ah, somewhat care-free. But, when it comes to flying, we are very serious."

"Explain more about your plan," said Hans.

"Actually, it is quite simple. You are to be pre-positioned in Gander, Newfoundland, to act as the relief crew needed to take the charter flight from Gander to Washington, D.C. Before you board the aircraft, you will be given two sets of latitude and longitude. The first set will take you to your, ah, drop zone. The second set will take your aircraft on auto-pilot to the White House.

"People who know about such things tell me the auto-pilot on your aircraft will have something called a 'Stage III auto-land feature.' That means it can fly a hands-off approach to any point on earth. So, all you have to do is make the proper settings, get your aircraft pointed in the direction of the White House, make your way to the rear of the aircraft and use the parachutes we will provide. You will land in the State of Maryland, well north of the aircraft's target."

"But we don't know much about parachuting," protested Hans. "Our only training was in the ejection seat for the MiG-17 and that was just a simulator."

"Our advisors tell us that all you do is attach something called a static line to the back of your parachute. You attach the static line to the hand rail of the air stair and jump out. The static line opens your chute for you. It could not be simpler."

"But we don't know anything about this Maryland place," protested Fritz. "We will be rounded up like the Nazi saboteurs of World War II, and shot!"

"Don't worry. Certain operatives will be there on the ground in Maryland to meet you. They will take you to a safe location where you will be paid in full. As soon as I hear you have properly performed your duties, then no harm will come to your parents. I suspect, however, they will be saddened to learn of your demise.

"No doubt, the American authorities will assume you both died in the blazing crash. Again, do not worry. Our operatives will have new identities and new passports for you. You will fly to Venezuela where Hugo Chavez has agreed to let you fly for the airline he has nationalized. You could afford cosmetic plastic surgery. You could afford many women. So, *Meine Herren*, what is your decision?"

"What choice do we have?" asked the brothers, as they each shook the hand of the casino manager.

✵ ✵ ✵

CHAPTER THIRTY-THREE

Berlin, Hotel Adlon

As the discussion with Abu Amed moved along, Dolly pondered the thought of pressing the panic button on her cell phone. It contained the same kind of technology that had allowed the CIA's Hong Kong Station case officers to rescue her from her captivity in a Chinese Junk in Aberdeen harbor. But considering Walter Zantner's story of a large gathering of Arabs at the Wannsee Mansion the next day might lead to a larger blow against al-Qaeda than the capture of Abu Amed, she kept her finger off the emergency button.

"Hold the phone, Mr. Amed," said Buck, reading Dolly's thoughts. "You've arranged for us to meet here because you think we have influence with the American president?"

"Whether or not you, personally, have influence is immaterial. But it is clear you have access to a secure means by which you communicate with your president directly or almost directly. I also know your president may have had a role to play in this phony book signing tour which has occupied your time in recent weeks. So, I am hoping to open what you Americans call a 'back-channel' communication."

"Why a back-channel?" asked Dolly. "Why don't you just deliver a video tape or DVD to al-Jazeera Television like you usually do? Better yet, contact one of our many diplomatic missions. Use the official channels."

"The answer should be obvious. The overblown and overly-mature bureaucracies inside your Department of State, your CIA, your Department of Justice, your FBI, and your Department of Homeland Security have become islands unto themselves. They are filled with middle-level functionaries who think and act like they are immune from the orders of your elected president. It makes no difference which of your political parties controls the White House or your Congress. The permanent bureaucracy knows it will be in place when a new president arrives and it will be in place when the old president departs."

"I can certainly agree with you about the State Department," said Buck. "When I worked in the Pentagon, we used to say we should appoint an ambassador to the State Department because it seemed the only logical way for us to have contact with the foreign-policy mandarins over in Foggy Bottom. We joked how we needed to have a State Department Desk and they needed to have an America Desk."

"Indeed, Colonel. Your State Department is in the hands of Eastern Establishment liberals who view Arabs as children who must be ruled by strong dictators. Their only saving grace is many of them come from wealthy, white, Anglo-Saxon, Protestant families who, in their inner convictions, are anti-Semites.

"We are not disposed to 'deal' with any of your bureaucracies. But I will grant Hollywood one thing. One of the themes running through some of your better television programs depicts the agents in the field as working for bureaucratic superiors who are complete buffoons. While we despise the TV series '24' for its overt racism against Muslims, '24' is a perfect example of why agents who work in the field should be distrustful of those who send them out, perhaps, to die.

"We have identified you and Dr. Madison as trusted and capable case officers who have access to the American president. And, by the way, when you gained access to our diesel fuel supply in Tora Bora, what chemical did you use to contaminate it?"

"Actually, a capsule of *Cladosporium Resinae* was hidden in the heel of my boot. That's what I put in the tank; however, to get the bacteria to reproduce, water and salt were needed. So, when I heard your guards approaching the fuel tank, I knew I was running out of time. To provide the water and the salt, I merely urinated in the tank."

"I'm sure you felt urinating in our diesel fuel supply was insulting."

"So, why did Osama bin Laden faint when I showed the letter from the American president?"

"I must confess not even I know what was in that letter. Do you know?"

"Haven't the foggiest. It was given to me sealed and I gave it sealed to Mr. bin Laden."

"Well, whatever it said was very upsetting to Mr. bin Laden. As you know, it prompted a severe drop in blood pressure. And, as you also know so well, Dr. Singh became catatonic and you had to step in and resuscitate Mr. bin Laden. At the time, that act saved your life. In fact, the decision was made to let you live your little lives in Grand County without further interference. Well, that was until we learned the truth about what you did to stop the dialysis machine that was saving Mr. bin Laden from renal failure."

"Look," said Buck, "All I know is Mr. bin Laden looked weak and fatigued, he was thin, his skin was very dark for someone living in a cave. He looked like someone suffering from renal disease. But he also kept licking the index finger on his right hand and putting it into a small bag tied to his waist.

"Sounds like Mr. bin Laden suffered from Addison's Disease as well," said Dolly. "Those are the classic symptoms. Diabetes, renal disease and Addison's can occur in the same patient."

"Forgive me, Dr. Madison, but I was not aware you are a medical doctor. I thought your doctorate had to do with Oriental languages, in particular, Chinese."

"My parents were missionaries in China before the communist takeover. My mother and I fled to Hong Kong – the New Territories, actually – to Rennie's Mill Mission, a place for refugees from communism. I was trained as a medical assistant. I even delivered a few Chinese babies. We screened and treated thousands of refugees for a variety of diseases. When we found Chinese carrying little bags of salt, we usually found Addison's disease. So, my diagnosis of Addison's Disease fits what I learned at Rennie's Mill Mission."

"You mentioned the ineffectual Dr. Singh," said Buck. "Is he still treating Osama bin Laden?"

"Dr. Singh was a Hindu. We needed a Muslim."

"Was?" asked Buck. "Does your use of the past tense suggest what I'm thinking?"

"Dr. Singh is no longer employed. Dr. Ayman al-Zawahiri is a skilled physician. Whatever medical needs we have are met by Dr. al-Zawahiri."

Changing the subject, Abu Amed said, "Forgive me, Dr. Madison. Would you like something different to drink?"

"Yes, I would like some tea. Thank you."

Calling the waiter over, Mr. Amed ordered, "*Herr Ober*, please bring Dr. Madison some Earl Grey. No sugar. No cream. I assume that is correct."

When the waiter withdrew, Dolly said, "Yes, correct. You know too much about us," said Dolly. "While you are at it, would you like to tell us the names of the moles you have placed inside our government?"

With another smug look, Abu Amed said, "We even know Colonel Madison hails from Oklahoma, plus other details of his early life."

"Are you aware that I'm an honorary member of a Native American tribe?" asked Buck.

"Of that, I'm afraid we are unaware."

"Yes, I'm a renegade Squattopee. It's a matriarchal tribe. We males are supposed to conform to the ways of the women," said Buck. Dolly had to bite her lip and focus on her napkin.

"Obviously, our intelligence is not quite complete. Why are you considered a renegade?"

"I keep standing up."

"Colonel, this must be another one of your stupid Americanisms. But let's just say we have enough intelligence on you to meet our needs. Your being a Squattopee is of no consequence, Colonel Madison. For now, anyway, you are both immune from further attacks. Revenge has its appeal; however, at present, you are both much more valuable to us as the back-channel between our movement and your president. Besides, the two of you have, so far, proven too wily. Too many of my best men have martyred themselves in the effort to kill you."

"And you're running out of virgins?" jabbed Buck. "We didn't mean to cause a shortage."

"Please, Colonel, do not mock my religion. I have not insulted yours."

"No, you have not. I apologize."

"Buck can back off if he wishes; however, as a woman, I am offended by what your society does to its women. They must go around completely covered up, they cannot go to school, cannot have a job outside the home, cannot vote, cannot drive a car, cannot dance, sing, play games or listen to music, and must submit to genital mutilation. If they do get to Islamic Paradise, they must perform as sex slaves for a bunch of terrorists. I'm sorry Mr. Amed, but I don't buy it!"

"My dear Dr. Madison," responded Amed, "you overlook the rewards of motherhood within our society."

"Look," said Buck. "Let's get back to the business at hand. There has to be more to this request by al-Qaeda to use our good offices, as it were, to communicate with our president. Has the world shifted in some way while we've been fending off your assassins and signing books? We haven't had access to Fox News of late, you know."

"Yes. The sands, as you might put it, are shifting with regard to Iran and the Shiites. As you know, Osama bin Laden and I are both Saudis. Our faith is Sunni-Wahhabi. Dr. Ayman al-Zawahiri is Egyptian, he believes in the movement founded by the Egyptian scholar, Sayyid Qutb. Fortunately, our belief systems are closely tied together.

"I might add Sayyid Qutb became radicalized, as you would put it, while attending college in Greeley, Colorado, in the late 1940s. In his book, *The America I Have Seen,* he wrote about how he was disgusted by the co-eds he saw on the Greeley campus. He wrote of Colorado girls showing off their large breasts, their full buttocks, their shapely thighs and sleek legs, and trying to seduce him."

"Living in Colorado," said Dolly, "we are already aware of the ridiculous attempt to say some sexy Colorado co-eds are to blame for Sayyid Qutb's hatred of America. Who knows what was in Qutb's mind? Maybe, he was AC/DC or even impotent. Whatever it was, maybe he hated himself for it and transferred his hatred to America."

Ignoring Dolly's remark, Abu Amed continued, "At Cambridge, I came to admire Lord Palmerston's credo: 'Nations have no permanent friends and no permanent enemies. Only permanent interests.' So, we of al-Qaeda sometimes align ourselves with various Islamic groups; however, our main focus is always the restoration of the Caliphate across the Crescent of Islam. But the first and most necessary step toward our ultimate goal is the destruction of the United States as a world power. Or, at the very least, to reduce the United State to no longer being the world's only superpower."

"But al-Qaeda is not a nation-state like Great Britain or Germany or even Belize, for heaven's sake," said Dolly.

"Technically, you are correct. But I like to think we are acting in the long-term best interest of our Saudi Arabian homeland. As you know, one of our goals is to topple the corrupt and apostate House of Saud and return Saudi Arabia to true Wahhabism."

"In other words, you want to go back in time," said Dolly. "Why do you think your form of Islam commands you to do that? Don't you get tired of waging jihad?"

"Frankly, Dr. Madison, I must confess the Sunni, pan-Arab world and the even the Shia in Iran suffered a deep loss of confidence in 1967, at the end of what you call: the Six-Day War.

"In 1967, as the forces of five Arab armies prepared to attack Israel, we were confident we could present the United States and the other allies of Israel with a *fait accompli*. You encouraged us in that belief.

"The United States and the United Nations stood meekly by when President Nasser expelled the U.N. observer force from the Sinai Desert. The U.S. and the U.N. did nothing when President Nasser closed the Strait of Tiran to Israeli shipping, an act designed to deal a crippling blow to the Israeli maritime economy.

"Under internationally understood rules of war, closing the Strait of Tiran with a 'close-in' blockade was an act of war. Still, the U.S. and the U.N. did nothing. We concluded Allah, be He glorious and exalted, would look with favor on what we were about to do.

"Then, on the eve of an all-out assault on Israel by all of its surrounding Arab nations with, I might add, the exception of Saudi Arabia, General Moshe Dayan did what he did best. He surprised us and the world with a preemptive attack on our airfields. In moments, the Soviet-supplied MiG fighters and fighter-bombers we were going to need to have air superiority over the battlefields to protect the movements of our armored forces into Israel were in flames."

"When you lost any chance of air superiority, why didn't you call off the attack?" asked Buck.

"Unfortunately, our ground forces were already concentrated right on the borders of Israel, some were even across the line. We could not bear the humiliation of pulling them back. Besides, in those days, a portion of Israel was only nine miles wide. Mistakenly, even without air cover, we still thought we could race across those nine miles, cutting Israel in half.

"It was not to be. Somehow, Dayan and his generals were able to move their vastly outnumbered infantry from front-to-front within the borders of Israel. Everywhere we attacked, we were met by surprising numbers of Israeli forces. Within six days, the Israeli Defense Force repulsed all of our attacks. Most of our tanks were in flames. It was the greatest defeat to Arab Islam since we were repulsed at the gates of Vienna in 1529 and, again, in 1683."

"Excuse me, Mr. Amed. I might add to your list the defeat of Muslim naval forces at the Battle of Lepanto in 1571," said Buck.

"Dr. Madison, I do not envy your living with a pedant such as Colonel Madison."

"Well, he did teach history at the university level for awhile. I've learned to live with it."

"At the risk of seeming immodest, Mr. Amed," said Buck, "I must confess to having played a very, very small role in the Six-Day War."

"Come now, Colonel, we happen to know you were serving in Vietnam in June of 1967."

"True. But in the late summer of 1966, General Moshe Dayan came to the 1st Air Calvary Division in Vietnam to learn more about air-mobile operations. At the time, our forward command post was near Pleiku. Back then, I was one of the junior operations officers for the division. One of my duties was to assist with the evening operational briefing for the commanding general and his staff. General Dayan, as you might imagine, was our honored guest – even during our top-secret briefings.

"General Dayan's sharply pointed questions kept us on our toes; however, we came to like him very much. He flattered us by saying he was our student. In all, General Dayan spent about two weeks with us. Well, except for the time when he disappeared."

"Disappeared? How could you let someone who was then the world's most famous general disappear?"

"That's what the Pentagon and the White House wanted to know. In fact, until General Dayan popped back up, our commanding general thought his career was at an end. You see, without telling anyone, General Dayan hopped on a helicopter carrying one of our long-range reconnaissance patrols. The mission of the patrol was to perform surveillance along the river between us and Cambodia. The patrol was instructed to keep its radios turned off unless, of course, it came under attack and needed one of the 1st of the 9th Cavalry's Blue Teams to come to its rescue.

"When we could not find General Dayan, we called all our units, even those ordered to radio silence. But the patrol harboring General Dayan thought it was a NVA trick. The patrol Dayan was with would not answer our radio calls. Some of the patrols responded; however, none of them had seen the missing General Dayan. But one of the Pathfinders on the division helipad did recall seeing General Dayan hanging around looking like he was trying to catch a ride somewhere.

"Then, after a few days, General Dayan flew back to the division helipad. He was all sweaty, grimy, disheveled and grinning from ear-to-ear. But his famous eye patch was firmly in place."

"So, what happened to your commanding general?"

"His two-year tour was almost over, anyway. Shortly after General Dayan reappeared, he left for the States. But he had to be

hospitalized with an ulcer in Hawaii. We always thought that was
due to General Dayan."

"What happened to the patrol?"

"The patrol leader was commended for observing radio silence.
Also, he could not be faulted for allowing General Dayan to accompany his patrol. Sergeants rarely argue such points with general
officers.

"On the eve of his return to Israel, General Dayan gathered us all
together to tell us he expected the Arab armies surrounding Israel
to launch an all-out assault to drive his people into the sea. He figured it would be in the summer of 1967. General Dayan knew his
forces would be vastly out-numbered. His only hope was to learn
airmobile operations as a means of quickly moving the limited
numbers of troops he had within the interior of Israel to where
they were most needed. But he also knew he had to have air superiority over the battlefield in order for those helicopters to survive.

"Less than a year later, the Six-Day War began. Needless to say, we
were pleased with the outcome. We felt we played some small role
in General Dayan's success."

"You realize, Colonel, you are just adding to the many reasons to
have you killed."

"Look, I can't change history. By the way, did you reach any con-
clusions based on the defeat of the Arab armies in 1967?"

"Yes. We concluded that Allah, be He glorious and exalted, con-
trary to our expectations, was not on our side during the Six-Day
War. Otherwise, we would have won. So, we had to ask ourselves
why Allah, be He glorious and exalted, did not allow us to drive
the Jews into the sea?

"Why? Because the Arab nations were apostate. Our leaders had
fallen so far away from the teachings of the Koran and the Hadith

and, especially, the teachings of Muhammad ibn Abdul Wahhab, to the point we no longer enjoyed the favor of Allah, be He glorious and exalted. We concluded our only salvation was to wage jihad in the name of a return to the true path of Islam and, by so doing, we could restore the Caliphate. In other words, we needed to re-incarnate the Islamic theocracies completely across the Crescent of Islam; thereby, restoring the favor of Allah, be He glorious and exalted.

"But our apostate rulers, like the princes of the House of Saud, had the strong support of the United States. We, the stateless jihadists, commanded no regular armies, we had no armored vehicles, no super-sonic fighters or bombers, no submarines, no ships, no cruise missiles. All we had was our faith in Islam and our willingness to die for our beliefs.

"As your vaunted Infantry School has taught for so long, 'Man is the ultimate weapon.' We have lots of men. And, I might add, women. Thanks to Mr. bin Laden and his backers, we have an adequate amount of money which increases each time you Americans fill your cars with gasoline derived from the oil of the Middle East. So, we have the money to buy the explosives we need to blow up every gathering of those who oppose us, and even those Muslims who will not join with us in jihad. To paraphrase your president, those Muslims who are not with us are against us."

"Do you suppose we could take a break so I can go power my nose?" asked Dolly.

"But, of course, how thoughtless of me. Hopefully, you won't take the opportunity to call for my capture."

"It crossed my mind," said Dolly. "But I don't want to spoil our chances of learning about what we hope will be a step toward peace between us."

"You will not be disappointed," said Abu Amed. "Meanwhile, shall I order you some more tea?"

"Thank you, no. That's why I need to visit the powder room."

While Dolly was away, Buck said, "Look, Mr. Amed, I can buy some of your western cultural imperialism line; however, I don't think that is truly at the heart of your particular problem."

"And what would that be, Colonel?"

"Just looking at your background and that of Osama bin Laden, Dr. al-Zawahiri, Sayyid Qtub and others I could name, none of you were born in rags, none of you were burning camel dung for cooking fires. Instead, all of you grew up in relative comfort, some of you in the midst of great wealth and comfort, allowing you to have advanced educational opportunities, even at some of England's most prestigious universities."

"Colonel, why are you boring me with facts of which I am already well aware?"

"Here's why: You and your senior jihadist colleagues are not motivated by love for the downtrodden. Nor are you motivated by your desire to restore the Caliphate across the planet. Your primary motivation is hatred – born of rejection.

"Face it, Mr. Amed, no matter how much money you have, no matter how many advanced degrees from prestigious western universities, no matter how many exclusive London men's clubs to which you are granted membership, no matter how many British or American landmarks you can buy up: You have the feeling of not ever being fully accepted by western Europeans and Americans.

"While Anglo-American oil executives and Anglo-American investment bankers may pat you on the back and tell you that you are a jolly good fellow, you feel, and you may be correct, that you will never, ever, truly be accepted as an equal. That is the basis of the hatred that drives you to dupe the less fortunate in your society to strap on their suicide belts, thinking they are dying for a great cause when, in truth, they are dying as payback for the slights you have endured."

Buck watched as Abu Amed's eyes narrowed and Buck saw flashes of hatred alternating with almost tearful admission of the truth of Buck's ripping the scab off the scars of the countless slights endured by Abu Amed at Cambridge. Obviously, no one had ever spoken to Abu Amed in such a direct manner.

It took a moment for Abu Amed to recover from Buck's verbal onslaught. But then, he said, "You speak much truth, Colonel. Those of us who have operated in western society as you describe have 'suffered the slings and arrows,' as the illustrious Shakespeare would say; however, there is such a thing as objective justice. And, in that regard, you cannot claim the western colonial powers have treated my people as they would wish to be treated. Isn't that what the Prophet Jesus, may His name be praised, calls upon you to do? You accuse me of being a hypocrite. I throw that right back in your face!

"Colonel Madison, our religion teaches us something you have little of and that is: patience. We had to suffer through a Richard Nixon, may his memory be cursed, to get to a Jimmy Carter, may his name be praised, to get a branch of Islam on the Peacock Throne in Iran. In your mind, you had to suffer through a Jimmy Carter, may his name be praised, to get to a Ronald Reagan, may his name be forever cursed!"

✳ ✳ ✳

CHAPTER THIRTY-FOUR

Hotel Adlon

Just as Dolly finished washing her hands, her cell phone rang. The initial warbling tone told her the transmission was going to be secure. She pressed a special button on her cell phone that sent back a warbling tone, confirming a secure electronic handshake.

"Did I catch you at a bad time?" asked Mac Macallan.

"I told you not to call me at the office," said Dolly, keeping her voice low so the restroom attendant could not hear.

"Well, despite all the wine and whisky-drinking, I suppose you are at work. A little birdie tells me you are meeting with Mr. Abu Amed."

"Would the little birdie be our waiter?

"Yes, he's my Joe."

"In other words, you haven't told Langley because you are afraid there's a mole back there."

"Correct."

"How's he being paid?"

"It isn't much. It's out of my pocket."

"You are dedicated to your mission. But we don't want your Joe or you to interfere with our discussion with Mr. Amed."

"Are you in any danger?"

"No, we don't think so. Not as long as Mr. Amed thinks we can be of some use."

"Okay. Keep me posted."

"Wilco," said Dolly, closing the circuit as she headed back toward Buck and Mr. Amed.

As Dolly resumed her seat, a visibly exercised Abu Amed was lecturing Buck. Amed looked like he had a wee bit too much alcohol. The old World War II slogan: "Loose lips sink ships," came to Dolly's mind.

"It is not in the best interest of either Saudi Arabia or Egypt or any of the Arab-Sunni nations for the Shiite Iranians to have hegemony over the Middle East," opined Abu Amed. "While it would, on one level, please us for Iran to eradicate the blasted Jews with nuclear weapons, it is not in the best interest of Saudi Arabia or Egypt for Iran to be so powerful. It is not in the best interest of Sunni/Wahhabism for the Iranian Shiite theocracy to prevail and, perhaps, infect the Islamic peoples who live to the east of Iran with their way of thinking. As you know, far more Muslims live east of Baghdad than live west of Baghdad.

"To his credit, the American president and his neo-con advisers foresaw Iraq as the key piece of terrain in the struggle between Sunni and Shia. Moreover, Iraq is the key piece of terrain between Saudi Arabia and Iran. It would not be in the best interests of Saudi Arabia, or even Egypt, for Iraq to become a satellite state of the Shia mullahs who control Iran. I might add, however, it must be very unsettling for the ordinary citizens of Iran, who are under such strict control by their mullahs, to observe the relative freedom now being enjoyed by their Shia co-religionists in Iraq. I must confess we Sunnis find Iran's internal unrest to our liking."

"Mr. Amed," interrupted Buck, "let's say you are suddenly calling all the shots for Saudi Arabia. How would you handle the Iran-Israeli confrontation over nuclear weapons?"

"It is very simple, my dear Colonel," responded Abu Amed, taking another sip of wine and slurring his words just slightly. "I would make a secret offer to Israel of a secure air corridor across Saudi Arabia for the Israeli fighter-bombers to wipe out Iran's nuclear facilities. That would end Iran's nuclear plans to achieve nuclear hegemony over the Persian Gulf and the Middle East.

"Next, when the Israeli fighter-bombers are on their way back from Iran, I would close the air corridor and use the Saudi Air Force to shoot them all down.

"The Arab nations surrounding Israel would be so enraged over the Jewish attack on Iran that they would launch another Yom Kippur-style attack on Israel. This time, having already shot down Israel's best aircraft, we would have air superiority. This time we would achieve total success, pushing the cursed Jews into the sea. No more Israeli, only Palestine. Saudi Arabia would resume its rightful place as the hegemon of the Persian Gulf and the Middle East."

"Except for one aspect, your plan is sound," said Buck.

"What aspect is that?"

"Rumor has it that the Israelis have a lot of nuclear weapons. They won't be driven into the sea without using them in self-defense."

"Yes, but Israel is a very small geographic area. They could poison themselves and their land by using their nuclear weapons in a confined area such as Palestine."

"Speaking of Palestine," said Buck, "I'm reminded of a story from the Old Testament. You do accept the Old Testament as being the true history of the Jewish people?"

"Of course we do. We also accept the New Testament's Jesus Christ as a true prophet."

"That's good. Anyway, when Joshua led the Jews across the River Jordan into the Promised Land, he got his sandals muddy. He washed them off and set them out to dry. But, when he went to retrieve his sandals, some Palestinians had stolen them."

"Wait. No, Colonel Madison, that could not possibly be true. The Palestinians were not there then."

"Thank you for making my point," Buck said to Abu Amed, who suddenly looked like a deer caught in the headlights of history.

"When we destroy the infidel Jews, you will not feel like mocking me!" retorted Amed.

"Granted, with air superiority, you might prevail; however, I'd be wary of those Israeli nukes," said Buck, deciding to mollify Abu Amed just a tiny bit. "I was commanding an armed cavalry squadron up on the East German border at the time of the Yom-Kippur War. President Nixon stripped U.S. Forces-Europe of virtually all the ammunition we had and rushed it to Israel. The Israeli Premier, Golda Meir, said Richard Nixon was the best friend Israeli ever had."

"Yes, that ugly old witch, may she be damned in hell, decided Nixon was not an anti-Semite after all," said Amed.

"Mr. Amed," said Dolly, interrupting. "We fully understand what you are saying. From your perspective, it makes absolute sense. But this is here and now. Are you prepared to come to the negotiating table? While my husband and I do not have any authority in that area, I would venture to say secret negotiations could occur at a place of your choosing."

"Dr. Madison, apparently unknown to you, secret negotiations have already taken place. Sadly, to no avail."

"If that is so, it took place above our pay level," said Buck. "What were you proposing? What did you hope to achieve?"

"At that time, we were asking the United States to eliminate Muqtada al-Sadr, along with his private Mehdi Army, also Abu Deraa, and all the Shia cells inside Iraq while, at the same time, giving every support to the Sunni forces. Our interests would be served by the re-establishment of a Sunni-dominated government in Iraq."

"You have a lot more folks who speak Arabic and Farsi than we do," said Buck. "The assassination of al-Sadr ought to be easier for you than for us."

"Yes, it would be easier for us to do; however, we cannot afford to have the Iranians trace the death of al-Sadr back to us. It is better for us for you Americans to do it."

"I don't mean to whine," said Dolly. "But it seems everyone wants America to do whatever heavy lifting needs to be done around the world. Don't you suppose we get tired of being everyone's patsy?"

"Yes, we do. But isn't it interesting how your pacification of Iraq turned out to be more difficult than your president thought it would be and how our cowing of the American Left turned out to be easier than we thought it would be."

"But how did you get what I call the Sinistra Media to be so cooperative?"

"Sinistra Media. From my studies at Cambridge," said Amed, "I recall how the Roman forts had a left gate and a right gate. The right or dextra gate was used in the daylight hours for the receipt of supplies and honored guests. The left or sinistra gate was used at night for the passage of spies and other unsavory people. So, sinistra came to mean both left and sinister. I congratulate you, Colonel Madison, on your choice of words.

"Truth be told, your Sinistra Media hate your president more than they love their liberal values which, by the way, are really quite opposite to what we Islamists believe. It's all rather odd. Is it not?"

"Okay," said Buck. "Let me understand all this. Saudi Arabia and Egypt don't want to be seen as killing off the Shia in Iraq for fear

of provoking the Iranians. When, and I say when, not if, the Iranians produce nuclear weapons and mount them on North Korean
missiles that can reach, not just Israeli, but all over Saudi Arabia
and even Cairo, you don't want to be in the position of having
provoked the Iranians to nuke Saudi Arabia and Cairo? Right?
So, once again, it's up to Uncle Sugar to fix things. I suppose you
even want the U.S. and Israel to prevent the Iranians from having
nuclear weapons in the first place?"

"Look," said Abu Amed, "You couldn't stop the North Koreans or
the Pakistanis or the East Indians from having nuclear weapons.
So, why do you think we, in al-Qaeda, can stop the Iranians from
having nuclear weapons?"

"Good point," said Buck. "So, what was the bottom line of the deal
you tried to make in secret?"

"Let me express the deal in American slang: We wanted the U.S.
to throw Israel under the bus. We wanted you to throw the current
governments of Saudi Arabia, Egypt and Jordan under the bus.
We wanted you to withdraw your active support from Israel, Saudi
Arabia and Egypt. We wanted you to sell them no more weapons
systems. We already have control over Syria and Lebanon. So, they
did not figure in our demands.

"In return, we offered a truce. No more attacks by al-Qaeda on
U.S. soil. In addition, we will stop our attacks within Iraq so you
can build a more stable bulwark against the expansion of the Iranian Shia. That will leave us free to restore Saudi Arabia, Egypt and
Jordan to the true faith. In additions, we were offering to cease our
attacks on you as persons. You could live out your remaining years
in safety."

"So, what happened?" asked Buck.

"Your president flatly rejected our proposal. So, we may try to
strike an accord with other powers."

"By others, I suppose you mean the former Soviet Union," said Buck. "But if you think American cultural imperialism is bad, wait until you get into bed with the Russians. Granted, since the collapse of the Soviet Union, they have allowed the Russian Orthodox Church to resume some of its pre-1917 roles. But the Russians will insist on control over your oil production. They will want to reduce how much you pump so they can sell their own much more expensive oil on the open market. Your people are going to be the used Mercedes dealers, instead of driving them.

"The EU isn't going to help you. It can't even get all of its own members to use the Euro. The Europeans couldn't even sort out the mess in the former Yugoslavia without American help. No, Mr. Amed, you are stuck with us."

"Look," said Dolly. "We think you are making a maximum effort against American forces around the world right now. Are you saying you are going to do something even worse than the atrocities of 9/11?"

"We made the mistake of going into those secret negotiations before we demonstrated our ability to bring Europe to its knees. So, yes, we are planning something far more damaging than 9/11. Something the Europeans, the Russians and the United States cannot ignore. Obviously, I will not reveal our plans to you. You would make them known to your precious General McClure and to your president in moments."

"Ah, the old carrot and the stick," said Buck. "Look, we'll transmit your proposal; however, the chances of the president selling out our allies and being less than an honest broker between the various factions inside Iraq are somewhere between slim and none. You may not like his foreign policy, but he is a man of rock-ribbed character."

"That, I grant you," said Amed. "You see, that's all the more reason for our side to negotiate from a newly-demonstrated position of strength."

"Beg your pardon, Mr. Amed," said Buck, "but I really don't see how you are in a position to make an ultimatum. If you think your terrorism is going to convert the world to Islam, you will be disappointed. Hopefully, we have learned the lessons of 9/11 and the lessons of the bombing of the London subway and the trains in Madrid."

"We are the ones who learn lessons, Colonel Madison. When we blew up your Marines and the French paratroopers in Beirut, we learned violence causes Americans to withdraw. When we attacked your troops in Mogadishu, you withdrew your troops. When we blew up your embassies in Kenya and Tanzania, the response of your previous president was to lob some relatively harmless missiles our way. We blew up your naval vessel, the *U.S.S. Cole* and killed 17 of your sailors. Other than repair the *U.S.S. Cole* in Norfolk, Virginia, you did nothing.

"Your public and, especially, the liberals in your Congress, have no stomach for the losses necessary to prevail against us. Colonel Madison, we understand your Sinistra Media better than you do.

"Your Sinistra Media are the handmaidens of the liberal left in your country. They are our Fifth Column in America. You are surrounded in your own country. Therefore, we will prevail.

"The ultimate winner of a struggle is always in a position to dictate the terms of surrender. Just on the basis of demographics, we will, eventually, prevail.

"Colonel Madison, let me suggest your country should employ the services of some really good and unbiased demographers. Let them compare the birth rates of the Scandinavians, Germans, French, Danes, Dutch and Britons with the birth rates of the Muslims already living in those countries. It is only a matter of time when Muslims will use your principle of 'majority rule' against you and come to be the majority in your parliaments or other legislative bodies.

"As long as it is the custom of western civilization to use birth control, to support homosexuality, to support same-sex marriages and to desire small families, then it will only be two more generations before the devotees of Islam will control your governments. So, that is what I mean when I say 'for now.'"

"Mr. Amed," said Buck, "when you say 'prevail' do you think you can turn the calendar back to the 16ʰ Century? Do you think you can restore the Caliphate to the power and territory it had back then?"

"Yes, we do. When we demonstrate, once again, that we are not to be trifled with or ignored and we have gotten your attention, this will be our offer: Tell your president we will accept a negotiated peace that leaves Islam in control of all the lands between Madrid and Baghdad and, of course, includes Palestinian control over Israel."

"I take it that you are counting on us to be your messengers," said Dolly. "So, I assume Buck and I are safe for now. Well, at least long enough for us to get back to the White House to deliver your request for more negotiations. Correct?"

"Yes, you are both safe for now," said Amed. "But if your country does not come back to the negotiating table, either secretly or openly, our little 'hospitality' arrangement is null and void. Be on your guard."

"You do the same, Mr. Amed," said Dolly, draining her cup. "Thanks for the wine and the tea. Enjoy whatever time you have left in Berlin."

"Oh, I plan to do that, Dr. Madison, although others will not."

✫ ✫ ✫

CHAPTER THIRTY-FIVE

Berlin. The Wannsee Mansion

Shortly after noon, a chartered tour bus deposited Senor Cristobal Garcia-Diego and his 30 Muslim brothers in the circular driveway fronting the Wannsee Mansion. When they were assembled in the reception foyer, they were greeted by the curator, *Herr Doktor* Manfred Langsam.

"Welcome to the Wannsee Mansion," said Dr. Langsam, in English. "Please allow me to provide you with a brief tour of our exhibits before escorting you to the conference room itself. I can conduct the tour in English, as I am now, or in German or French. Unfortunately, none of my staff can speak Arabic or Spanish."

Speaking in English for the group and letting the curator know who was in charge, Senor Garcia said, "English will be fine *Herr Doktor*. I was educated at Cambridge. I even lost my Castilian accent. As needed, I can translate for my colleagues. Please, as we are on a tight schedule, let us begin the tour."

During the tour, he made sure his colleagues understood the contributions made to the concept of the Holocaust by the Muslim uncle who had adopted a young Saddam Hussein and who shaped the Iraqi dictator's conceptions of how to run a dictatorship and how to deal with the Jews.

The brief tour completed, Senor Garcia thanked Dr. Langsam for his courtesy. The Muslims for Peace entered the conference room and locked the door behind them. The group took their places around the same long conference table that had once held the notepads of the men who had plotted the demise of the Jewish people of Europe in 1942, the men who had drafted the Wannsee Protocol.

Sitting at the head of the table, Abu Amed began, "Today, my brothers, you have seen with your own eyes how a determined leadership united under their ideology of purification of the

German race organized for the elimination of the filthy Jews. It is a pity the Americans, the British and their allies intervened in the purification process.

"But we shall not fail in our duty to Allah, be He glorious and exalted, or will we fail the writings of the Koran calling for the conversion of all peoples to Islam or their extermination. So, without further ado, I will bring you up-to-date on an item of current interest and on the plan to strike against the infidels here in Berlin."

"First, I will review the status of the Madisons. For now, they may be able to play a useful role by taking a certain proposal to their highers. So, if you have any agents stalking the Madisons, they are to be called off. Besides, we can always kill them later.

"Now, a few administrative details: The chartered bus has been released. We will return to my villa by tour boat. Should you have to use the sanitary facilities, please so indicate by raising your hand. Unlike the Wannsee Protocol, we will not be taking notes of this meeting. Keep all your belongings in this room because, at the end of our conference, we will proceed directly down to the dock for our evening tour of the lake, and then to our villa across the way.

"My brothers, let us start planning the truly important work we must do here in Berlin. I will begin with some historical background on the first of our targets – the Brandenburg Gate. Atop the gate is a statue of an infidel goddess in a chariot being drawn by four horses. Originally, the statue was a symbol of peace; however, the Nazis redesigned it as a symbol of victory. Only now, the victory will be ours.

"As a diversion, a team from this room will destroy the Brandenburg Gate. Then, just as the German authorities and, indeed, the entire German nation and Europe are focused on the destruction of the Brandenburg Gate, another team from this room will use a combination of explosives and poison gas to kill perhaps as many as 20,000 people watching the Berlin Thunder football team play the Amsterdam Admirals in a game of American-style football in the Olympic Stadium.

"Just prior to the Anglo-American invasion of Iraq in March of 2003, we were able to remove, along with Saddam's other weapons of mass destruction, a large quantity of Zyklon-B – the same poison gas used by the Nazis to eradicate the cursed Jews at Auschwitz and the other concentration camps.

"At the Olympic Stadium, fireworks are planned for display during the intermission or half-time activities. Unknown to the German authorities, we will have replaced the canisters that normally produce the colorful fireworks with canisters containing Zyklon-B. When the panicked spectators try to escape the stadium, we will set off explosives to close off all of the exits. A combination of the Zyklon-B and their own trapped panic will cause the deaths of thousands. Their virtually naked and shameless cheerleaders will feel the vengeance of the Law of Sharia. The two attacks here in Berlin will make the events of September 11, 2001, look like the work of amateurs.

"The American Left and its friends in the European and American media will force the American government to opt for peace on our terms. The progress of Islam, stopped by the Europeans at the gates of Tours in 732, and at the gates of Vienna in 1529, will be avenged and reversed. The Crescent of Islam will assert its rightful rule over the entirety of Europe.

"Our people, who have been forced to live in the ghettoes of Europe, will occupy the grand palaces of Europe. Our brothers and sisters who have already infiltrated Europe will rise up, giving the native Europeans the three choices dictated by the Koran: convert to Islam or submit to Islam or die. The pathetic French, who profited from the Oil-for-Food Program by taking bread from the mouths of the Iraqi children, will renounce Catholicism even more than they have already and embrace Islam.

"The Americans will shrink back into a Fortress America mentality. Israel, with no allies left to protect it, will be destroyed. Every last one of the cursed Jews will be driven into the sea. The House of Saud and others who still supply oil to the Americans and other infidel nations will quickly rally to our side and al-Qaeda will join its

Wahhabi brothers in complete domination, not just of the entire Arabian Peninsula, but of the entire oil riches of the Middle East.

"Foolishly, the Americans have neglected to develop their own oil, coal and gas resources. Without the oil of the Middle East, the entire American economy will come crashing down. Mules will be more prized than Mercedes. Plows will be more valuable than Porsches. Those without the means of self-protection, such as fire-arms, will be slaughtered by the criminals their courts have failed to incarcerate or have let loose. The riots of the 1960s will revisit America until all of her vaunted institutions are reduced to smol-dering ruins.

"Now, my brothers, for our planning purposes, we will divide into two teams: One for the Brandenburg Gate and one for the Olympic Stadium. When I am satisfied each team has mastered the details of its mission, we will take a rest from our labors by embarking on an evening cruise around the shores of the Wannsee. Our boat tour completed, we return to my villa to complete our preparations.

"But I want you to take special note of some of the villas dotting the shoreline. Some of them were built prior to and after World War I by wealthy Jews. When the Nazis, may their memory be praised, sent those money-grubbing Jews off to the concentration camps – a fate planned in this very room – some of the leading Nazis appro-priated the villas as their homes. Unfortunately, the heirs of some of the Jewish families have reclaimed the villas and are living in them today. I want you to keep all this in mind to steel your hearts for the destruction we must accomplish in the days to come."

They spent the rest of the afternoon finalizing their plans for the destruction of the Brandenburg Gate and for the deaths of the thousands of spectators expected to watch Berlin Thunder play Amsterdam Admirals in the Olympic Stadium two days hence.

✠ ✠ ✠

CHAPTER THIRTY-SIX

The final voyage of the *Valhalla*

Walter called Buck to say Buck and Dolly should arrive at the Mansion at 1630 hours. They should tell the receptionist that *Herr Doktor* Langsam was expecting them. While a mere half-hour would not do justice to the exhibits, the objective was for Buck and Dolly to have a plausible reason for being in the area. The Muslims for Peace were supposed to vacate the conference room at 1700 hours, and then come down to the dock for their boat tour of the Wannsee.

After a day of shopping and sightseeing, and dressed like typical tourists, they were ready for the museum tour, Buck and Dolly had the doorman put them into a taxi and they headed off for the Wannsee. On arrival at the Wannsee Mansion, everything went exactly as Walter had outlined over the telephone. Buck and Dolly were greeted as *Herr Oberst Doktor* Madison and *Frau Doktor* Madison, a sure sign Walter had done a good PR job on his friend, Dr. Manfred Langsam. [See front view of the Wannsee Mansion at: www.buckanddolly.com]

Dr. Langsam was most gracious, although he was clearly doing Walter a favor by taking his time to squire two Americans around the exhibits he had seen untold times. While Buck and Dolly were being shown around by Dr. Langsam, Walter was pacing up and down the shoreline, casting soulful glances at his beloved *Valhalla*.

Deciding they had a few more moments before they needed to go down to the dock to shore up Walter's resolve, Buck inquired of the curator, "*Herr Doktor* Langsam, do you suppose we could sneak a look into the conference room? We realize it is still being used. But we promised *Herr* Zantner we would wish him farewell before he gets busy with the tour group. After that, we must leave for our flight to America. We would not like to come all the way to the

Wannsee Mansion without having a peek at the infamous conference room. Maybe you have one of those little spy holes?"

"Of course," said Langsam. "In fact, I often look inside the conference room myself just to see if all is well. You know, it was the
former dining room of the Mansion. The waiter had a peep hole
so he could see when it was time for the next course. Come, I will
show you my secret."

With that, Dr. Langsam led them to the conference room's main
door. Quietly, Dr. Langsam pressed gently on an ornate panel.
With the panel open, a fish-eye lens provided a wide-angle view of
the conference room.

"*Bitte, Frau Doktor und Herr Oberst Doktor*," whispered the curator,
stepping away from the door. "Look inside."

Dolly applied her eye to the small opening and then stifled a gasp.
Seated at the conference table was Abu bin Kahlil, the tango whose
passport they had stolen in Barcelona.

"Is something wrong, *Herr Doktor*?"

"Oh, no, "said Dolly, stepping back. "It's just everything inside
looks just so stately, so civilized. I find it hard to believe what took
place in that room in 1942."

"Yes, it is difficult to comprehend. *Herr Oberst Doktor* Madison, it's
your turn."

Just as Buck was putting his eye to the peephole, one of the terrorists Buck had not seen before indicated to Abu Amed his need
to visit the restroom. Granted permission to leave the conference
room, his hulking figure was looming toward the conference room
door.

"Scatter!" whispered Buck, as he hurried away from the door.

Dolly and Dr. Langsam turned on their heels and walked away from the door as did Buck. As the man burst out the door and headed toward the men's room, all three of them pretended to be looking at some of the grisly black and white photos displayed on the walls.

After the man was inside the men's room, Dolly said, "Forgive us, Dr. Langsam, we should not have been trying to intrude on that meeting in there. Perhaps we can look in on the conference room some other time."

"Yes, of course," said Dr. Langsam. "We were just not quick enough."

Not wanting to be caught out in the corridor, Buck quickly added, "Dr. Langsam, we cannot thank you enough for taking your valuable time to give us an unscheduled tour of the Mansion and the secret peek into the conference room. We are in your debt more than you know. Is there a quick way out toward the lake? We'd like to join *Herr* Zantner before he is inundated at 1700 hours by the people in the conference room.

"Yes, indeed, *Herr Oberst Doktor.* I'll just let you out this set of French doors. I need to walk with you just a bit to show you the break in the hedge which, I might add, is quite formidable." [See lake view of the Wannsee Mansion at: www.buckanddolly.com.]

After Dr. Langsam led them to the break in the hedge, he said, "Simply walk straight down to the lake. It is getting dark now, so please watch your step. As you can see, the lights of the villas around the lake are starting to rim the shore line."

After Buck shook the hand of Dr. Langsam and Dolly's hand was kissed, Buck and Dolly made their way down the path leading to the shoreline and Walter's kiosk.

"Is everything okay?" asked Walter.

"Everything is as we planned," said Buck. "Just make sure you tell the rag heads that life jackets are not required."

"Good thinking, Buck. In fact, I'm a step ahead. I've already put the passengers' life jackets down below."

"Terrific. Even though I see signs in English, French and German saying smoking is *verboten,* do not warn the terrorists against smoking. Given their reduced lifespan, I don't think they'll be in danger of cancer. Mr. Amed is fluent in English. But the others may only speak Arabic. Give your tour spiel in English. Amed will probably translate into Arabic. Keep him busy. Maybe he won't think about life jackets.

"Then, when you get them out in the middle of the lake, carry out your plan. Send them all to enjoy those 72 virgins earlier than they had planned. Can you do that, Walter?"

"Of course, Buck. If you say they deserve to die, then they deserve to die. But all those lives. You are asking me to do something terrible."

"Okay," said Buck. "Let me put it this way: Those terrorists sitting inside the conference room right now are some of the same terrorists who plotted the destruction of the Twin Towers in New York City, the attack on the Pentagon and, if some brave souls on a fourth airliner had not died trying to stop them, the 9/11 terrorist would hit the White House or the U.S. Capitol.

"But they also ruined your business here as well. Their terrorism is one of the reasons why Gentile and Jew alike are avoiding your boat for fear of being blown to bits. God knows what they have been plotting all afternoon up there in the Wannsee Mansion."

"Buck, I know what they have done in the past."

"Walter, think about what these terrorist will do in the future. You have the opportunity to save many, many more lives than will be lost out on the water tonight."

"Okay, okay, I'll go through with it. When my lovely *Valhalla* is in the middle of the lake, I'll dash below and unscrew the cap on the fuel drain hose. Since I just pumped the bilge completely dry of water, I know exactly the level of fluid needed before the bilge pump activates and causes a spark. I'll be over the stern just before it happens. Saving the lives of untold innocent women and children will be my guide and my comfort."

"And so it will," said Buck, as he detected some movement up by the Wannsee Mansion. Led by Abu Amed, 30 jihadists were strolling down the path leading toward the *Valhalla*.

Dolly gave Walter a big hug. Buck shook his hand and said. "We've got to go before Amed sees us. But don't worry, Walter. Even before we see the blast, we'll be back here at the kiosk, ready to call the lake patrol and the *politzei*. And, if the patrol isn't quick enough, I'll swim out and get you."

With their backs to the Wannsee Mansion and the advancing group of jihadists, Buck and Dolly walked hand-in-hand along the shoreline, two lovers out for an evening stroll.

As he neared the dock, Abu Amed took notice of the couple walking away along the water's edge. Even in the gathering darkness, something about the tall man's bearing seemed familiar. The woman seemed familiar as well. But his thoughts were interrupted when the captain of the *Valhalla* rushed up to greet him and asking if he spoke English. Flattered by the attention, Abu Amed explained about his Cambridge education and how he was, indeed, the person in charge.

By the time Buck and Dolly were 300 meters from Walter's kiosk, Walter had all of the jihadists on board and the *Valhalla* was headed toward…well, *Valhalla*. When the boat was so far away across the lake they could not be recognized, Buck and Dolly reversed course and made their way back toward the kiosk. On arrival, Buck hunted around for a rock large enough to shatter the glass cover on the emergency call box. Finding a suitable rock, Buck held the rock in readiness.

Sound travels well across calm waters. They could easily hear Walter using the boat's public address system to draw the attention of the Muslims for Peace to the villas which had, at one time, been occupied by various bigwigs of the Nazi regime. Walter turned the darkness to advantage by explaining how the lights beginning to appear along the shore made the lake even more beautiful than in the full daylight of summer. He started to explain some of the homes were already decorated with Christmas lights, then thought better of it.

Some years earlier, Abu Amed visited the Wannsee during a break from his studies at Cambridge. Much of what the captain was saying was old hat to him. Growing bored, he looked around the boat. Because he could not swim and he was becoming uncomfortable on a strange boat without wearing a life preserver, he moved toward the bow where he saw a box painted in international orange. The box was labeled: "*Schwimmguertel.*" Abu Amed sat down on the box. Resting on a box of "swim belts" made him feel much safer.

Sensing Abu Amed would probably remain close to the box of life preservers; Walter exited the wheel house and went down the ladder into the bilge. Using the wrench, he unscrewed the cap on fuel hose. Raw gasoline gushed down into the bilge pump recess. In moments, the pool of gasoline forming under the base of the bilge pump would raise the float high enough to trigger the electric motor and make the spark Walter was counting on.

Quickly, Walter closed the hatch over the bilge and climbed up out of the engine compartment. He made his way around the little table at the stern. Walter opened the compartment containing his automatic personal floatation device.

Just as Walter was donning his PFD, Abu Amed noticed the boat's captain had ceased his little monologue. Abu Amed got up off the *Schwimmguertel* box and turned around. He saw the boat's captain was no longer in the wheel house. Scanning the deck, Amed saw the captain standing at the very stern of the boat, putting on a strange-looking type of life vest.

Amed stared at the *Valhalla's* captain who stared right back. Amed watched as the captain climbed up on top of the stern rail. Amed started to shout for someone to stop the captain, but realized he was too late when the captain raised his one fist toward Amed with the forefinger and little finger of his hand extended, making the hex sign so abhorred throughout the Middle East.

Shoving his startled colleagues left and right to get out of his way, Abu Amed pushed his way toward the stern, but he was too far away and too late to stop the boat's captain. He watched in horror as the captain hurriedly launched himself backward off the stern. By the time Amed reached the stern, the captain was swimming away from the *Valhalla* just as fast as he could. Abu Amed climbed up on the stern rail and was about to jump when the *Valhalla* was blown to bits.

If Buck and Dolly had not been standing behind the kiosk, they would have been knocked off their feet. The blast was so strong they had to support the kiosk to keep it from toppling over on top of them. In moments, a mini-tsunami was rolling outward from the epicenter of the explosion. When it reached the shoreline, it swamped the *Valhalla's* dock and flooded the base of the kiosk. Then, bits and pieces of the *Valhalla* and the Muslims for Peace began to rain down on the lake and the surrounding shoreline. The rain of debris forced Buck and Dolly to take shelter under the eaves of the kiosk.

Dolly screamed when someone's hand landed on her side of the kiosk. Buck almost vomited when a severed head landed next to his feet. For a moment, the head spun like a top. When it stopped spinning, gravity gripped it and the head rolled down into the roiling waters where it bobbed up and down with each wave of surf. One eye was still open. It seemed to be staring up at them, accusingly.

Buck used the rock in his hand to smash the glass case marked *Dringendes Gespraech* so he could extract the telephone. Immediately, Buck's call was answered by the lake patrol. In German, Buck gave the patrolman who answered a description of the horrible, burning scene out on the water. To add an ironic point, Buck called it a Holocaust. With Teutonic efficiency, it was only a few moments before a patrol boat was speeding toward the scene of the disaster. Even though the boat had a powerful spotlight to counter the darkness, the spotlight could only identify some bits of flotsam and jetsam floating here and there.

Buck and Dolly could hear Walter shouting at the patrol boat. As the spotlight illuminated Walter, Buck and Dolly could hear Walter calling out: *"Ich bin okay! Helf den anderen!"*

Despite the horror unfolding before their eyes, it was all Buck and Dolly could do to keep from laughing at Walter's shout to help the others. Soon, two more rescue boats arrived on the scene. They continued to search the waters while the first boat, carrying a half-drowned Walter, headed for Walter's dock. Apparently, Walter may have been the only survivor.

Shortly after the patrol boat deposited Walter on his dock, the *Kriminalepolitzei* (KRIPO) burst a patrol car through the opening in the hedge and raced right down to the shoreline. Dr. Langsam ran along behind the police, wringing his hands, upset about the damage to the hedge and to his lawn.

The KRIPO required the water-soaked Walter to fill out an accident report. As the only other eye-witnesses, Buck and Dolly were directed to write a brief report on what they had seen. The KRIPO said English would do. A medical team arrived. Walter was examined and, other than some nicks on his head and face from falling debris, and being soaking wet and chilled, he was found to be relatively unhurt. Their reports completed, Walter asked if his American friends could take him immediately to his flat so his wife would not be worried about his safety.

The police were reluctant until Dr. Langsam stepped forward to vouch for Walter and his friends as people who could be trusted. Reluctantly, the police agreed on the condition Walter and the

Madisons would come to their offices first thing the next day for more questioning. With fingers crossed, they readily agreed.

Buck and Dolly put their arms around Walter and walked him back up to the Wannsee Mansion. Poor Walter was carrying his life jacket, now deflated, but still bearing the name: *Valhalla*. Walter began to sob. But Buck and Dolly knew it was not a lament for the terrorists. Walter's lament was for the *Valhalla*.

At Dolly's request, Dr. Langsam called a taxi for them. While they were waiting for their taxi, Dr. Langsam graciously invited Walter to use his telephone to call anyone he wished.

Walter used the phone in Dr. Langsam's office to call Anna at her relatives place in Fulda to let her know of the "accident." Anna said she would watch for news of the accident on TV. Buck and Dolly couldn't tell if Anna was in on the plot to "sell" the *Valhalla* to the insurance company or not.

With Anna away and his noisy neighbors sure to descend on him once news of his accident appeared on TV, Walter said he didn't want to go to his flat. Buck and Dolly didn't think it would be wise to take the disheveled and still dripping Walter into the Hotel Adlon. Because Walter had, at one time, worked for the Agency, the three took a taxi to a street corner a few blocks from the address Mac Macallan told Buck to memorize.

✷ ✷ ✷

CHAPTER THIRTY-SEVEN

Berlin, Safe House

The safe house was located inconspicuously near the *Kurfeursten-damm* in the middle of a block of flats reminiscent of New York City brownstones. Waiting until the street was deserted, the three walked up the steps leading to the street number provided by Macallan. Buck rang the door bell which was answered by a matronly *Hausfrau*. "*Guten Tag. Was wollen Sie hier? Wir brauchen kein Verkaeufer.*"

"*Wir werden ins haus gehen,*" said Buck, (continuing in German). Please consult your access list for a Colonel and a Doctor Madison; however, our friend here, Herr Walter Zantner, may not be on the list. Herr Zantner has just been injured in a terrible explosion. He will need some minor first aid and to be debriefed by Herr Macallan. Please remind Herr Macallan that Herr Zantner and he were, at one time, colleagues. Thank you."

"*Moment mal,*" she said, closing the door in their faces while she, no doubt, phoned for instructions with regard to Walter. After a few moments, she reopened the door, announced her name was Helga and bade them all to enter. She said Herr Macallan would join them shortly. Helga showed them the location of the bar and told them to help themselves while she prepared some wet towels to clean the face of Herr Zantner and do whatever else was needed to make him comfortable. Helga said she remembered Herr Zantner from the old days. After the initial grime had been removed, Helga pointed Walter toward a bathroom where he could take a shower. She had laid out some dry clothing she hoped would fit.

Buck found a nice Merlot for Dolly. Apparently, the safe house was still being used to debrief some fairly high-level defectors or detainees. If this was one of the "secret prisons" so offensive to the American Left and their friends in the media, then the Agency's "rendition" program was treating the detainees rather well. Even better than Club Gitmo. The whisky section of the bar was stocked with Glenfiddich, Bowmore, Talisker, Macallan, Laphroaig and Famous Grouse. Buck decided on a very large portion of Laphroaig and one drop of spring water.

They were just ready for a second round when Walter returned from the bath, wearing some fairly presentable street clothes. Then, just as Buck handed Walter a Warsteiner, Mac Macallan came up from the basement. Mac gave no explanation as to how and why he entered that way; however, it obviously had something to do with counter-surveillance.

Mac headed for the bar and poured himself a double shot of, what else, the Macallan single-malt. As Helga applied some soothing ointment to Walter's debris-scratched face, Mac said, "I just heard from our **KRIPO** contacts about the explosion on board the *Valhalla*. Well, Walter, you gave us all quite a scare. You haven't put yourself in that much danger since the old days and the tunnel you helped the Agency dig into East Berlin back in 1953."

"Jolly close that," said Walter in the posh accent he had perfected many years ago in England as a British P.O.W. "If it weren't for the KGB mole, George Blake, we might have tapped their phones right 'till the Wall came tumbling down'

"But while I hated to lose my boat," said Walter, with a wink only Buck could see, "those bloody WOGs deserved to drown. If they do reach Paradise, I hope all of them 72 virgins have the French Disease."

"Interesting thought," said Buck. "I wonder if the Islamic Paradise permits Wasserman tests. If Wasserman was Jewish, then I doubt it."

Ignoring Buck, Mac said, "Just in case you were wondering, the German Chapter of CAIR was being led by Mr. Abu Amed himself. Tomorrow, our liaison with the **KRIPO** will be pressing for positive IDs; however, I'm told the folks who were the last people to sail on the *Valhalla* are missing so many body parts the KRIPO may never know their identities."

"How about DNA?" asked Dolly.

"The political correctness crowd over here in the E.U. isn't keen on advance DNA data collection. But E.U. passports seem to come in everyone's cornflakes. So, we do have some passport fragments to work with."

"Let's hope the KRIPO does whatever it can," said Dolly. "Can you put poor Walter here up for the night and can you tell us how we are going to get back to the land of the round door knobs?"

"Indeed. Walter is welcome to stay here tonight. In fact, all three of you are staying here tonight. My case officers have already checked you out of your hotel. They are bringing your belongings here. Walter, old boy, please forget about ever being here."

Walter, pouring some schnapps to chase with his beer, nodded his assent.

"Now, I have someone to bring up from the basement. Someone, who should be a great deal of help to you tomorrow when you leave for Washington-Dulles International Airport. Turning on his heel, Macallan went to the door to the basement and beckoned someone to come upstairs.

"Dr. Madison, Colonel Madison, Herr Zantner, allow me to introduce Heidi Schnell. She and Helga already know each other because Heidi is another one of our assets. Heidi is retiring to Florida where she can continue to work on her gorgeous tan."

After everyone had shaken hands – the German custom never broken unless the government decrees a flu epidemic so bad as to forbid the practice – Macallan gave Heidi a generous portion of whisky. "For a number of years Heidi has worked as a flight attendant for LuftCondor. She speaks several languages quite well, to include Arabic."

"Yes, when I was a young, they called us stewardesses or *hôtesse de l'air* back then," offered Heidi, "I foolishly married a Saudi Prince and lived for a time in a fabulous palace in Saudi Arabia. But then, after he decided to divorce me for an even younger woman, I was able to escape captivity and resume my career with LuftCondor."

"Well," said Dolly, "I find it difficult to believe any man could find anyone more attractive than a tall, blue-eyed blond such as you."

"Actually, it had to do with a mistake I made in redecorating our bedroom in the palace. The Saudi Prince wanted a canopy bed with a mirrored ceiling. I wasn't careful about where I got the mirror and it had some printing on it that said: 'objects in mirror may appear larger than they are.' He thought I was making fun of his… well, you know. So, after the divorce, I decided to go back to being a virgin."

"As you can see," said Macallan, "Heidi has a wicked sense of humor and some of her self-deprecating stories may be a bit, ah, apocryphal. But I dare say Heidi has been invaluable to us by letting us know who is going where on LuftCondor; especially, in the Middle East and Africa.

"While you can see her blue-eyed, blond beauty has not faded, Luft-Condor retirement rules are rather strict. So, we have arranged for her to begin a new life in the USA by serving as the head flight attendant on the charter flight you two are taking tomorrow to Dulles. It departs Berlin Schoenfeld International Airport at 1400 hours local time."

"Wait a minute," said Buck. "As much as Dolly and I would enjoy flying with Heidi, we were expecting to fly first class on a Lufthansa 747 direct from Berlin to Washington. I was planning on free champagne and caviar followed by a long nap."

"Yes, that was the plan; however, you and Dolly won't be using the first-class seats I reserved for you on Lufthansa. Two of my case officers, a married couple, will be flying in your place. A few hours ago, I received orders from General McClure and from Langley saying you and Dolly are to be put aboard a special charter flight from Berlin-Schoenfeld to Washington-Dulles. Now, let me explain the charter flight you'll be on.

"The German Marshall Fund was formed in 1972 at the suggestion of former German Chancellor, Willy Brand. The idea came with a gift of over 150 million Deutsch Marks from the people of West Germany. In 1986, the Germans raised the fund's endowment to 245 million Deutsch Marks. More than just a thank-you for America's post-World War II generosity to re-build a devastated Germany, the Fund has played a key role in promoting German-U.S. understanding and cooperation. Today, the Fund has offices in Berlin, Belgrade, Bratislava, Brussels and Paris.

"Each year, some of the more affluent members of the German Marshall Plan Society journey to D.C. where they say *Danke Schoen* to America for the Marshall Plan. Our government, in turn, hosts them at a black-tie dinner in the White House with the president and the first lady. The next day, the charter aircraft will drop them off for some fun at Disney World. That's where Heidi gets off as well, and remains. From Orlando, the Society members return to Germany via Lufthansa.

"The reason they return to Germany on Lufthansa is because their LuftCondor charter aircraft is an old Boeing 727 headed for the aircraft bone yard near Tucson. As you probably know, the venerable 727 has three, jet-fuel guzzling engines and, without expensive modification, is too noisy for American skies.

"Because of the 727's limited range of only about 2,500 miles, you will fly from Berlin to Shannon, Ireland, to refuel. Your next stop is Gander, Newfoundland, to refuel again. From Gander, you fly direct to Washington-Dulles.

"As you may know, the 727 has both a forward entry door and a set of hydraulically operated, integral aft stairs in the tail cone or ventral area. The aft stairs make the 727 popular in developing countries because expensive jet ways are not needed for boarding or deplaning. Also, the 727 has an internal auxiliary-power unit, so it can start its engines without help from a ground unit. So, it works well in the developing countries where ground support is scarce or even non-existent.

"Tomorrow, all passengers will board via the ventral air stair. There is no first-class compartment. It is all one-class seating. Counting the two of you, the aircraft will be almost fully loaded.

"Buck and Dolly, you will wait in a private room we have arranged for you until the other passengers are on board. You will not be subjected to the usual security screening. Thanks to Heidi here, you will have the luxury of three seats. That's the good news. The bad news is your three seats are next to the aft galley and not far from the two aft lavatories."

"Oh, great," said Buck. "We'll be up all night while beer-swilling Germans troop back and forth to the lavatories. Sorry, Walter. No offense intended."

"Quite all right, old chap," said Walter, as Macallan handed Walter another beer.

"As I said, Buck, I wanted to send the two of you home in more comfortable circumstances; however, I have been overruled by Langley and by General McClure. Because you and Dolly spent the last few weeks causing havoc among al-Qaeda's operatives, I can only suspect the Agency does not think it prudent to put the two of you on board a packed 747 that could turn into another Lockerbie massacre."

"So, why aren't the members of the German Marshall Plan Society in danger?" asked Dolly.

"Apparently, General McClure thinks the terrorists will figure the increasingly famous or, should I say 'infamous,' Madisons will insist on first-class travel on a jumbo jet. By putting you on the unscheduled LuftCondor charter, I can only assume General McClure thinks all involved will be safer."

"But Abu Amed says we arc King's X for now," said Dolly.

"You know the Koran authorizes Muslims to lie to infidels. If you choose to believe a cold-bloodied killer, be my guest; however, I have my orders."

"Okay, but what if the Islamists make a mistake and blow up the regularly-scheduled Lufthansa flight, to include your two case officers?" asked Buck.

"Working for the Agency can be risky at times. Anyway, with regard to the two of you, the Agency's hands will be clean. Won't they?"

"John Le Carre could not have said it better," said Buck.

"Any questions, so far?" asked Mac.

"Yes," said Buck. "What about our personal weapons?"

"Good point. We don't expect trouble on the LuftCondor charter; however, we have done a few background checks on your fellow passengers and on the crew here in Berlin. So far, they all check out.

"As for your 'kit,' as our British cousins like to say, I have, at considerable trouble I might add, rounded up a fresh supply of the items you, ah, seasoned operatives seem to require. I was able to locate some inflatable pillows, ear plugs, extra hearing-aid batteries and extra reading glasses for Buck, replacement cell phones batteries, a package of large-size cable ties (apparently, one of your hobbies is arresting people), insect repellant, anti-diarrhea pills, handi-wipes, laxatives, iodine tablets – all the stuff on a long list I just got from General McClure."

"The cable ties are for kinky sex," said Dolly.

"Right," said Macallan, ignoring her. "Anyway, a shoulder bag and a briefcase filled with this 'stuff' will be given to you in your waiting room. I have good news and bad news about your handguns. The good news is: you can carry your handguns on the LuftCondor charter. The bad news is: someone at Langley is uncomfortable with the mayhem attending your every move. Apparently, head-quarters doesn't want you blowing bullet holes in the aircraft's pressure vessel. So, unless absolutely necessary, do not fire your handguns while you are in the air."

"Hold it," said Buck. "If there is trouble between Berlin and D.C., what are we supposed to use?"

"On my own initiative, I was able to procure a blackjack for each of you. That's another reason you are not going through the normal passenger security screening. Also, I would prefer you make no mention of the blackjacks to anyone – especially, back in Langley."

"You have our word. But do you mean 'blackjack' or 'sap'?" asked Buck. "Given a choice we would like flat saps, preferably made by Bucheimer or Bianchi."

"Actually, you will find flat saps, not blackjacks, in your briefcases tomorrow. Unfortunately, Bucheimer went out of business and Bianchi no longer makes them."

"So, what's the brand of the flat saps you found for us?" asked Dolly.

"*Gestapo.*"

"Oh, great," said Dolly." Hopefully, the leather covers aren't embossed with *Arbeit Macht Frei.*"

"Good point," said Buck. "One more thing. What do we tell the other passengers? That we bought our charter tickets from Berlin to Washington on eBay?"

"Buck's right," said Dolly. "During those two refueling stops, we are sure to be drawn into conversations. So, what's our cover legend?"

"Use your real names," said Mac. "Here's your legend: You are writers and scholars who have been doing research for a book on the history of the Marshall Plan. Dolly, tell them your publisher wants you to accompany them on their flight to Dulles. Once you are in the USA, you will be interviewing some of them so you will have some fresh quotes for your book. Okay?"

"Sounds plausible to me," said Dolly. "But shouldn't we do some reading on the Marshall Plan?"

"Indeed, you shall. Upstairs, in your bedroom, you will find some brief, but comprehensive, materials on the Marshall Plan, it origins and its impact on the post-World War II economic recovery of Europe.

"Walter, try to get over the loss of your boat. Buck and Dolly, the next time you will see Heidi is when she is waiting for you at that 727's rear stairs. She will show you to your seats.

"Oh, by the way, in the cargo bay, will be a plain, U.S. government-issued casket. Unfortunately, it has been used quite often. It contains the remains of an intelligence officer who rendered enormously useful service to our government before he died, apparently of natural causes. After the Wall fell, some kindly former East Germans told us where he was buried. Using old dental records we were able to identify the remains of this particular officer.

"But only a handful of people know who he was and what he did. I am told Langley has been in contact with the slain officer's superannuated sisters and they will be present at a private memorial service inside the rotunda at Agency headquarters. I am also told the sisters wish to remain anonymous and will be heavily veiled.

The small handful of senior people in attendance will think the veils are only because of their grief. But the veils are to disguise the identity of the sisters. Apparently, some secrets will be kept forever.

"But, as you know, the Agency's heroes and heroines are remembered by the embedding of an anonymous star in the wall of the rotunda. Prior to the service, a very senior person will escort the two sisters and show them the latest star.

"As you may have gathered," continued Macallan, while pouring himself and Heidi more whisky, "the Agency went through some difficult times under the Trimmer Administration, leading to our failure and that of the FBI to detect and prevent the events of 9/11.

"When Trimmer's cockamamie attorney general and her deputy built a wall preventing the FBI's intelligence division from sharing leads with its criminal division and with the CIA, the 9/11 screw-up was virtually inevitable. So, 9/11 wasn't so much a failure to collect the information as it was a failure to connect the dots and produce actionable intelligence.

"Back in the days when you two and Walter were active, it was a lot easier to conduct penetration operations and to gather some very useful intelligence. Trimmer's second pick for DCI issued orders designed to keep us from recruiting foreign nationals whom the PC crowd deemed 'unsavory,' or had criminal records or were guilty of any kind of human-rights violations.

"Somehow, he failed to understand the kind of person we might induce to betray his or her country and provide us with intelligence is not likely to be the local altar boy or the soldier-of-the-month. Not only did we lose eight years of opportunity to recruit human intelligence operatives, we lost the ability to work with the usual hired assets such as: counterfeiters, forgers and cat burglars. Surreptitious entry became a thing of the past."

Batting her long lashes and doing a breathless Marilyn Monroe impression, Heidi said, "Even seduction was forbidden. Those bloody restrictions cost me a lot of expensive, candlelight dinners."

"She never tried to seduce me," complained Walter.

"That's because you were before her time. Also, you were on our side," said Macallan.

"I knew I should have defected," said Walter, downing more schnapps.

"Stop it, Heidi, Walter," said Macallan. "Our visitors will get the wrong impression. Besides, it's time Heidi and I must be going. Tomorrow, she has to see you safely to Washington-Dulles. I have to go back to the embassy and see what our KRIPO contacts have learned about the sinking of the *Valhalla*. The only name Dr. Langsam can remember is: Christobal Garcia-Diego. As for the German chapter of CAIR, Langsam was never given a by-name list of attendees. So, other than a body count of about 30, it is not likely we will know much more.

"Okay, that's it for now. Any more questions?" asked Mac, starting to help Heidi with her coat.

"Yes, what's the in-flight movie?" asked Buck.

Ignoring Buck, Mac said, "All right then. Come along Heidi, I'm sure these folks want to visit with Walter. After tomorrow, they may not see Walter for quite some time. Walter needs to be filing an insurance claim tomorrow. Also, Buck and Dolly have some reading to do."

"But wait," said Buck. "Can you tell us something about the agent whose remains we will be escorting?"

"Very well," said Macallan, with a nod to Heidi to take off her coat and prepare another round of drinks.

☆ ☆ ☆

CHAPTER THIRTY-EIGHT

Augie

"The agent's cryptonym was 'Augie,'" said Macallan. "In fact, I have Augie's file right here, although it's been heavily redacted. Even so, it tells an amazing story of unselfish service to our nation. In short, he was a hero. So much so, his quiet exploits have been made part of the instruction materials at the Farm.

"He lived in East Berlin from approximately 1945 until his death in 1990. He never came out, not once. And, except for Walter here, who sometimes serviced his dead drops, and a handful of folks at Langley, no one knew anything about him.

"Actually, I didn't have much to do," said Walter. "My job was to avoid surveillance and service the three different dead drops Augie set up for us."

"Was Augie a computer-generated cryptonym or was it his own invention?" asked Buck.

"The cryptonym was Augie's invention," said Macallan "He saw himself cleaning out the Augean Stables of the godless communists in East Berlin."

"Unless he could divert an entire river to do it," said Dolly, "it sounds like a pretty menial task."

"Menial," said Macallan. "That's the right word for Augie and his operation. For almost the entire time he was our best covert asset in East Berlin. He worked as a janitor in the headquarters of the East German Intelligence Service or EGIS, later known to the West as Stasi. On occasion, he would be detailed to work as a bus boy when Stasi officials would hold a dinner to entertain visiting KGB or GRU mandarins from Moscow. He helped us ID some of their top people. To put names to faces and vice versa.

"Augie would swipe a glass or a small plate from those dinners, take them back to his flat and dust them for fingerprints. He would lift off the fingerprints and make an ink image of them and do close-ups of the prints with his camera."

"My job," added Walter, "was to pick up the Minox cassettes and bring them back to Berlin Station."

"Just fingerprints?" asked Dolly.

"More than that. Once Augie got his janitor's job at Stasi head-quarters, he had access to the trash containers. Or, dust bins, as the Brits would say. After awhile, he was trusted to take the burn-bags of highly classified documents to the incinerator. Augie kept a sub-miniature camera, a Minox, hidden near his work-place. Depending on the circumstances, he could, sometimes, photograph pages of documents before they made it to the incinerator.

"In the later years, when the Stasi was equipped with document shredders, his production slowed down. But he had a photo-graphic memory. If he got to read a document lying unattended on a desk, he would memorize it. When he got back to his little flat, he would write out what he had read in long hand and then photograph what he had written with the other Minox he kept near his flat."

"My gosh," said Dolly, "how on earth did the Agency get someone with Augie's talents to work at being a janitor and living in a hovel, as you call it, for all those years?"

"Augie, like you, Dolly," said Macallan "was the child of Christian missionaries. In fact, he went to college to prepare himself for the ministry. At the University of Oklahoma, he was a Letters Major – meaning he studied the classics. He was a member of the elite Pe-et Senior Honor Society. He studied Greek, Latin, Hebrew and Philosophy. This was in the late 1930s. While he was at university, his parents were sent to China.

"Because he wanted to read the German philosophers in the original, he also learned German."

"I can't believe he worked all those years as a janitor," said Buck.

"Wait," said Macallan, "the story gets even more amazing. At university, Augie also made Phi Beta Kappa and was selected as a Rhodes Scholar. In 1939, he was just finishing up at Oxford when Hitler invaded Poland. As Britain mobilized for war, Augie wanted to do something to help; however, he was a pacifist at heart. He read everything St. Augustine and Thomas Aquinas wrote about the Doctrine of the Just War. Still, he could not bear the thought of shooting someone.

"While at Oxford, he fell in love with a Scottish girl from a family possessing one of those hereditary titles. For his gallant service in World War I, her father was elevated to the peerage and given the title: Lord Stirlingbridge. So, she was the Lady Stephanie Stirlingbridge. But she didn't like formality. She just wanted to be called by her Christian name.

"Here's her photograph," said Macallan, passing it around. "As you can see, she was lovely, a cross between Deborah Kerr and Greer Garson. Even though the photograph is in black and white, you can tell she had that lovely peaches and cream complexion along with the reddish- blond hair that caused the French to think of the British Isles as the Land of the Angels or *Angleterre*. Note her wonderful smile. For a Scottish or English woman of the time, she had remarkably good teeth.

"She and Augie were very much in love. His scholarship so impressed the Oxford faculty he was going to be asked to stay on to do research and to teach. They were planning a wonderful postwar life together.

"To do her patriotic duty, she volunteered to be in the Auxiliary Territorial Services, the ATS. At no pay, I might add. Because of her upper-class status, she was assigned as sedan driver for the top British and American military brass. Princess Elizabeth and Churchill's daughter, Mary, also served in the ATS. So, it was definitely the proper thing to do.

"As Lady Stephanie drove, she would sometimes overhear the generals talking about the atrocities being committed by the Nazis and by the Red Army. Those stories she shared with Augie. About that time, Augie got word his parents had been captured by the Japanese in China and executed."

"That's what happened to my father," said Dolly. "Only he was beheaded by the Red Chinese, with his entire congregation watching. Then, just for being Christians, they were all shot. Now it is the Muslims who are persecuting the Christians and, as usual, the Jews."

"I'm so sorry, Dolly. So, I know you, of all people, can understand Augie's motivation. The death of his parents, plus the urgings of Lady Stephanie, made Augie decide to put aside his pacifist leanings. Through her father, Lord Stirlingbridge, Augie was introduced to Colonel William Donovan who, because of Augie's German and French, got Augie commissioned as one of the first junior officers in the brand-new Office of Strategic Services, the OSS.

"Eventually, Augie took parachute training and was assigned to lead one of the Jedburgh Teams. Just prior to D-Day, Augie kissed Lady Stephanie goodbye and his team parachuted into occupied France to help the French resistance disrupt the Nazi's lines of communications.

"When the Jedburgh mission was over, Augie was detailed to move forward with General George Patton's Third U.S. Army as it advanced across France and into Germany. The unit he was with had just breached the Rhine when Augie got the news that a German V-2 rocket hit the staff car she was driving. Lady Stephanie and the senior officers with her were obliterated.

"Even though Augie and Stephanie were not married as yet, Colonel Donovan arranged a special leave for Augie to go back to

Scotland for her funeral. If Augie had been dedicated before, he was demonic when he returned to his duties in Europe.

"When the Russians reached Berlin, Augie was dispatched ahead to Berlin as part of a liaison team. Actually, they were sent to keep an eye on the Russians because General Patton already saw the communists as a larger threat than the shattered Nazi Army.

"Wandering around the rubble of Berlin, Augie conceived the mission that would consume the rest of his life.

"When Colonel Donovan, by that time promoted by FDR to brigadier general, visited Augie in Berlin, Augie opened his heart to Donovan. He told the OSS chief how he wanted to submerge into the communist-occupied Zone and do what he could to wage war against the atheists. As you might tell by now, Augie had always shown signs of being a religious zealot. Avenging the death of his one true love became his *raison d'etre*. As the file here shows, Donovan tried to talk him out of wasting his enormous talents behind what Churchill would later call: the Iron Curtain. But Augie was adamant."

"But the Nazis killed Stephanie, not the Communists," said Buck.

"No matter. To Augie, Nazi evil was bad and Communist-atheist evil was even worse," said Macallan.

"Did you pay him? Did he need supplies?" asked Dolly.

"Basically, all he wanted was a sub-miniature camera and film," said Walter. "Even though he never asked for money, we would sometimes include a little money with the replacement film cassettes. He had chosen the life of a monk, living in that hovel of a flat on the pay he got as a janitor. But it made us feel better to think he could afford a little extra butter or, maybe, some extra coal, some warm clothes now and then.

"Before they parted for the final time, Donovan gave Augie one of the original Minox sub-miniature cameras, one made in Lativa before the war. Over the years, we were able to upgrade his camera to the Minox II and so on. Eventually, we provided the Rolls Royce of sub-miniature cameras, the Minox III B."

"How did you know about the dead drops? Their locations? When to service them?" asked Buck.

"Augie was a genius," said Walter. "When he met with Donovan, Augie had his tradecraft all worked out. His main concern was whoever came to service the dead drops was expert at counter-surveillance. He told Donovan there would be no brush passes. Moreover, he bristled when Donovan thanked him for wanting to spy for the OSS. Augie insisted a spy was someone who betrays his country. Augie felt he was a penetration agent working behind enemy lines on behalf of the United States of America."

"Augie had that right," said Buck. "The media and, consequently, the general public rarely understand the distinction between spy and agent."

"Augie told Donovan he intended to be a sleeper for a long time. But, when he detected U.S. intelligence had developed some kind of capability in East Berlin, he would contact the OSS using a means he shared with Donovan. But President Truman disbanded the OSS and Donovan was out of job. It was pay-back time."

"What do you mean, pay-back time," asked Dolly.

"When then Lt. Colonel William Donovan commanded an infantry battalion in World War I, he complained to the Rainbow Division Chief-of-Staff, then Brigadier General Douglas MacArthur, that the artillery support his battalion was getting from a certain artillery battery was lousy. The artillery battery commander was one Captain Harry S. Truman.

"General MacArthur called Captain Truman up on a field telephone and sent a rocket up his backside. Truman never forgave MacArthur or Donovan. And, as they say, the rest is history.

"After the CIA was created, and Donovan was cast aside, Donovan gave the notes of his Berlin meeting with Augie to someone he trusted in the CIA.

"One of the post-war agreements with the Russians gave the commies three military liaison missions inside West Germany. We only got the one mission in East Germany."

"How did the Russians end up with three missions and we only had one?" asked Dolly.

"Because, when it came to negotiating with the Russians, our State Department was way out of its league. The Russians argued West Germany was divided into the British, American and French Zones. So, they claimed the need for a mission in the British, American and French Zones. They only had one Occupation Zone – all of East Germany. So, we ended up with just one tiny contingent of intelligence types on the outskirts of Berlin, in Potsdam.

"Augie watched our guys get set up in Potsdam. He found a cheap flat within view of their offices. Then, he used the prearranged code he had given to Donovan to say he was ready to make contact. It resulted in the one and only time anyone met him in person. Walter was sent over there. So, I'll let him tell the story."

"At the time," said Walter, "there was absolutely no reason for Augie to be under surveillance. He had yet to get a job with the EGIS. I, on the other hand, had to make sure I was 'clean' before we met. It was the typical park-bench meeting you see in the espionage movies, two strangers on a park bench reading newspapers and feeding pigeons. Actually, when I met Augie, he was wearing a disguise – masterfully applied make-up – it made him look like your run-of-the-mill-refugee. So, despite sitting on the same park bench with him that one time, I would not know the undisguised Augie if he walked into this room right now.

"Augie told me how he had engaged a flat that could be viewed with binoculars from our Potsdam Mission. The flat had three windows facing toward our guys. Each window had one of those Rolladen shades. You Americans call them 'roller shades.' You know, the kind of wooden slats we Germans roll down on the outside of our windows to not only darken the room inside but to provide insulation against the cold and, even more importantly, a semi-solid bulwark against intruders. Memories of the Thirty Years War die hard over here.

"Augie had devised a code using his three Rolladen. From the viewpoint of our mission, the Rolladen on the left was "A." The middle one was "B." The one on the right was "C." All of Rolladen all of the way up meant one thing. All of them all the way down meant something else. Positioning them half-way up or half-way down provided another set of positions. The result was a large number of combinations and permutations, if you will. Augie sent General Donovan a master code list showing how Augie could vary the positions of the Rolladen to even spell out messages.

"Each morning, an officer of the U.S. Military Liaison Mission in Potsdam was to scan Augie's windows. From how the Rolladen were positioned, he would learn if Augie needed to have a dead drop serviced and, if so, which one. Augie even had a code for emergency extraction; however, he never used it.

"The only time I saw him, albeit in disguise, his hair was long. He had a beard. His clothes were appropriately post-war, East-German shabby. There was nothing remarkable about his gait. He was just one of those 'little people' of whom the communist *Nomenclatura* would take no notice.

"Augie told me the locations of the dead drops he had selected. His tradecraft was excellent. The dead drops could be serviced without attracting attention. He said he wanted a second Minox because he intended to keep one hidden somewhere near his flat so, once he gained access to classified documents, he could photograph them. If he got to clean offices at night, he hoped to use that camera to photograph documents.

"Sometimes, he would write out a list of needed supplies, like more cassettes and batteries for the Minox B's built-in light meter. He would photograph the list."

"We suspect he kept his flat sanitized at all times," said Macallan, taking up the story. "If the police were to raid his flat, other than his books on religion and philosophy, there was nothing to find. If he got wind of a new version of the Bible in German, he would ask for that. Apparently, he spent much of his time studying religion and philosophy. Karen Armstrong was his favorite. So, we kept him supplied with her latest books. In German, of course.

"In time, even the East Germans began to have black and white TV sets. Eventually, not having a small TV would have been suspicious. Augie must have used some of the pittance we gave him to buy a television set. Sometimes, at night, our guys could see the flickering light from a TV."

"Did you have to push him to do other things?" asked Buck.

"The KGB developed a surveillance dust," said Macallan. "The Agency developed its own version, although we added a small amount of a scent that dogs related to. The idea was to spread the almost invisible dust in places where the communist agents would walk in it. If they came over to the West to contact their agents or service dead drops and eluded our surveillance, we had dogs trained to sniff for the surveillance dust. We uncovered several KGB dead drops that way.

"We borrowed another idea from the KGB, only this dust really was invisible to the naked eye. But under a certain kind of lamp, you could see it. It helped us track letters being mailed by the Stasi to their agents in West Germany or to their agents in our zone in Berlin. Our agents would look for the places where the East Germans hung up their coats. Our guys would put some of the invisible dust in their coat pockets in the hope the East Germans would put letters to be mailed in those pockets.

"All the mail posted from East Berlin or even posted in West Berlin was screened by the *Bundespost*. We supplied Augie with both the dust and the powder. He employed them to good effect. Thanks to Augie, we uncovered a number of hostile agents operating in the West.

"Then, about a year before the Wall came down, we noticed Augie's rolladen never moved again. Nothing. After a few weeks, someone opened the Rolladen fully and we could see what appeared to be a cleaning crew inside. We suspect Augie died in his sleep and it took awhile for his body to be discovered. He died as he lived – unremarked.

"But someone, possibly a neighbor, had Augie buried in a Potsdam cemetery. After German reunification, Augie's sisters went to Potsdam. They were able to find his grave. But it has taken all this time to get the current German government to allow us to have his remains. We suspect they have been checking to make sure whatever Augie had been doing all those years does not reflect badly on them. We also suspect he was never properly embalmed. We think his remains are quite desiccated by now. So, essentially, the coffin you will accompany to Washington will contain the little that is left of the remains of Augie.

"But his remains and his legend are very important to the Agency. His story of dedication to duty and sacrifice is probably unsurpassed in the annals of clandestine intelligence. The photographs of documents he provided from inside the Stasi and, sometimes, the GRU and the KGB were priceless. Augie helped the Agency's counter-intelligence staff uncover a number of moles in MI-6, in the Agency, and some in military intelligence, as well. Doubtless, he saved the lives of many of our agents. Ironically, the Augean Stable he cleaned out was as much ours as theirs.

"Now, you know all we know about Augie," concluded Macallan.

"It will be our honor to escort Augie's remains to his homeland," said Dolly.

☆ ☆ ☆

CHAPTER THIRTY-NINE

Berlin, Schoenfeld, International Airport

With Berlin time six hours ahead of Washington, the 1400 hour departure time from Berlin meant the German Marshall Club would reach Washington-Dulles International Airport about 2000 hours, Washington time. Despite the re-fueling stops in Ireland and Newfoundland, the Germans would still have time to get to their downtown D.C. hotel and get a night's rest before they would begin a round of briefings the next day at the Pentagon. The following evening, the Germans were slated to attend a black-tie dinner at the White House with the president and the first lady.

In fact, the president and first lady were hosting black-tie dinners two nights in a row. About the time the German Marshall Society would be landing at Washington-Dulles, the Secretary of Defense, the Secretary of State, the members of the Joint Chiefs of Staff, the Director of National Intelligence, the DCI, and the staff of the National Security Council would be filing into the White House for their annual dinner with the president and the first lady.

Buck and Dolly looked down through the glass wall of the VIP waiting room onto the airport tarmac of Berlin-Schoenfeld. They could see Heidi and her staff of four flight attendants bantering with the Berlin-based pilot and his first officer just before the cockpit crew began their normal pre-flight checks of the aircraft. Other than the still-svelte Heidi, the other flight attendants looked more grandmotherly than the fetching stewardesses from back in the glory days of the airlines when flight attendants were called stewardesses and gave flight to thousands of "coffee, tea or me" male fantasies, some of which were realized.

Their walk-around complete, the flight-deck crew boarded the aircraft followed by Heidi's four flight attendants. When it was time for the passengers to board, Heidi beckoned to someone inside the terminal. A stream of eager passengers emerged. Each member of the German Marshall Plan Society was greeted with a smile by Heidi and started on his or her way up the stairs into the aircraft. [See photograph of passengers boarding at: buckanddolly.com.]

Finally, Buck and Dolly came down from the VIP lounge to over-see the loading of the coffin. Buck was asked to sign a receipt for the coffin. After securing the receipt in his briefcase, Buck joined Dolly who was waiting for him at the base of the ventral air stair.

"*Guten Tag, Frau Doktor Madison und Herr Oberst Madison,*" said Heidi.

"Nice uniform," said Dolly, commenting on how nice Heidi looked in her sky-blue flight attendant outfit.

"Blue becomes you. I love the pill box hat. But I notice some flight attendants wear the tan version of your uniform while others are in blue. What's the difference?"

"*Danke sehr.* I tell the passengers the flight attendants who wear tan will 'do it' and the ones wearing blue will not," said Heidi with a wink, as she escorted Buck and Dolly up the air stair and to their seats at the very rear of the aircraft.

Buck asked for and received a comfy blue blanket to roll up for the small of his back. That would take some of the strain off of his aging back. Dolly kept her shoulder bag within easy reach, on her lap. Buck slipped his notebook computer into the seat pocket ahead of him. He hoped to continue to work on their book.

The seating was arranged so Buck and Dolly did not have anyone else on their side of the aisle, giving them an empty seat between them. The extra room was appreciated. It also meant they could have some privacy. Buck had the window seat. Dolly, as was her preference, sat next to the aisle.

Across the aisle from Dolly was a somewhat flashily-dressed Ger-man businessman who looked like he was wondering why the two newcomers, who were obviously Americans, had three seats and he was packed in with the two passengers to his left. He immediately engaged Dolly in the kind of conversation almost universally engaged in by airline passengers meeting for the first time: Why are you on this special charter flight? What do you do? Where do you live? They conversed in English.

Dolly said, "I am a writer working on a history of the Marshall Plan. Perhaps, we can talk more once we reach Washington?"

"Yes, I suppose we could. What does your husband do?"

In an effort to reduce, if not end, further conversation, Dolly handed the German one of Buck's phony business cards. "*Ach,* I see," said the German, reading the card. "Your husband is the editor-in-chief of *The Journal of Septic Tank Living.*"

"Yes, would you like him to take my seat and explain all the nuances of septic systems?"

"*Nein,* that will not be necessary," said the German, turning what Dolly took to be a cold shoulder.

Buck whispered to Dolly, "Works every time."

As the Boeing 727 began to taxi, Heidi's voice came over the passenger cabin speakers: "*Guten Tag, Meine Damen und Herren* (continuing in German), Welcome on board your German Marshall Plan Society charter flight to Washington, D.C. Our Boeing 727, as you may know, is classed as a short-to-medium-range airliner. Our charter is operated by LuftCondor. Our initial crew is based here in Berlin. We will do all in our power to make your flight as comfortable as possible. The actual flying time to America is nine hours and 54 minutes; however, with our refueling stop in Ireland and with the second refueling stop in Newfoundland, our total time en route will be about 12 hours.

"At Shannon Airport, we will be on the ground for about one hour. The same will hold true at Gander, Newfoundland. We urge you to deplane at each stop and stretch your legs a bit. You may leave your belongings in place. They will be safe. Please do carry your passports and your boarding passes with you at all times.

"Now, I have good news and I have bad news. The bad news is there are no first-class seats on this flight. The good news is all seats on this entire charter flight are first-class. That means whatever you wish to drink is without charge, and the food is going to be much better than you can get on a regular airliner these days. As we taxi out for takeoff, please give your attention to your flight attendants for the safety briefing. If you have any electronic devices such as cellular telephones, please turn them off now.

"Shortly after each takeoff, we will begin our bar service.

"Our final leg is from Gander to Washington Dulles International Airport, located about 19 miles northwest of the District of Columbia. At Gander, our captain and first officer will deplane and be replaced by a new flight-deck crew. The flight from Gander to Dulles will be just under three hours.

"So now, *Meine Damen und Herren*, sit back and relax and please let your cabin staff know of any desires you may have. Again, welcome aboard LuftCondor to America. *Danke Sehr!*"

The refueling stop in Shannon went as planned. And, as scheduled, Heidi and her cabin crew served an airline meal en route to Gander.

"What did you think of the chicken?" asked the German from across the aisle.

"Chicken? I thought we were eating Spotted Owl," said Buck. "But, maybe, it was American Bald Eagle. It's hard to tell them apart." Dolly rolled her eyes. Sensing the American was pulling his leg, the German went back to reading his book.

Following the meal service, Buck put in his ear plugs, donned his sleep mask and slept the rest of the way to Gander. Dolly, the ever watchful, reviewed her notes that would become part of the book they had been writing about the events of the last few weeks.

Dolly prayed this would be the last time they would be called on to go abroad. Dolly sensed their luck would run out soon. While their adventures or, misadventures, as she thought of them, might make good reading, it would be only a matter of time before the jihadists would come after them once again.

But then, she also worried about living at home. She knew Abu Amed's promise of immunity was a sham. The Koran authorizes Muslims to lie to infidels. The U.S. government could not protect them forever. The president had already stretched his authority to the limit to provide the protection he ordered for them following the terrorists' thwarted attack on the Panama Canal. But he would be going out of office soon. Who knew what the new president would think about two superannuated cold warriors? Who knew if the new president would even fight the so-called War on Terror?

Maybe, there could be some sort of federal protection program, like the changed circumstances given to gangsters who rat on their fellow gangsters. Buck had changed identities before, but she never had. What would it be like to live somewhere else, to adapt to a new name, maybe to have an altered appearance, maybe to live under a brand-new legend made up by some bureaucrats in the FBI or the CIA? Could they be trusted?

Yet, she knew Buck would never willingly leave their mountain home. If they had to carry side arms all the time, that is what they would do. Their home was already fortress-like enough. A moat and a drawbridge were the only missing elements.

The cabin temperature was cooler than she wished, so she pulled the airline blanket around her shoulders. The cold made her mindful their aging bodies were coming toward the time when knowledge of the martial arts would not avail them much against younger, faster assailants. They would have to rely on that great equalizer of the Old West, the pistol. Or, the short-barreled, 12-gauge shotgun Dolly kept under her side of the bed.

Still, while sailing or skiing or hiking or even riding in a car, they could be picked off by a skilled marksman. The radical jihadists weren't going to go away. The jihadists were like some kind of horror-film monsters. Each time one leg or arm or head was cut off, a new one would grow in its place.

She and Buck had not asked to be put in the position in which they now found themselves. She felt a wave of anger. Why couldn't they just be retired? Why did the Cubans have to shoot down their airplane? Why did the terrorists choose their cruise ship to scuttle inside the Panama Canal? Why did they have to traipse through Europe daring al-Qaeda to kill them?

Maybe some kind of witness-protection program would be the answer. Maybe they could just disappear. Start a new life somewhere else. When and if they got home, she would talk with Buck about it.

The landing at Gander was routine. In fact, everything about Gander was routine. The only thing different was when Buck and Dolly went around thanking many of the airport staff for the hospitality they provided to the passengers of the aircraft that were turned back from landing in the United States on 9/11. The wonderful folks living in and around Gander had taken stranded passengers into their homes and fed them for four long days and nights until they could get back to where they came from or on to where they were going. Merchants opened their stores and let the stranded passengers take whatever clothing or anything they needed. None of them would accept payment for anything.

On the wall of his den, Buck framed one of the shortest-ever documents published by the United State Government. While its brevity was notable, its content was shocking:

"Due to extraordinary circumstances in the interest of public safety the airspace of the United States is closed until at least noon, EDT Wednesday, September 12, 2001."

Actually, it was four days before the airspace was open to commercial aviation. Meanwhile, selected general aviation aircraft, those small planes, were tasked to fly medical personnel, blood and plasma to where they were needed most. Dolly prayed American airspace would never, ever have to be shut down again.

The crew day for the original flight-deck crew from Berlin expired at Gander. Even an air charter like LuftCondor operated under rules mandating that flying officers had to have a certain amount of rest within each 24-hour period.

It was late afternoon in Gander as the weary passengers stumbled back on board, Heidi used the PA system to say, "*Meine Damen und Herren*, a new flight-deck crew is already on board and will be flying us the rest of the way to Washington-Dulles. We will be airborne shortly. Our flying time should be just under three hours.

"This flight, *Meine Damen und Herren,* is historic because you are flying on the next to the last flight this particular aircraft will ever make. After we land at Dulles, this airplane will be flown to Tucson, Arizona, where it will be retired and will then serve as a source of spare parts for the Boeing 727s remaining in service in the developing world. Because so many of you are staying in the United States to pursue various travel or business agendas, your return to Europe will be via the regular scheduled airlines.

"For my part, this will be my last flight. I have purchased a condominium in Florida and I will be going there to retire and to work on my suntan. I hope you enjoy your dinner at the White House tomorrow evening. I'll be thinking of you in your formal attire. I hope you'll be thinking of me in my bathing suit."

Everyone on board gave Heidi a round of applause.

☆ ☆ ☆

CHAPTER FORTY

Skyjacked

The LuftCondor flight started out as a normal charter flight from Berlin to Washington-Dulles International. But the flight segment between Gander, Newfoundland, and Washington-Dulles turned out to be anything but normal. The ordeal began when Heidi grew suspicious of the relief pilots who came on board at Gander. The captain and the first officer were new to her. She greeted them in German, drawing barely audible responses. Moreover, they were wearing something under their raincoats. Heidi was reminded of the Hunchback of Notre Dame.

The relief crew's refusal to allow Heidi to stow their raincoats in the closet just aft of the flight deck caused Heidi to become even more curious. Just before take-off, she brought coffee to the captain and the first officer. The captain was already in the left seat; however, he was still wearing his raincoat. He was sitting so far forward she doubted he would be able to fasten his safety belt. The first officer took the coffee tray from Heidi. He gave her a dismissive *Danke Schoen* and locked the door to the flight deck.

About 20 minutes after take-off, Buck was trying to decide between working on their new book and taking a nap. The nap was about to win out when Dolly nudged his arm. A worried-looking Heidi Schnell was moving quickly down the aisle toward them.

Heidi knelt in the aisle with her back to the passenger who had been led to believe Buck was an expert on septic systems. She whispered, "I've never flown with this flight-deck crew before and they seem, well, weird. If they don't know how to fly this airplane, none of us will live to retire."

Alarmed, Dolly whispered in Heidi's ear, "The German right behind you is trying to listen to what you are telling us. Maybe you could offer him a better seat up front?"

Without further word, Heidi turned to the German and said, "*Mein Herr* (continuing in German) it seems very cramped and stuffy back here. I can offer you a seating arrangement like that enjoyed by the Americans. It is even over the wing where the ride is much smoother."

The German had no choice but to accept Heidi's offer. After he gathered his belongings, she led him forward to the seat she offered. Once the man was seated, Heidi hurried back to Buck and Dolly.

"You said the captain and the first officer were acting weird." said Dolly. "What does that mean? Lots of pilots are weird. I'm married to one."

"When they came on board, I asked to take their raincoats and hang them up, but they brushed on by with hardly a word. I hurried along the aisle after them to offer coffee or tea, even sandwiches. Just to get some kind of response, I was even tempted to offer me. The captain paused just long enough to tell me they had everything they needed and would let me know if they needed anything more. He spoke with a Prussian accent.

"Also, it is customary for the captain or the first officer to come on the PA and welcome the passengers. As you may have noticed, they have not done that. Both of them went right onto the flight deck. After I handed the first officer their coffee, he locked the door. Of course, after 9/11, that's required by regulations.

"Anyway, I just thought I should let you know."

"Do they look like Arabs or Iranians or Turks?" asked Dolly.

"No, they are Nordic. Blond as I am. Well…ah, they could be natural blonds."

"They seem to be flying okay," said Buck, looking out the starboard side and down at the lights from the ships making their way along the East Coast of Canada.

"Buck, you're the lawyer," said Dolly. "Do we have legal grounds to do anything?"

"Quiet please. No one on board knows I'm a recovering lawyer." That drew another nudge from Dolly.

"Seriously," said Buck, "all we have right now is circumstantial evidence. The dowager or hunchback humps, however, could be parachutes. It occurs to me this is the same kind of airplane used by the infamous D.B. Cooper to parachute with a bag full of extorted cash into the wilds of Oregon. So, there is a certain insane connection between parachutes and the Boeing 727. And, as we all know, this particular 727 has a ventral air stair that works."

"So what if we do nothing and the pilot and the first officer bail out on us?" asked Dolly.

"For one thing, they would have to walk right by us."

"Yes, but they may have guns. Some pilots are allowed to have guns. If we try to stop them, they could shoot us. Recall, Mac Macallan cautioned us about shooting onboard."

"Good point," said Buck. "But what if our suspicions are without merit and we do something overt which could, in some narrow-minded U.S. Department of Justice quarters, be viewed as skyjacking? This is an international flight. Would an American president have enough clout to give us a get-out-of-jail card? So, in a way, I suppose this comes down to Pascal's Wager."

"What's that?" asked Heidi.

"Blaise Pascal was a brilliant 17th Century mathematician and philosopher. When asked if he believed in a life after death, he said he didn't know for sure. And, since he didn't know for sure, he was going to come down on the side of religion and wager on a life after death. If correct, he would gain Heaven. If wrong, he had nothing to lose, anyway."

"So, what does that tell us?" asked Dolly, impatiently.

"It tells us Heidi needs to very quietly ask the other flight attendants to come back here to the aft galley so I can brief them on our plan."

"What's our plan?" asked Dolly.

"I don't know," said Buck. "We'll think of a plan while Heidi is gathering her gals and getting them back here."

When all the flight attendants were crowded into the aft galley, Heidi asked her comrades if they thought the flight-deck crew behaved rather strangely. To a person, they voiced their concerns. All of them felt something was seriously wrong.

Buck took over to explain it might be necessary to use a ruse to determine the identity and intent of the crew on the flight deck. He said everyone was to remain calm and go about their duties. If, however, Heidi told them to do something out of the ordinary, they were to obey her orders without question.

"What are you, some kind of air marshal?" demanded one of the older flight attendants.

"Actually, I am a marshal," said Buck, omitting his actual title was 'honorary' deputy sheriff back home in Grand County, Colorado.

"Look, my wife and I are both experienced pilots. Are you willing to support us if we find it is necessary to take control of this aircraft?" The flight attendants nodded their support.

"Okay, here's the deal. We are going to burn a rubber band inside the starboard-side lavatory. Heidi, you get on the intercom to the first officer who, during this en route phase of flight, isn't doing much anyway. Convince him to come back here to investigate some suspicious smoke. Tell him it smells like an electrical fire.

"Heidi, you and I will be standing outside the lavatory. I will be pretending to want to use the lavatory; however, you are holding me back until the first officer can investigate the strange smell. Just as he looks into the lavatory, I will use one of the flat saps you are about to hand me, Dolly, to render him unconscious or, with luck, semi-conscious. With you two ladies lining up outside the lavatory door as if you are waiting your turn, I will apply some enhanced interrogation techniques to get him to tell me his life story. If he and his colleague turn out to be as pure as the driven snow, then I owe him an apology. I could also be in big trouble.

"Fortunately, I have enough money from Uncle Sam in my carry-on bag to send at least one of his children through college. Money may be the root of all evil, but it can also buy a lot of forgiveness and pain killers."

"Let's do it," said Dolly. "What do you need us to do?"

"Dolly, from your shoulder bag, I need a flat sap, three sets of plasti-cuffs and one of the Ketamine syringes. Next, we are going to need two gags. Ladies, I need two sets of panty hose. Any volunteers?"

One of the flight attendants hurried off to get her shoulder bag. When she came back, she pulled two unopened packages of panty hose from her bag and handed them to Buck.

After thanking her, Buck said, "Heidi, I need a book of matches and a rubber band. Now, everyone go back to your duty positions. Try to act normal."

Heidi reached into one of the aft galley drawers. She produced a book of souvenir LuftCondor matches, and a rubber band. Stepping into the starboard aft lavatory, Buck struck a match and applied it to the rubber band. When the acrid smell filled the air, Buck said, "Heidi, it's time for you to get the first officer to come back here."

Heidi picked up the intercom to the flight deck and spoke a few words in German. After a few moments, the first officer emerged from the flight deck, pausing to lock the door to the flight deck with his key. As the first officer made his way aft, Buck noted the man was wearing what commercial pilots often wear: a uniform coat, a white shirt, a black tie, black pants, and black shoes. No raincoat. If he brought a parachute on board, then the parachute was still on the flight deck. In a galley drawer, Heidi found a sign announcing in German, "Lavatory out-of-order."

When the first officer reached the aft lavatory, he found Heidi motioning for him to enter. Just as he put his head inside the lavatory to sniff the air, Buck hit him on the back of the head with the sap, buckling his knees. Buck lifted the collapsing first officer into the lavatory. Heidi closed the door firmly shut on both of them. She heard a click as Buck pushed the "occupied" sign into position. Dolly and Heidi lined up outside the door as if they needed to use the facilities.

Inside, Buck subjected the first officer to a few moments of "enhanced interrogation." Satisfied with what he learned, Buck gave the first officer a shot of Ketamine. A few minutes later, Buck opened the lavatory door to reveal the unconscious first officer all trussed up like a Christmas Turkey and gagged with panty hose. While Dolly and Heidi watched, Buck arranged the first officer on the floor of the lavatory. Buck closed the door. Heidi installed the "lavatory out-of-order" sign.

"Here's the short version of his miserable life story," whispered Buck. "He and his brother are being paid to set this aircraft on a course to crash into the White House. But they plan to parachute out the back."

"*Gott im Himmel!*" cried Heidi.

"Yes, that's where we are going to join Him unless we can take control of this aircraft," said Buck.

"Vat must ve do?" asked Heidi, her normally impeccable Oxbridge accent losing ground.

"First of all, I want you to assemble your flight attendants at the forward galley. Explain to them that it will be necessary for Dolly and me to replace the pilots. Tell them to stand up around the door to the flight deck as if they are just gossiping among themselves. Actually, they will form a screen to keep the passengers for seeing what the three of us are going to be doing at the door to the flight deck. We don't want the passengers to get excited and interfere, thinking they are going to prevent a skyjacking."

"What about the first officer?" asked Heidi, regaining some composure.

"I've got his key to the flight deck in my pocket," said Buck. "He'll be out for a couple of hours. No worries.

"Once you have your flight attendants briefed and in place, Dolly and I will come forward with our saps, a panty-hose gag and more plasti-cuffs.

"We'll use the first officer's key to open the door. I'll rush in and hit the captain with the sap. Together, we'll pull the captain over into the space where flight engineers used to sit. We'll gag the captain with panty hose and hog-tie him with plasti-cuffs. Dolly will administer a shot of Ketamine. I'll slip into the left seat. Dolly will take the right."

Heidi assembled her flight attendants as instructed. They were both alarmed and relieved by what Heidi told them. They engaged each other in animated conversation as they arranged themselves between the passengers and the door to the flight deck

Buck and Dolly looked at each other. When Dolly nodded, Buck unlocked the flight deck door with the first officer's key. Hearing the door open, the captain turned his head slightly to the right, expecting to see his brother. Before the captain could utter a sound, Buck brought his sap down on the right side of captain's head so hard that Buck thought for a moment he might have killed him.

Dolly, Buck and Heidi pushed onto the flight deck, locking the door behind them. The flight attendants drifted back to their assigned areas. After the captain was bound, gagged and given a shot of Ketamine, Heidi left the flight deck to use the PA system to address her passengers.

"*Meine Damen und Herren* (continuing in German), I am sorry to wake those of you who are sleeping. But I have some good news and I have some bad news. The good news is we now have a wonderful new set of pilots, two officers from a U.S. intelligence service. They will fly us safely to Dulles International Airport. The bad news is the pilots who joined us in Gander were imposters. But have no fear. The two imposters have been bound and gagged and rendered unconscious.

"Eventually, the imposters will be placed into the hands of the American authorities. For right now, I just ask for your patience and cooperation. I am confident the worst part of this disruption is one of the lavatories at the rear of the aircraft will be closed for the rest of the flight. That leaves us with two lavatories. So, with your cooperation, we should be just fine.

"Meanwhile, I'm asking the flight attendants to serve champagne to everyone for the duration of our flight to Dulles. *Danke Sehr.*"

Turning around, Heidi reentered the flight deck.

"Well done, Heidi." said Buck. "You and your ladies performed admirably."

After reassuring Heidi that he and Dolly could fly the airplane, Buck said, "Now, please go back to the passenger cabin and help your ladies keep everyone calm. Maybe sing some German songs or something. Dolly and I have a few things to arrange up here."

✳ ✳ ✳

CHAPTER FORTY-ONE

On to Dulles

After they secured their safety belts and adjusted their seats, Dolly said, "Now, our only problem is how to make a safe landing at Dulles."

"Actually, we need to do something before we get to Dulles."

"What's that?"

"I don't think any reasonably sane person would parachute out into a cold, December night in Maryland without having made prior arrangements for some ground transportation. Whoever has been tipping off al-Qaeda to our itinerary and where we would be staying might be waiting on the ground. This could be the FBI's big chance to break up a spy ring within the State Department or the CIA or even the Pentagon."

"You are suggesting we make a low pass over that lat/long and throw them out the back?"

"Yes, I'm thinking about 3,000 feet AGL. That's the initial instrument approach altitude for Dulles anyway. Look, we get someone on the radio to tell us how to slow this baby down to about 130-knots. Then we drop the two skyjackers into the waiting arms of the FBI.

"So, first thing we do is contact air traffic control. We explain our situation to Washington Center and give Center the two lat/longs. We ask for two FBI teams. We need one FBI team to stake out that place north of Frederick and another team to meet us at Dulles. We could still have another tango on board and not know about him or her.

"Then, we ask Center to put an experienced 727 pilot on the radio. He or she can talk us through a low pass over that first lat/long.

Before hand, we rig the parachutes of the false relief crew so we can pitch them out the aft door. How's that for a plan?"

"I'd say we are going to be very busy. But, if we drop those stairs down into the slipstream, won't they act like a down elevator, pitching our tail up and our nose down?"

"Good point. We, but more likely you, will have to apply a lot of nose-up trim. My larger concern is the slipstream won't allow the opening to be wide enough to exit two jumpers. But I know there's some way to do it. One of my best Army buddies led an evaluation team testing an early-model 727 to see if it could be used for dropping the Delta Force from extremely high altitudes. They must have figured it out because I know the Delta Force does it.

"Unless we step out on the wing, our satellite phones won't work up here. So, for now anyway, we can't reach Jack McClure. Do you have you any ideas on how we can contact Washington Center?"

"Okay," said Dolly. "What if I squawk 7500 on the transponder, and listen on 121.5 – the emergency VHF frequency?"

"That should work. When Center sees us squawking the 'skyjack' transponder code, we are certain to get a call on 121.5." Dolly set the transponder to 7500.

After a few moments, a male voice with a Chuck Yeager-like southern drawl asked them to confirm their transponder setting.

"Roger, Washington Center," said Buck. "We are a LuftCondor charter in-bound for Dulles. We are squawking 7500 on purpose. We just prevented a skyjacking of this aircraft. My wife and I are now in command. Both of us have lots of hours in small aircraft. I even have an hour of 727 simulator time. But we are going to need some help from an experienced 727 pilot. Also, we are going to need some help from the FBI in a couple of locations."

"Roger, LuftCondor. Just in case some other aircraft need this VHF frequency for an emergency, let's switch over to a UHF frequency. Also, UHF will be more secure. Can ya'll do that?"

"Affirmative. Which one?"

"Ya'll try to meet me on UHF 225.8. If ya'll don't hear me on 225.8 in two minutes, come back to VHF 121.5, and we'll try something else."

"Roger. Meet you on UHF 225.8."

Dolly left one VHF radio on 121.5. Reaching over to the UHF radio, she set it to 225.8.

Buck radioed, "Center. This is LuftCondor on 225.8. Do you read?"

"LuftCondor, I have you loud and clear. How me?

"Same. Same."

"LuftCondor. Change your transponder to 0218."

Dolly reset the transponder. Buck said, "Squawking 0218."

After a moment, the controller said, "Okay. That's fine. I've got a positive ID on my radar screen. Now, LuftCondor, did ya'll say you need FBI help in two locations? Seems like ya'll oughta be happy just to land at one location."

"Center, we need a FBI SWAT team to report to what is probably an open field just north of Frederick, Maryland. The skyjackers' accomplices may be waiting for them to land on that field. It will save the FBI a lot of time and effort if they can capture the skyjackers and their accomplices all at once. The other location is Washington-Dulles."

"LuftCondor, Center. Surely, ya'll wouldn't be planning an off-airport landing in that Boeing 727, would ya'll?"

"Negative, Center. The skyjackers are wearing parachutes. We are going to throw them out the back."

"Holy… ah, what then?"

"We are hoping you will have rounded up someone with a lot of 727 hours to coach us into making a normal landing at Dulles. Look, we have a cabin full of high-powered Germans in the back. In fact, they have a dinner date at the White House with the president and the first lady for tomorrow night.

"They've been told about the skyjackers. Naturally, they are pretty upset. But we are hoping to find some former *Bundeswehr* types to help us eject the skyjackers out the back."

"Roger, LuftCondor. If I was one of them Germans, I'd be more scared than a Jew in a canoe in the Suez Canal. Ya'll wait a minute. Someone is talking in my ear. Wait. Wait. Okay. The FBI is now telling me a SWAT team just scrambled from D.C. by chopper and is headed toward Frederick. Also, they've got me patched by land-line to a General McClure in the Pentagon. Ya'll know him?"

"That's affirmative."

"That's good because he just gave me your names. So, would ya'll have a lat/long for that place north of Frederick?"

Dolly came on the radio. She read off the latitude and longitude.

"Thank you, Ma'am. Copy good. General McClure says ya'll's a pilot, too, Ma'am."

"I have more total hours than he does, but zero time in a 727 simulator."

"Well, ya'll don't worry your pretty little head none. I'm sure ya'll do just fine."

Condescending, male-chauvinist, thought Dolly.

"Okay, LuftCondor, I'm handing ya'll over to Rod, my good pal. He's a former 727 instructor pilot with thousands of 727 hours. Ya'll have a good evening now."

☆ ☆ ☆

CHAPTER FORTY-TWO

Farm field, ten north of Frederick

The couple huddled together against the cold of the December night. Now and then, so they could run the heater, they turned on the engine of her Japanese-made SUV.

The man had been reluctant to go with her into the Maryland night to some mysterious open field. But the promise of more sex with the dark-eyed beauty overcame his reluctance. He drove because her driving skills were limited. But not because she was too young. It was because in her culture women were not permitted to drive automobiles. But, as far as what they did together, she was in the driver's seat.

She used the Garmin GPS stuck on her dashboard to find the place she wanted to be. She had him back the SUV into a tree line overlooking a moonlit farm field. Then, she told him the sex would have to wait until after they had made their rendezvous with some people she was supposed to meet. Once the rendezvous was made, they were to transport the people to the Baltimore International Airport. She said the life of her family depended on it.

If some mysterious people were to be taken to Baltimore, the man wondered why the woman had brought along the two body bags he had seen in the SUV's cargo area. Hopefully, the bags had nothing to do with the people they were supposed to meet.

Every once in awhile, she would roll her window down a bit so she could listen for a sound she apparently expected to hear. Since sex was not in the immediate offing, and he was tired from a day of chasing meaningless paper in his government office, he slunk down in the driver's seat and went to sleep. She, however, was caffeine-wired to the point her hands were trembling.

Far across the field, she could see an all-night light shining down
from a pole onto some farmer's barnyard. Parked by the barn,
she could make out the shape of what must be the farmer's family
sedan. She tensed when she saw the dome light in the vehicle go
quickly on and off. But it was only 8:00 p.m. Maybe the farmer or
someone had just come back from town. She relaxed a bit.

✿ ✿ ✿

"Kraemer, you idiot," said the SWAT team leader. "Where'd you
get this hunk of government junk with the dome light still hooked
up?"

"I'm sorry, sir," said Special Agent Kraemer. "On short notice, it
was the only sedan the motor pool could give us."

"At least it gives me a place where I can radio General McClure,"
said the black-clad, balaclava-hooded SWAT team leader. "Kraemer, you are wearing civies. Go inside and try to reassure the farm
family. I scared the crap out of them when I tried to do it in my
SWAT-team gear. Explain we do not expect any shooting. We are
just here to make an arrest. But, if anything gets damaged, tell
them Uncle Sam is good for it. Hell, tell them we'll even pay for
walking across their freaking winter-stubble field. Now, disconnect that blasted dome light before you go. Meanwhile, I'll call
McClure to see if he has an ETA for the skyjacked 727."

✿ ✿ ✿

"LuftCondor, this is Rod. I understand you want to make a low
pass north of Frederick and then transition to Dulles for landing.
Correct?"

"That's affirmative, Rod."

"LuftCondor, I need to tell you the ventral air stair door on the
727 is not designed to be opened in flight. You can do it. But be

advised that you probably won't be able to get it completely down. Also, you probably won't be able to close it all the way back up."

"Roger, Rod. But since we'll be at low altitude and so close to Dulles by then, will a partially open door be a big problem?"

"Negative. Not a big problem. It just means some extra drag."

"Okay. Rod, I need some power and flap settings for 130 knots. We've been studying the Dash One, but we'd like to hear the numbers from you."

"Is your first officer prepared to copy?"

"Affirmative," said Buck, as Dolly brandished a ball point pen over her kneeboard.

Rod dictated the appropriate descent power and flap settings to Dolly. Then, he said, "LuftCondor, let your autopilot/GPS take you to the lat/long north of Frederick. But turn off the altitude hold feature so I can talk you down. Then, we'll depressurize the aircraft. How high do you need to be for your...ah, parachutists?"

"We need to be at 3,000-feet AGL. I doubt these skyjackers are skilled jumpers. Let's give them plenty of altitude."

"LuftCondor. General McClure gave us your names. So, we were able to call up your FAA certificates. You've both got some twin-engine time; however, you've got three engines to deal with. No matter. Just keep all the throttle levers even with each other, just like you would in a twin."

Rod talked Buck through the power and flap settings Dolly had written on her kneeboard. They began to descend at 500 feet-per-minute – the standard, initial descent rate for most instrument approaches.

When they were almost at 3,000-feet AGL, Rod instructed Buck to increase engine power to maintain altitude, re-trim the aircraft and reset the altitude hold for 3,000-feet AGL. Next, Rod talked Buck through the procedure to depressurize the aircraft. When the aircraft was depressurized, Rod told them to set their altimeter to 29.92 inches of mercury, the standard setting.

Buck said, "I need to let my co-pilot fly for awhile so she can get used to this aircraft. In a few minutes, I'll have to go aft to supervise the exit of the skyjackers. Okay?"

"Roger. Ma'am, is your altitude hold set?"

"Affirmative," reported Dolly.

"Roger. Maintain current altitude, maintain 130 knots. When the ventral air stair gets down into the slipstream, you'll have to trim the nose up. The air stair will act like a downward-deflected elevator back there. You got your hand on the elevator trim?"

"That's affirmative."

"Okay, LuftCondor. Report when the skyjackers are…ah, away."

"Wilco."

As she shifted forward in her seat to put her hands on the control yoke, Dolly looked out the small window at her right side. She could see the twinkling lights reflecting off the little patches of snow scattered across the Maryland countryside. Some of the houses had Christmas lights running along the eaves of their roofs. She thought about all the families down there, some rich, some poor, but all warm and safe in their homes. At that moment, she would have gladly traded places with the poorest among them.

Before Buck left Dolly alone on the flight deck, he called Heidi on the intercom. "Heidi, see if you can find two strong Germans to come up here and help me move the captain to the aft galley. Also, I'm going to need two former parachutists from the *Bundeswehr*, two *Fallschirmjaeger*, if at all possible. They are going to have to be pretty brave because it occurs to me it may be necessary for us to be doing a high-wire act on those stairs without a net."

After several minutes, Heidi knocked on the door to the flight deck. Buck opened the door to find two rather robust Germans standing in the forward galley. Buck asked them to carry the captain to the aft galley.

Made limp by the Ketamine, the captain was difficult to carry; however, the Germans managed to carry him, parachute resting on top of his stomach, down the aisle by grabbing his shoulders and his feet. Some of the passengers recoiled at the sight of the bound, gagged and unconscious captain.

Buck thanked the two burly Germans for their help. He went back onto the flight deck and waited awhile until Dolly indicated her comfort at the controls. Then, Buck picked up the first officer's parachute and took it with him as he made his way aft. He drew some terrified looks from the passengers. Buck stopped to chat, in German, with some of them. He assured them only the skyjackers would be using parachutes.

When Buck reached the aft galley, Heidi handed him a headset. It was connected to the intercom to the flight deck. Buck called Dolly. He asked her to provide him with the distance-to-go numbers from the GPS. At five miles out, he said she should tell Heidi to open the aft exit. At one-half mile out, he would start expelling the skyjackers. With luck, they should drift to somewhere near where they were supposed to land.

In German, Heidi made a formal introduction of two fit-looking German volunteers. Both of them had served in the *Bundeswehr* as *Fallschirmjaeger*. In German, Buck explained he wasn't exactly sure how the air stair door was set up or even how much room they would have to work with. Buck said if they didn't feel like they could get out on the stairs with him, he would understand. When Buck finished his spiel, they both came smartly to attention and saluted. They would do just fine.

Buck pulled the unconscious first officer out of the latrine, un-cuffed his hands, and had the Germans wrestle him into his parachute harness. Then, Buck un-cuffed the captain. When the Germans finished with the first officer, they strapped the captain into his parachute.

Memories of his time in Jumpmaster School came back to Buck. It would go against his training to put someone out the door with-out a proper parachute inspection. With the first officer in his parachute harness and lying face-down, Buck inspected the first officer's parachute. The chute was a brand-new model T-11, the parachute replacing the venerable T-10 which had served the U.S. military so well for so many years.

Inside the static line sleeve, Buck found the universal static-line snap. It was properly attached to the static line. Tracing the static line with his fingers, Buck came to a small flap. He knew the flap was there to protect the curved pin that prevents the pack tray from premature opening. Buck lifted the flap to look underneath. Someone with a very sharp knife had severed the static line.

Without a word from Buck, the *Fallschirmjaeger* leapt to inspect the parachute on the back of the captain. The captain's static line had been severed as well. In both cases, the sabotage had been covered over by the protective flaps over the curved pins.

Part of the curved pin includes a closed metal ring. Buck took the severed end of the static line and stuck it through the metal ring and then brought about a foot of the static line back and tied it in a knot. To make sure the bitter end would not come loose, he signaled Heidi for some duct tape. In Vietnam and Cambodia, damaged helicopters were often held together with duct tape until a proper repair could be made.

While one of the *Fallschirmjaeger* held the knot in place, Buck put a dozen wraps of duct tape around the knot. The integrity of the static line was restored. Even at 130 knots, that many wraps of duct tape were not likely to come loose.

When they finished with the first officer, they duct-taped the static line of the captain back into place. Otherwise, both of them would have plummeted to their deaths. Buck and the *Fallschirmjaeger* did a high-five. The irony was not lost upon them.

Over the intercom, Buck reported what they had found to Dolly. "Dead men don't tell tales," said Buck. "Whoever is behind this skyjacking wasn't entirely forthcoming with the skyjackers. If someone is waiting on the ground for the skyjackers, then it must be for the purpose of removing their bodies."

"You just saved the lives of the two Krauts who were going to kill us," said Dolly.

"Well, yes. This way they can talk to the FBI. Listen, Dolly, this headset cable isn't going to stretch all the way back where I will need to be on the air stair. I'm going to give this headset back to Heidi. We'll use Heidi as our go between. Here's Heidi."

Heidi donned the headset and kept nodding as Dolly repeated Buck's previous instructions. To close the communications loop, Buck had Heidi repeat what she had just heard from Dolly. Heidi was all set to do her part.

Turning to the two Germans, Buck went over their roles once again. They were not only game, but grinning with anticipation. Buck explained the captain would be the first to exit the aircraft, followed by the first officer. The Germans knew it was an airborne custom for the most senior person to jump first. They each flashed Buck a big smile.

Buck explained how they were going to stack the two skyjackers with the first officer on the bottom and the captain on top. Buck couldn't think of the German equivalent for "daisy-chain," so his actions would have to take the place of explanation.

Suddenly, Heidi pressed on the ears of her headset as if to hear Dolly better. Then, Heidi moved to the ventral exit door and swung the big unlocking level to the unlocked position. When she pulled the door inward, there was a slight rush of air from the main cabin and into the cavernous tail cone. Heidi stepped away so Buck could look inside the tail cone.

Lying on top of the air stair was another T-11 parachute. Buck wondered: *Is this just a back-up chute or is there another jumper on board?* Buck picked up the additional parachute and handed it to one of the *Fallschirmjaeger* who dumped it onto the galley floor.

With the chute out of the way, Buck could see the ventral air stair had two parts. The air stair door itself, and a small, aluminum panel at the far aft end that looked like its function was to un-lock and re-lock the aft end of the air stair in place. Buck nodded his head for Heidi to step aft to drop the air stair.

On Heidi's left was the control panel for the ventral air stair. Right next to the control panel were the so-called black boxes, only they are really international orange in color.

Heidi reached one hand back to Buck who took it in his strong grip. With the other hand, Heidi pressed the button that activated the hydraulic pistons. The pistons struggled against the 130-knot slipstream. The roar from the slipstream was deafening. Paper cups, paper napkins, and other bits of litter came rushing from the main cabin and shot out into space.

Rather than burnout the motor, Buck signaled for Heidi to stop. The air stair was not fully down; however, with some added weight, it looked like the opening could be made large enough to eject the two skyjackers.

Buck pulled Heidi away from the door opening and into the aft galley. As the cabin pressure adjusted to the ventral door being open, the rush of out-going air abated to the point Buck felt it was safe to approach the head of the air stair. He could see how D.B. Cooper did it. Cooper must have crawled on his belly out to the end of the air stair and dropped off into the night. But getting two unconscious and trussed up skyjackers out the narrow opening was going to require some extra weight toward the end of the air stair.

The air stair itself was less than a yard wide and no more than seven feet long. Fortunately, the air stair was equipped with side panels the tops of which were designed to be used as hand rails by boarding and deplaning passengers.

Gripping the beginning of the hand rails, Buck turned around and backed out onto the head of the air stair. He motioned for his helpers to bring him the unconscious first officer with his head face-down and facing aft. Buck's weight combined with the first officer caused the air stairs to drop lower into the slipstream.

Suddenly, Dolly felt like she had applied some down elevator which, of course, she had not. Quickly, she rolled the trim wheel toward her to give the aircraft some nose-up trim. She held the aircraft steady at 3,000-feet AGL.

With the Germans pushing and Buck pulling, they got the first officer another three feet down the air stair. Buck reached into the parachute's pack tray and extracted the first officer's universal static-line snap. He handed the snap to one of the *Fallschirmjaeger* who pulled out enough static line to reach a D-ring in the floor of the galley. After making certain the static-line snap was secured to the D-ring, the *Fallschirmjaeger* gave Buck the okay sign.

Satisfied, Buck signaled for the Germans to try to stack the captain on top of the first officer. After a lot of pushing and shoving, they got the captain's head to reach the middle of the first officer's pack tray. That would have to do.

The combined weight of Buck and the phony air crew increased the downward angle of the air stair even more. Dolly applied more nose-up trim as she attempted to maintain 3,000-feet AGL. The slipstream was forcing the air stair to bounce up and down. Buck began to fear that he, sans parachute, and the skyjackers might be pitched out into space.

Buck reached down into the captain's pack tray, pulled out the static-line snap and attached it to an equipment D-ring on the first officer's parachute harness. Then, Buck crawled forward over the top of stacked flight crew until he was sitting on the captain's back-side.

On the flight deck, Dolly was worried that she was about to run out of nose-up trim. The airspeed was degrading. Dolly began to fear the aircraft would stall. In case she needed to add power she had her left hand on the power quadrant.

Buck could feel movement underneath. The captain was raising his head up, trying to look around. The Ketamine must be wearing off. Also, the cold air and the noise were enough to wake the dead. If the captain had any idea of where he was, he must have been terrified.

Buck looked down to make sure his legs were not tangled in any of the static lines. If so, he could be swept out of the aircraft along with the skyjackers.

Although somewhat more steerable than the old T-10 parachutes, the new T-11s were not by any stretch of the imagination steerable parachutes. The T-11s were designed to have a slower rate of descent than the T-10s. While that would reduce the number of broken legs and sprained ankles, staying aloft longer increased the exposure to enemy ground fire. Buck doubted the phony air crew would know how to steer a parachute anyway. So, if there were much of a crosswind, they might do a Mary Poppins, landing who knows where?

Buck nodded to Heidi that all was in readiness to make the drop.

Buck and the two *Fallschirmjaeger* stared at Heidi so hard that she felt like she had forgotten to put her clothes on. After what seemed an eternity to Buck, Heidi must have heard Dolly say they were one-half mile from the lat/long displayed on the GPS. Heidi gave Buck the half-mile signal.

The Fallschirmjaeger put their hands on the first officer's derriere to be ready to help Buck boot the skyjackers out into space. To the casual observer they must have looked like a Rugby scrum.

Buck was gripping the hand rails so hard his knuckles were white. Buck was just ready to shoot one leg out backwards with a Karate kick when he looked up at Heidi.

The German Heidi had reseated over the wing was holding Heidi's head in a hammerlock with his right arm. Over her left carotid artery, he held the four-inch, hardened-plastic blade of an Executive II letter opener, the kind of deadly weapon that slips by most TSA magnetometers.

Above the roar of the open ventral exit, the German shouted for Buck and the *Fallschirmjaeger* to bring the captain and the first officer back inside the aircraft. When one of the *Fallschirmjaeger* turned to stand up to see who was behind him was shouting orders, the *Fallschrimjaeger's* bulk caused the German with the knife to lose sight of Buck's left hand as it dropped to Buck's left ankle. When Heidi saw Buck's hand drop down to his ankle, she tilted her head leftward just enough to expose a portion of her captor's head. A red dot appeared just above the German's right eye which was followed instantly by a bullet from Buck's Walter PPK/S.

The deadly letter opener dropped to the galley floor. Heidi's assailant fell as if his legs had been kicked from under him. Heidi fainted on top of him. The *Fallschirmjaeger* scrambled off the pile and helped Heidi to a seat. Buck struggled his way back into the cabin and examined the dead German. There was no exit wound.

Reaching forward to Dolly's seat, Buck grabbed Dolly's shoulder bag, extracted a tampon, pulled off the protective cover, and stuck the tampon in the small hole in the German's forehead.

Then, Buck got back out on top of the pile and summoned the *Fallschirmjaeger* to assist. They reformed the scrum. With Buck kicking backwards and the *Fallschirmjaeger* pushing, the captain and the first officer tumbled off the air stair, through the roaring 130-knot slipstream, and then into the quiet blackness of a cold December night.

The three of them watched as the first officer's static line jerked against the D-ring in the galley floor. The shock of the opening of the first officer's parachute would jerk the captain's static line and the captain's parachute would open as well. Hopefully, they would fall into the arms of the FBI.

The sudden weight reduction brought the air stair back up in line with the cabin floor; however, the opening was far from closed. On the flight deck, Dolly was rolling the trim wheel forward like mad in an effort to cancel all the nose-up trim she had applied when the air stair was way down in the slipstream. When she was done, she called Washington Center, "Rod, LuftCondor. Jumpers away!"

Buck looked down at the dead German blocking the path to the air stair. Buck nodded to one of the *Fallschirmjaeger* who picked up the body and pitched it out the opening. The body bounced once in the middle of the air stair, twisted off to the side and was gone. Buck wiped up the little bit of blood on the galley floor with a towel and then let the slipstream suck the soiled towel out of his hand and out into the void.

Buck bent down to pull the first officer's static line back inside the aircraft. He rolled it up and threw it on the galley floor. Buck and the *Fallschirmjaeger* inspected the extra parachute. The static line was intact. It had not been tampered with. *Obviously, management has its perks,* thought Buck.

The irrepressible Heidi was back on her feet and ready to help. When she saw the first officer's static line was clear of the stairwell, she returned to the aft exit and pushed the button that would cause the hydraulic system to raise the air stair up into its locked position. The roar of the slipstream began to subside somewhat. Struggling against the slipstream, the main part of the air stair came close to snapping back in place but did not close completely. The small locking panel could not overcome the slipstream. It was still hanging down and flapping in the wind.

Heidi beckoned Buck to come look. Buck did so and told her it was no big deal. He helped Heidi close and lock the ventral exit door. When the lever snapped shut, the relative silence seemed almost eerie. Heidi, Buck, and the *Fallschirmjaeger* looked approvingly at each other. They had a group hug.

Buck nodded his thanks to the *Fallschirmjaeger* who saluted, did another high-five and grinned their way back to their seats, pausing along the way to receive the congratulations of their comrades.

Over the PA system, the fully-recovered Heidi announced all of the airplane's lavatories were now available for use. Inside the cabin, the Germans cheered the news.

As Buck walked briskly forward to rejoin Dolly on the flight deck, the Germans on the aisle seats held out their hands for Buck to give them a friendly slap. The others gave Buck the "V" for victory sign.

Buck slipped into the pilot's seat and said, "Good job. I've got the aircraft."

A relieved Dolly asked, "How'd it go back there?"

"A small part of the ventral exit door closure is still flapping in the breeze. It's just some added drag."

"I meant what happened to the skyjackers?"

"Apparently, they didn't like the meal service. So, they left. Assuming I rigged them correctly and assuming their parachutes work, they should be safely on the ground. Did you tell Rod?"

"That's affirmative," said Dolly.

"Actually, there was an extra jumper you could not have known about. The German in the flashy suit. Apparently, he was on board to make sure the captain and the first officer did their jobs. He had his own chute stashed behind the ventral exit door."

"What happened to him?"

"He used a knife to take Heidi hostage, so I shot him. She's okay. Just shook up. We threw the third skyjacker out the back. By the way, I owe you a tampon.

"Rod, LuftCondor here," radioed Buck. "We are ready for vectors for landing, Dulles."

✡ ✡ ✡

CHAPTER FORTY-THREE

Dulles International Airport

"LuftCondor, this is Rod back with you. We have cleared all the airspace around Dulles. No worries about other traffic. I am going to vector you out west of Dulles and then back around to line you up on runway 36 Left. What little wind there is will be right on your nose.

"I'm not going to hand you off to Dulles Approach Control as ATC normally would. Instead, I'll be with you all the way down. Even though I know you have done plenty of ILS approaches, I am going to talk you through this particular ILS approach. I think you could shoot this approach all by yourself; however, given the circumstances, I'm going to vector you all the way onto the Localizer. Do you have the approach chart for Dulles ILS 36 Left?"

"Affirmative. But what about the Cat III auto-land system? Can't we use that?"

"Negative, I'd have to teach you how to use it. I say again, do you have the chart for Dulles ILS 36 Left?"

"I have it in my lap. As we speak, Dolly is dialing in the frequency for the Localizer/Glide slope."

"Okay. When you come around and I get you centered on the Localizer, you will be near the Outer Marker. I want you to intercept the glide slope from just a little bit below. At the Outer Marker, have your first officer drop the gear and deploy the flaps. Establish a descent rate of 500-feet-per-minute. I need you to give me an approach speed of 124 knots indicated. But adjust the power so you can keep the glide slope needle level. When you get over the runway threshold, I'll tell you to come back on the power. Beware the aircraft will want to sink quite rapidly. So, you may need to add some power. You will have plenty of runway ahead of you. Just let it fly itself onto the ground.

"We've giving you your own ground control frequency. It's 123.0. Once your roll out, call me on 123.0 and I'll direct you to a special area we've set aside.

"A follow-me vehicle will be at the north end of 36 Left. It will show you where to park. You will be surrounded by a security force. There will be transportation for the Germans and the flight attendants. For you, there is a Marine helicopter that is going to take you and your wife to someplace. I asked the aircraft commander where, but he wouldn't say."

With the engines throttled back, Buck and Dolly could hear Heidi leading the Germans in the kind of songs sung in German beer halls. The Germans must have been linking arms and swaying from side-to-side. They were causing the wings to rock. Not a great deal but enough to bother Buck who was worried about nailing the instrument approach.

"Dolly, call back there," said Buck. "Tell those Germans that you have a message from Montezuma."

"What's that?"

"Knock off that singing in the halls."

Dolly could tell that Buck was nervous. So, she called Heidi on the intercom and suggested that every other aisle rock one way and the alternate aisle rock the other. The wings stopped rocking, but the singing continued. Buck stopped complaining about the Germans and focused on the ILS approach.

The landing at Dulles went just the way Rod said it would go. It wasn't perfect. Dolly held up two fingers. Buck wasn't sure if that was the victory sign or where she placed his landing on the Richter

Scale. Buck followed the follow-me vehicle until the driver stopped, got out, and signaled for Buck to park.

As soon as Heidi let down the ventral air stair, some Kelvar-armored and seriously-armed FBI agents bounded up the stairs. The passengers applauded. A young woman in the uniform of an airline captain accompanied the FBI agents. After patting Buck on the back, the captain told Buck and Dolly that she would take care of shutting down the engines and securing the aircraft.

Buck felt he had one more duty. He called Rod on 123.0 and thanked him for getting them all down safely. They agreed to meet in person, someday.

Buck retrieved his notebook computer from the seat pocket. Then, they grabbed their carry-on baggage and followed the exultant Germans down the air stair.

On the ground, the Germans formed a circle at the base of the ventral air stair. They waited for Buck and Dolly and Heidi to deplane, then mobbed the trio with hugs and kisses. Buck and Dolly told everyone that Heidi was the real hero of the ordeal. Heidi pointed to her fellow flight attendants, and they were mobbed as well. Buck got the Germans to be quiet long enough to explain that an air traffic controller named Rod was the person who kept them safe. The Germans gave three cheers for Rod.

A Special Agent from the FBI asked everyone to gather around while another agent handed them statement forms to be filled out in either German or English. The passengers were instructed to fill out statements as to what they observed during the flight. The FBI would collect the statements when they reached the Willard Hotel near the White House. An official from the State Department would be at the Willard to take care of passport matters. Turning to Buck and Dolly, the Special Agent said they would be interviewed later by a very senior person.

After the Germans boarded the waiting buses and headed off for downtown, Buck and Dolly saw Brigadier General Jack McClure standing off to the side next to a black, Army-issue sedan. Dolly gave him a hug. Buck saluted. They both thanked McClure for all the protection he gave them.

"I was starting to think that I had goofed when I put you on that charter flight," said McClure, "but it looks like you averted a disaster even worse than 9/11. That alone, made your so-called book-signing tour a success. But remind me to stay as far away from you guys as humanly possible."

"So, what now?" asked Dolly.

"Your checked baggage will be unloaded right here because, in a few minutes, you will board the Marine chopper that is shut down over there. It will take you to Camp David for the night. As we speak, the president and first lady are holding a White House dinner for our national security team. Before he goes to bed tonight, POTUS will be made fully aware of what you guys just pulled off."

While they were thanking General McClure for his help, the cargo door in the belly of the aircraft began to open. A ground crew member drove a baggage truck with a conveyor belt up to the cargo door. The conveyor belt was raised into position. A baggage handler crawled up into the cargo bay. The first items to ride down the belt were the Madison's checked baggage. A Marine in a flight suit came over. He grabbed the Madison's carry-on bags and their checked luggage. Using a small handcart, he took everything over to the helicopter.

"Look, I have to get back to the Pentagon," said McClure. "Dolly, give me your shoulder bag. The weapons go back into my little armory. You won't need them where you're going."

"I'm afraid two items are missing," said Buck. The bag is short one round of .380 and one tampon."

"Don't tell me. You shot someone on the plane and plugged the hole with a tampon?"

"Affirmative. There was a third skyjacker. Tell the FBI to look for a body without a parachute. Besides, the tampon was your idea."

"If and when you two ever get back to Colorado, give me a call. Hopefully, it will be long distance."

General McClure slipped into the right rear seat of the waiting staff car and was gone. As the Madisons waved goodbye to Jack McClure, a black, Cadillac hearse rolled quietly up to the aircraft and parked. The driver was alone. He dismounted, walked around to the rear of the hearse and opened the rear door. Like many of the cab drivers in the D.C. area, the driver had a dark complexion. He wore a dark suit, a white shirt, a black bow tie, and black shoes.

The next item on the conveyor belt was an unfortunately well-used, standard GI casket. The driver struggled without success to pull the casket off the baggage truck. Buck hurried over to help. In accented, but workable English, the driver explained his usual partner had called in sick. The casket wasn't really heavy. It was just unwieldy. Working together, Buck and the driver were able to get the casket off the baggage truck. They carried it over to the hearse and eased it onto the rollers in the floor of the hearse. As the driver closed the rear door, Buck noticed a crack in the cover of the right-rear tail light. That suggested the old hearse had seen a goodly number of funerals or, maybe, was just rear-ended by a taxi or someone talking on a cell phone. Buck pulled the paperwork for the casket out of his briefcase and told the hearse driver to sign for the casket. The driver scribbled something illegible on the form. Then, the driver nodded his thanks to Buck for his help and drove away with the casket. Buck put his copy of the receipt into his pocket.

✡ ✡ ✡

CHAPTER FORTY-FOUR

Camp David

The helicopter crewman beckoned Buck and Dolly toward the helicopter. The crewman helped them strap in and gave them each a headset. The aircraft commander said, "Welcome aboard. We understand you flew that 727 in here this evening. You retired from the airlines or something?"

"Oh, we're retired all right," said Dolly. "We just can't get anyone around here to believe it."

"Did I hear we are going to Camp David for the night?" asked Buck.

"Yes, sir. Someone will meet us on the helipad and take your bags to one of the cabins. Then, we take this bird back to Andrews."

"We've never been to Camp David," said Dolly, "cabin living sounds rather rustic."

"Ma'am, I think you'll find it a few notches above rustic. You'll see."

The pilot pulled pitch and the Marine helicopter lifted off. Ten minutes later, the helicopter was making a corkscrew descent over Camp David. As soon as the chopper landed, the crew chief dismounted. He helped Buck and Dolly down onto the helipad.

Two golf carts were waiting. A sailor came forward to help the chopper crew put the baggage on one of the golf carts.

Buck snapped a salute toward the aircraft commander. Dolly gave him a wave. When they turned around, they were greeted by a naval officer.

"Welcome to Camp David. I am Navy Lieutenant, junior grade, John Pfeifer. Please come aboard this golf cart and I'll take you to Maple. The other cart will bring your luggage."

"Maple?"asked Dolly.

"Yes, Ma'am," said Lt. Pfeifer. "The cabins aren't numbered. They are all named after trees. You'll be staying in Maple. It's just a short walk from Aspen, the president's lodge."

"Are you stationed here?"

"Actually, I'm the Public Works Officer, in charge of the facilities. My wife and I live here full-time. It's a very interesting assignment."

"Are you an Academy grad?" asked Buck.

"No, I'm only Christmas help. You know, Navy OCS, just doing my three years of active duty."

"I'd say you lucked out," offered Dolly.

"We think so. Okay, here we are. Maple is all yours. You will find a Navy steward inside. He will get you whatever you may require. Food, drinks, tooth brushes, if yours are lost. I'm told you will be having breakfast tomorrow with POTUS and the first lady in Aspen. It's been my pleasure to meet you. Enjoy your stay." Lt. Pfeifer snapped Buck a pretty good salute and drove away.

The white-jacketed Navy steward who greeted them at the door showed them around the cabin. Maple turned out to be anything but rustic. While the décor did give the impression of a rustic ski lodge in Colorado or Maine, the quality of all the furnishings was almost on a par with Buckingham Palace.

The steward asked if they needed anything. Dolly said their luggage contained everything they would need for the night; however, she wondered if it would be possible to have some clothes pressed. The steward said he would be happy to see to it that any suits or dresses would be pressed and that any laundry would be washed and back at the cabin before first light.

While the steward went to fetch a laundry basket, Buck and Dolly pulled from their bags all of the items that needed washing or pressing. They gave them to the steward and wished him a good evening.

At last they were alone and in a, presumably, safe environment for a change. Even so, Buck went around making sure all the windows and doors were secured. He was pleased to see a Marine guard walking around outside the cabin.

After they climbed into the California king-size bed, Buck rested the notebook computer on his lap. He took a few minutes to bring the notes for their book up-to-date. Ever since they left Gander, he had been too busy.

"I've mentioned this before about spy novels, but isn't this the time when the hero and heroine make love?"

"Sure, right after they have flown an aircraft they have never flown, dropped two tangos in parachutes out the back, shot another one, landed the plane at one of the world's busiest airports, ridden a Marine helicopter to Camp David, and have no idea what tomorrow will bring. In your dreams."

"Oh, I agree. Turn out the light. Let's get some rest. We might get to go home tomorrow."

✫ ✫ ✫

As was his habit, Buck awakened just before dawn. As was her habit, Dolly slept on. Wearing a thick, terry cloth robe bearing a Camp David logo and some bedroom slippers, Buck went out into the living room. Their laundry was all done and stacked neatly on a table. The clothes that needed pressing were on hangars.

On the coffee table, he found a tray bearing an envelope, some coffee, some tea and some crescent rolls. Laid out were copies of

The Washington Times and *The Washington Post.* Next to the newspapers were two of the famous Camp David windbreakers, with the names "Colonel Buck Madison" and "Dr. Dolly Madison" already stamped on the front. A note said they were welcome to keep the windbreakers as souvenirs of their stay at Camp David.

On the back pages of the newspapers and below the fold there were stories about how the FAA's air traffic control helped a Boeing 727 charter carrying members of the German Marshall Club to land at Dulles International Airport after the flight crew became confused and had used the wrong radio frequencies and transponder codes during their approach. Quick thinking on the part of personnel in the FAA's Air Route Traffic Control Center resolved the incident without loss of life or injury. The aircraft in question was not damaged.

As usual, *The Washington Times* story was straight newspaper reporting. As usual, *The Washington Post* spun the story to imply the entire incident might have been avoided if the White House had better relations with the union representing the air-traffic controllers.

All of the accounts took on a nostalgic tone about how the old 727 was being retired after long service in the Third World and was going to be flown on its last flight to the aircraft bone yard near Tucson, Arizona. It would be cannibalized for spare parts. There was no mention of the FBI.

Buck had just finished scanning the newspapers when Dolly, wearing a similar robe and slippers, joined Buck in the living room. After pouring a cup of tea, Dolly opened the envelope. "It says the president and first lady request the honor of our presence at breakfast at the Aspen Lodge at 8:00 a.m."

"I'd say it sounds like a command performance," said Buck. "Let's ask if we can go home today. In fact, we should check the airline schedules out of Dulles and Reagan National. We might even get home before dark."

Going to the phone, Dolly rang up Lt. Pfeifer. "As you know, we are invited to Aspen for breakfast. What should we wear?"

"Ma'am, I can only go by previous experience; however, up here, the president usually wears cowboy boots, jeans, a flannel shirt and, if it's cold, a jean jacket. The first lady wears slacks, some kind of sweater and penny loafers. I might suggest you wear the Camp David windbreakers while here. I hope that's helpful, Ma'am."

"Yes, thank you, Lt. Pfeifer," said Dolly, hanging up the phone. "Buck, we can wear our travel clothes and the windbreakers to breakfast. But, for the airline trip, let's just tuck the windbreakers in our luggage. We've attracted more than enough attention as it is."

After their coffee, tea and a crescent roll each, they got dressed for the breakfast with the president and the first lady. Then, they packed for what they hoped would be a commercial flight for Denver. Dolly called the airlines to get some idea of what flights might be available. A 3:00 p.m., non-stop from Dulles to Denver looked attractive. When they finished packing, they heard what sounded like three or four helicopters flying around Camp David. It was almost 8:00 a.m.

In a few minutes, a Marine guard rang the doorbell. Buck and Dolly joined the Marine on a golf cart and headed for Aspen Lodge. In casual attire, the president and the first lady came forward to greet them. The president and Buck shook hands. The first lady hugged Dolly.

The first lady motioned them toward a spacious dining area. When they were seated, the president said it was their custom to hold hands while he asked the Blessing. Dolly said that was their custom as well. As the four held hands, the president recited a brief prayer of thanksgiving for their food and gave thanks that Buck and Dolly had returned safely. A sailor wearing cook's whites appeared. He put a platter of bacon, ham, scrambled eggs, and hash-brown potatoes on the table and withdrew. They would eat family-style.

The president said, "I'm told if you two hadn't taken control of that Boeing 727 last night, our entire national security team would have been killed along with the leadership of the German Marshall Plan Society. We don't know how to thank you."

"Mr. President, when you consider our lives were on the line last night as well," said Buck, "we can't claim our actions were entirely altruistic. As you know, Mr. President, we were supposed to be carrying a proposal to you from Mr. Abu Amed. But with the destruction of the *Valhalla*, that became moot."

"Oh yes, Mr. Abu Amed. I had some Swiss intermediaries meet with Mr. Amed some time ago. But his ideas were so off-the-wall we told him to take a hike."

"Mr. President, I can assure you Mr. Amed's latest proposals were equally off-the-wall. Again, we are pretty sure he's dead. End of story."

"Mr. President, if you want to thank us," said Dolly, "I will be so happy when we are allowed to go home."

"And so you shall," said the president. "However, Buck has one more duty to perform this afternoon. The sisters of the intelligence officer who served so nobly and died all alone so many years ago in Potsdam are aware you escorted the remains of their brother. The sisters have asked for Buck to be a pall bearer at the memorial service for their brother. Assuming you are agreeable to serving the sisters as they desire, I propose the four of us fly on Marine One to Langley for the service."

Although disappointed, Buck and Dolly nodded their acquiescence.

"I'll get to what we'll be doing this afternoon in a moment," said the president. "But I'm curious as to how you two uncovered the plot to crash the German Marshall Society into the White House. How did you get the skyjackers to confess?"

"Mr. President, you better than anyone would know we don't use torture as defined by the Geneva Conventions," said Buck. "But, when we rendered the skyjackers unconscious, I must admit I came close to the line. Even so, the blows I used to gain control of them were no worse and probably a lot less traumatic than our soldiers and Marines face on the field of battle. Given what the skyjackers planned to do, even the use of lethal force would have been justified under anybody's rule book, to include the International Red Cross.

"I used what some might call 'harsh' interrogation techniques on the first officer to get him to confess how he and his brother were planning to crash us all into the White House. To my mind, we were faced with a 'ticking time-bomb' scenario. If I had to rough him up a bit to save the lives of hundreds of others, I was justified in doing so.

"What I did was similar to the techniques used on me and count- less other GIs during Survival, Evasion, Resistance and Escape or SERE training, as it is usually referred to. Bear in mind, Dolly and I did not just save the lives of the German Marshall Society, we saved the life of the first officer I slapped around and that of his brother, the pilot, as well. Their parachutes had been rigged to fail. Unwit- tingly, they would have jumped to their deaths.

"Fortunately, the first officer wasn't nearly as dedicated to his cause as your typical, hard-core Islamic jihadist. Turns out, he was just a mercenary, although he said something about his parents being at risk from the jihadists. Once Dolly and I learned the nature of the plot, the rest was relatively easy. Well, the hard part was flying an airliner neither of us had flown before.

"Mr. President, I hope you will hang some sort of civilian medal on our friend, Rod, over at Washington Air Traffic Control. Rod is the one who got us down safely. We don't know his last name; how- ever, I'm sure you can find out. I think any competent private pilot could have followed Rod's instructions and landed as we did."

"Yes, Buck," said the president. "Soon, we'll have Rod's full name. He doesn't know it yet; however, he will be brought to the White

House for a secret medal ceremony. Although I'm sure our German friends will be talking to the media about their horrifying experience, we want to protect your friend, Rod, from any possible reprisals from whichever wing of al-Qaeda was behind the White House plot.

"But there was another plot you don't know about. Abu Amed and his lieutenants were conspiring to poison gas thousands of people in the Berlin Olympic Stadium. Herr Zantner's motives may have been dubious; however, blowing up his boat saved the lives of an untold number of Berliners. By the way, the German team won the football game."

"So, that's what Abu Amed was hinting about when he told Dolly and me of his need to get your attention and the attention of the western European leadership."

"Apparently, so," said the president. "But let's turn our attention to this afternoon's activities. Buck, you are to wait on the steps with the other pall bearers while we three walk into the rotunda for the memorial service. After you and the other pall bearers place the casket in the center of the rotunda, you are to take a seat beside Dolly and we will have the service. Following that, a Marine helicopter will drop you two off at Dulles where an Air Force Special Air Mission C-21 will be waiting to fly you back to your local airport. The first lady and I will chopper back over to the White House for the dinner this evening with the German Marshall Plan Society. Is that acceptable?"

"Of course, Mr. President," said Buck. "But we can catch a commercial flight. As I recall, the C-21 is the military version of the LearJet 35. A Lear 35 is a bit posh for two retired spooks."

"It's the least we can do. I'm told your community airport can handle bizjets like the C-21. It even has jet fuel."

"Yes, Mr. President, it does," said Dolly. "The C-21 will save us tons of time, and I'll even help refuel it myself."

"Okay," said the president. "Then, we all know what we'll be doing for the rest of the day. Of course, I've had almost daily updates on your adventures or, should we say, misadventures; however, we need to hear directly from you. Was the book-signing tour worth all the time, trouble, expense and danger we put you through?"

"With respect, Mr. President," said Buck, "we don't have the full picture right now. We don't even know what happened last night with the skyjackers we threw out of that 727."

"Of course you don't. Nor do I have all the details. But do you remember the CIA officer who came over to brief you at Blair House?"

"Yes," said Dolly. "He had one of those stuffy Ivy League names. He didn't seem too happy about briefing a couple of retired spooks."

"Then, you might not be surprised to learn Catesby Fawkes and his lady friend were waiting in that open field for the skyjackers to land. He, she, and the skyjackers are being questioned by the FBI as we speak. At this point, it is unclear if this Catesby Fawkes person understood if he was going to be meeting live parachutists or some dead parachutists. Also, Fawkes may not have known your aircraft was supposed to crash into the White House. So, for now, we don't know if Fawkes is a traitor, or a jihadist or a common criminal. In any event, he's in a world of hurt.

"As the nation's chief law enforcement officer, I must be careful not to make any public statements that are prejudicial. If Fawkes were not a U.S. citizen, I would say just between us that he is both a traitor and a jihadist. Again, other than to acknowledge last night's arrests, I'm not saying anything more in public.

"As for the third skyjacker, the one who was shot, the FBI has his body downtown. He has been identified as the manager of an Arab-owned casino in Baden-Baden," the president concluded.

"Anyway, Mr. President," said Dolly, "all this explains how the Abu Amed wing of al-Qaeda placed the bombs at Harrods and at Charles DeGaulle Airport. It also explains how al-Qaeda seemed to know our itinerary and our accommodations almost as well as we did."

After breakfast, Buck and Dolly were excused to go back to Maple to get some rest and get ready for the memorial service. When they left Aspen, they found they had been assigned their own golf cart. A placard hung on the cart bore their names and the name of their lodge.

When they got back to Maple, a steward was waiting for them. He held up a dark, pin-striped business suit, a white shirt and a maroon tie for Buck. For Dolly, he had a simple black dress topped with a box jacket adorned with some understated embroidery, also done in black. Her kit included the kind of pill box hat made popular by the late Jackie Kennedy. The hat was done in a soft black cloth with wide-mesh veil that could be worn up or down.

Everything was a perfect fit. General McClure must have been at work. Carefully, they hung up the funeral attire. They flopped on the bed and took a nap.

At noon, a steward arrived with a cart full of food. The steward explained the president and first lady were hosting a luncheon for a foreign dignitary. The grilled chicken was for Dolly and the grilled sole was for Buck. They were to share the Caesar Salad. Having a quiet meal in a secure setting suited the Madisons just fine.

"Someone knows I don't eat fish," said Dolly. "Don't you find that kind of spooky?"

"What's spooky is how you eat tuna fish in a tuna salad. Isn't tuna a fish?"

"That's true; however, I just call it tuna salad, not tuna-fish salad. There's a difference."

"Apparently. Anyway, I'm sure Jack McClure has a complete dossier on both of us. I just wish we knew as much about those people who are trying to kill us."

After they finished their lunch, they dressed for the memorial service. When the telephone rang, it was Lt. Pfeifer. He said he was coming to escort them to the helipad where they would be joined by the president and the first lady. The staff would get their luggage and place it on Marine One.

As they left Maple, they thanked the stewards for their kindness. Boarding the golf cart, Buck asked, "Could you get used to this kind of life?"

"No way," said Dolly. "All I want to do is get home."

✲ ✲ ✲

CHAPTER FORTY-FIVE

CIA Headquarters, Langley, Virginia

Just before the president and first lady arrived at the helipad, Lt. Pfeifer asked them to board Marine One. The standard protocol observed by the western democracies calls for the most senior person to board last and to deplane first. After the president and the first lady were on board, he gave Buck and Dolly a thumbs-up. The pilot pulled pitch. Marine One did a cork screw climb above the Camp David compound until it reached a cruising altitude above the range of any hand-held ground-to-air missiles. From somewhere came a trio of Marine helicopters identical to Marine One. As Buck and Dolly watched in awe, four helicopters engaged in what amounted to a helicopter shell game, continuously changing positions within the flight of four. The purpose, of course, was to disguise the "real" Marine One.

After a few moments over the Maryland countryside, the president pointed out in the distance to the antennae belonging to the National Security Agency. Other than some posh horse-country farms, that was it for sight-seeing. Shortly, they crossed over the Potomac and into Virginia. When Marine One arrived over the Langley campus, it quickly lost altitude with another series of downward corkscrew turns. The other helicopters recovered somewhere else.

After the helicopter shut down and the rotor wash abated, the Director of Central Intelligence came forward to greet them. Introductions were hardly necessary; however, they were made anyway. Hands were shaken all around. The DCI's photographer asked them to pose with the DCI.

"Thank you for coming," said the DCI. "The two surviving sisters of the deceased are already inside with the other mourners. As you approach the entrance to our headquarters, allow me to ask you to stop and say a few words to six rather ancient honorary pall-bearers all of whom knew the deceased from the early days in the OSS. They are among the very few who know who is being honored today."

Turning to Buck, the DCI said, "Colonel Madison, as you know, the family has asked for you to be one of those who will actually carry the casket into the headquarters rotunda. You will be assisted by five of our younger case officers who, of course, never knew the deceased. It is appropriate for us to greet them as well."

After all the pall-bearers, both honorary and actual, were greeted and thanked, Buck watched as the DCI escorted the president, the first lady and Dolly into the Agency's main entrance. Buck noticed some of the honorary pall-bearers, just to keep standing, were relying heavily on their rubber-tipped aluminum walkers.

Once the official party was inside, a shiny-black hearse glided to a smooth stop at the curb. It was not the same hearse Buck saw at Dulles. Or, maybe, someone had fixed the crack in the right-rear tail light cover and gave the old hearse a wash and a wax job.

A funeral director emerged from the front passenger seat. He was outfitted in a dove-grey morning coat complete with dove-grey gloves. The driver was wearing a black chauffeur's outfit. Buck recognized him from the previous night at Dulles. Nodding to the pall bearers, the funeral director opened the back hatch of the hearse. The driver extracted a portable gurney and set it up. Then, the funeral director asked the pall-bearers to pull the casket out of the hearse and set the casket on the gurney. The funeral director instructed them to roll the casket to the massive front entrance of the headquarters and then carry the casket, doing the slow march, into the rotunda and place the casket on top of a catafalque.

The casket rolled rearward out of the hearse easily enough; however, when the weight of the casket was fully taken up by the six pall-bearers, Buck thought it was way too heavy.

Buck muttered to the other pall-bearers, "Let's set this hummer down. It must weigh over 1,000 pounds." His colleagues were happy to comply.

"Is there a problem?" asked the funeral director, archly.

"What's the deal?" asked a hovering Secret Service Agent.

Buck spoke up. "Last night, after the flight to Dulles, I helped unload a plain, GI casket weighing about 200 pounds. It was just me and the driver over there. It was easy. You can ask him. But this casket feels like it must weigh over 1,000 pounds. Also, the other casket had a lot of scratches on the lid. This lid is smooth."

"Oh, oh," said the Secret Service Agent. "The casket we inspected earlier this morning had some scratches. When we looked in, all we saw were some old bones. I don't know where this shiny-new casket came from. I'm not even sure if this is the same hearse."

"Well, something's wrong here," said Buck. "If this casket contains the desiccated remains of someone who has been dead for several decades, it should not weigh very much. But this casket is plenty for the six of us to handle. I think we need to look inside. Five minutes, max. Okay?"

The Secret Service Agent had no sooner agreed to a look inside when the funeral director and the driver quietly slipped into the hearse and drove off, leaving the back of the hearse still open. Using his lapel radio, the Agent signaled to his colleagues at the entry gate to hold the funeral director and the driver.

Unfortunately, the entry gate was designed more to keep vehicles from bursting in rather than from bursting out. Accelerating flat out, the hearse knocked the gate off its hinges and kept on going.

Surrounded by the now alarmed pall-bearers, the fit and the barely able, Buck and the Agent undid the latches holding the lid to the casket. They slid the lid aside to where they could look down into the casket. The casket was filled, almost overflowing, with white satin. Buck and the Secret Service Agent pulled the satin aside to see what was underneath. There were no human remains. What they saw was an olive-drab painted cylinder about 12-inches in diameter and about five-feet long nestled in even more white satin.

"Holy crap! What the hell is that?" asked the Agent.

"According to this stencil right here on the casing," said Buck, "This is a 'Warhead, Nuclear, Model W-9.' It's one of our earliest atomic weapons."

"Earliest? How the hell do you know that?"

"Many years ago, I served on a TPI Team. We inspected nuclear weapons. More to the point, we are now looking at a 15-kiloton atomic weapon."

"Get POTUS out of here right now!" barked the Agent, into his lapel microphone. Then, he remembered to add the appropriate code word for a presidential emergency evacuation.

"You better put POTUS, the first lady and my wife onto Marine One and fly them at least 30 miles to the West of here!" urged Buck. "At 15 kilotons, this baby will take out Langley and the entire D.C. area. And while you are on the radio, see if you can get an E.O.D. team over here right away. It's a good bet this thing has a timer or barometer set to make crispy critters out of us all. Meanwhile, I'll see what I can do."

The Secret Service Agent relayed what Buck had said to his boss.

"I need a screwdriver and a flashlight," said Buck.

Tugging at his belt, the Secret Service Agent asked "How about a Gerber Tool and my Mini-Maglite?"

"Perfect," said Buck, looking toward the helipad where he saw the rotors on Marine One already approaching take-off speed. The Secret Service was pushing POTUS, the first lady and Dolly on board Marine One. The mourners were streaming out of the headquarters building and headed for the parking lots. Two heavily-veiled women were being stuffed into a waiting sedan.

Buck used one of the tool's screwdriver blades to open an access panel. Holding the battery end of the flashlight in his mouth, Buck shined the light down into the maze of wiring connecting the barometers and other fusing and timing devices designed to keep the weapon from exploding at the wrong time and also designed to ensure that the weapon would explode at the right time and at a pre-set altitude.

"What do you want me and these pall-bearers to do?" asked the Secret Service Agent, acknowledging Buck's expertise.

Taking the flashlight from his mouth, Buck asked, "What's your name?"

"Special Agent Fleming."

"Special Agent Fleming, tell everyone to evacuate the Langley campus and try to find some kind of deep underground shelter. Meanwhile, I need you to stay here and shine your flashlight down inside this nuke."

Special Agent Fleming told all the pallbearers what to do. The younger pallbearers sprinted toward the parking lot. Buck had never seen octogenarians make walkers move so fast. Fleming remained on the other side of the casket facing Buck, his face betraying the fact that he would rather be someplace far, far, away: however, his sense of duty was telling him he could not abandon the tall, white-haired gentleman who needed his help.

Buck had never seen a nuclear weapon with an external countdown timer. Weapons to be dropped or fired had nothing on the outside. A wire ran from the timer and down into the access port. The timer indicated it had five minutes to go before reaching zero. Looking into the spaghetti-like array of color-coded wires, Buck realized he and Fleming were in deep kimchi. He was clueless as to what to do.

Buck figured one of the internal barometers had already been set to release the weapon at the same altitude as the Langley campus. That caused Buck to assume all the weapon was waiting for was to receive its final release instructions from the count-down timer.

No matter the consequences, Buck decided the timer could not be allowed to reach zero. The timer had to be receiving electricity from somewhere. But the weapon was so ancient, surely the original internal batteries would be dead and it was almost a certainty that no one would still be making new batteries for such an old and out-dated weapon. An additional power source had to be down in the casket somewhere.

Feeling around under the billows of white satin surrounding the weapon, Buck's hand hit on a hard object. With Special Agent Fleming pulling the satin aside, Buck found an automobile battery hidden down in the very bottom of the casket. Someone had drilled a hole in the side of the weapon's casing. A cable from each of the battery terminals ran through the holes and into the weapon.

Using the pliers function of the Gerber Tool, Buck started loosening the nut that was holding the cable to the positive terminal. Fleming held his breath. Buck prayed the device was not rigged with a current-interruption switch.

There wasn't even time for Buck's life to pass in front of him. Or, even time to think about Dolly. As Buck lifted the connector off of the top of the positive battery post, he glanced at the timer. The timer stopped counting down.

Now, Buck could only hope the weapon's many fail-safe systems were now in control of the weapon and they would remain in control until an EOD team could take charge.

"What now?" asked Fleming, wiping sweat from his face.

"I don't know. It could still explode. But I couldn't take the chance of letting the timer run on to zero. So, where are POTUS and the first lady? More importantly, where's my wife?"

Listening to his ear piece, Fleming said, "Marine One is taking them far, far away. Tell me, Colonel, how did you know to find that battery and disconnect it?"

"Actually, I didn't. And we still won't know for sure. Hopefully, the EOD team still has the technical pubs for the W-9. When this weapon was produced, I'll bet today's technicians were still in diapers."

Special Agent Fleming spoke into his lapel microphone for awhile. Looking around, Buck could see that the Langley campus was now deserted except for Agent Fleming, the 15-kiloton atomic weapon, the abandoned gurney, and some brave security personnel who were trying desperately to put the damaged entry gate back in place.

"Colonel Madison," reported Special Agent Fleming, "Marine One landed safely over in West Virginia. POTUS is aware you think the weapon is neutralized. In a few minutes, he and his party are going to relocate to another undisclosed location."

"Where's that?" asked Buck.

"You know I can't tell you that," said Fleming. "But I can tell you a second back-up helicopter is now on its way here to take you to the same place where POTUS and Marine One are headed."

After saying goodbye to Agent Fleming, and making a mental note to mention Fleming's courage to the president, Buck jogged over to the helipad. In a few minutes, he heard the characteristic wop, wop, wop of advancing rotor blades.

When the aircraft commander signaled for Buck to do so, Buck climbed into the second back-up helicopter for Marine One, secured his seat belt, and put on the headset offered by the crew chief. The helicopter lifted off and took up a northerly heading.

"Where are we going?" asked Buck.

The aircraft commander responded by saying, "Sir, you'll recognize the place when we get there." After awhile Buck began to recognize the Catoctin Mountains. The chopper was taking him back to Camp David.

On the intercom, the aircraft commander reported, "Sir, I just monitored a radio call from the leader of the EOD team. He says to relay his compliments to Colonel Madison for disconnecting that battery. The weapon is now safe."

"No amount of prior planning beats pure dumb luck," responded Buck.

CHAPTER FORTY-SIX

Camp David

After the helicopter landed at Camp David, Buck dismounted and snapped a salute to the aircraft commander. When he turned around there, once again, was Lieutenant Pfeifer.

"Welcome back, Colonel. Climb in. I'm supposed to take you directly to Aspen where the president, the first lady and your wife are waiting for you."

"Kind of you, Mr. Pfeifer," said Buck. "We must stop meeting this way."

When they reached Aspen Lodge, Buck thanked Lt. Pfeifer for the ride and was immediately greeted at the door by a naval aide who nodded him into the living room. The president got up off the leather sofa and came forward to shake Buck's hand.

Buck was immediately surrounded by Dolly and the first lady. There were hugs and kisses all around. "I'm beginning to think that it isn't safe to be around you two," said the president. "How can we ever thank you?"

"Mr. President, you can let us go home," said Buck. "Dolly and I are getting too old for this, well … crap."

"I can understand how you feel," said the president. "Come, we'll all sit by the fireplace. The steward will bring you whatever you want to drink. I already have my diet soda."

"I'll stick with my tea," said the first lady. Dolly said, "It's past 5:00 p.m. in Greenwich. I'd like a glass of Merlot and I suspect Buck would like a double shot of single-malt whisky with a drop of spring water. Please, no ice."

"Actually," said Buck. "My aging system is suggesting club soda."

"As you wish," said the president, with a nod to the steward. "Buck, once again, we are in your debt. How did you know to look for an add-on battery?"

"Dumb luck, Mr. President. But I figured the original internal batteries would be shot. That timer was getting power from somewhere. Timers are set to count down for a reason. I just decided to stop the timer from doing its job. We are lucky the nuke wasn't wired to explode if some amateur like me ran into a current-interrupter switch or some other kind of loop designed to get the unwary to cut it.

"Fortunately, I was being neighborly last night and helped that hearse driver with the unloading of a casket. Cast your bread upon the waters.

"Mr. President, we know your time is limited but we'd like to move on to ask you to take special notice of the work done by Brigadier General McClure and his staff. The support they gave us during the book tour was magnificent. Same goes for the CIA case officers we met out in the field. The officers, men and women of the *USS Enterprise* saved our bacon. They were truly professional. The Berlin Station Chief, Mac Macallan, was superb. Colonel Dawes of MI-6 and his Cessna Skylane were essential to our escape from Gibraltar. The prime minister might like to know about Dawes. Also, Heidi Schnell, the head flight attendant for LuftCondor was magnificent. Heidi can provide the names of the former German parachutists who helped me rig the phony air crew into their parachutes."

The president jotted down more notes.

Then, for the benefit of his wife, the president recounted all of the things that had happened to Buck and Dolly during their trip to Europe. The first lady just kept shaking her head in amazement.

At the end of his recitation, the president was grinning like the proverbial Cheshire Cat. Once again, he had proven the milk-toasts wrong. The president allowed as how the European-based leadership of al-Qaeda had gone to Islamist Paradise, although DNA had yet to confirm the demise of everyone who was on the *Valhalla*.

Dolly decided it was a good time to ask the president if some sort of federal pension could be arranged for Walter Zantner. The president said he would look into it. Buck took the opportunity to mention the bravery of Secret Service Agent Fleming and the gate guards who kept trying to repair the broken gate. The president jotted down more notes.

Dolly asked, "Mr. President, have the traitor or traitors who caused us so much trouble been identified?"

The president responded by saying, "As you already know, the traitor waiting in that empty field north of Frederick was Catesby Fawkes. But he wasn't working alone. With him was a gal who says her name is Aliyah. So far, all Fawkes will say is that she seduced him and that he wants a lawyer.

"The FBI has Fawkes, the girl and phony air crew locked up downtown. Germany doesn't have the death penalty, so the phony air crew is begging to be sent back to Germany. The German Government is saying it will put them on trial for air piracy. The fainthearts over at State want them returned to Germany.

"All of them have asked for lawyers. But I think they are terrorists, not mere criminals. Some of the wimpy lawyers over at Justice want to read them their rights under criminal law before they can be properly interrogated. But, until we can get their myriad violations of law sorted out, I think we should send all but Fawkes to Gitmo. Interesting how those who would destroy our freedoms are always eager to use our freedoms to their benefit."

"Mr. President," said Buck. "Don't be buffaloed by wimpy lawyers. In 1984, in *New York versus Quarles*, the U.S. Supreme Court found a 'public-safety' exception to the Miranda ruling. If there's a good possibility a criminal or a terrorist knows about a bomb or something that is about to harm the public, the apprehending officers can question the suspects right away in the interest of public safety, with no lawyers involved, and what the officers learn is still admissible as evidence against the offenders in a court of law.

"But the larger point, Mr. President, is not about winning court cases. The larger point to find out about the threat to public safety and shut it down before it kills people."

"Buck, I keep forgetting you were trained as a lawyer," said the president.

"Trained is correct, Mr. President," said Buck. "But I never practiced."

"So now we know Fawkes was the traitor," continued the president, "who was tipping off Abu Amed as to your accommodations and where you intended to go next. The girl, Aliyah, says she was under the control of a Saudi by the name of Mir Aimed Kasi. She says Kasi is based in Yemen. Unfortunately, Kasi was not out there in that field with Fawkes and Aliyah. But he was the driver of the hearse with the atomic weapon on board.

"At this point, we are clueless as to the identity of the funeral director. In any event, he and Kasi have disappeared. An all-out effort is being made to locate them. The FBI found the hearse abandoned near the Langley campus. They must have had a getaway car already in position. Or, someone picked them up. Again, we are clueless. No fingerprints. No human hair left behind. By the way, with so many terrorists still on the loose, I've decided to continue your protection back home.

"As for the terrorists we have in hand right now, I have directed that Aliyah and the Germans be taken to Gitmo. Fawkes is a U.S. citizen, so he'll stay here."

As he was recounting all the events of the recent past, the president could see Buck and Dolly were exhausted. The president explained that he and the first lady were due back at the White House that evening to host the German Marshal Society. The president suggested it might be a good idea for Buck and Dolly to repair to Maple and have their evening meal brought to them. The suggestion was gratefully accepted by the Madisons.

"But, before you go, I have another duty to perform," said the president, pressing a button on the side of his chair.

Two of the president's naval aides appeared. They must have been waiting in the pantry located behind the living room fireplace. The aides looked splendid in their blue uniforms with the gold-braided aiguillettes of their office hanging from one shoulder. The junior aide was carrying what looked like gift boxes for presidential cuff links.

The president told Buck and Dolly to stand at attention. The senior presidential aide, a Navy captain, read from an official-looking document. He said, "Attention to orders! By order of the President of the United States, the Presidential Medal of Freedom is hereby awarded to Melissa Rennie Dolly Madison."

The president took the medallion from the junior aide and hung it around Dolly's neck. He gave her a kiss on the cheek and then shook her hand. Dolly was stunned and choking back tears. Buck gave Dolly a big hug and a kiss. The first lady gave Dolly a big hug.

Then, the senior presidential aide coughed politely to indicate that he was not finished. "Attention to orders! By order of the President of the United States, Colonel James Buckley Madison is promoted to the rank of brigadier general in the United States Army Reserve."

The junior officer, a Navy Lieutenant, opened the other leather-covered box and showed it to Buck and Dolly. Inside the box were stars for a brigadier general.

"Because you are not in uniform," said the president, "we can't pin them on; however, Dolly you are permitted to kiss the Army's newest general officer."

With enthusiasm, Dolly did as she was told. The first lady gave Buck a big hug. For his part, Buck was too taken aback to speak. He thought he was just going to receive another set of presidential cuff links.

"Wait, there's more," said the president. "You get a flag with one star on it and you get a semi-automatic pistol, a holster and a leather belt with a special buckle. The pistol, I am told, is on loan to you, unless, of course, you wish to purchase it from the government when you retire. You get your choice of the M9, M15 or the Colt .380. Just tell my aide which one you want and it will be shipped to you."

"Because it is small," said Buck, "I'll take the .380. But, Mr. President, I am retired already."

"Yes, and that is why I could not promote you on the active-duty list. Congress controls that one while the president has more control over the Reserves. But I have to tell you, Buck, should the needs of the nation so require, you are subject to recall to active duty in your new rank."

"Mr. President," said Buck, "this is too much. We just happened to be at the wrong places at the wrong times."

"I've often thought the same thing about my time in the Oval Office."

When the senior aide asked the president if there would be anything else, the president thanked them for their assistance. The aides departed the way they came.

With a knowing wink, the president said, "Well, Sir James, and Lady Dolly, I know you are eager to head toward the mountains of Colorado."

Taken aback, Dolly asked, "Mr. President, how did you know about what happened to us that evening at Buckingham Palace? It seems like so long ago, I'd almost forgotten."

"The prime minister gave me a call the very next day. But now that you are home safely, we can talk about it."

"With respect, sir," said Buck, "let's wait until the next Honours List comes out. And then, it is only honorary and we do not plan to go around using those distinctions. Besides, I've always thought the O.B.E. stood for: 'Other Blokes' Efforts.' Regaining control of the Sandia *Seawind* was the work of many people, you included."

"Okay," said the president. "Until then, it will remain our secret. But I can't help it. Tomorrow, General Madison and Lady Dolly, you are to fly by helicopter from here to Dulles and from Dulles in a USAF C-21 to Granby, Colorado. Will that be okay?"

"Mr. President," said Dolly, "that's even better than a knighthood and a promotion combined. Thank you."

"It is the least I can do," said the president.

"Mr. President," said Buck, "you mentioned recall to active duty. Do you have something in mind?"

"Buck, this war we find ourselves in will not end soon. It has, unbidden, consumed my presidency. When the first lady and I came to Washington, our thoughts were on rescuing Social Security and Medicare, cutting taxes, making sure kids were being taught, getting people of faith more involved in helping people, and cleaning up the environment without crippling our economy.

"Going in, I had no idea how a disaster like 9/11 would set the tone for the rest of my years in office. Anyway, I get to retire soon. I have a color photo I'm taking home with me. It is a photograph of an Iraqi woman holding up her purple-ink-stained finger to show she voted for the first time in her life. It's really quite remarkable."

"I find it quite astonishing that the Muslim male has such fear of women," said Dolly. "They keep fifty-percent of their population, except for bearing children, from making the contributions so many of their women could make to the betterment of their society."

"Good point, Dolly," said the president. "But, as the leader of the nation that is the most accepting of diverse religions and races, if I tried to make the point you just made so well, I'd be labeled as a religious bigot or worse.

"Among the many threats we face, where do you place Iran?" asked the president.

"Mr. President, from the time that President James Earl Carter put a banana peel under the ailing Shah and helped the mullahs to power in Iran, it has been Iran, Iran, Iran. I can't say Iran enough, that has been at war with the United States of America and the West. While I don't think Iran has the geo-political power to be a major power, I do think an Iran with nuclear weapons could destroy Israel. The result would be a world-wide war like we have never seen before.

"If you look back at all the terrorist attacks since 1979, Mr. President, almost without exception they are the work, either directly or indirectly, of the Iranian mullahs. Mr. President, there will be no end to the War on Terror until those evil men are out of power and a more peaceful government in place."

"Unfortunately, Buck, I will soon be a lame-duck. So, it looks like all that will be the work of my successor and the Israelis. And, if my successor doesn't have the heart for it or doesn't care if Israel is destroyed, it probably won't get done. I'm well aware a single atomic weapon landing inside the borders of Israel means doom for Israel and the Jewish homeland."

"If push comes to shove, Mr. President, I think the Israelis will do another General Dayan. They'll launch a preemptive strike just like they did in 1967 and just like when they took out Saddam's nuclear reactor in 1981."

"Then, let's pray my successor doesn't stand in their way. Now, General Madison and Lady Dolly, we must be off to host your new-found German friends. I suspect they will be telling us many nice things about you. Get a good night's rest. You go home tomorrow."

EPILOGUE

The next morning, Lt. Pfeifer escorted them to the helipad and saw them off to Dulles where a C-21 awaited them. After thanking the Marine helicopter crew for the ride, Buck and Dolly walked over to the C-21 and greeted the Air Force crew. A Marine gave their luggage to the Air Force sergeant assigned to the C-21.

The aircraft commander, a major in the U.S. Air Force, said the weather would be clear all the way to Colorado; however, it would be necessary to refuel en route. "Do you have a favorite place to stop?" asked the aircraft commander.

"Yes, we do," said Dolly. "I learned to fly in Beatrice, Nebraska. The airport has first-class service for refueling and for picking up a catered lunch. Also, we would love to see, Diana Smith, the airport manager. Will Beatrice be in range?"

"No problem. So, Beatrice, it is," responded the major, as he set the airport designator BIE into his GPS. "I'll file a flight plan for Granby with a refueling stop in Beatrice. When we get close enough, I'll radio ahead so they will know you guys are on board."

During the flight, Buck worked some more with his laptop. Dolly napped. When they landed in Beatrice, Diana Smith greeted them and also Don and Evalyn Fitzwater, the retired airport manager and his wife; and Dave Morris, who taught Dolly to fly, and from whom Buck got his civilian instrument ticket. General Aviation pilots are a close-knit community, so it was like old-home week.

The flight to Granby provided the usual spectacular view of the Continental Divide and the Rocky Mountains west of Denver. As they neared the local airport, the co-pilot used the Common Traffic Advisory Frequency (CTAF) to announce their position and their intention to land on runway 27. In response, the pilot of a Cessna Citation said she would be taking off on runway 27, headed for

Palm Springs. To give her time to do that, the pilot of the C-21 held at the PENEY intersection over the town of Tabernash, south of Granby. After the Citation departed, the C-21 landed on runway 27 and then taxied to the fuel facility. Buck and Dolly helped the Air Force crew refuel, thanked them profusely, and waved goodbye.

When the sound of the C-21's twin-jet engines subsided, an eerie silence descended over the airfield. After being at the center of so much unwanted attention for so long, the Madisons enjoyed the quiet. None of the airport's thirty or so based aircraft were in evidence, although some of the south-facing hangars had their doors open to admit the warmth of the late December sun. Undoubtedly, some of the local pilots were performing maintenance on their aircraft or, perhaps, additional experimental aircraft were in the process of being built.

"The quiet is nice," said Dolly, as they watched a Red-tailed Hawk circling high above the airport, looking for the prairie rodents that infested the airfield and pooped inside the hangars.

"Sure feels like home," said Buck, "although I didn't mind those four- and five-star hotels."

"Unfortunately, they came completely equipped with people trying to kill us. You might say that was a downside."

Buck used his cell phone to call home and ask one of the Cornwells to come get them. With at least 15 minutes to wait, they walked the half-mile along the side of the back taxi-way to the hangar where they kept their aircraft. Buck pulled the prop through a few times to recoat the cylinder walls with oil. After relocking the hangar door, they saw Buck's extra-long Ford Expedition coming up the road.

"Welcome back," said Secret Service Agent, Benny Cornwell, coasting to a stop.

"Thank you," said Dolly. "Where's Prince?"

"Oh, he's waiting for you at home. Beth thought it best. Here, I'll help you with your bags and off we go."

When they reached home and Cornwell stopped the SUV, Prince ran out jumping and barking for joy. Beth Cornwell was with him.

Immediately, Buck, Dolly and the Cornwells gave Prince a short walk to the end of their cul-de sac and back. To reestablish their old routine, Buck put Prince through the commands that Prince enjoyed performing: Sit, Down, Stay, Come and Heel. As always, that was followed by a small treat.

The effect of the drill was to settle Prince down. The Cornwells were happy to report nothing out of the ordinary happened while Buck and Dolly were gone. Beth Cornwell expressed her thanks for the opportunity to live amidst such wonderful scenery around Lake Granby.

"It's been like living inside a picture postcard," said Beth, her earlier gunshot wound completely healed.

"Where do you and Benny go from here?" asked Buck.

"After we spend Christmas with Beth's folks in Wray, we are headed back for D.C.," said Benny. "But we are not leaving you without some protection. Apparently, you stirred up quite a ruckus in Europe."

"Let's just say our book tour was a great success," said Dolly. "But the flight back home did test our flying skills."

"We didn't hear much about your time in Europe," said Beth. "But once you landed back in D.C. it seemed like you two were on the cable news 24/7. So, will this be the end of your…ah, adventures?"

"We certainly hope so," said Buck. "We're eager to turn the notes we wrote on this trip into another book. We've decided to give any proceeds to a fund that helps wounded warriors and their families. The president said something about continued protection here. Do you have any information on that?"

"Yes, Benny and I have already been replaced by another detail. No suits and ties this time. These guys look like the loggers who go around here chopping down those poor beetle-killed trees. They look like the 'Ax Men' on cable TV. No one would take them for someone in the Federal Protective Service. But, they are. You will see them working around here now and then. But they will always have your Six."

"We don't know how to thank you," said Dolly. "You took such good care of Prince. I'm sure he'll miss you. Please, Benny and Beth, come by anytime you are in the area. Like our friend, Bob Price, you don't need to be on duty, you know."

After the Cornwells were gone and darkness had fallen over Lake Granby, Buck and Dolly settled down in their own bed for the first time in almost a month.

Suddenly, Buck sat up and said, "I should haul our little plastic Christmas tree out of storage. It's almost Christmas."

"Buck, you can do that in the morning. It's still two days until Christmas."

"Also, I have to get you a Christmas present."

"Not another push lawn mower, I hope."

"No, I was thinking about a self-propelled snow blower for the back drive."

"I hope it is silver."

"Why is that?"

"So it will match the extension ladder I got so you can paint the living room."

"Okay. That's settled. What now?"

"Aren't you going to turn out the light?"

"Yes, but I want you to see this envelope."

"What envelope?"

"I found it in the pocket of my raincoat."

"The only time you needed a raincoat was in London."

"That's right. We were out in front of the American Embassy. The old guy who looked like Neville Chamberlain gave me an envelope. But so many things happened I forgot all about it. Anyway, he said to open the envelope after we got home."

"Open it. The suspense is killing me."

Taking his pocket knife from the nightstand, Buck slit open the tiny envelope and extracted a tiny key.

"Look, Dolly, this must be the key to a safe-deposit box. See, it says Royal Bank of Scotland on one side. There's a number stamped into the other side."

"You said there's a note?"

"Well, just his business card. But there's writing on the back of the card. The hand is pretty shaky. All it says is: 'We know who killed JFK.'"

"Surely, we aren't going back to England or Scotland to find out who killed JFK? We just got home."

"Yes, we've had enough foreign travel for two lifetimes. But it is intriguing."

The End

ABOUT THE AUTHORS

William Penn is the *nom de plume* of a husband and wife writing team. After retiring from military service during which they gained first-hand knowledge of virtually all the places they describe in their novels, both authors pursued careers in state government, academe, political consulting, public relations, and journalism. Following that, they settled in Grand County, Colorado, to enjoy its myriad outdoor-sports opportunities, its scenery and the wonderful people who live there or visit. When not downhill skiing, sailing, flying, hiking, fly-fishing, volunteering, and writing, the authors try to be good companions to an Old English Sheepdog. This novel, like its predecessors, *The Grand Conspiracy* by William Penn and *The Panama Conspiracy* by William Penn, is part of a four-novel series featuring Buck and Dolly Madison. The final novel in the series, *The Umbrella Conspiracy,* is a work-in-progress. For more information, see: www.buckanddolly.com.

Photo credit: Leigh Taylor